THE ALTERNATIVE HERO

Tim Thornton was born in 1973. Despite a boarding-school education and a degree in drama, his adulthood has largely been spent playing the drums, most recently for indie/folk artist Fink. Along the way he has delivered daily newspapers in Copenhagen, changed light bulbs at Shepherd's Bush Empire, and pulled one of the first rickshaws in London. *The Alternative Hero* is his first novel.

www.thealternativehero.co.uk

TIM THORNTON

The Alternative Hero

VINTAGE BOOKS
London

Published by Vintage 2010

2 4 6 8 10 9 7 5 3 1

Copyright © Tim Thornton 2009

First published in Great Britain in 2009 by
Jonathan Cape

Vintage
Random House, 20 Vauxhall Bridge Road,
London SW1V 2SA

www.vintage-books.co.uk

Addresses for companies within The Random House Group Limited
can be found at: www.randomhouse.co.uk/offices.htm

The Random House Group Limited Reg. No. 954009

A CIP catalogue record for this book
is available from the British Library

ISBN 9780099531784

The Random House Group Limited supports The Forest Stewardship
Council (FSC), the leading international forest certification
organisation. All our titles that are printed on Greenpeace approved
FSC certified paper carry the FSC logo. Our paper procurement
policy can be found at www.rbooks.co.uk/environment

Printed and bound in Great Britain by
CPI Bookmarque, Croydon CR0 4TD

To Chris Bateson and John Kelley

PART

ONE

I am Zeitgeist Man
or so the papers said,
you might as well enjoy me now,
in six months I'll be dead.

Thieving Magpies, 'Zeitgeist Man'

THIEVING MAGPIES ARE FINISHED

You know how it is sometimes.

You're at a festival. You've been drinking all day, the only thing you've had to eat is one of those foul hog-roast sandwiches while watching the Longpigs, maybe a bit to smoke back at the campsite, a couple of tequila shots while waiting for your friends to put their trousers on; the evening draws in, you zip up your tent and set off to catch a few bits and pieces before the headliner.

Grab another drink. Perhaps nail that little half-pill you've been saving. See a few minutes of Mansun on the *Loaded* stage.

Then it all goes a bit peculiar.

First, you've completely lost all the others. You dimly recall one of them saying they were going to watch Gene, but you've no memory of which stage they were playing on. You try to cast your mind back – were you with anyone else when you saw that mad dude with the body make-up? – but your brain's not working very efficiently. Oh well, bugger it. You don't need them anyway. Plus, you're bound to bump into them by the pizza bus before the Magpies. Hang on, no

– this isn't Reading, this is Aylesbury. No pizza bus. Never mind. You can meet them where the pizza bus *would* be, if this was Reading. Genius. They'll probably be thinking the same thing. Who's on before the Magpies? You consult the dog-eared running order you pinched off that geezer behind the sound desk. Boo Radleys. Fair enough. Time to get something to eat.

Oh, and another drink.

Go on. Get yourself another drink, Clive. You clearly need it.

You try to walk over to the food stalls, but they don't seem to be where they were this afternoon. The main stage appears to have moved as well, but on reflection it must have been a different beer tent that you started out from. You pause to swig from your cup and get your bearings, but it's bloody difficult when the place is littered with people, slouching around in various states of fuckedness, trying to start those poisonous fires made from beer cups, newspaper and the free Aylesbury '95 souvenir poster that came with *Melody Maker*. It's rapidly darkening and grim-smelling smoke keeps getting up your nose and in your eyes, but you stagger on, accidentally kicking some bloke who's passed out next to one of the speaker stacks. At last you spot a tempura stand. Not quite what you had in mind, but it'll do. Four pounds for tempura and noodles. Hunger. Yes. You dizzily instruct the woman to spoon on lashings of sweet and sour sauce, stop off for another drink, then settle down just in time to see the Boos crunching their way through 'Find the Answer Within'.

A brief moment of contentment and serenity.

Which abruptly finishes when you drop most of your tempura on the grass. Bollocks. At least it wasn't your drink. You pick some of it up. A few clumps of grass have stuck to the sweet and sour sauce, but fuck it, it's all vegetable. Shove it in with some noodles and you'd never know the difference. You scoff the lot while Sice sings his little heart out, wash it all down with some more of whatever that is in your beer cup, and then . . . feels like time for a little rest. Get some energy up before the mighty Magpies. The glorious, world-beating Thieving Magpies, back to inject some quality and integrity into what's swiftly becoming an alarmingly overrated pop landscape. You lie back and settle yourself on the cool ground, the lawn threadbare from constant tramping over the last forty-eight hours. It's funny to look up and see a worm's-eye view of the festival: the darkening sky, festivallers walking past, hooded tops, strange hats, brainless conversations. And yes, what an amazing selection of sounds. It's only now you're lying down you can really take it in. The Boos pounding away in the foreground, of course, but there's assorted chatter and laughter, various stereo systems booming out from tents and stalls – and if you really concentrate you can actually make out the noises of the band on the *Loaded* stage. Hmm . . . sounds rocky . . . voice isn't up to much . . . that good bit when the band stops and he sings the verse by himself for a moment – *When he wakes there's no one there . . . He still loves her, the girl from* – and then they all kick back in.

Respect.

Respect for the real people.

Nah, it's not The Real People.

It's . . . um . . .

[From the September 1995 issue of *Craze* magazine.]

Lance knocks back the rest of his champagne and shrugs.

'It's all right. I mean, it's a decent crop of new bands and they're all doing fairly decently. It happens. I'm not convinced it's earth-shattering. I haven't heard anything that, like, radically influences me or sends me scratching my head back to the drawing board. But it's pretty healthy, I s'pose. A fuck sight better than the crap that was around when we first came out. I quite like Sleeper, she writes good lyrics. Supergrass are cool.'

A foreign writer asks who he's rooting for in the great Blur/Oasis single battle.

'Neither, I think both songs are shit.'

But which group does he prefer?

'Slade.'

CRAZE: *Do you see yourself as part of, or an alternative to, the current explosion?*

'I don't see why we have to be either.'

CRAZE: *Were you ever concerned that you'd be superfluous to it?*

'How do you mean?'

CRAZE: *Rendered unnecessary?*

'I knew this was coming. I dunno. You tell me. Why would we be?'

CRAZE: *You're part of the old guard. Pretty much everyone else has been swept away.*

'Like who?'

CRAZE: *You know. The Cure. The Wonder Stuff. The Mission. James. Pop Will Eat Itself. Carter. Jesus Jones.*

'Yeah, and you've forgotten Ned's Atomic Dustbin, Eat and Kingmaker, and why don't you throw in Gaye Bikers on Acid and Dumpy's Rusty Nuts while you're at it?'

About half the room laugh. The others look puzzled. Lance continues.

'You must've got that list off the back of an old Camden Palace flyer. You see . . . we've never had much in common with that lot. We've always been more than capable of moving on, and we're not stopping now just 'cos there's suddenly a cool new scene for all you cool new people to shake your record bags to. I mean, why shouldn't people continue listening to us? Why is it such a surprise? It's not as if we're doing something completely contrary to what's happening now. We use guitars. We're British. We write real pop songs about real life. And we still rock harder than anyone. A lot of the new bands rock about as hard as Simply Red.'

CRAZE: *But you represent a bygone era.*

'No. That's just what you've decided, because the goths and grebos used to dig us, and 'cos we're from Reading. It's a complete fallacy. I bet you won't be asking Shaun Ryder the same question.'

CRAZE: *Does a backlash scare you?*

'From the press? We've already had four of them. One after each album. We'd survived our first one probably before you finished your GCSEs.' [Laughs]

CRAZE: *What about from the public?*

'No,' he scowls. 'You read *Music Week* – look at the sales figures, mate. The record's already gone platinum, and it'll probably be double by the time the Blur album comes out. And that's just Britain. So I don't think anyone at BFM's losing sleep just yet.'

Deciding the conference has reached a natural conclusion, he rises, delivers one of his characteristic cheeky grins, gathers up his routinely silent bandmates and departs. Although slightly more defensive than we've come to expect, the consensus is that his acerbic style is on fine form and that it's business, for the foreseeable future, as usual.

So it comes as some surprise five hours later when, in front of fifty thousand people, Lance Webster single-handedly ensures that the significant portion of his own musical career is drawn to a rapid close.

'Summer's gone, days spent with the grass and sun . . .'

Hang on.

'I don't mind, to pretend I do seems really dumb . . .'

You've woken up. Which means you must have fallen asleep. The last streak of daylight in the sky has gone. So has your good mood. You're pissed. In the British *and* American senses of the word.

That last little half-pill has wormed its way into your bloodstream, blended with the alcohol and made your head hurt, in that sort of non-hurting way that ecstasy does. Your mouth is dry. Anything left in the beer cup? Nope. Better get another one.

But they're playing your favourite Boo Radleys song. Hell, it's *everyone*'s favourite Boo Radleys song this summer. Apart from those who liked them before they turned into The Monkees. You struggle to your feet. The tune is blasting out. The crowd's loving it. Impressive stuff. Wake up, Boo. There's so many things for us to do.

Like dance. Sod it, it's a pop song. What's a little head-throbbing. You frug away, belting out the lyrics with the rest of the mob. But something else is strange. The chanting mob in question are quite far away. There are lots of other people next to you, though. Huh. Truth is, these particular neighbours don't seem to like this breezy little indie-pop song much. One look at their faces explains why. The hair, pallor and interesting beards. And the T-shirts. Fear Factory. Sepultura. Slayer. Cradle of Filth. You're surrounded by them. And they're not happy. Christ knows why they're here. Probably because Skunk Anansie played earlier and now they're too drunk to move. But you're dancing, jumping, hollering ('*You can't blame me, not for the death of summer*') without a care in your boozed-up and loved-up world. Although . . . it *does* make you feel a little self-conscious, behaving like this, alone, in a sea of dark metal. Why don't they like it? What's wrong with a little . . . *frivolity* occasionally? Why does music have to continually refer to crucifixes, disorder unleashed, seasons in the abyss and principles of evil made flesh in order to get these corpses moving?

'Am I the only one enjoying this?'

Apparently you are.

'What's wrong with you?'

You're shouting.

'Why are you all so fucking miserable?'

Hang on. You're shouting. That's why they're all turning round, looking strangely at you.

'Why don't you all piss off back to your tents and stick on some fucking Napalm Death?'

No. Not nice. Rude. Pretty dangerous too, as there are about forty of them and only one silly little pissed indie wanker.

'Just because you've spent the last fucking ten years listening to the same Iron Maiden record.'

'Leave it, mate, all right.'

One of them has spoken to you. Quietly, almost kindly. *You won't like me when I'm angry.* A threat you skilfully ignore.

'You're all dull as shit. Oooh, look at me, I'm so dark and damaged.'

'Mate, why don't you just mind your own fucking business?'

Another of them. Less quiet, not particularly kind at all.

'I was! But you're fucking . . . *prohibiting* me from enjoying myself!'

Ah. The logic of the heavily intoxicated.

'Go and stand somewhere else then!'

A girl this time. Knee-length black hair, face jewellery, Nine Inch Nails T-shirt. Apparently about three feet tall.

'I was bloody here first!'

'It's not fookin' reserved seating, mate.'

Birmingham accent.

'Yeah, but it's a bloody festival, you could at least fucking—'

'I've heard about enough of this shit.'

New guy. Big guy. *Enormous* guy. Shaved head. Beard you could store cigarettes in. Sick of It All T-shirt.

'If you don't button it or fuck off, I'm going to personally see to it that you finish your evening locked inside an overturned Portaloo.'

Sometimes a hopeless drunken argument is assailed by a moment of clarity. This is such a moment. But you're still drunk. To completely back down now would be as unnatural as mooning in front of your girlfriend's parents. So, unable to bend, you break.

'Yaaaaaaaaaaahhhh!!!!'

This is you. You're screaming. You're hurling out limbs in every available direction, pushing past the massive dude and tearing through the comatose herd of metallers. As only the very fucked can, you leap and shove and sprint, hollering abuse in a language that doesn't resemble English but perhaps Hungarian, ignoring the various observations ('Oi, watch it, you cock') that drift into your ears as you pass. On and on you race, until the black and Judas Priest give way to the brown and Teenage Fanclub, then finally the white and Oasis. Not that you prefer this brand of people, but they're at least dancing and the danger is over. The Boos are on their last song by now, you're about twenty yards away from Mister Carr himself, you've got that sweating-buckets heatrush thing going on and the stage lights are illuminating everyone in your immediate vicinity. Suddenly the festival seems very small, intimate, like it's taking place in a school sports hall with oversized equipment. You look around frantically for something to drink. A girl next to you has a pint, but . . . naaah, even you can surmise that she won't want some gurning fool nagging on her beverage. Instead you approach a nearby Graham Coxon lookalike who has a camping water bottle dangling from his rucksack.

'Mate, can I have a sip of your water?'

'Nah, man, it's vodka and blackcurrant.'

'Wicked.'

Although this isn't perhaps the reply he expects, Coxon shrugs and hands the bottle over. You've drunk about half of it before he grabs the bottle back.

'That'll do.'

You acknowledge his generosity with a grunt and a belch. It's only then that it hits you how strong the mixture was. The guy probably just added a small carton of blackcurrant juice to a whole bottle of vodka. Oh well. Needs must when you've an evening of meat-and-potatoes guitar music to get through. You catch your breath slightly at the hot tingling sensation all over your body and turn your somewhat flexible attention back to the action on stage.

[From the *Daily Telegraph*, 14 August 1995.]

POTTED MAGPIE

Lance Webster, 28, vocalist with the indie-rock group Thieving Magpies, was arrested on Saturday night for drunk and disorderly behaviour. Webster had brawled with security staff and repeatedly insulted the audience at the Aylesbury Festival, during a headline appearance which was abandoned after twenty-five minutes. The band, best known for their 1992 album *Bruise Unit*, have subsequently cancelled several concerts in Europe and the US.

'*I stare at my face, I know every trace, and I make it hard to get along, to get along with me . . .*'

'Yeah.'

'*Bills and heartburn . . .*'

'Yuh . . . ills and s-soaps . . .'

This is you.

'*And flickin' through the books you've read before . . .*'

'Read befo-ooore-ah . . .'

You're singing.

'*Tears come easy . . .*'

'. . . ears come easyyyyeeeah . . .'

You can't sing. But you're singing all the same. To a song you've never heard before.

'*Words come hard, but there really isn't much . . .*'

'Much to say no moooo-ooorre.'

'*I stare at my face . . .*'

'Yeahh-aaye stare at maaah face . . .'

'Sorry, man.'

It's Coxon again.

'Uh?'

'Sorry, pal, can you give it a rest?'

'Give what a rest?'

'The singing. Sorry. Trying to listen.'

'Am I not allowed to sing?'

'Sorry, friend. It's just that—'

'What?'

'It's, um, not very good.'

'Who are you? Freddie Mercury?'

'No, but . . . the words . . .'

'It's a fucking gig.'

'I know, but—'

'Everyone's singing.'

'Well, not really to this one—'

'Uh?'

'Well, it's a new song. He said it's a new one.'

You puff yourself up.

'Well, *I* know it.'

'Um . . . how?'

'How?'

'Yes. It's brand new.'

'I have the album.'

'Mate, the fucking album isn't out yet.'

'I got an advance copy.'

'Bollocks.'

'I'm a music journalist.'

'Fucking right, man. I'm a music journalist too, and they haven't even finished recording the damn thing.'

'They gave me some demos.'

Coxon is shaking his head, exasperated.

'Mate, you're full of it.'

You ponder this charge for a moment as the band play on. Unable to fully disagree with the man, you change tack.

'Who d'you write for anyway?'

He ignores you.

'Come on! Who d'you write for?'

He turns back to you and gives a wide, sarcastic smile.

'*Craze.*'

'*Craze*? That pile of crap?'

First he looks astonished at your intuition, then turns away. 'Fucking weirdo,' he mutters.

'You're a bunch of clowns, man,' you continue. 'That rag is so fucking superficial they should give it away for free with packets of chewing gum.'

'Fuck off.'

'Are you proud of your work when it comes out?'

'Why, who do you fucking write for?'

You've become an expert at sidestepping this particular question.

'Plus, you're the only pieces of shit that gave the Magpies album a bad review.'

Finally at his wits' end, Coxon spins round and grabs you by the neck of your T-shirt.

'I know! I wrote it!'

He glares at you for a few seconds then pushes you away. The rest of the crowd are now heartily cheering as the triumphant Boo Radleys leave the stage. You, however, are oblivious to this.

'You're Tony Gloster?'

He has his back turned now, joining in the applause.

'Oi! Are you really Tony Gloster?'

This has clearly impressed you, one way or the other. You tug on his rucksack.

'Tony!'

'Piss *off*!' he roars, shoving you off again. 'What do you want from me, knobhead?'

He angrily turns to go.

'Hey! Tony! Where you going? You'll miss the Magpies.'

Gloster glowers at you for the last time, then spits out five words that contain not one trace of doubt.

'The Thieving Magpies are finished.'

[From *Melody Maker*, 18 August 1995.]

LANCE: WHAT THE F*CK HAPPENED?
Oh dear. And it was all going so well.

As you surely know by now, Lance Webster put a slightly unusual slant on the Thieving Magpies triumphant come-back appearance at Aylesbury last weekend. At the moment no one – not even the *Maker* – has the slightest clue *why* any of this happened, but we can provide you with an eyewitness account of precisely what went wrong . . .

Approx. 3 p.m. Thieving Magpies tour van arrives on festival site. Band disembark and disappear into dressing room.

4.30 p.m. Band arrive in backstage bar for press confer-ence. Lance sipping champagne. Lance seems argumentative and a little unhinged in responses.

6 p.m. Lance and Magpies drummer, Craig Spalding, spotted watching dEUS on second stage, Lance with pint in hand.

7.15 p.m. Lance seen strolling around backstage area with girlfriend Katie.

9 p.m. Lance due to be interviewed by Radio 1 in back-stage bar – no sign of him. Craig Spalding and guitarist Martin Fox interviewed instead.

10 p.m. Magpies' scheduled onstage time.

10.15 p.m. Magpies walk onstage to enormous applause and launch into current single, 'Contribution'. Lance performing normally.

10.20 p.m. Halfway through second song, 'The Cool and the Crooks', Lance abandons usual lyrics and starts to sing Blur's 'Country House'. During final chorus he sings '*the c*nt and the c*nts*'.

10.25 p.m. Lance straps on acoustic guitar, swigs heavily from red-wine bottle and begins extremely raucous solo rendition of Oasis's 'Roll with It'. Audience enthusiastically sing along. Lance messes up some lyrics and chords. When he reaches line '*I know the road down which your life will drive*', he stops and shouts at crowd: 'Why the f*ck are you singing that sh*t? That's enough. Whoever was singing that b*llocks can f*ck off and watch something else.' Uneasy looks from other band members – eventually Dan Winston speaks quietly to Lance and persuades him to continue with scheduled performance.

10.27 p.m. 'Try Blinding' – all is well until after first chorus. Lance wanders away from microphone, stops playing guitar and makes 'wanker' signals at an unidentified person in front of stage. Remains on lip of stage until band have reached second chorus, at which point he returns to microphone and sings as usual. Remainder of song passes without further upset.

10.31 p.m. Lance hands guitar to roadie, grabs red-wine bottle and addresses audience: 'So who are you here to see? Elastica? F*cking Menswear? [Neither band is playing at Aylesbury.] Cast? The Bluetones? [Both bands completed their sets earlier on.] Well, f*ck off and see them, then. I've got no songs for you. F*ck off. We're not playing another note until you leave.'

10.32 p.m. Several audience members start to voice dissatisfaction with the evening's entertainment. Hearing this, Lance screams, 'Yeah, you can say what you f*cking like, you miserable little c*nts. I'm the one up here with the guitar getting paid. I can play the same song fifteen times in a row if I want.'

Someone evidently shouts something like 'Go on, then': Lance nods, utters something off-mic involving the F-word, grabs guitar back from roadie and plays opening chords to 'Try Blinding'. Crowd roars disapproval. Dan Winston and guitarist Martin Fox attempt to stop him. Webster stops playing, throws guitar down and leaps offstage to where security are standing.

10.34 p.m. Webster punches male member of security staff in the face. Chaos ensues. Martin Fox and drummer Craig Spalding quickly join melee. Dan Winston strides over to main microphone: 'Sorry everyone, our singer's decided to be a cock tonight, thanks for your patience.' Four security guards restrain Webster, while Fox and Winston – shortly joined by Thieving Magpies manager Bob Grant – attempt to placate assaulted party.

10.37 p.m. Incredibly, situation briefly improves. Assaulted bouncer is led away, Webster is encouraged back onstage and band resume positions. Audience by now extremely restless, although numbers do not appear to have dwindled.

10.39 p.m. Martin Fox optimistically cranks out opening riff to 'Look Who's Laughing'. Crowd cheers. Lance approaches microphone, draws breath to sing, glances over towards where previous action took place, shouts 'F*ck this', throws guitar down *again* and dashes off into wings.

10.40 p.m. Thieving Magpies' 1995 appearance at Aylesbury Festival is over. General confusion, audience hurling beer cups, band members departing as speedily as possible.

10.41 p.m. Pursued by security staff, festival staff, roadies, band members and manager, Lance Webster storms into backstage area where he spots previous adversary being consoled by security management. Webster hurls himself at him. This time assaulted party fights back, scoring a direct hit.

10.43 p.m. Compère Jonny Malone announces to furious crowd: 'Well, sorry, everyone, that appears to be it for the main stage this evening – you can still catch the end of Dodgy's set on the *Loaded* stage . . .'

10.45 p.m. Fight still raging backstage. Roughly fifty people involved now – a large proportion of whom seem to be restraining Webster.

10.50 p.m. Festival police appear. Following swift assessment of situation, Lance Webster is handcuffed and firmly requested to assist authorities with their enquiries.

10.51 p.m. Heated negotiations commence between Live-Time Security, Bob Grant Management and Thames Valley Police.

11.10 p.m. Negotiations transfer to Aylesbury Police Station.

Approx. 3 a.m. Negotiations suspended. Lance Webster is released but instructed to reappear for questioning on 21 August.

Blimey. So what – as just about everyone must be asking this week – the f*ck happened?

MY LIFE COMPLETELY CHANGED AFTER I SAW LANCE WEBSTER COMING OUT OF THAT DRY-CLEANERS

It starts with an unusual dream.

Of all the dreams I've had in my life that feature Keith Richards boisterously playing the piano at the side of a large stage while a veiled Adam Ant slow-dances with Syd Barrett, this one is definitely the best.

Before my rapidly moving eyes, the dancers separate and prance about like banshees, emitting the appropriate hysterical shrieks and sobs. Then, in an almost biblical vignette, Ant weeps at the edge of the stage while Barrett affectionately wraps the veil around his head, moaning, 'Weep no more, Stuart – weep no more.'

'Roger, you have healed me,' Ant replies, and they embrace.

Keith Richards laughs heartlessly and continues his piano torture, pausing occasionally to yell at a TV audience that the donation target has yet to be reached and could we please all go to the website now.

Even through my beer-induced slumber, it intrigues me that while Richards is every inch the rancid present-day specimen we barely believe can still manage a chord shape, Syd Barrett appears exactly as he did in 1966: long brown hair, chiselled features, pretty and infinitely capable, Pink Floyd at the height of their psychedelic powers. My dream also features the Adam Ant of yesteryear, in his case the 1982 model, youthful, dark and dashing, having newly lost his Ants. But the presence of the Internet and other *mise en dream* suggests a far more recent happening. Of course, dreams can fuck with time and space whenever they feel like it, but there lingers in my brain a certain relevance to this particular warping. Similarly, as the dream's end credits roll, a final bewildered utterance from Barrett seems also to signify something fairly important: 'I've lost Geoffrey. Where's Geoffrey? I'm looking for Geoffrey Webster.'

Geoffrey Webster?

Who the hell is Geoffrey Webster?

The question bounces around my aching head as I rise, clean my teeth, fling on some clothes, down a few Alka-Seltzer and rush out of my flat. I must've had a few more drinks than I can recall last night, for I'm ashamed to say the bus has trundled over halfway to Old Street before it hits me who Geoffrey Webster is.

Lance Webster.

The man who, as far back as 1984, decided his given name could and would not be the name of an internationally famous purveyor of alternative rock 'n' roll, ditching Geoffrey for the infinitely more viable abbreviation of his grandfather's Christian name, Lancelot.

The frontman whose charmed, platinum-selling world plummeted headfirst into the contents of a rancid festival toilet before the eyes of the indie cosmos one wretched summer night in 1995.

The former star ('the closest thing Britain's ever had to its own Cobain', as I once wrote in some dreadful fanzine) whose subsequent career became an increasingly pitiful series of cock-ups and false starts until he finally gave up in 1999.

And the man who I more than partly blame for the way my life has steered itself over the underwhelming course of the last nineteen years.

But enough of that.

Why was Syd Barrett looking for him?

Now, I know trying to explain dreams is an ill-advised and mostly fruitless endeavour. If there's any deep-seated, sinister Freudian reason for the fact that members of my family (particularly the male ones) have been known to morph into my ex-girlfriend halfway through dream conversations, I really don't want to know it. But usually dreams at least feature people that I actually care about, or have thought about recently. I've never been remotely bothered about Pink Floyd, and Keith Richards is an overrated guitarist in one of the planet's most overrated rock bands, as far as I can tell. It's true I've developed a keen interest in Adam Ant's early career over the last few years, but why he was hanging out with these other cocks I have little idea. So, I'm forced to analyse this dream a bit. Plus I have a moderate hangover and there isn't much to do at work: ideal circumstances for ruminating over reveries.

The best explanation I can come up with is that Keith Richards was presiding over a charity television show at which pseudonym-using, fallen-from-grace pop stars had the old wounds of constant media buggery healed via a dancing ritual performed by their lookalikes, while a watching audience donated money. Lance Webster was next on the bill (perhaps a duet with Gary Glitter) but, true to form, had vanished before his allotted stage time.

Great. I'm glad to have sorted that one out.

Apart from a cursory glance at Google to see if Webster has been up to anything new that the universe might be alerting me to, I make no other attempt to find a reason for his reappearance in my psyche. My obsession – as my ex-girlfriend termed it – with Webster died in about 2002, when I'd finally tired of waiting for a follow-up to his debut solo album (*Commercial Suicide*, released in the

same week as Oasis's *Be Here Now*), but certainly his spectre has
continued to clatter about in my skull like a bad relationship. It's
therefore not particularly surprising that I'm still dreaming about the
man – or, more to the point, the *absence* of him.

It's an otherwise uneventful day at the office. I do my usual
blend of fatuous emailing, a few token work-related tasks, mindless
web-surfing and keeping an eye out for Ron or Michael's sudden
approaches.

'Clive, this document,' announces Ron, just as I'm shutting my
computer down for the day, 'is an application for insurance.'

'Yes,' I answer.

'It arrived,' Ron continues, staring out of the window and
fingering the sheet of paper dangerously, 'at ten-thirty this morning.'

'Yes,' I repeat, still unable to argue.

'Is there any particular reason why it remains in your tray,
unprocessed, at a quarter to six?'

I glumly restart my machine and stay at work for another forty
minutes, fantasising over what it might be like to work for a company
where sometimes, just occasionally, someone looked up from their
desk at half past five on a Friday evening and suggested a quick pint
before home.

At some point my mobile bleeps, summoning me to some uninteresting chain pub in Islington where I stand around with a few
of my uninteresting friends as they ruminate about their week's
uninteresting highs and lows and prepare themselves for the night's
main activity: a visit to their latest uninteresting clubbing discovery.
I make my excuses at ten-ish and sidle off homeward, ignoring their
usual protestations. A kebab, another can of lager, a short round of
commiseratory masturbation (Katherine Heigl, if you're interested;
one in a long queue of second-tier Hollywood actresses I've recently
become excited about – last week it was Anna Faris, the week before
Carrie-Anne Moss) and another painfully predictable Friday evening
is over.

The next day, however, proves significantly more intriguing.

Via the least intriguing of activities, of course. I am sent by my heavily hungover flatmate, Polly, on a mission to buy some of that rank, fruited malt loaf she sometimes favours for Saturday breakfast, plus a light bulb, paracetamol and some tampons (one of those strange selections at the checkout that I sometimes picture mixed up in a wok together – to universal funny looks from anyone I might share this musing with). The high street is crawling with shoppers and prams as usual, so I make a swift detour into a café to wolf down my favourite sandwich (bacon and mushroom), and then continue up the street. Imagine my surprise, half a minute later, when I see a Lance Webster lookalike emerging from the dry-cleaners with a sizeable pile of plastic-covered items.

Except, of course, it isn't a Lance Webster lookalike.

I'm not certain at which point in the following twenty seconds I realise this. All I know is that something about him – the way he walks, the quick glance up and down the street before he sets off, possibly his shoes (rather ostentatious shiny light-brown brogues) – whatever it is, it propels me to make an about-turn and hurry back down the street after him. God knows. It certainly isn't his face, which suggests a slightly fat elder brother of my former hero. But I don't believe any rational thought contributes to my arrival at this decision; my body seems to move of its own accord, almost as if I *smell* that it's Lance Webster.

I ought to point out, this isn't the first time this has happened. A few years ago I walked past Björn Ulvaeus on Oxford Street. Again, his appearance had become less blond Swedish male pop star and more bearded, kindly uncle, but before I knew what I was doing I was running back up the other side of the road so that I could walk past him again; it's a funny old thing. As I approached him for the second time I ran through various lines I could maybe say to him ('Sorry to bother you, I'd just like to tell you that ABBA made my childhood slightly more bearable'; 'Sorry, I thought you ought to know that *ABBA: The Album* kicks the shit out of *Pet Sounds* and *Sergeant Pepper* as a classic, flawless pop masterpiece'; 'Sorry, but can I just say that "My Love My Life" is the song I want played at my funeral', etc.) but wisely decided to merely saunter past, enjoying a few seconds of being metres away from a genius. Besides, what if he'd been having a bad day and had told me to piss off? I'd have probably hurled myself in front of a passing 73 bus.

Which is partly why I don't want to address Mr Webster. The other part being that I haven't a clue what to ask him. My feet carry on moving up the street while I try to arrange the myriad questions and possibilities that now present themselves like a line of hopeful auditionees. Could I talk to him? Could I make friends with him? Could I interview him? Could I finally find out the truth about 12 August 1995? Could I finally find out the truth about Gloria Feathers? Could I succeed where others had failed? Could I sell the interview for vast sums of money? Could I build a successful career as a music writer on the back of that one, earth-shattering exclusive? ('It sounds like a cliché, but it really is true,' I'd tell Zane Lowe. 'My life completely changed after I saw Lance Webster coming out of that dry-cleaners.') Most of them wholly implausible of course, but when, I am afraid, has that ever stopped me before? And let's not forget, I have back-up from the dream-world. Of *course* I can do all those things. That's what my dream was telling me to do. Look for him. Look for Geoffrey Webster. Don't just let him go. It was nothing less than a cosmic heads-up. All is clear.

Minutes later I'm tailing him round the corner of my own street. I've never really followed anyone before. I'm not doing any of the things I imagine one is supposed to do, such as keeping a reasonable distance: when he swings left down a little path to a fairly standard Victorian townhouse I'm probably about two metres behind him, so I have to swerve clumsily and walk straight past – which is stupid, really – had I been slightly further back I could have seen whether he'd pressed a bell or let himself in, or caught a glimpse of what was behind the door, whether or not it was a flat, all sorts of useful stuff. But no.

I'm left standing halfway up my street with now raging curiosity but no further details, no plan, no desire to go back home – and crucially, no light bulb, tampons, paracetamol or foul malt loaf for the waiting mess of headache and nausea that is Polly. Not wishing for a tricky weekend, I glumly venture back towards the high street. This is the way it's always been with Polly and me: she bails me out, I run her errands in return. Ever since university, when she spared me from a five-hundred-pound library fine by pretending to be dead. Long story.

I spend pretty much the rest of the day in a daze, playing Thieving Magpies songs, scribbling things in my notebook, hammering stuff out on my ancient laptop and drinking cans of lager and so on. Polly's hangover lasts until about six, at which point she buggers off to have a meal with Problem Sarah (a friend from university for whom Polly conducts weekly counselling sessions, to which I am rarely invited), leaving me the flat to myself so I can do all sorts of exciting things like fall asleep in front of *Parkinson* and spill lager all over my bowl of Doritos.

It's now Sunday. My twenty-four hours of thinking and recovering from the mini-encounter are just about up. And it's fairly reasonable to announce, I have something of a plan.

But I'm not due at the pub for another half an hour. There's time for a bit of a history lesson.

Unless you were a boring, unadventurous middle-class teenager living in a boring, unadventurous middle-class southern English town during the latter half of the 1980s, it's almost impossible to conceive the seismic impact a man like Lance Webster and his band of Thieving Magpies could've had on someone like me.

Nowadays, even if you have only a passing, superficial interest in popular music, you'd be well aware of a fairly balanced selection on offer. If you're after pure pop, you can get it. If you're after 'quality' indie, there's *heaps* of it. There are entire radio stations devoted to it, for God's sake. If it's a middle-of-the-road, singer-songwritery thing that floats your boat, you're inundated. And of course your myriad other genres and subgenres – metal, hip-hop, electronica, dance, folk, etc. – whatever you want, it's on a plate, in the high street, on the World Wide Interweb, at your polygenre multi-entertainment enormoshop. But in 1987 or 1988, as far as the cautious, conservative me was concerned, you had shit pop – *and that was pretty much it.* It was Stock/Aitken/Waterman acts (Kylie, Jason, Rick Astley), almost-as-bad non-Stock/Aitken/Waterman acts (Five Star, Yazz, Swing Out Sister), pointless bands signed on the back of U2 (Then Jerico, T'Pau), watery trios signed on the back of A-ha (Breathe, Johnny Hates Jazz), rapidly declining Norwegian trios (A-ha), rapidly declining former teen idols (Duran Duran, Spandau Ballet), desperate attempts to find new teen idols (Bros, Wet Wet Wet), desperate attempts to find the new Smiths (The Housemartins), woefully worthy adult pop (Dire Straits, Phil Collins), woefully worthy stadium rock (U2, Simple Minds) . . . and the Pet Shop Boys. It's an anxious state of affairs when the Pet Shop Boys can be described as a saving grace.

There I was, up to my waist in 1988, leafing through *Smash Hits* looking for, ooh, I don't know, some really interesting article about Terence Trent D'Arby, when I saw it. *Smash Hits* isn't widely remembered for its ground- breaking coverage of new rock talent, but back then the last embers of its early eighties credibility heyday were still smoking. Can't remember now who the piece was written by, Tom Hibbert or Ian 'Jocky' Cranna perhaps, but I can recite the review's finest ingredients word for word to this day:

> The hair may be long and the guitars loud 'n' thrashy, but these gents from Reading manage to make glorious pop the way it should be: spiky words, catchy melodies and beats to make you jump around the kitchen, complete with brilliant titles such as 'Have You Stopped Talking Yet?' and 'I Always Hated Love Songs' – like Morrissey but less pretentious.

As enticing as the rest of it was, that last bit was what grabbed me: 'like Morrissey but less pretentious'.

I didn't *get* Morrissey. I do now, of course, now that my balls have fully dropped and we have The Smiths' whole career to look back on, but I was too young in 1984 when they were doing the really good stuff, and by the time I was old enough to appreciate them, their output seemed limited to strange ditties about girlfriends in comas or disco dancers meeting sticky ends. And they were northern. Not that I have anything against northerners, but my blinkered, never-set-foot-north-of-Luton teenage self couldn't understand how a foppish, posh-singing geezer with flowers protruding from his arse could hail from a city that looked, whenever I saw it on TV, like the set of *Coronation Street*.

But these Thieving Magpies sounded *wicked*. Guitars that were 'loud 'n' thrashy'? Pop music 'the way it should be'? All in the same band? *In 1988?* Get me to a record shop NOW. And the fact they were from Reading, rather than East Kilbride, put a nice, cosy Home Counties spin on the whole thing. Clearly they were the band for me.

So I got me to a record shop. For such an occasion I decided to go somewhere a little more special than my town's usual chain retailers, partly because I anticipated blank looks when mentioning the band name, but mainly because I felt this total departure from my usual buying habits (the few things I heard on the radio that didn't disgust me) warranted a total change of scene. This was to be, after all, the very first time I had bought a record without previously hearing a note of its contents. I rose one Saturday morning, donned (in all probability) a Level 42 T-shirt, muttered something to my mum about having some homework to do with a friend and boarded the train to London.

An hour later I was struggling up the escalator of the world's windiest tube station, Kentish Town. I'd been reliably informed by someone at school that Kentish Town was *the* mecca of specialist pop music, bursting with stockists that were unlikely to shirk at a request for the obscurest of discs, let alone something that had already been featured in *Smash Hits*. So, imagine my surprise when I found myself wandering down a breathtakingly dull, rainswept high street, punctuated by a few scary-looking Irish pubs. I walked and walked, but the only hints of anything remotely cutting-edge were a shop that sold drums and an ironmonger's, which were hardly of interest. When the shops finally ran out I plucked up courage to ask a passer-by where I might go to buy records: 'Loads of places in Camden Town,' came the reply. Bugger. My idiot school informant had messed up the names. I strode the half-mile back up to Kentish Town station and, blissfully unaware of the finer points of London geography, travelled the one stop to Camden, eventually locating a likely looking emporium that happened to be about two hundred metres south of the spot where I'd just asked the passer-by for help.

Things didn't get any less confusing once I was inside. I'd seen few shops that looked less like my local branch of WHSmith. Here was a world of odd, multicoloured posters and flyers advertising appearances by groups whose names I couldn't even pronounce; of black-clad, black-haired, pale-faced characters floating aimlessly around; of background music that sounded like the neighbours were being murdered, and thousands of records arranged in no comprehensible order. What was 'US New Wave'? What was 'Industrial'? What was 'UK Indie'? And – most significantly, for me – where was the 'Rock and Pop' section?

I decided the best way of coping with my predicament was to also float around aimlessly, letting these strange new names and phrases creep into my head. Gothic. Post-punk. Front 242. Nitzer Ebb. Reading Festival. The Marquee. Spacemen 3. The Men They Couldn't Hang. Green On Red. Fulham Greyhound. Hüsker Dü. What *was* all this?

I must have been in the shop for twenty minutes before the guy behind the counter (dressed in a T-shirt that announced – to my continued bemusement – 'Death to the Pixies') asked me if I was all right.

'Uh . . . yeah,' I lied. But then, realising I didn't much want another perplexing, fruitless quarter of an hour to pass, added, 'Um . . . you got any Thieving Magpies?'

'Over there,' the assistant pointed. 'UK Alternative section.'

'Cheers,' I grunted. Alternative to what?

I located the appropriate rack and fished around, eventually reaching, via The Godfathers, Transvision Vamp, All About Eve, Voice of the Beehive and The Cult (some of whom I'd actually heard of), a plain, black cover that bore the legend 'Thieving Magpies/Shoot the Fish' in the favoured mock-typewriter-print font of the day. Nothing else was on the sleeve, apart from the tracklist (which included, to my amazement, a song called 'If I'm Still Sober, You're Still Ugly') and a small photo of some spotty, long-haired oiks on the back, standing next to a pond.

Energised by my successful hunt, I relaxed, rifled through the other racks, chatted amiably with the assistant and eventually saun-tered happily out of the shop with the Happy Mondays' *Bummed*, My Bloody Valentine's *Isn't Anything*, the twelve-inch of 'Touch Me I'm Sick' by Mudhoney and The Cardiacs' BBC Session EP. I then celebrated with a fortifying pint of Guinness in the Camden Stores.

I'm lying, of course. I shuffled out with my sole purchase, ignored everything else in Camden, bought a Marks & Spencer's sandwich and went home.

[From the Christmas 1988 edition of *Slade Lane School Magazine*.]

If you haven't heard of the Thieving Magpies yet, you will soon. They are a new pop group from Reading that I discov-ered recently, and their debut album, *Shoot the Fish*, has been literally glued to my turntable for the last three weeks. It's full of rocky guitars but the songs are brilliant. The singer is called Lance and he writes really good words, like in the song 'Soapbox':

Yesterday I spent just lying in the sunshine
Now my tan is fading and I don't feel so good.

Most of the songs are fast and loud, but they have two really good slow songs called 'Chopped Heart' and 'Have You Stopped Talking Yet?'. The second of these is an example of how the singer writes really angry words but juxtaposes them with a ballad melody.

None of their songs have got in the charts yet but they will soon. In fact, I predict that by this time next year they will be a household name!

Ask for *Shoot the Fish* this Christmas. You won't regret it!

Clive Beresford, Form 4B

Okay, I know. It has a distinct *eau de GCSE coursework* about it. But it was my first piece of 'proper' writing. And that was the edited version. The first draft was *much* better, and it included the lyrics I actually wanted to quote (the bit in 'Now That You Are Fashionable' that goes *'you're standing on a sinking ship . . . you might find someone who gives a shit but I doubt it'*). But anyway, it gives you a basic flavour of how I was feeling at the time: not two weeks after arriving home with the record, I had been prompted to begin a glittering career in music journalism – albeit one that could be mainly followed through dodgy fanzines and various publications' letters pages. I've tried many times to describe quite how I felt when I played that Magpies record for the first time (through headphones on my dad's record player, as it happened), but to this day the very best I can offer you are two desperately underwhelming clichés:

1.   When I heard that pounding drum intro, followed by the jagged guitar and the first snatch of Lance's searing vocal – everything felt *right*. Not quite a psychologically nourishing, 'all is right with the world' feeling, but certainly a feeling that everything was right with what I was hearing. The music did *exactly what I wanted it to*. The lyrics seemed every bit as cutting, cheeky and menacing as the titles suggested. They delivered on their promise. Unlike other bands of the time, it required no compromise on my part, no leap of faith, no 'ignore the singing and it's great' qualifiers (as I had to keep in mind when I first heard *The Stone Roses* the following year).

2.   The album gave me an unprecedented sense of *belonging*. Or at least, the potential of belonging. That may sound hopelessly daft and romantic, but bear in mind that at the age of fifteen – woefully shy, covered in spots and bollocks at sport – the concept of belonging to at least *something* other than the Tears For Fears fan club was fairly attractive. In this music I heard things I could identify with, and therefore the promise of something important: if I could find others in whom it also pushed the right buttons, I might just unearth a pocket of humans I could relate to. Those who were also bored to death of the utter nonsense on *Top of the Pops*; tired of listening to old Madness, Blondie, Police, Jam and XTC records in the absence of anything that could excite in a similar way; bewildered by simply making do with the latest Bon Jovi or INXS album because they at least happened to use guitars; too scared to try acid house, indifferent to heavy metal and harbouring a perpetual, passive and terribly English inner rage for the mundane, mainstream or familial. But too damn straight-laced to misbehave, to stand on street corners and take drugs or mug people,

and also not rich or cool enough to holiday in the Mediterranean, go skiing or have a few practice rounds of golf with Daddy. I had to find this section of similar people to whom I might belong; I had to find them *now*.

A set of circumstances that traditionally had driven similar disenfranchised youths to at the very least seek out the radio output of the late, great John Peel. Fuck it, I didn't even have the sense to try *that*. Nor did it immediately occur to me that this world I sought was the very same world to which the Camden record shop belonged. But I found out. It took a while – six months, to be precise – but I got there. And to my credit, I succeeded because I bypassed everything else and went straight, in the spring of 1989, to a Thieving Magpies gig.

I convinced my parents to let me go by pinching a piece of letterhead from the school office and typing a likely looking note from one of the lesser-known teachers stating that, on the strength of my magazine piece, the class trip would be to see the Thieving Magpies at the Hammersmith Odeon (it was actually Brixton Academy, but I thought that would set my mother's antennae twitching). There was also an upfront request for fifteen pounds in cash for the ticket and travel, which I innocently took to school one day in a brown envelope. Looking back on it, all sorts of things could have gone wrong, but luckily my parents were swayed by the power of the school emblem on the letter and – apart from a little vague muttering from my dad over his gin and tonic that 'surely the Science Museum would be more educational' – never thought to question it. So, rigid with excitement, I went.

The first thing that threw me was how bloody massive Brixton Academy was. The 'academy' bit brought to mind a sort of school hall, so I was amazed enough when I wandered up to the huge, domed building, but what really astonished me was the sheer number and variety of people who milled and queued outside. I really don't know what I was expecting – a few lonely individuals who'd also seen the *Smash Hits* review, perhaps – but I certainly wasn't prepared for an army of enormous, tattooed geezers wearing black vests, long shorts and dark boots; girls dressed similarly with dyed hair of every conceivable colour; some cheery-looking blokes with massive baggy jeans and fishing hats; a healthy yield of the kind of pale-faced, black-clad weirdo I had seen in the record shop (although there was nothing aimless or floatsome about most of them today, in fact spirits were quite unfeasibly high); and a large collection of boys and girls who were a bit like older versions of me but with longer hair (mine was still an entirely nondescript short-back-and-sides job at this stage), groovy boots or trainers with coloured laces (I wore my school shoes) and far more interesting T-shirts (thankfully I had selected something neutral for the evening, and not another gem from my small but horrific selection of pop garments). It was this final, slightly more 'normal' group of fans that intrigued me; could this be the long-sought crowd to which I wanted 'in'?

Hefty bottles of cider and cans of beer were guzzled and discarded before the whole throng streamed through the doors into the foyer. The gig hadn't even started but the air inside was already pungent with sweat, beer, smoke and another ever-present aroma that I later identified as patchouli oil. Alternately out of my depth and oddly at home, I found myself swept along with the tide of people towards the doors of the cavernous auditorium – where I got my next surprise. The support act (a concept I'd vaguely heard of) that began as I entered only consisted of two people: a bloke fiddling with a sort of synthesizer/record-deck combo, and another chap screaming incomprehensibles while thrashing away at a guitar. When they'd finished their opening 'song' the singer acknowledged the ripple of applause in a decidedly well-brought-up voice: 'Thanks! Good evening. We're International Brian!'

While International Brian screamed through their set I gaped at the huge hall with its incongruous white villa-style decoration, laughed at the clutch of people directly in front of the band who leapt, slammed into each other and flung their arms around (out of boredom, perhaps), bought myself a Coke (those were the days), marvelled at the collection of slogans emblazoned across people's chests ('Dinosaur Jr', 'Info Freako', 'Unbearable', 'Heroin Satan Fuck') and then at last prepared myself for the arrival of the mighty Magpies. I was to be disappointed. The quartet of blond-haired goons who flounced onstage to a modest cheer were in fact a second support band. What they did next beggared my already shaky belief. They kicked into their first number at such a ferocious pace that I half expected them to levitate, spontaneously combust or keel over into the pit. Guitars and hair flew in all directions, drums were mercilessly tortured and what passed for vocals were entirely indistinguishable from everything else. The storm raged for ten minutes and then crashed to a halt as the band demolished all their equipment and left. I was ready to laugh, but my fellow audience members roared their appreciation. Was that good? I had so much to learn.

As I made my way to the loo I became concerned that it might be the custom at this sort of concert for the performances to get shorter the further up the bill you went. Therefore, if International Brian's set was half an hour and this last lot played for just under a quarter, how long would the Magpies play for? Seven, eight minutes? That was barely time for two songs. Oh well. At least I'd be home on time. Or perhaps all the groups went around again, for another go?

'Beresford!'

Eh?

'Beresford! Clive!'

Odd. Someone had the same name as me.

'Clive! Over here!'

I glanced in the direction of the voice. Sitting cross-legged on the floor next to the bar, to my amazement, was a face I recognised.

'Potter! Sorry, Alan!'

'Beresford, what the fuck are you doing here?'

'I'm . . . well. You know.'

Alan Potter was in the year above me at school, which officially meant we could have nothing to do with each other, but he'd always seemed a friendly enough chap; one of the lower-sixth-formers less likely to punch you in the nuts as you carried your dinner tray. He wore black jeans with a blue and white stripy T-shirt, and was accompanied by a small purple-haired girl who stared silently at the carpet for the duration of the conversation.

'I never knew you liked alternative, Beresford.'

That word again.

'Well, I sort of, you know . . . Thieving Magpies. They're pretty good.'

'Yeah, but did you see Birdland? Fuck!'

Did I?

'Apparently they did their shortest set ever the other day, and it was *six minutes*,' he enthused, as if this represented the very pinnacle of artistic achievement.

'Wow, amazing,' I replied uneasily.

'D'you want some of this?' Alan asked, handing me a plastic glass of bright red liquid.

'Uh, yeah.' I took a sip. Blackcurrant. With some sort of alcohol.

'Who you here with?'

'Er . . . no one,' I admitted.

'No one? Fuck, man. You can hang out with us if you like. But don't tell anyone at school.'

If I was heartened by this gesture, I soon discovered the pay-off. After I settled down next to the pair, I attempted to make conversation by asking what Alan had meant by 'alternative'. After he stopped laughing at my evident naïvety and ignorance, he provided me with a definition so compendious that I began to assume he'd memorised a school essay on the subject. Alternative, he began, was the name of the musical movement to which the Thieving Magpies belonged, so called because it formed an alternative to basically everything else.

The criteria under which a band qualified to call itself alternative was subtle, somewhat intangible and often contradictory, but Alan advised keeping in mind a mental tick-box chart, on which the group in question must score at least two or three, as a reliable identifier:

- Guitars, often distorted or effected, but with a minimalist playing style (i.e. few solos)
- Straightforward, raw production on recordings
- 'Gigs' (as opposed to 'concerts') at which . . .
- . . . 'rucking' took place (as opposed to 'moshing', which only happened at heavy-metal shows)
- A loyal group of fans, often with its own collective name (e.g. The Mission's followers, who were known as 'eskimos'), sometimes even with an exclusive costume or dance
- A down-to-earth, ironic, self-effacing attitude (which therefore excluded most heavy-metal bands)
- Participation at outdoor festivals
- Coverage in the music papers *Sounds*, *NME* and *Melody Maker*
- Public denouncement of mainstream pop music
- A paucity of clichéd/excessive references to love in lyrics (with the exception of goth bands, who could pretty much get away with anything)
- 'Experimental' nature of song composition/arrangement
- An appreciation of (but not necessarily over-indulgence in) alcohol and/or drugs

And so on.

The overall *sound* of the music mattered less than one might think, Alan explained. Crucial to the issue was the band's aesthetic relationship with punk. An act could, for example, mainly use electronic instruments – the staple of decidedly non-alternative acts like

Eurythmics – but throwing in the occasional punky power chord and having a 'punk attitude' would instantly put them in the alternative bracket, as in the case of Renegade Soundwave or The Shamen. Punk was also a key factor in how a band *ceased* to be alternative: U2, for example, had almost certainly been alternative when they started out, but had recently steered themselves so far off the punk map with releases like *Rattle and Hum* that they'd been expelled. (It was theoretically possible, Alan argued, for a previously mainstream group to *become* alternative, although it rarely happened – Depeche Mode being one of the few recent examples.)

He pointed out that a lot of people described all of this as simply 'indie' music, on account of the greater share of alternative acts being signed to independent labels, but earnestly warned me that using this term could be misleading in the extreme, for not only could it accidentally include unwanted horrors (most of the acts produced by Stock/Aitken/Waterman, for example, were signed to Waterman's own label, PWL, so were technically speaking 'indie'), but it could also discount a whole crop of dyed-in-the-wool alternative bands (e.g. New Model Army, Balaam and the Angel and Thieving Magpies themselves) whose output was administered by major record companies. 'Alternative' was therefore a far more reliable moniker.

Alan sat back, clearly delighted with this dissertation, and took a swig of his red stuff. I was just about to comment when he embarked on the appendices – a bewildering rundown of the many subgenres that sheltered under alternative's umbrella (goth, grebo, punk-metal *et al.*) – but then he must have sensed that I'd switched off, for he rapidly reverted to the Magpies themselves.

'They're the most likely to,' he stated.

'Most likely to what?'

'Go mega. Become huge, man. They're gonna be the biggest alternative band in the world. They've got the goods. They're streets ahead. No one else has got the songs, man.'

'That's right,' I agreed, knowledgeably. I considered asking him if he'd seen my school-magazine piece, but decided it might be neither the time nor place.

'But their attitude as well. Webster's got it sussed. He knows *exactly* what he's doing. He can run circles round those cunts.'

I nodded uncomfortably.

'So, do you go to a lot of these, er . . . gigs?'

'Not many,' Alan grumbled. 'Only about once a week. I can't afford much more. I try to see smaller bands; they're always cheaper. Tickets for this place are seven quid now, man. With travel and a few jars that's almost a score. I only get paid fifteen.'

'Fifteen – you work, then?'

'Sainsbury's on Saturday, man. It's a pisser, but . . . uh-oh. Hold up. We'd better get going.'

A slight change in atmosphere had alerted Alan to the imminent arrival of the main attraction. He and his female friend rose, grabbed another pint of alcoholic Ribena from the bar and then proceeded to barge their way through the now heaving and shoving capacity crowd until we reached a position of quite alarming proximity to the stage. I was also overjoyed to notice we were squashed right next to the scary tattoo brigade I'd spotted outside, who were drunkenly roaring various phrases at each other ('Theeeeevers!', 'Wankaaaaah!', 'Yooou're shit! Aahhhh!'). I must have had a face like a wet lettuce, as Alan grinned and nudged me in the ribs.

'Don't worry, man. Just watch out for the MFM.'

'The what?'

'Mass Forward Movement.'

I didn't need to ask what it was, because just as Alan said it, it happened. The lights blacked out, four thousand voices emitted a roar louder than I considered possible, the opening piano flourish of The Boomtown Rats' 'I Don't Like Mondays' blasted out of the giant speaker stacks and everyone instantly decided they wanted to stand where I was standing. I was carried several yards forward as people of both genders rammed themselves against me in time with the music. Quite why we were listening to Bob Geldof hoarsing his way through this old classic – let alone bouncing around to it as though it were a Motörhead song – was the least of my worries. The Magpies hadn't even taken to the stage yet and I was already bobbing threateningly near the yellow-shirted bouncers who glared at the melee and occasionally, I was horrified to see, hoicked people out who had evidently got too close. Where did they go after that, I wondered? I had visions of some terrifying backstage torture chamber where the guards wrenched the most foul confessions out of hapless Thieving Magpies fans ('Okay, okay! I admit it! I did quite like the last Deacon Blue single!') for their own amusement.

It's a strange feeling to have so many of your preconceptions flattened in so few minutes. Virtually nothing about the evening so far had been what I expected. But from the moment the onstage lights kicked in and the audience's ovation reached an alarming crescendo, as four blokes I vaguely recognised ambled onstage and picked up their instruments, everything was somehow a little more familiar. From then on, God knows how, I knew exactly what was going to happen. I suppose the music on *Shoot the Fish* contained a strange sort of semiotic coding which transferred information directly into the brain of the eager listener, so that he/she really would expect the drummer to have that cool, energetic but nonchalant approach to beating his kit, the guitarist that way of spanking his instrument like it was a naughty child even on the mellowest tracks, that the bassist would remain in his corner doing, well, absolutely nothing but playing the bass, and that Lance Webster had a habit of remaining on the lip of the stage, confrontationally staring out the crowd, until it was almost too late to return to the microphone to bellow out the lyrics. I was also magically aware that Webster would not utter a word of greeting until after the fifth song, finally acknowledging the audience's presence by demanding, 'So what, is it your fucking bedtime already?' before launching into a seething rendition of

'Scared of Being Nice', with its tender refrain '*I don't respect you but I'll fuck you anyway*'. A sentiment I was still blissfully ignorant of, but on that night I'm sure I knew what he meant.

Above the bouncing, kicking, screaming, ramming, hollering and gurning stupidly with unfettered delight, the proceedings were presided over with breathtaking authority by Mr Webster: equal parts scary teacher, football coach, rock 'n' roll fuck-up and demigod. His vocals were clear, faultless and a hundred times more powerful and emotive than on the record. His regular insults ('We didn't come all the way here to entertain a room full of idle wankers') were perfectly executed, just the right side of totally abusive, and you knew you were never too far away from a cheeky grin. And those songs shone out across the vast theatre to the point where, for the first time in my fifteen-year-old life, I experienced a profound unity, of almost five thousand people, most of whom had never met before and would barely meet again, welded together by a common focus, taste, purpose, anger, release and enjoyment. A unity this Lance Webster was able to control with virtually the flick of an eyelid.

I am still − some eighteen years later − *astonished* to report that when the band left the stage for the third and last time (after a brutal rendition of 'Zeitgeist Man', a B-side that had now become their standard gig finale) I staggered up to a similarly soaked Alan Potter, put my hand on his shoulder and burst into tears. I don't think I'd actually cried at all since I trod heavily on a large nail when I was eight, but I was so physically and emotionally exhausted and consumed by the knowledge that I'd finally found my own world, and that Lance Webster was its *de facto* president, that I couldn't do anything else. Alan clearly understood enough to not need ask what was wrong, and patted my shoulder in a matey sort of way.

'Yeah, all right, man, that'll do,' he said after a few seconds.

Although the journey home began with much lively banter and comparing of notes, I was all too aware as the train neared our town that our temporary friendship was coming to an end and that we were simply in a different year at school once more. Like a fool, in the station car park, as Alan walked away to his parents' car, I gushed, 'Let me know when you're going to some more gigs!' To which he responded curtly, 'Yeah, we'll see what happens, all right.'

As I trudged home I felt the evening quickly evaporate, and started to come to terms with the fact that my day-to-day life would remain, for the moment, unaltered. School trips could not be synthesised in this way very often, if ever again, really. But I had hope. I suppose I saw Alan as perhaps the keyholder of that hope but, wisely for an immature fifteen-year-old, I calculated that simply striding up to him in the dinner hall and saying brightly, 'Hello! So who are you seeing this week, and can I come?' was precisely the wrong thing to do. The solution would be to somehow have something that he wanted from *me*. My current set of possessions, attributes and circumstances presented nothing of the kind, of course, but I was sure that if I thought hard enough I would come up with something.

But that's enough for now – I'm late for the pub.

YOU CAN TELL US TO FUCK OFF IF YOU LIKE

Alan is already halfway through his first pint and tenner on the fruit machine by the time I appear. He's always been punctual. I find it quite annoying. I used to bitch to others that it was because he had nothing else to do. Now I realise he's just efficient. Which is probably why he is the owner of a successful business and is loaded, and why I am not.

'Hello, mate,' I begin.

'Hi.'

Can't talk to him now, he's three nudges away from victory. I get a drink instead.

'Shit,' he observes, petulantly slapping the side of the machine as I return. We sit down, Alan switches off his phone. 'All right then, what's this amazing piece of news?'

I take a deep breath.

'Lance Webster is living in a house at the end of my road.'

'Oh, fucking hell.'

This is not the reaction I hoped for. But I remain hopeful.

'Is that a good "fucking hell"?'

'No, it isn't. Are you serious? Is that really what you have to tell me?'

'Yes!'

'Oh, for God's sake, Clive. I thought you were gonna tell me you're getting back together with—'

'And you really think *that* would be good news?'

'Well, I'd think so.'

'Well, it wouldn't be,' I assure him. 'Can we get back to my original subject?'

He exhales theatrically. 'Lance Webster.'

'I saw him yesterday picking some stuff up from the dry-cleaners. Then I followed him home.'

'You sad bastard.'

'He lives at number 3 on my road. Possibly 3A.'

'How d'you know he actually lives there?'

'He must do. Unless he's started a dry-cleaning delivery service.'

Alan smirks. 'It might really have come to that.'

'I'm going to interview him.'

'How?'

'Not sure yet.'

'I didn't think he did that any more.'

'That's 'cos people have approached him the wrong way,' I proclaim. 'I'm going to do it differently. Informally. He might not even know he's being interviewed.'

'So what, you're going to chat him up in a bar or something?'

'Maybe. Something like that.'

'Why do you want to interview him?'

I take a large gulp of beer.

'Because I think it's time for the definitive story.'

'Of the Magpies?'

'Yeah, partly. But the whole scene as well. And I want to find out what really happened to him that night.'

Alan snorts. 'No one knows what happened to him that night. I doubt even *he* knows what happened to him that night.'

'Well, I'm going to find out.'

'Right.' He shrugs and looks around the pub. At first I think he is impressed by my resolve, then I realise he's probably heard me make these grand statements of intent before. 'Well, good luck,' he offers.

'You could be a bit more enthusiastic. If I'd told you this ten years ago you'd be camping outside his house.'

'Let's not have that argument again, Clive.'

He's referring to a frightful drunken row we had a year or so ago when I accused him of becoming a total sell-out to consumerist society, with all attendant charges concerning lost youth, forgotten dreams, rampant global capitalism, blah blah. Not entirely unfounded, but not a conversation I particularly want to have again either.

'There must be a flicker of interest in there somewhere,' I insist.

Alan sighs. 'The guy's dead, man. I mean, the Lance Webster I used to know, we used to know. He's old news. He's the past. And . . . well, if I really think about it, I'm probably still a bit pissed off with him.'

'All the more reason to try and speak to him.'

Alan makes that weird noise he always makes when he's a bit sceptical, sort of a cross between a scoff and a belch.

'I'm not really sure how far you'll get.'

'Well, I've been thinking of doing something quite radical about it.'

'Like?'

'Spying on him for a few days.'

'Careful, man. You remember . . .'

'Yeah, I know, but I'd be really subtle. Nothing sinister, only to find out where he goes, what he does. Where he drinks. Where he eats. And then – go undercover.'

'Explain.'

'Like – I dunno, get a job in the pub he goes to, or—'

'You could start working at that dry-cleaners,' Alan deadpans, sipping his drink.

'No, somewhere that might require banter. Like his music shop.'

'You're mad. Anyway, I don't think he even plays music any more.'

'He's bound to do something, though.'

'What does he look like these days?'

'Pretty much the same. Slightly fatter perhaps. Same kind of hair, like it was after he cut it. Receding a tad. Dresses smartly. A bit like Mick Jones, but younger.'

'Facial hair?'

'No.'

Alan ponders for a moment, then his eyes light up slightly. I think I've got him.

'I'd love to ask him about Gloria Feathers.'

I open my hands with what I hope looks like an air of benevolence.

'All this may be possible.'

Alan grins stupidly at me for a few seconds, like a toddler who's just been promised an ice cream. Unfortunately it doesn't last.

'So where exactly do I fit in?' he frowns.

'Well,' I smile greasily, 'quite apart from wanting to share my plan and its subsequent progress with my oldest friend . . . I was sort of hoping you could lend me something.'

'What?'

'I'll be really careful with it.'

His frown becomes a glare.

'Oh no.'

'Oh, come on.'

'Clive, no. You don't understand. That thing is under lock and key.'

'I know.'

'And it's falling to bits.'

'I know! I won't take it anywhere.'

'That book is valuable. Some of the ticket stubs are worth—'

My turn to scoff. 'Worth what? They're fascinating, but they're not *worth* anything.'

'That Jesus Jones ticket, man. Kilburn National, May 1990. Blur first on the bill, Ned's second. That's worth *money*, man. The geezer on XFM said so.'

'Well, whatever. It's not really the ticket stubs I'm interested in. It's the other stuff.'

'Why do you need it?'

'Partly for research purposes. But . . . well, put it this way, if . . . sorry, *when* I meet the bloke, I'm gonna look a whole lot more impressive with that on my bookshelf.'

'You actually reckon you're going to get him round to your house?'

'I'm using the word "bookshelf" figuratively.'

'Yeah, exactly – which is another way of saying my precious scrapbook will be knocking around in your bloody rucksack for weeks on end. I tell you what, man, you set up a meeting with him, or provide me with some . . . evidence that you're making headway, and you can borrow the book.'

I shake my head in disbelief.

'Arse. "Provide me with some evidence" – for God's sake, you're beginning to talk to friends like you're conducting an audit.'

Alan shrugs, Shylock-style. 'Those are my terms.'

'Thanks, but it really would be better if I could have the book first . . .'

'Perhaps, but I'm not budging on this one. Not after what happened to my Curve twelve-inches.'

'Oh, come on, some of the reviews in there are mine anyway.'

We continue in this manner for another ten minutes, after which an unsteady compromise is reached. I will be able to view the scrapbook within the confines of Alan's house, but it is not to be removed until some contact with Webster has been made, the nature of which will be evaluated by Alan at the time. I am happy with this, up to a point. The next debate is whether my initial scrapbook visiting time could be this very afternoon – which, after some resistance, I win.

We jump into Alan's Mini and head to Crouch End. He goes a really stupid route via Highbury Corner so it takes ages and I have to endure most of the Kooks album, but the *en route* banter suggests he is a little more upbeat about my proposed project than he originally let on. Finally he swings the little car into a spot outside his palatial residence.

I cannot possibly overstress how different Alan and Liz's place is to the sort of dwellings that Polly and I end up grumblingly sharing. Potter Heights, as only I call it, is a four-storey townhouse entirely owned and occupied by the Potter family and their Bulgarian nanny, who has her own flat on the top floor. It's clean and immaculately decorated; carpet in rooms that require it, real varnished wooden floors in those that don't. It's always warm. Alan and Liz each have an office on the first floor. The lounge *cum* dining room, which can be one or two separate rooms depending on what mood you're in, is bigger than our entire flat. The basement *is* the kitchen, where the fridge groans with produce from posh local delis and organic-mongers. There are five loos. It's the sort of house even Alan's parents describe as large. All of this from a bloke who only five years ago was living on 25p packets of noodles, sneaking cans of lager into the pub and buying albums on cassette in their first week of release.

We go inside and, emphasising that this is strictly a business mission rather than a social call, Alan leads me straight up to his office.

'Coffee?'

I can't help giggling.

'Yeah. And a blueberry muffin.'

Alan laughlessly pads over to the corner of the room where he unlocks a large, battered and sticker-covered record box (some things thankfully never change) from which, with the greatest of care, he extracts the bulging, spiral-bound A5 notebook and solemnly places it on his desk in front of me. He looks at his watch and almost, I am convinced, says something like 'you've got fifteen minutes' but clearly thinks better of it and departs for the kitchen. Strange bastard.

But never mind all that. For the item now in my hot little hands makes everything worth it. Alan's greatest labour of love (apart from his daughter, perhaps). A chronological record of every gig he attended between 1988 and 1995. A total of 284 separate events: where they were, who he was with, a list (where possible) of what songs were played, the ticket stubs, press cuttings, sometimes his own photos, even details of how he got home – all brought to the thin sheets in glorious Anal-Alancolor. It's been almost half a decade since I held this masterpiece of indie-pop accountancy, so this afternoon's rifling session is particularly satisfying. Aside from the first few pages (when I was probably sitting at home memorising French irregular verbs), I can open the book anywhere to be instantly assailed by the most vivid of memories: PJ Harvey at the White Horse in Hampstead, The House of Love at Cambridge Corn Exchange, EMF supporting Carter USM at ULU ('they were great, some cocks tried to attack the singer, though . . . Neil Tennant showed up'), Paris Angels at Manchester Hacienda ('I have seen the Paris Angels and I believe'), Power of Dreams at Camden Palace ('they're amazing, why aren't they massive?'), Loop at Our Price in Reading ('without question the best thing I have ever witnessed in my entire life'), Madonna at Wembley Stadium ('me and Clive were the only people wearing Ned's Atomic Dustbin T-shirts in the whole place, which kind of made it worthwhile'), Björk at Wembley Stadium, supporting U2 ('she was so good we decided to leave straight afterwards'), Nine Inch Nails at Wembley Stadium supporting Guns N' Roses ('they were so good we decided to stay for Guns N' Roses'), Jane's Addiction supporting The Wonder Stuff at Brixton Academy

('I thought they were shit, Clive thought they were amazing – big row'). And of course, looming large throughout the volume, no less than eighty-six entries concerning the Thieving Magpies.

Although not the very first band Alan saw (that honour went to – oh, the shame of it! – The Blow Monkeys), the Magpies were certainly the first group whose live appearance Alan deemed worth commemorating. The opening entry was probably made a while after the occasion itself (he actually chanced upon a supporting set of theirs while seeing, as further disgrace and hilarity would have it, Status Quo) and in fact is executed in such an uncharacteristically girly way one would almost suspect Alan's younger sister were behind it. Spread over two pages, an early, catalogue-esque photo of each band member glued in and framed with multicoloured felt-tip flourishes, their names written lovingly underneath, the ticket proudly displayed above, with the Quo's name blacked out and the Magpies' logo glued over the words 'plus special guests'. And, weaving its way around the pictures and assorted bunting, Alan's hysterical write-up – again, one suspects, written with the benefit of hindsight:

Tonight we saw the group that's going to change my life, weren't expecting much when they walked on but oh my God they were brilliant. The energy was mind-blowing, they started with 'Scared of Being Nice' and then roared through the rest. Lance took the piss out of the crowd, telling them Francis Rossi had an accident and was going to play in a wheelchair. All the songs were well good, 'You're Still Ugly' and 'Have You Stopped Talking Yet' and 'Siamese Burn' and 'Marlow Meltdown' (B-side of Soapbox) were all WICKED. Brill bit in 'Chopped Heart' when he started singing Pictures of Matchstick Men. I don't think the audience thought it was funny. But fuck, I'm going to see them again . . . loads . . . this is the beginning of the future!!!

Indeed, how prophetic. Although, as if to prove he hadn't quite left mainstream late-eighties hell, the second entry was a very small passage concerning a Steve Winwood concert.

I skip to the end. It's some token of the huge part the Thieving Magpies played in this music fan's life that his tome is bookended by accounts of their performances: the first bursting with naïve colour, fresh, exciting discovery and a fifteen-year-old's unjaded optimism; the last, black as fuck and weighed down to drowning point with bitter disappointment, as the last spluttering breaths of a golden era and its crowned champion went gurgling down the alternative-rock drainpipe. Alan must have used the entire contents of a permanent marker to blacken the two-page spread, the centrepiece of which bears the succinct description 'TWAT' scrawled in red across a cheery snap of the man himself. Above, meanwhile, an advert boasting the Aylesbury line-up is roughly pasted, a neat rip straight through the heart of the very same band logo so proudly boasted seven years previously, and languishing below, the entry's sole – and the scrapbook's final – sentence:

CONGRATULATIONS, ZEITGEIST MAN, YOU'VE DONE EXACTLY WHAT THOSE BASTARDS WANTED YOU TO DO.

Alan had angrily ripped out the book's remaining few blank pages.

But like all intense love affairs, Alan's with Webster and his group didn't end as instantly as his final instalment suggested. For many months afterwards he continued to scour the pages of the music press and expectantly phone the Thieving Magpies fanclub for any sign that normal service would be resuming, and their final album remained in perpetual proximity to his CD player. But, as sales of *(What's the Story) Morning Glory?* went stratospheric, while Tony Blair contacted removal men for his imminent arrival at Downing Street – and bands like Rialto suddenly discovered they had a career – something definitely withered and died in Alan. I suppose it would have died eventually anyway, few people are able to sustain the same level of fanaticism for something as frivolous as a pop group once real life kicks in, but for Alan, when Lance Webster stormed off that stage in a blaze of violence the proverbial dream really was over. The very next week he went and got his hair cut.

'Eurghh,' Alan cringes, returning with the coffee. 'For Christ's sake, don't show him that page.'

'That's the best bit.'

'The sentimentality of youth,' he frowns, handing me a muffin. When you ask for something to eat at Alan's, you get it. Even if you were joking.

'So I'm just trying to find,' I begin, leafing through the book, 'the gig that we spoke to him at.'

'Beef, I think. New Cross Venue.'

'The Heart Throbs at the Square,' I correct him.

'He was *at* that gig. But it wasn't where we spoke to him the first time. Sorry, Clive, could you be a bit more gentle with the pages?'

'Sorry.'

'It was the Beef gig. I approached him halfway through that cover they used to do.'

'"You Sexy Thing"?'

'No, the other one. "These Boots . . ." and so on.'

I shake my head. 'I'm sure it was at The Heart Throbs.'

'Depends which conversation you're talking about. I've had more than one chat with him, you know—'

'Here it is,' I interrupt, triumphantly. 'The Square, Harlow, *the seventh of April nineteen ninety*. "We spoke to Lance Webster!" – in very excited pre-pubescent handwriting, I must say.'

'Piss off.'

'"We asked him what the real lyrics were to the bridge of 'Me in a Room'."'

'Oh, *that* conversation,' Alan huffs, tidying some papers.

'"Dominic drove us, but finally was a wanker." Ha! I remember what *that*'s about.'

'He was never quite as useful as we planned, was he?'

We had befriended Dominic Browne for the sole reason that he'd just been given a car by his wealthy and spoiling parents. Driving the family jeep while holidaying in Spain meant that he was ready to pass his driving test practically by the time he'd finished breakfast on his seventeenth birthday. I was still sixteen at this point; Alan, much to his annoyance and embarrassment, had already failed the test twice. Credit where it's due, Dominic had a fairly respectable alternative track record: he'd attended both Glastonbury and Reading the previous year, he'd used his new set of wheels to follow Claytown Troupe around the country during half-term and had already, we were envious to learn, been to a Faith No More show. The items that weakened his case to be a *genuine* gigging companion were that he excelled at sport *and* academic work, drank little, insisted on wearing a rugby shirt and proper shoes to indie clubs, was generally a bit full of himself and, we suspected, wouldn't deliberate too long about screwing you over if it made his own life easier: a hunch that was conclusively proved correct that particular evening in Harlow.

The three of us had piled into Dominic's convertible Volkswagen Golf (a car that further downgraded his indie credentials, we considered), ploughed up the M11 and, tradition dictated, necked a few cans of Strongbow before our arrival at the Square, an externally unpromising club that had nonetheless already played host to some pivotal musical evenings for me. We were standing around watching the support band, trying to think of witty chat-up lines for some of the tie-dyed lovelies scattered around the room – when Lance Webster ambled past, followed, as was often the case, by the pile of blond dreadlocks known to most as Gloria Feathers.

'Did you see that?' I whispered to Dominic (Alan had gone to the toilet).

'Yeah,' he shrugged. 'So?'

That was the other thing about Dominic. A fan of pretty much all the other bands we liked, he thought the Magpies were 'a bit too commercial'. Whether he really believed this or just said it to endow himself with a highbrow opinion, I never quite worked out.

'Fuck,' I muttered to no one in particular. 'I've got to try and speak to him.' Cautiously I looked over to where he and Gloria stood. A third party had joined them now, perhaps The Heart Throbs' guitarist. As usual Gloria was doing all the talking.

Alan returned from the loo and instantly noticed the new arrival. 'The fuck's he doing here?'

'Dunno.'

'Maybe he goes to the out-of-town ones so he doesn't get hassled,' Alan mused.

'Funny that, I was thinking of hassling him myself,' I commented.

'Forget it, man. You'll never get past Gloria.'

The support band finished and the DJ, perhaps thinking it would serve as a welcome to the venue, stuck on the Magpies' 'Me in a Room'. I glanced in Webster's direction; he had rolled his eyes and buried himself deeper into the conversation. Dominic feigned disgust and went to get another Diet Coke; Alan and I, normally happy to dance anywhere, self-consciously swayed a bit and tried not to mouth the words. I couldn't relax, knowing who was a few bodies away from me. I needed to somehow reach out to him, give him some small indication of the happy turmoil he was helping my life plunge into; but without appearing to be some kind of gibbering Super Fan. Whatever I said to him needed to have a *point*. A minute later the angrily sung, incomprehensible middle-eight of the song kicked in and the man himself gave me my answer.

'I'm going to ask him what he's singing here,' I declared to Alan suddenly.

'Okay,' Alan nodded, without debate.

'Can you come with me?'

'You sure?'

'Yeah. In case Gloria hits me or something.'

We paused for a moment. I felt like I was standing outside my headmaster's office, preparing to knock.

'I'm not sure, man,' admitted Alan. 'He might tell us to fuck off.'

'Part of me doesn't care.'

'Shall we try and have a drink first or something?'

The DJ swapped the Magpies tune for 'Sensitize' by That Petrol Emotion. A small whoop went up from Webster's corner and Gloria skipped off to dance near the stage with some others.

'Now,' I commanded.

We nudged our way past a few people until we were directly in front of him. We stood there foolishly for what seemed like ten minutes until I remembered I was meant to be doing the talking; I drew breath to speak but then heard Alan's voice next to me.

'Er, excuse me, man. Sorry to bother you . . . you can tell us to fuck off if you like . . .'

Webster grinned cheekily. 'Fuck off, then.'

We all laughed. Phew!

'We were wondering,' I continued, taking the reins back from Alan, 'what the lyrics were to that bit in "Me in a Room"?'

'"Me in a Room",' Webster repeated, narrowing his eyes at me strangely. *He's short*, I thought. *He's wearing a long, brown and decidedly non-alternative suede jacket. His hair looks scruffy and knotted.* But – *he's Lance Webster.*

'The bridge bit,' Alan added.

'Sounds like you're singing "*the system eyes all grind around the fuck*",' I pointed out, laughing nervously.

'That's probably because I am singing that,' he smiled. 'I think it began life as something else, perhaps "*I sit, I stand, I sleep, I drink, I fuck*", but we recorded it one night when I got pissed out of my head on Black Russians and had to keep doing it over and over . . . the more pissed I got the more I changed it, until it just became that. I can't believe it, you bastards have picked my one nonsensical lyric!'

'Sorry,' I muttered.

'We never play it live anyway,' Webster sneered. 'Shit song.'

'No, it's great,' Alan and I chanted in unison.

'All right,' Webster laughed, 'you really *can* fuck off now.'

Class dismissed.

'Nice one,' stammered Alan, turning to go.

'See you at Rivermead,' I said stupidly, and followed.

We returned to where a smirking Dominic stood, clearly delighted at how short the exchange had been.

'So, what did he have to say?'

'What a geezer,' Alan began.

'Top bloke,' I added.

'Yes, but what did he actually say? For God's sake, Beresford, your bloody hands are shaking.'

He was right. My adrenalin rush had reached its peak, coupled with the sweet satisfaction at having actually pulled off a Nice Little Chat with my hero. Just like three mates, we'd been, shooting the breeze in a bar before watching a great band. I was one of *them*. Despite the fact he'd essentially told us to fuck off twice in the space of one conversation.

'Oh, we were just talking about his lyrics, you know . . .'

'Which lyrics?'

'The guy's so fucking creative, man,' Alan explained. 'He was telling us how he wrote the song as one thing, then—'

'. . . decided on the spur of the moment he wanted to do something different.'

'He's indecisive, you mean.'

This from Dominic triggered two glares of unbridled outrage.

'Oh!' I coughed, unable to phrase my indignation.

'He's an *artist*,' managed Alan. 'It's *improvisation*.'

'Whatever. Did you ask if he'd do an interview for *Peanuts*?'

'It's called *Vorsprung Durch Peanut*, Browne,' I spat. 'Or the *Peanut*, if you must shorten it. And no, I didn't. That wasn't the point.'

'Like he'd have said yes anyway.'

'He *does* do fanzine interviews actually. Give us a sip of your Coke, will you.'

'No. Why don't you ask Lance Webster for a sip of his snakebite?'

'Like a Daydream' by Ride came jangling out of the speakers, to increased frugging from the room's swelling crowd.

'Ahh,' sighed Dominic. 'Now we're talking about artists. This guy. Lance Webster's a fucking ironmonger by comparison.'

'Bunch of wimps, man,' Alan summarised.

'Mark Gardener's just a pin-up boy,' I elaborated. 'He does fuck all. The guitarist's the main one. And anyway, they're shit live.'

Neither of us really meant all this. We'd thoroughly enjoyed seeing Ride at ULU a few months back, but when it came to defending the Magpies we had ears and eyes for no one else.

Dominic sipped his drink and shook his head sadly.

'You two. You just won't stop living in your little dreamworld of Magpies and Atomic Dustmen and bloody Wendy James. [Alan had a particular weakness for Transvision Vamp, something I didn't completely share.] Aren't you ever interested in something more mature?'

'Mature!' Alan barked. 'What's so bloody mature about The Darling Buds?'

'They're exquisite. As are Soho, who you're also unable to appreciate.'

'Pile of shit, man. And what was that wank you were listening to the other day, the dance stuff?'

'"What Time Is Love?", KLF,' responded Dominic confidently. 'It's gonna be huge.'

'Well, I don't like it, man. And The Shamen. It's all a load of toss. And that fucking Gary Clail bullshit. If I wanted to listen to dance music I'd hang out with Jamie Eisner.'

Dominic put his drink down and squared up to Alan.

'You just hate stuff that doesn't fit into your neat little boxes, don't you?'

'No, I—'

'It's okay, Alan, I understand. I realise it takes a while for your brain to allow all this horrible new stuff past your little elitist alternative checkpoint. It was exactly the same when I introduced you to Jesus Jones—'

'That's utter bullshit, *I* discovered *them*—'

'Don't worry, Alan. I don't mind. But for the moment, if you don't like what I play in my car, don't fucking get into it.'

Thankfully The Heart Throbs took to the stage at this point, because I thought it was getting a bit out of hand. Dominic wandered off to another part of the room, as he sometimes did, and after Alan calmed down we pushed forward, as we always did. There's nothing quite like a slice of blissful, slightly dreamy guitar pop to take the edge off, and soon we were back where we started: watching a top gig, having just passed the time of day with our favourite musician. Only once did a nag of doubt resurface in my mind.

'You don't think he's gonna fuck off without us, do you?'

'Nah, man,' Alan replied. 'I've had worse arguments with him before. I stole that bird off him at the See See Rider gig and he still gave me a lift home.'

Adequately reassured, I allowed myself to drift back, as the band swept into their finest tune, 'Dreamtime'. One of those orgasm-points in gigdom followed, when everyone and everything seem to be as one: the Carlotti sisters' harmonies, the guitars, the lights, the colourful, dancing crowd – all melted together, as I looked over to see (I mean, could life possibly get any better?) Lance Webster, looking pretty enrapt himself as he gently bopped next to the rather more animated Gloria Feathers. I felt fairly certain there were few places closer to the centre of the alternative-rock universe than where I was standing at that moment. I didn't even wince with envy a little later when I caught sight of Dominic, who'd somehow got talking to a pretty girl in a Bomb Disneyland T-shirt.

A girl who later received a lift from Dominic in his convertible Volkswagen Golf; unaccompanied, I hardly need add, by Alan and me.

'Cock!' yelled Alan for probably the fourth time, as we sprinted down the dark street towards the station. 'I'm gonna fucking crucify him on Monday.'

My luminous DM laces were flying everywhere as we pelted round the corner in time to see the 23.59 gently moving off in the direction of London.

'No!!'

We stood there hopelessly for a minute or so, trying to get our breath back. A recent regime of sitting in the park necking cider and vodka had done its work on our teenage bodies and we were now almost comically unfit.

'What an unbelievable arsehole,' Alan finally summarised. 'When the hell did he leave?'

'No idea,' I responded, miserably doing my laces up.

'He was still there after they came off stage?'

'Yeah, he was there for ages, talking to that girl's mates. I looked over at him while "Fatman" was playing.'

'They played "Sheriff Fatman"?'

'No, "Fatman" by Eat.'

Alan blew his nose loudly, turned and started walking slowly away. 'Of all the fucking gigs to do this, man.'

'You sure that was the last train?'

Alan didn't bother to answer this, but simply carried on up the street.

'Where do you think the motorway is?'

A bloody long way away, was the answer. We trudged along the dual carriageway, half-heartedly sticking our thumbs out, the sickly yellow street lights the only reminder we were anywhere near civilisation, singing various songs to keep us going ('*how was it for you, how was it for you?*' . . . '*I didn't like you very much when I met you, and now I like you even less'* . . . *'you're not the sort that I like helping out . . . look who's laughing now'*, etc.). My DM laces were perpetually giving me gyp.

'You should get longer ones, man. Tie 'em round the top of the boot, like I do.'

I grunted in response. The inspiration for my outfit (black jeans, Ned's Atomic Dustbin T-shirt, unbuttoned purple shirt worn as a jacket) was so far exclusively Alan, but there were certain things I was determined to avoid copying in the hope of remaining just slightly individual.

'Nice bird,' he volunteered.

'Uh?' I replied, looking around pathetically for any specimens of feathered wildlife. Alan giggled.

'Knob-end. I was talking about the blonde before.'

'Oh, right. Yeah.'

Alan and I had been pushing our precarious luck before we left the Square by attempting to join the Webster circle again, which had expanded to include three of the four Heart Throbs, a pair from the support band, indie DJ Gary Crowley, the ubiquitous Gloria Feathers and the aforementioned blonde girl, who was near the edge of the group and seemed the most likely to give us the time of day. But the stupid thing back in those days was that we rarely had a drink in our hands, either due to diminished funds or over-scrupulous bar staff (I've a feeling it was both on this occasion) so we always looked more hanging-around than hanging-out.

'I'm sure she was someone, man.'

'Someone?'

'The blonde.'

We were distracted briefly by the sound of approaching dance music. A throbbing Transit van roared past us, ignored our out-stretched thumbs and hurled a half-full can of cider in our direction.

'Tit!' Alan shouted after the Transit.

'There's some left,' I exclaimed, bending to pick the can up.

'Don't be a pleb, man.'

I shrugged. I'd have done worse if I'd been on my own.

'Anyway, I was saying. She's a singer or something, I'm sure of it.'

Alan would later claim to identify her as Sarah Cracknell, soon to be of Saint Etienne – although God knows how he arrived at that conclusion. He didn't have a chance to consider it for much longer back then, for soon the cider-flinging van was speeding back down the wrong side of the deserted dual carriageway towards us.

'Probably coming back for their cider,' chuckled Alan; although as the van neared we halted and stepped backwards nervously.

'Maybe he didn't like being called a tit,' I suggested. The van spun round, came to a crazy diagonal stop in the middle of the road and stuck its hazards on. A bearded, mad-looking bloke with muddy dreadlocks stuck his head out the window and yelled delightedly above the pounding din.

'Where ya goin'?'

'Bushey,' Alan bellowed back, injecting as much rock 'n' roll as possible into the word. 'Where you going?'

'*Where?*' came the response.

'Yes, where?' repeated Alan, a little too enthusiastically, as events would prove.

'Cool, us too!' the guy shouted back. 'Come on!'

'No, where!' repeated Alan.

'Tha's all right, mate, we're all goin' same place, jump in the back, we'll drop you by the Royal Oak or somethin' in the town centre. That'll do you, eh?'

'The Royal Oak! Perfect,' I beamed, at the sound of a pub less than fifteen minutes' walk from my house. Alan looked a little stunned, then shrugged approval.

'Yeah, man, the Royal Oak's cool. Cheers.'

What brilliant luck! There was nothing to this hitch-hiking lark. We plodded round to the back of the van. The doors opened and we were met by two scruffy mongrel dogs on threadbare leads, held by two equally mangy dreadlocked geezers in New Model Army

T-shirts. A small girl lurked further back, looking fairly spaced-out in a Spacemen 3 top that she'd fashioned into a dress.

'Come on in, don't be shy,' grinned one of the chaps. 'I'm Barry, this is Welpo, Liz over there, Si up at the front and this,' indicating the two dogs, 'is Margaret and Steve.'

We climbed in and settled ourselves on the purple rug. Welpo slammed the doors and Si, after turning the music down just a touch – to ear-splitting rather than brain-crushing volume – began to wildly reverse back up the road.

'Sorry I chucked the can at you,' he shouted. 'You looked like you needed a drink.'

The makeshift lounge they'd created in the back was lit by an ultraviolet torch and surprisingly cosy, once I'd got used to Steve's arse in my face. Alan looked content enough, having temporarily abandoned his concerns as to where the hell we were going. I accepted a swig from Welpo's can of cider and tried to familiarise myself with the music.

'Who's this?'

'You what?' Barry frowned, cupping his ear.

'Who's the music?'

'The Shamen!' he exclaimed. I looked over at Alan to see if he would repeat his earlier view that they were 'a load of toss', but he was already being snogged by the spaced-out girl.

I'm still amazed we got as far as we did without noticing our ridiculous error. I remember remarking into Barry's ear that it was quite a coincidence we were all from the same town, and being somewhat puzzled when he mentioned something about living near 'the river'. Perhaps if the music hadn't been so loud I might have asked him where the hell a river was in Bushey; then again, perhaps if Alan wasn't having his faced sucked off he might have noticed from Si's driving style that we were clearly not on the motorway. As it was, we only smelled a rat when the van stopped after fifteen minutes and Si announced our arrival.

'Already?' stammered Alan, breathlessly.

'Yup,' laughed Si, as Welpo opened the doors. 'I don't hang around.'

Alan and I gingerly peeked out and were greeted by the sight of a pub that was indeed called the Royal Oak but was blatantly not in Bushey.

'Where the fuck are we, man?'

'*Where!*' Barry responded, in surprised and slightly pained tones.

'Yes, where!' Alan repeated. 'Where have you driven us?'

'*Where!* In Hertfordshire! W-A-R-E!'

Oh, the hilarity.

By the time we arrived home at around lunchtime the following day, after a tortuous, meandering train journey, a few significant decisions had been made: we would no longer (as if we had any choice) rely on Dominic Browne for gig transport, we would not accept a lift from anyone until we had made them repeat our town of destination at least three times, Alan would try to abandon some of his inbuilt prejudices concerning dance music, and I would make it my top priority – as I resolved through my near-hallucinogenic tiredness, having spent all night sleeplessly listening to Alan enjoying the sexual appetite of a tripped-out, twenty-something Spacemen 3 fan a few metres away from me – to lose my virginity as soon as possible.

Back in Alan's office, I sip my coffee, nibble my muffin and continue flicking through the scrapbook's heavily encumbered pages.

'So weird, isn't it?' I comment wistfully. 'If that happened these days . . .'

'We'd get a fucking cab and be home in time for last orders.'

'Yeah,' I nod – but the fact that I don't necessarily consider this a good thing is lost on Alan.

Further research is abandoned at that point, for Alan's three-year-old daughter, Jocasta, races into the room and delightedly begs us to play hide-and-seek, which in the enormity of Alan's house is a game so riveting I'd almost choose it above, say, tenpin bowling as a drinking sport. Soon Alan's businesslike guard is dropped and we horse about, Liz joins in, beers come out and it quickly turns into A Fun Afternoon. We play for a good hour, then sit around chatting for a bit, pizza goes in the oven, more beers emerge and it's just about to turn into A Fun Evening when my mobile bleeps and I remember I promised Polly I'd have Sunday-night lasties with her. My work is done, though, for as I'm putting on my coat Alan mutters 'bugger it', runs up the stairs and returns with the scrapbook, wrapped up in a strong transparent plastic bag, as though it's some untouchable legal exhibit.

'Just be bloody careful with it,' he quietly asserts.

I smile gratefully. 'I'll make it worthwhile.'

'Yeah, yeah . . . get outta here,' he grins, giving me a hearty slap on the back that doubles as a friendly push out the door. 'Good luck.' Then, out of earshot from his wife and child, he adds touchingly, 'Try not to fuck it up.'

'Thanks. Vorsprung Durch Peanut . . .'

'Vorsprung Durch Peanut,' he counters.

As I wander towards the bus stop I have a brief moment of paranoia that he's really given me the book because he can't bear me coming round the whole time to look at it. But, deciding this is probably stupid, I board the bus and head home.

WHAT AN EXTRAORDINARY WAY TO BEHAVE

And now I am alone.

The funny thing is, I really am going to do this. It's an odd feeling when you reach an absolute decision within yourself to do something rather peculiar and ill-advised, knowing nothing can change your mind. Alan's probably thinking, 'Oh, it's just another of Clive's loser-esque schemes. He'll have forgotten about it by the middle of the week.' And yes, on the surface this is remarkably similar to the others. But – unlike the episode years back when I announced to everyone my intention to seduce the actress who played Lauren Carpenter in *Neighbours*, giving rise to a weekly trail round all the pubs in Fulham where I'd heard she was living (a plan that was also the product of an unusual dream, now I come to think of it) – the key factor this time is that Lance Webster *really is here*. On my street. I've narrowed down his whereabouts to the nearest twenty metres. No detective work is needed. All I need is a little patience, luck, some of the social skills and intelligence I must surely (surely?) have amassed over the last thirty years, and it really should be easy. Oh yes.

But how do you follow someone? I'm not the sort of slick individual who can lithely creep around unnoticed. I decide that I'd better do a little research. I pop into my local bookshop and glance at one of those absurd stocking-filler manuals called *How To Do Difficult Stuff* or something, but it only tells me how to escape from a straitjacket or how to have sex on a plane. The Internet is my next stop, and of course some knob has taken the trouble to write down his methods in some detail. 'Prepare the proper attire,' he begins. 'Black is a bad idea. At all hours, you'll stick out like a sore thumb. Red attracts attention. Wear greys and greens. If the weather permits it, wear a hooded sweater or jacket.' All my clothes are grey and green anyway, but what does he mean, 'if the weather permits it'? As in, if it's not too hot and sunny? Clearly not written by anyone British.

'Spot your target,' he continues. 'See which direction they're headed in, and how fast they are moving.' Okay. I've already worked out I'm going to have to sit at the top of our basement steps until I see Webster emerge from his house (let's hope he actually does, or I'm in for a boring weekend). The instructor then enters into a complex discussion regarding parked cars, outracing your target and making fake calls on a mobile, occasionally offering such use-free nuggets as: 'If the weather isn't cold enough to make a bent head plausible, keep looking down at your watch.' What the hell does that mean? My attention kind of wanders off after that bit.

I take a fleeting look at the 'Things You'll Need' section, which comprises little more than 'the ability to lie convincingly' (I was once told my lying is so unconvincing that I'm actually convincing; I've managed to lap myself in believability terms), and finally a cautionary glance at the warning note:

Only ever follow a person to play a practical joke on them or engage in a similar harmless activity. You and you alone are responsible for your actions. Using these instructions to commit a crime does not void you of responsibility for your actions, nor does it annul the damage you have done to the lives of other people.

Well, this *is* just a harmless activity, isn't it? I won't be damaging anyone's life. I just want to know what he gets up to. It's not like I'm going to blackmail him or stalk him or anything, is it?

So, as Churchill once blethered, the era of procrastination is fast disappearing down the resolutional plughole. It's Saturday morning. My clock radio says 8.04. Time to get on with it.

I don appropriate clothing (black jeans, grey T-shirt, green hooded top, black woolly hat), knock back a cup of tea and a piece of toast. Polly is still passed out on the kitchen sofa from last night (we have no lounge) but briefly raises her head to utter a few words of encouragement ('Don't do anything stupid'). I climb the metal steps from our basement flat to street level. It's a little chilly, but not raining. I look up and down the street. No sign of anyone. Hope I'm early enough. 8.15. Settle myself on the second step. Reasonably good view of the steps coming down to the pavement at number three. Wait.

Wait.

People walk past occasionally. No one seems to take much notice. Around nine, an old lady I've never seen before looks quizzically at me as she shuffles along, then stops to ask if I'm all right. I reply that I am. Her next question is surprising.

'Are you a terrorist?'

For some reason, maybe because I'm already bored, I say yes. She hurries off looking concerned. Perhaps that wasn't the best thing to do. It'll give her something to talk about on the bus though.

More waiting.

9.45-ish, Polly emerges blearily with a cup of tea – which I think is for me until she sips from it, informs me that my mother has just been on the phone ('You'll be pleased to know I didn't tell her what you were really doing') and unsmilingly disappears back inside.

Some brief action occurs at 10.25, when a male figure trots down Webster's steps. The music to *Mission: Impossible* strikes up in my head as I scramble to my feet and sprint after him. Hearing the flat-footed clatter approaching from behind, my quarry, who is clearly not Lance Webster, whips around and frowns at me, startled. With very few other options I carry on running past, mutter a feeble 'sorry, mate' and streak round the corner of the adjacent street.

Fuck it. I'm going to have to get a whole lot better at this.

I hide in the newsagent's until the faux-Webster has left the scene then return to base, my dress rehearsal complete. This time nothing remotely relevant happens until around one, when Polly, in a rare fit of being-nice-about-my-bloody-silly-ideas, brings me a Marmite sandwich and yesterday's *Evening Standard*.

Over the long, uneventful course of the afternoon I rattle through several stages of doubt about several different things, starting with this project and why on earth I am bothering, then my life in general – how I managed to reach this age with so few career prospects and pounds in the bank – then my ex-girlfriend and why it didn't work out, then my trip to New York last year and why I decided it was tall but overrated, then my visit to Lisbon the year before and why I decided it was completely underrated, then back to what I'm doing right now (if I had an ounce of sense I'd have made myself a little survival pack with some fruit, water, at the very least a Thermos of coffee like they do on TV), then finally, as usual, my job.

God, I hate it. It was only meant to be for a week when I started, and that was three years ago. Now I'm like some fucking senior there, without the benefit of really being in charge of anyone. It's the most ridiculous set-up. Ron and Michael, the two owners, are like a comedy double-act minus the comedy. Ron's a diminutive, bespectacled fifty-something divorcee with high blood pressure; a trained accountant from a relatively humble background, who in the eighties managed to make a lot of money, all of which he's gambled on this funny little glorified telesales business. He mooches about at work, apparently channelling all his energy into the most menial of tasks – emptying the recycle bin, ripping up cardboard boxes, hoovering the meeting room – then suddenly pounces on one of your documents to pick a thousand holes in it, or yells at everyone for chatting too much, or sacks a secretary. He's fairly unnerving. On first meeting him you think his sense of humour has been wiped out by some freak mental accident, then you realise it's not so much absent as dry as a Mormon's birthday party. Sometimes you find him alone in a far corner of the office, laughing at one of his own jokes. The only other human who gets them is Michael. Michael is the kind of man who I'm sure would be hysterically funny if he wasn't your boss, or your friend, or in the slightest bit connected to you. He's a painfully old-fashioned Chelsea-dwelling upper-class Hooray Henry; again, made a load of cash in the eighties, added it to his sizeable pot of 'old' money, fulfilled his every geek-boy fantasy, dated a couple of models, married and divorced one of them within a year, probably did a pile of coke, then went rather publicly bankrupt after the ex got a big settlement out of him. He's still only in his late thirties. He's a blond giant, totally manic and overbearing, has absolutely no sense of personal space whatsoever and possesses a razor-sharp, ruthlessly logical business mind of the sort that would have come in very handy in 1987 (he refers to the Internet as 'the connected computer'). He is occasionally capable of hilarious wit, but is generally pretty charmless. In fact, if you want a good description of Michael, have a listen to the Blur song 'Charmless Man', which I've always been convinced was written about Michael – the bloke in the song is identical in every way (Michael also hangs out at the Soho House members' club, as Damon Albarn did around the time the song was written – they could easily have met). Michael and Ron understand each other in a puzzling way that somehow works, inasmuch as they haven't murdered each other yet. You'll sometimes walk over to their part of the office and find them working, ostensibly in complete silence, until Michael will suddenly exclaim, 'Ron, I'll tell you a fourth time if you wish,' continuing a debate that has probably been simmering for hours.

Once an argument exploded over whether Markham Street in Chelsea was the ninth or the tenth street on the right as one travelled down King's Road. Unable to quench their excitement by consulting the *A–Z*, they jumped straight into a taxi and raced over there to prove one or the other wrong.

'I must insist, Michael, that although Markham Square has two exits, it can still only be counted once,' Ron calmly stated upon their return.

Michael laughed incredulously.

'You still can't accept that I'm right, can you, Ron? What an extraordinary way to behave.'

In terms of employees, the pair favour a ragbag of misfits and occasionals, often advertising vacancies in the *Stage*, they being of the shaky belief that under-employed actors are reliable and have a good telephone manner. Various other weirdos drift in and – often very swiftly – out: musicians, students, travellers, general under-achievers, attracted by the reasonable hourly rates, flexible shifts and relaxed attitude towards contracts of employment. An actor, for example, can bugger off for a month to appear in a Christmas pantomime, then slot straight back in come the New Year. The advantage of this arrangement for Ron and Michael is they have absolutely no responsibility towards their employees: no holiday, sickness or maternity pay, and they're free to hire and fire with little or no red tape. But the downside, which in my three years they've never come close to grasping, is that no one who works for them gives the slightest fuck about the fate or fortunes of the company, each person doing as little work as humanly possible (the weekend shifts, with Ron and Michael rarely there, are an absolute joke); the only motivation for anyone's presence is the cheque they are grudgingly presented with at the end of each week – or, in my exceedingly unusual case, month. I alone managed to negotiate what passes for a full-time salary a year or so ago at the insistence of my then girlfriend, for I had progressed to what Ron and Michael laughingly describe as a managerial role.

This consists of little more than showing new staff the ropes and then ploughing on with the same tedious old shit as everyone else: answering the phone, talking to corpses all over the country – Grantham, Horley, Bideford, Dumfries, Wantage, Bingley – jotting down the crap they witlessly spew on badly photocopied pieces of paper. I say and hear the same words every minute of every hour of every day, five days a week, fifty-two weeks per year. It's hell. My fellow losers are inoffensive enough – we all get along, to a degree – but since everyone is timetabled to arrive, go to lunch and knock off at completely different times, no one really knows. I suppose things could be worse, but I frequently find myself going home angry, tired and despondent. If things don't change soon . . . well, I may be forced to do something about it.

Sorry. Don't mean to moan. But as it's nearing four o'clock and Mr Webster still hasn't graced the outside world with his presence, there really isn't much else to talk about.

Now, I know what you're hoping. Thirty seconds before I decide to call it a day, maybe around six, Lance Webster finally emerges from his lair and mooches off down the street, bowls into the nearest pub, orders himself a cider and settles down in front of the football, whereupon I station myself locally and strike up idle banter. If only. What actually happens is hardly as straightforward, possibly more interesting.

Ten past five, I am visited by a traffic warden. A male one. Fifty-ish. I am still dressed in woolly hat and hooded top and seated unsteadily at the top of our metal steps, so I suppose I still look like an outside bet on a burglar, or a granny-basher, or at the very least someone who should soon be taking his evening medication. The warden asks me several questions, some of them stupid, most of them slightly bemusing, all of them tempting me to ask, 'Why do *you* want to know? You're a traffic warden.'

'Hello,' he begins.

'Hi.'

'Can we help you?'

I look around him a bit, and further down the street. He is alone. Perhaps he is royalty.

'Erm . . . no?'

'Just wondered what you were up to, y'know. Sat there. Second time I've seen you today.'

'Oh, yeah? First time I've seen you.'

He is not smiling.

'What are you doing?'

'Erm . . . just chilling.'

'Bit nippy today, yes,' he laughs humourlessly. 'Seen anything interesting?'

'No. You?'

'Hmm,' he replies, biting his top lip and frowning down the street. 'There's been a couple of complaints.'

'About me?'

'Well, about people like you.'

God knows what he's meant to be doing. Happily, however, at that moment he must start being a traffic warden again, for who should we see – I mean, really, who the *arse* should we see – but Lance Webster, frantically jingling a set of car keys, cantering up from the other end of the street towards a nondescript vehicle.

'I'll move it,' he shouts.

All right. Again, I must apologise. You understand. Three words. Three everyday words. But that voice, that slightly harsh but impossibly articulate intonation, that hint of Berkshire accent (if Lennon had been from Reading, etc.) – I know, I know . . . take a cold shower, get a hotel room, whatever. But. When you've spent your life hearing that same voice spitting out those glorious lyrics: *'I can't recall if we really have sex, all I can feel are the after-effects'*; outsmarting interviewers on late-night radio: 'No, no, hang on, there seems to be some theory that being taken up the arse at boarding school disqualifies you from making valid rock music. Well, I dunno. Ask Kurt Cobain. I'm quite sure he'd have preferred being occasionally buggered by a prefect than the mountainload of shit he had to put up with as a youth'; berating the crowd for sluggishness: 'Oh, what's the matter, did [support band] Daisy Chainsaw tire you out, little children?' – you can't ignore a little tingle down your spine when you hear that voice again, even if it is employed for something as mundane as telling a traffic warden not to ticket his car. Which, as it turns out, is too late.

'You got a ticket anyway,' states the warden, ambling up to him.

'Aw, come on, mate – I live right there. I only parked outside so I could take my cat to the vet. I've only been there five minutes.'

'Fifteen.'

'Yeah, well, maybe, sorry, but . . . look, I had to dash to the shop to get some pet food, because otherwise I can't get her into the box, but I didn't know I'd run out, and . . . oh, it's complicated.'

'Nothing I can do. Once I press the button, that's it.'

Webster huffs and rips open the little plastic packet placed under his windscreen wipers.

'Eighty quid!'

'Forty if you pay within a fortnight. There's an address on the back if you want to appeal.'

I'm hiding further down my stairwell while watching this riveting exchange. I can just see Webster's lower half, his carrier bag (Kent's – 'Everything for Your Pet') swinging as he hopelessly stamps his feet. I didn't really have him down as a cat lover, but there you go. I cast the obvious thought aside (how the hell did I manage to miss him leaving his flat, retrieving his car, parking outside, going inside and coming out again, when I've been sitting here patiently since eight o'clock this bloody morning) because an idea has just struck me. Probably the first genuinely astute idea I've had all day. I pull my hat down, hurry back up the steps and stride purposefully past the warden and the still fulminating ex-pop star, continue up the street, do a left onto the main road, cut down the little alleyway which chops off the one-way system, then out onto the high street and stop by the pub next to the Morrisons. There, a comfortable distance from the homeless dude who sits next to the cash machines, I wait.

I don't have to wait long. Five minutes, if that. I actually spot him in his car, driving past and turning right before the MFI, finding himself a spot, getting out with the cat box and hurrying back to the high street. He reaches the vet's, just across the road from where I'm standing, presses the buzzer and enters.

As bright as my previous brainwave was, I've no idea what to do now. Okay, so he occasionally takes his cat to the vet. Great. There seems little to be gained from barging in there and trying to chat to him as he waits for his pussy to be dewormed, or whatever it is. Lacking any startling inspiration, I simply wait. This is not difficult. I've been doing it all day.

But just in case life was getting too easy, it starts to rain. That strange, jerky rain you often get in the springtime; oversized raindrops. Initially this is not a problem. Ten minutes later it's a little bit stupid. The unremarkable assortment of Saturday-afternoon traffic, buses, screaming police cars and thundering HGVs continues for a short while longer until, thank Christ, Webster emerges and sprints back to his car. But there's something missing. It takes me a few moments to spot what's missing: something which, in a fairly tenuous manner, gives me my opportunity.

He hasn't got his cat with him.

I hang on for a moment to check he's not simply running back to grab something, but no; he drives off. I cross the road and look at the opening times tacked to the door. 'Closed Sundays. Monday–Saturday, 8.30 a.m.–6.30 p.m.' Without thinking too much, I whip off my hat and enter. The small waiting room is mercifully empty apart from the blondy-grey-haired lady who sits behind the counter, surrounded by cash register, phone, toys, packets of catnip, photos of various animals ('A few of our furry friends') and other assorted pet paraphernalia. I give her my best, non-nutterest smile.

'Hello,' I start, wondering whether she'll remember me.

'Oh, hi!' she exclaims, looking up from some paperwork. 'How are you?'

'Fine,' I reply. 'Long time . . .'

'That's right,' she nods. 'How's – erm . . .'

'Cookson?'

'Cookson! That's it.'

'Ah,' I shrug, mock-ruefully. 'I lost the custody battle, I'm afraid. He's now in Camberwell with his mum.'

'Oh! I'm sorry.'

'Don't be,' I laugh. 'He's got a garden now. Cat flap and everything.'

'Aw, good,' she beams, glad it was a happy, cuddly ending for the feline in the relationship. 'So what can we do for you today?'

'Well . . . a couple of years ago I remember you telling us it sometimes got pretty swamped in here, and you asked for people to help out?'

'Oh, yes. Still do actually. Not that we're inundated with volunteers . . .'

'Well, I just thought . . . I'm free on Monday, and I wondered whether you could use any . . . you know . . .'

Suddenly her voice takes on a tone of desperation.

'Monday?'

'Yes . . . I know you're probably not terribly busy on Mondays, but—'

'We are *overwhelmed* this Monday! There's a full day of appointments, dozens of pets to be fetched from the surgery and I've got to go to pick my mother up from hospital.'

'Ah. Where's she in hospital?'

'Bournemouth.'

'Right – so, er, Monday would be good, then?'

'Yes!' She stands up, reaches out and clasps my hand. 'Oh, my goodness, we're in such a spot! You couldn't have come at a better time!'

I'm not making this up, honest. In fact, her reaction is so embarrassingly over the top that I start backtracking.

'But, surely . . . you need to be a *current* customer to volunteer?'

'Oh, no! Don't worry about a little thing like that,' she chatters, brushing the very thought aside. 'Hang on, let me go and tell the vet, she'll be thrilled!'

She scampers off to the little consulting room. Shit. Of course, I'm assuming Webster actually needs to come and pick up his bloody cat on Monday. He'd damn well better do, as I seem to have inadvertently got myself a hard day's voluntary toil. I'll have to pull a sicky as well – from my real job. I must be insane.

The same female Australasian vet who occasionally jabbed a needle into my ex-cat emerges from the consulting room, her face lighting up with recognition.

'Ah, yes! Mr Beresford!'

I hold up my hand in reluctant acknowledgement. 'That's me.'

'So good of you. What time can you start?'

'Er . . . well, whenever, really.'

'Do you drive?'

'Do I drive?'

'The animals need to be picked up from the weekend surgery at nine.'

'Ah. Yes. Where's the weekend surgery?'

'Stevenage. The van will be in Stanmore, though, where the weekend driver lives. Is it possible for you to collect it tomorrow evening? So good of you!'

'Er, well, yeah, I guess so . . .'

'Jackie will give you the address, if you could bring the animals back here. They need to be fed, and then the other vet arrives around eleven. After that it's just managing the till and waiting room until we close.'

'Ah.'

'Whatever you can manage really. The whole day would be great.'

My dad has an expression that always used to irritate me as a child: 'How do I get into these things?' But in recent years I've come to recognise its accuracy and its myriad uses. Hell's bells. All this had bloody better be worth it.

Jackie, the blondy-grey-haired lady who suddenly has a name, gives me the address of the van place ('It's just a little walk from Stanmore tube – about twenty minutes or so'), then the weekend surgery place ('It's not really Stevenage – it's out the other side of the town, village called Walkern, round the back of the trading estate near a water mill – you can't miss it') and briefly apprises me of the nature of my cargo ('Not too many this weekend: five cats, a guinea pig and a ferret – only three dogs, but then one of them is Nigel the boxer, and he can get a little frisky'). Just on my way out, my head spinning with the intricacies of a world hitherto as remote to me as that of tap-dancing, I stop and ask what is almost certainly a rather peculiar question.

'You haven't, um . . . the vet, she . . . erm . . . has she had to put any animals down today?'

Jackie frowns.

'Yes. She has, I'm afraid. Why?'

'Oh, no reason,' I smile unconvincingly, and stumble out.

I hurry home, trying my damnedest to recall how long Webster was in there. Fifteen, twenty minutes? Maximum. Is that long enough?

Polly is sitting at the kitchen table when I stumble through the door, her black mop of hair all over the place, still wearing her mangy dressing gown and those rank, oversized animal slippers from way back, splattered with a few years' worth of toothpaste drips. She's smoking, sipping red wine, calmly dipping cream crackers into a tub of margarine while reading the Saturday *Telegraph*. It's a fairly typical scene.

'How long d'you reckon it takes to put a pet down?' I ask, without preamble.

'Put a pet down?'

'Yes. You know. Kill it. Put it to sleep. Out of its misery, via lethal injection.'

'How long?'

'Yes!' I repeat irritably, extracting a can of beer from the fridge and cracking it open.

'Why do you want to know?'

'What does that matter? D'you reckon ten minutes, fifteen?'

Polly sits back and thinks.

'We had an Alsatian that once suddenly became demented while Dad was on the toilet,' she begins. 'It wouldn't let him out of the bathroom. Each time he tried to escape it would hurl itself at the door and attack whatever part of him was protruding. Almost bit one of his fingers off. He had to stay there until Mum came home a few hours later. Then it tried to attack her. Eventually she managed to whack it over the head with a paving stone.'

'Did she kill it?'

'No, just stunned it. They called the vet but the vet was busy, so they got the farmer from over the way to come with his shotgun. The dog woke up before the farmer got there, so Mum tried to hit it again. Problem was she missed and hit Dad's foot. Broke his ankle.'

'So what happened in the end?'

'It chased Mum into the garden, so she jumped in the swimming pool. It was normally the only place the dog wouldn't go. But the fucking dog just leaped in and swam after her. Finally the farmer appeared and shot the dog.'

'Dead?'

'Yeah.' Polly sighs and takes a large swig of wine. 'Loads of blood, though. We had to drain the pool.'

Polly's examples are always as entertaining as they are thoroughly useless.

'So, you've no idea, then.'

'About what?'

'Oh, never mind.'

I take the beer to my bedroom, stick on a CD (The Sundays' *Reading, Writing and Arithmetic* – always good for a rainy evening when you've just come back from the vet), pull off my soaking jeans, then collapse onto the bed. So. Day one of my fantastically well-thought-out campaign, and what have I achieved? Well, aside from a lot of waiting, scaring a granny, confusing a traffic warden, prancing about in the rain and offering my voluntary services for the day – not an awful lot. But unless he really was taking his cat to unwittingly meet its maker (which I've decided probably wasn't the case – I mean, fifteen minutes would be pretty tight for a spot of pet euthanasia, even in today's money; plus he looked wet but hardly heartbroken on the way back to his car), the odds are that I'm actually going to have some sort of exchange with the man on Monday.

And how do we feel about that?

I jump up and turf Harriet Wheeler's pretty meanderings off the CD player, sift through the jewel cases that litter my so-called desk, and locate a particularly bashed-up one with that familiar cover: a schoolboy, in dirty blazer, shorts and cap, standing on a hill and holding a helium balloon, on which the legend '*Lovely Youth*' is scrawled.

Of course, this isn't the first copy of the Thieving Magpies' flaw-less second album I've owned. I think I've owned three in total: the first, a cassette, as a lot of my albums were back then, long since lost. Then I bought it on vinyl in about 1993, partly so my DJ friend Archie Landless could play tracks from it at the indie disco over which he presided at our university. The bastard ran off with it in the end, along with several other gems: my vinyl copies of *Complete Madness*, The Wonder Stuff's *Never Loved Elvis*, The Police's *Regatta de Blanc*, Jellyfish's *Spilt Milk* (an absolute *classic* – which also holds my personal accolade of having the best Side One ever), my limited-edition picture disc of Nirvana's 'Smells Like Teen Spirit' (God *damn it!* Why did I lend him that?) and finally – this one hurts – my never-to-be-found-again copy of the very first *Now That's What I Call Music* compilation album (original pig cartoon, 'Victims' by Culture Club,

'Safety Dance' by Men Without Hats, *two* Kajagoogoo songs and Phil Collins wearing a flat cap on the front). But losing *Lovely Youth* is the real killer. I had to make do with a taped copy of Alan's pristine vinyl version until 1996, when just about every bargain bin in the country contained a few Thieving Magpies albums. After meticulously comparing prices I eventually purchased my current copy for three quid, but it's simply not as good on CD. Aside from the usual bollocks about the warmth of the vinyl sound, the booklet, inexplicably, doesn't contain half the photos the inner record sleeve or cassette inlay did, and Lance's individual song notes have been cruelly omitted. This feature of the Magpies' records became as much a part of the acquiring experience as hearing the music itself, and gave the listener a pretty good insight into what went on in the singer's head. Whenever I glance at Alan's copy of *Lovely Youth* I go straight to the passage that accompanies 'Pit Pony': 'Someone once asked me what I thought of the fashion industry. This is my response – although I still think this is too polite.' And I love the annotation for *Shoot the Fish*'s 'Have You Stopped Talking Yet?': 'Written in the loo during an argument's cooling-off period. The answer is no, by the way.' While this tradition was clearly deemed too silly for the mainstream-busting earnestness of *Bruise Unit*, it was reinstated for the final album, *The Social Trap*, which bristled with such back-on-form attacks as: 'This one's dedicated to a clutch of ex-friends for whom cocaine has replaced personality. I'd rather gouge my eyes out with this pen than be at a party with you again. Goodnight and fuck off' ('A Good Time Was Had by None') and 'Ooh, look at me, I'm so dark and damaged' ('Keep It Out of My Face').

Anyway, I digress. Although *Bruise Unit* unarguably marked the point at which the diverse compound of the band boiled down nicely, enabling them to make a unified, uncomplicated but accomplished album that would prove their career zenith, it's *Lovely Youth* that I need to hear right now. If all successful bands experience Neil Tennant's much-referenced 'imperial phase', where everything they touch turns to platinum, this must be reached via a 'territorial phase', during which the group's best work is normally produced and they are in possession of a factor that can be (sadly) best described as 'cool': referenced by all the right journalists, played by all the right DJs, namechecked by all the right colleagues, remixed by all the right producers. This period's length varies enormously from act to act: usually it lasts for just one album, often their debut (Oasis, The Killers, The Strokes, The Stone Roses), sometimes their second or third effort (Blur, Manic Street Preachers); occasionally a band manages to stretch it slightly longer (Radiohead, The White Stripes). In a few isolated cases this era actually never finishes (The Smiths), or is sometimes so fleeting in length it's as though it hasn't actually occurred at all (Coldplay, Snow Patrol). For the Thieving Magpies, *Lovely Youth* encapsulates this period. As snotty as their debut, containing some of their loudest, punkiest efforts ('Tube Screamer', 'Everyone Behaves Like a Cunt So Why Can't I'), it also finds them stretching their sonic palette, experimenting with samples and sequencers ('War on the Floor', 'Camp David'), and is home to one of the most robust pop compositions of their career ('Look Who's Laughing'). But more importantly, it's the *freshness* of the record that strikes you; the excitement of writing and recording such an article seeps unstoppably through the speakers until there's no doubt that you're listening to something genuinely rare and thrilling. Fifteen months after hearing their debut, during which time I had changed more than I can possibly describe, hearing the adrenalin rush of opening track 'Rancid/Putrid' escape from my cassette deck was . . . well, certainly more exciting than losing my virginity, which I'd been permanently parted from the previous month.

And what sort of man was Lance Webster back then? Well, the geezer Alan and myself nervously chatted to in Harlow would have been basking in the knowledge that, two months after its release, *Lovely Youth* had sold its one-hundred-thousandth British copy, prompting the incongruous appearance of a gold disc in his Kentish

Town flat. In the post-Britpop music business this statistic would be simply described as 'a good start', but back in 1990 their label BFM were more than happy with the Magpies' progress. Previously average sales – it had charted high but quickly fallen, as most alternative albums tended to do – had been inflated by the release of the afore-mentioned 'Look Who's Laughing' as a single, which by early March had leapfrogged The Stone Roses, Primal Scream, Inspiral Carpets and even Bros to insert itself at a confident number nine, sharing the top ten with the likes of Michael Bolton, New Kids on the Block and Jive Bunny (the only alternative act who charted higher was Depeche Mode). A sell-out European tour was about to commence – the band retaining their integrity by eschewing an economically sensible offer to play Wembley Arena in favour of an equivalent three nights at Brixton Academy, and even America was pricking up its ears, as the album floated around the high sixties of the *Billboard* chart thanks to heavy rotation on college and alternative radio.

Lance Webster, it could therefore be safely assumed, was feeling pretty pleased with himself. At an age when most of his school contemporaries were just finishing university and embarking on exciting careers in law and accountancy, Webster was Out There, playing to packed clubs and theatres in Britain, Europe and America, straddling the covers of *Sounds* and *Melody Maker* on an almost monthly basis; his waistcoat and shorts, long brown hair and – when slightly more pretentious occasion called for it – round glasses becoming as much an outfit *du jour* for the fans as the baggy flares, flowery shirt and fishing hat of the Madchester set. He could walk into any indie club in the country with a test pressing of a new song; the DJ would greet him like an old friend and spin the disc instantly, always resulting in frenzied grooving and bouncing from the kids. But although he was the champion of the T-shirted masses, who felt relatively comfort-able (as we did) wandering up to him at a gig and saying hello, Webster's slightly more intellectual slant, way with words and lyrical references to books, films and art undeniably put him far apart from the melee, and well removed from the aesthetic concerns of, say, a member of Ned's Atomic Dustbin. Simply put, he was not one of us – nor did we want him to be. Admired and in many cases counted as a friend by a wide cross section of alternative luminaries – Robert Smith, Clint Mansell, Wayne Hussey, Jim and William Reid, Bill Drummond, Steve Mack, Billy Bragg, Jim Bob, Mark Arm, Bobby Gillespie, Tanya Donnelly, Tim Smith, Billy Duffy, even Nick Cave and Michael Stipe – his ready wit and low tolerance of bullshit made him one of the coolest new kids on the indie block. For a while this meant he could get away with virtually anything and still come out looking like a hero. I don't mean in the traditional zones of 'sex, drugs and rock 'n' roll – in fact, he mostly seemed to frown on all this as 'old hat', although there never seemed to be any shortage of stunning girls around him – but more in the way he addressed his constituents. Mostly this behaviour revealed a graduate of the Johnny Rotten school of insults, but at times Webster seemed to address them as a PE teacher would some recalcitrant kids, or like they were particularly dumb sheep in a field. Stranger still, no one complained. 'We're gonna play a cover of "Centrefold" by the J Geils Band,' he announced at one show. 'Anyone got a problem with that?' Of course, some old-skool-punk dissenters down the front roared their disapproval, to which Webster barked, 'Right, you can fuck off, the exits are clearly marked'; and then actually waited for the culprits to leave the pit before the band launched into the song. In June of 1990, the Magpies were given an evening slot on the second (now 'Other') stage at Glastonbury. A minute or two before their published stage time, Webster wandered onstage wearing dark glasses and a bowler hat, and began to speak in a fake posh accent. 'Ladies and gentlemen, you are about to watch the Reading-based rock band commonly known as Thieving Magpies. Before you do, you are legally required to repeat the Glastonbury Second Stage Oath.' General looks of amused confusion from the audience, some of whom hadn't yet realised who this figure was. 'Repeat after me: I do solemnly declare [the crowd repeated] . . . that the second stage at Glastonbury . . . has the shittiest sound in the world . . . most of it disappearing . . . across the plain . . . and into the valley behind . . . or drowned out by the rain . . . which will almost certainly begin . . . halfway through the set . . . but I promise . . . to enjoy myself anyway . . . and not shout out for any songs . . . because the band choose the fucking set [a particular bugbear of Webster's] . . . and we are merely . . . lowly audience members . . . who aren't fit to lick . . . the grease off Craig Spalding's kick-drum pedal.' And with that, he introduced his own band. The assembled masses, having obediently chanted every word, rewarded him with a louder ovation than ever.

And oh, we lapped it up. We would have done anything the man asked us to. For if Webster was satisfied with his own success, it meant even more to the likes of Alan and me, treading water as we were in a drab pond filled with A-levels, applications for universities we had little interest in going to and girls who had little interest in going anywhere near us; all this to a soundtrack (unless we were controlling the tape deck) of mindless Stock/Aitken/Waterman pop and punchable Euro-dance acts such as Black Box and Snap. But the Thieving Magpies, and a batch of similarly heroic groups, represented our triumph, our foothold, our flag on the world's musical map. We were as evangelical as a bunch of canvassing Scientologists, proudly sporting our various bits of merchandise, quickly indoctrinating anyone who showed even the vaguest interest by carting them off to a pub, feeding them a few pints of cider and black, playing them a compilation tape and giving them a copy of the fanzine (yeah, I'm going to have to fill you in on that one shortly). Whenever the Magpies ascended the charts or appeared on television or mainstream radio, we genuinely saw it as *our* achievement.

But on a personal level, we knew next to nothing of Webster. He'd seemed pleasant enough when we spoke to him, but privately,

who had any idea? He'd once memorably described himself as
an 'arrogant, overbearing and selfish tosser' – which at the very
least seemed likely to be an exaggeration – but any reports reaching
us suggested a rounded character whose only crime was an occasional inability to hold his drink. He was certainly an expert in
self-promotion, developing Morrissey-like notoriety for giving
incredibly good interviews, often for publications that had little interest
in his music but who were simply after a few choice *bon mots* and a
spark of controversy. I often forget, when re-reading these, how
insanely young he was at the time; that he was so unapologetically
self-assured still strikes me as bloody impressive, especially remembering what a clueless little fart I myself was at the age of twenty-
three.

But was he really happy? An odd thought, perhaps, but one I
feel the need to address on the eve of meeting him again, some
seventeen years later, his life so profoundly different. And yes, I know
I'm only going to be serving him in a vet's surgery, but still. Imagine
I'm not. Imagine I'm actually going to be sitting down, tape recorder
and all, for a proper interview. What would I ask him? Where would
I start? Having scaled such heights, he's now living in a small flat in
a boring north-London suburb, and no one knows who the fuck he
is. Having sold a good seven or eight million records over the course
of his career, he's now arguing with traffic wardens about eighty quid.
Am I being hopelessly naïve, or is he likely to be really, *seriously* pissed
off about this state of affairs? And, as Noel Gallagher once charm-
lessly scribbled, where – why – *how* – did it all go so fucking wrong?

NOW, THAT NAME RINGS A BELL. REMIND ME WHO THEY WERE?

Okay. It's 1.30 a.m. after one of the more unusual days in my life, and there are five things to report. Some good, some bad.

1. Webster showed up (good).
2. I've had more interesting conversations with my toilet seat (bad).
3. I think his cat's on the way out (bad).
4. I've just been out on a date with the Other Vet (good).
5. She just left (bad).

Blame Snow Patrol for that last one. And Coldplay. And possibly Keane, although I can't really remember now. And, in a roundabout sort of way, Lance Webster.

I'll try to race through the day's more mundane elements. Picking up the vet's van on Sunday night was a relative doddle, for I had the genius idea to call my mother and suggest an impromptu Sunday lunch visit ('Oh, darling! What a lovely idea! It's not like you to actually *volunteer* to come round'), then announced to my dad halfway through my second helping of pudding that I needed a lift to Stanmore. Even the most cursory of glances at the map had baldly displayed Jackie's woeful understatement with regard to Van Man's house being twenty minutes' walk from the tube station. It took virtually twenty minutes to get there by car. The other thing she had neglected to fully describe was how much of an utter nightmare this boxer dog Nigel was. 'Frisky' my arse. I'm usually all right with animals, having harboured a few in my time, but fucking hell. He spends most of his time trying to walk on his hind legs, 'affectionately' biting everything in sight. He'd eaten almost all my jumper by the time the pets were in the vehicle. On a previous jaunt he apparently managed to undo a cage door and swallow a whole chinchilla, so now he has to ride up front with the driver. He did most of the steering on the motorway. I decided to stop at Alan's house for a break, also to tell him the good news about my impending meeting ('Sod off and don't come back 'til you've got something proper to tell me') – when I returned to the van Nigel had chewed the road atlas to shreds, changed the channel on the radio and taken off the handbrake; the van had rolled backwards and was resting perilously against the bumper of Alan's Mini. That Alan didn't notice is a bloody miracle.

It's also somewhat miraculous that I was able to safely transfer the various creatures into the back room of the surgery, inexpertly shove some food in their direction and take up my position at the front desk before Lance Webster himself strode through the door at ten to eleven. Trust the contrary bastard to be early. I was hot and sweaty from my exertions and had damn near forgotten what I was there for in the first place. He was looking shabbier today, unshaven, wore a pretty hideous striped granddad shirt that suggested a rather ill-advised purchase from Marks & Spencer, and eyed me with a look of distrust that made my body temperature drop about ten degrees.

'Where's Jackie?'

'Jackie?'

'The usual assistant,' he responded crisply.

'Oh, *Jackie*. Well, she . . .'

I froze mid-sentence. He was doing it again! Narrowing his eyes at me strangely! He's *exactly the same*. With shorter hair. I might as well have been sixteen and back at the Harlow Square. What *is* it with that look?

'She's picking up her mother. I'm the . . . um . . .'

'Well, I've got a cat to pick up: Jessica.'

He fiddled about in his pocket and gave me a handwritten chit, which I studied blankly. My eyes were doing that annoying thing they do when I'm really nervous, which is water, basically. I could vaguely make out 'Jessica – Webster' and the date. Not that it mattered.

'Is she back?'

'Um, yeah, I'll go and get her,' I spluttered, and hurried off down the corridor. Weird. I'm not really sure what I was expecting, but he seemed . . . *rude*. Without actually being rude. The best that could be said for the whole thing so far was it proved I'd not been tripping and that it actually was him. Oh, the hilarity, if the chit had said 'McAllister' or whatever.

I unlocked the backroom door and was greeted with a gargantuan lick from the perpetually upright Nigel. I'd tied his lead to the handle of a filing cabinet in the far corner, which he'd pulled right across the room.

'Not now,' I growled, pushing him away and grabbing the yellow cat carrier which contained Jessica. But then I stopped for a second and took a few deep breaths, marvelling at the surreal position I'd squeezed myself into. I reflected that if it all ended now, at least I'd have done this. At least I'd have returned an ailing cat in a yellow box to my all-time musical hero. All was suddenly quiet. Even Nigel was momentarily still. I let Lance Webster (yes!) wait for a few seconds longer, then pushed open the door.

He was alternately glancing at one of those information posters ('Is your pet overweight?') and texting someone when I reached the waiting room. One of the two activities must have cheered him up a bit, as his manner was appreciably different.

'Ahh . . .' he smiled, upon seeing his moggie. 'How's she been?'

Oh, no. Please don't start asking me technical questions.

'Okay,' I replied. 'She's, um, eaten some breakfast.'

'Good.' He poked a finger through the mesh door of the carrier, which Jessica acknowledged with a sniff. 'It's just prolonging the inevitable, of course, but . . .'

'Ah.'

He sighed, sadly. 'Yes. Mind you, it would help if the other one wasn't terrorising her the whole time. Actually, while I think of it . . . have you got any of that hormonal stuff that you spray to stop them urinating everywhere?'

Thank God I once owned a cat.

'Feliway? Yeah, I think so . . .' I looked at the products stacked up on the shelf and located a little purple box. I then tried to hand it to him, but he was still busy with his creature, so I was left standing awkwardly with my arm out for a few seconds. I was going to say, 'Here's your spray,' but that sounded peculiar, so I settled for a cough.

'Oh! Sorry!' he exclaimed, took the box, looked up and then treated me to a full-strength, 1991-style Lance Webster grin, dimples and everything. Blimey. Christ knows what sort of look I must have given him in return. I fear that my eyes probably widened, my mouth opened slightly, as if I'd just been injected with something. We held this tableau for what seemed like about five minutes, then Webster himself coughed.

'So . . . are you going to take some money off me?'

'Oh, shit! Yes.' I moved round to the other side of the desk and sifted through the bills that Jackie had clipped together. 'That's . . . wow, five hundred and fifty.'

'Plus this?' he asked, waving the spray.

'Ah. Sorry. I'm, um . . . new here. Has it got a price on it?'

'No, not that I can see.'

'Right.' I fought the temptation to say 'Hey! – have it on the house. Have an operation, get the pissing spray free.' Instead, boringly, I settled for phoning Jackie. Webster didn't seem to mind. He sat down while I rang, busying himself with his chequebook. Finally she answered and gave me the correct price.

Thinking back now, from the vantage point of lying on my bed in the small hours drinking the last of a bottle of leftover wine, it seems hard to accept there was nothing I could have done to take more advantage of the situation, but I'm afraid it's probably true. I'd like to be able to say it was enough, just as it was with Björn from ABBA, to share the company of musical brilliance for a few fleeting minutes and, in this case, at least to talk about *something*; but I don't think I can. I was pretty pissed off as he left – bearing his doomed animal, still grinning, admittedly a far cry from the curt so-and-so who'd entered the building five minutes before – although of course I didn't show it. I even managed a proper smile. I toyed with the idea of saying 'thanks, Mr Webster' just for a laugh, but thought better of it. I shut the door behind him and then took a look at his cheque. HSBC. Reading Broad Street branch. Funny, you don't expect people like him to bank in normal places – but I suppose that's just silly. His writing was a mess. 'Five-six-seven-fifty.' How strange. He writes cheque amounts like Ron at work. Now I think about it, his dad was an accountant. That must be it. Then I eyed his signature. Mr G W Webster. Funny; I thought he'd changed his name to Lance by deed poll. Clearly not.

I fished around in my bag for Alan's scrapbook, which I'd brought along for moral support. It didn't take long to find what I was looking for. Please excuse the fact that Alan is going through his 'interesting handwriting' period and seems to have abandoned the use of most upper-case letters:

FRIDAY 24 AUGUST 1990
mega city 4, mudhoney, MAGPIES, faith no more
fucking brilliant only gonna be breif cos the pens running out, what a cracking day. janes adiction pulled out which was a right pisser but megas were amazing, mudhoney good stuff although had to pick clive up about 4 times because we'd had about three bottles of mendip each, some shit irish band came on and nick cave was well boring so we just drank more then MAGPIES who were absolutely splendid, lance on good form, he did this brilliant thing before look who's laughing cos there were loads of rockers showed up to see FNM. he made all the rockers put their hands up, then all the indie fans, then got the indie fans to go to the rockers and say 'good evening, welcome to reading festival, this is our festival now but thank you for coming anyway, this is the thieving magpies who are from reading and they're about to do one of their top ten hits' – it was well funny, the bloke I said it to was okay but clive's told him to piss off after about five words, I reckon there must have been some fights. then FNM played who were great but their sound was shocking, patton finished hanging off the scaffolding, didn't bother with the cramps but went and found a magpies bootleg and lisened by the tent with more mendip but the BEST THING WAS that I met LANCE BY THE TOILET after FNM and got his autograph, all right it's a bit [word I can't make out, but I think it's probably 'unco', i.e. uncool] but I was bladdered and couldn't be arsed to think of anything good to say. READING IS AMAZING . . . neds tomorrow

You can imagine what Alan's entries were like when he wasn't being 'breif'.

Stapled to the page is a label from one of the bottles of 'mendip' (full name actually Mendip Magic, a strong cider we had bought in bulk from a crustie) which Alan had hastily ripped off and presented to the passing Webster. I remember being obscenely jealous of this. Alan had a knack for spotting members of bands while out and about, often for striking up relaxed banter with them. I never spotted them, apart from that one time in Harlow. But Alan was constantly seeing the fuckers, like he had a sixth sense for it. And in the most incongruous places. He once saw Carl McCoy from Fields of the Nephilim in Boots. Barry Mooncult from Flowered Up in (honestly) a florists. Andy whatsit from New Fast Automatic Daffodils on a platform at Manchester Piccadilly station (he even claims they went for a pint together). I remember wandering around Reading that year desperately trying to spy my own exciting crop of indie celebs, but to little avail (I think the best I managed was Jonathon, the indie DJ at Camden Palace, but you saw him everywhere). So, anyway – Webster's autograph is just a scribble and the originally black ink has turned browny-green over the years, but I held up his cheque and compared the two scribbles, made under such wildly different circumstances, and I have to admit the similarity sent a little tingle down my spine.

I sat back in the vet's now silent waiting room (apart from the occasional muffled whimper from the perpetually vocal Nigel) and my mood plummeted. Not only had Lance Webster already been and gone, leaving me with bewilderingly few options for taking the matter further, but I still had a day's arsing around with animals to get through. For free. I glanced at my watch and, to be frank, the idea of fucking off occurred to me. The Other Vet would be arriving any minute. If I just left the keys on the desk and snuck out the door, letting it lock behind me, that wouldn't be too bad, would it? The animals would only be alone for, what, two minutes. I'd helped them out with the day's most important and arduous task; they could surely manage the rest of the day? I mean, what would they have done if I hadn't offered? I gathered up my belongings and stood up, giving myself a last-minute karma check. Was this okay?

But by the time eleven o'clock had struck, two things had magically happened: one, I had been transformed into a selfless hero of the hour, possessed of endless public spirit and generosity, sensitive, thoroughly modern, masculine and (perhaps) attractive; two, I had decided to rub along through the day after all. The power of women, eh?

All right, bearing in mind that our fourteen-hour relationship has just come to an abrupt and fairly acrimonious end, by which I must be slightly influenced, I can still say that she wasn't *that* attractive. I think it was more the initial shock of her bursting through the door (carrying her bike), actually being female and close to my age, then the fact that she spent the next five minutes telling me how wonderful I was for giving up a whole day and how much she'd heard about me from Jackie (eh?), all the time flashing her eyes and doing that tactile thing. I mean, I suppose it's just nice to be flirted with, and complimented and stuff, because to be frank (and I don't mean the violins to come out here) it's been a while. So when she finally put on her white tunic and disappeared inside the consulting room, I was gasping a bit. Okay, I'm being unfair. It's also because she's ... you know. Pretty. An ingredient not lost on me when, some eight (nonetheless knackering) hours later, she (yes, she) suggested we go for a drink.

Now, before you start worrying that this is all getting perilously close to the Nick Hornby zone, there's a good reason for telling you all this. Here we have, or had, a fairly standard thirty-year-old London-dwelling English woman. Born in Kent, I think, normal school, studied to be a vet in London. Likes doing normal London things: drinking, partying, eating out, going to the cinema. Clearly – although we didn't discuss it properly until much later – enjoys music, as she mentioned she had tickets to this year's Glastonbury. But halfway through the evening, which was going very nicely thank you (a few pints in, chat flowing, the pub buzzing but not too crazy), the following exchange occurred.

'Well, at least you only have to talk to them on the phone,' she was despairing, on the subject of the general public. 'I actually have to meet the fuckers. Tell 'em what's wrong with their bloody pets.'

'You don't enjoy it?'

'I love the animal part.'

'You love animals' parts?'

'Silly,' she laughed. 'I love the actual vet bit. It's the bloody public-relations bit I can't bear.'

'Right.'

'You know what I wish?' she began, playing with an empty crisp packet. 'I wish it could be a vet drive-through. They drop the animals off at a kiosk, bugger off and wait in the car park. Then they get called over the loudspeaker when I've finished, drive to a second kiosk where they get their pet back and a print-out of what's wrong with them.'

'That's a great idea. I should think they've got those already in America.'

'Probably.'

'But you do get relatively interesting characters in your place,' I suggested, deciding the time was right.

'Like?'

'Well, the guy today, who picked up Jessica the cat. Just before you arrived.'

'Jessica? That old tabby with lymphoma?'

'Lymphoma,' I winced. 'That's like cancer, yeah?'

'It is cancer. Poor thing.' She drew her index finger sharply across her neck and shrugged.

'Curtains?'

'Weeks, I'm afraid. Maybe less. The guy's heartbroken though. He keeps taking her in for pointless treatment. Seems to not care too much about the cost.'

(Ah. So maybe he has got a few bob stashed away somewhere.)

'Well,' I confided, 'you know who that guy is, don't you?'

'His name is . . . um . . . Webster.'

'Yeah,' I smiled, patiently. 'Lance Webster.'

'Okay,' she nodded, still expecting something more.

'Lance Webster,' I repeated. 'Used to be the singer with Thieving Magpies?'

She frowned and swallowed a mouthful of beer.

'Now, that name rings a bell. Remind me who they were?'

There it is.

I mean, I ask you. This kind of bloody thing happens all the time. *Remind me who they were.*

Usually, depending on who has said it and how much I've had to drink, such a comment heralds the arrival of a rather large argument. Not because I'm *offended*, you understand – it's just that I'm genuinely confused. Nah, bewildered. Flabbergasted. I just can't understand it. It doesn't compute with the way my brain operates. *Who were they?* Only the biggest British alternative band in the world, between the years 1991 and 1995. With the arguable exceptions of The Cure and Depeche Mode. Oh, and maybe New Order. 'Bad Little Secret', their biggest UK hit (although far from my favourite song of theirs, as it happens), held the number-two position on the singles chart for three weeks (only kept from the top spot by that stupid 'Please Don't Go' song). *Bruise Unit*, the 1992 album that propelled them into the same arenas around the planet as the likes of Nirvana, Pearl Jam and REM, shifted *four million* copies. Between 1989 and 1995, the Thieving Magpies sold out Brixton Academy a record-breaking *twenty-five* times, including three four-night runs. In addition to goodness knows how many NECs, G-MEXs and festival-headlining slots. But no one ever remembers all this. They just have vague memories of a band who were kinda fun down the student disco, but who were ultimately forgettable. Or, if a music journalist is talking, an outfit who represent quite how bad indie music managed to get, before Britpop came along and, by the grace of its fucking hairdo, corduroy jacket and afternoon drink at the Good Mixer, saved us all.

Or, even worse, a recollection like the one my 'date' offered me.

'Oh, I know – they did that song that went *"Nothing ever happens, dum-dum de dum-dum de dum . . ."*'

'No, that was Del Amitri.'

'Oh, sorry.'

I have no idea how people do it. But they do.

'You remember,' I coaxed. '*"You still don't know how . . . look who's—"*'

'*" . . . laughing now",*' she finished off.

'There you are! You know them.'

'Yeah, I know that one. Christ, that was *him?*'

'Yup.'

'Blimey,' she remarked. 'I always kind of preferred the Mondays and the Roses, though.'

'Ah.'

'You're a big fan, I take it?'

'Um, yeah,' I mumble.

'Wow. So it must have been quite a kick for you, meeting him today?'

'Sort of, yeah – I've met him before, though.'

Technically not lying, but all the same I decided it was a good time for a toilet visit. The last thing I wanted was my noble, gallant and (not to mention) date-acquiring day's activity to be exposed for the devious, self-interested and ultimately useless exercise that it really was. I regrouped with the assistance of the mirror in the gents'; I get pretty flustered on this sort of occasion and need to check that I'm still with the programme, especially after a minor blow like this one. It's funny, if I'd mentioned the Magpies and she'd exclaimed, 'Oh my God! Not *them*! He was the most hideous creep and all their videos sucked!' – I'd have been happier. Marginally. But it's the *indifference* that does my head in. The predictable, let's-ring-up-XFM-and-ask-them-to-play-'I Am the Resurrection'-for-the-fifteenth-time-today-style ennui which leaves me gagging. The sort of musical apathy that drives a listener straight into the arms of . . . well. You'll see.

Having said all that, I am nothing if not a nine-months-single, thirty-something loser with a few pints inside him who wouldn't mind a shag. I returned from the loo and the evening rolled happily along, music remaining firmly on the conversational reserve bench, and before I knew it they were chucking us out of the pub. How the decision was made to come back to mine I can't now remember, but I do recall being glad that Polly was still at her parents' house, and then having a bit of a snog in the kitchen. That, unfortunately, was as good as things got.

'You got any music?' came the enquiry, after I'd poured us a glass of wine each.

'Of course! What do you want to hear?'

(Mental note: never ask this question. Just select. It's so much easier.)

'You know what I love, love, *love* to listen to on nights like this?' she enthused, already starting to dance a bit.

'No,' I replied, hoping I had whatever it was.

She took a sip of wine and proclaimed, with some drunken passion:

'Snow Patrol.'

Oh God.

'*If I lay here . . . If I just lay here . . .*'

She closed her eyes and started to sway her hips.

'*Would you lie with me and just forget the world?*'

'Oh, really?' I asked, feigning innocence.

'Have you got that?' She beamed. 'Or Keane?'

'Um . . .'

'*Is it any wonder I'm tired . . . Is it any wonder I feel uptight . . .* Oh, such a good song.'

'Yeah, I suppose . . . I'm not sure we have it . . .'

She clapped her hands, gave me a big kiss and asked excitedly, 'Okay, what do you have? Show me. Which one's your room?'

Before I could respond she'd skipped off down the corridor. I followed, hoping my quarters weren't in too much of a state. She turned into Polly's room and snapped on the light.

'Ah, that's my flatmate's room.'

'Bloody hell, what a tip! So this one must be yours,' she smiled, bursting into the room opposite. 'Oh, *such* boy colours . . .'

She settled down next to my unruly stacks of CDs while I folded a few items of clothing and generally tidied up a bit. Her fingers skipped through some titles that clearly didn't register and it was a while before she spoke; each time she did, it irritated me.

'Nirvana, cool . . . Oh, you've got the *Pulp Fiction* soundtrack! Excellent . . . Mondays . . . Oh, I love the first Oasis album . . . Who the fuck are *they*? [I think she was eyeing a Butthole Surfers album at this point] . . . The La's. Oh my God, "There She Goes" is so amazing . . . Loads of people I've never heard of! . . . Oh, here's a Thieving Magpies album – let's have a look . . . Oh my God, it really is him!'

'We could put that on if you like?' (It was the MTV *Unplugged* album.)

She frowned. 'Not terribly romantic stuff, though, is it?'

I was rapidly losing interest in the whole thing.

'Chili Peppers . . . Oh, it's an old one though . . . Wonder Stuff. Has this one got "Dizzy" on it? [I didn't bother to reply] . . . Christ, have you actually got anything recorded recently?'

'Yeah, loads! I think there are some Elbow albums in there . . .'

'Boring.'

'Fratellis? Boards of Canada?'

'Yeah, shall we try to stick to people I might've even vaguely heard of?'

'Or Arctic Monkeys?' I held up their CD hopefully.

'Bit punky for late at night, perhaps?'

'There's vinyl too . . .'

'Oh, bit of a palaver. Has your flatmate got some music?'

Without my say-so, she strode back into Polly's room and to her diminutive CD rack, where, I knew full well, some true horrors lurked. I hovered in the doorway, huffing a bit.

'Oh, this is a bit better! . . . Björk . . . Moby . . . Scissor Sisters . . . Oh my God, she's got Snow Patrol! [She extracted this for later use and continued] . . . Bluetones . . . Leonard Cohen . . . The Verve . . . Oh, Joni Mitchell. I love this . . . Coldplay! Is this the one with "Fix You" on it?'

'It had better not be,' I grumbled.

'Cheer up, Granddad!' she laughed. 'Can we hear this?'

'Um, I'd rather not . . .'

'Oh, come on. It's gooorgeous. Better than your Snoozing Magpies,' she chuckled, giving me another kiss. My sour face must have said it all. She frowned again, this time genuinely. 'Seriously, Clive, brighten up! It's only music.'

'It's *not* only music,' I snapped, and stomped off to the kitchen.

Okay, I know what you're thinking. She's right. Lighten the fuck up, sad boy. Let her stick on her Chris Martin claptrap, or whatever she damn well wants, have another drink, forget about it, and get ready for some action. But no. I'm sorry. Perhaps I'm getting old – or older, at least – but I can't be arsed with that sort of thing any more. I was going to spare you the cringesome details of the next ten minutes but you ought to hear them really, as it gives you some insight into what really goes on in my head. Put differently, it demonstrates what a fuckwit I am. Especially when I've had a few.

She followed me into the kitchen, her face a picture of uncertainty; although it was pretty close to a certainty that the useful part of the evening was already over.

'I've a feeling I've done something to offend you,' she began, gently, 'but I can't say I know what it is.'

'No, it's not you,' I sighed.

'Well, that's good to hear,' she commented, with a healthy twist of sarcasm.

'It's just . . . oh, I don't know.'

'Well, if *you* don't know, then . . .'

'Sorry,' I muttered, taking a swig of wine. Bloody hell, I thought I'd seen the back of this kind of discussion.

'Is it your ex?' she asked, suddenly.

'My ex?'

'Well, in the pub you said your ex had a pretty shit taste in music.'

'Well . . . yeah, but not really,' I dithered. 'But I suppose it does still kind of depress me that, um . . . it begins with having sex to Kings of Convenience, then finishes with fighting for the CD player over Queens of the Stone Age versus KT Tunstall.'

'Uh-huh . . . it sounds like it *is* your ex.' She picked up her mobile and checked her text messages: always a sign that an evening is going well.

'But then, you think . . . if it *begins* with fighting for the CD player, then where does that take you?'

She looked up, appalled.

'Oh, what the fuck is your problem? For a start, *we* weren't fighting for the CD player; *you* were. And plus, what makes you think this is the beginning of anything? We were having fun, having a laugh, and now suddenly you've made it into something awfully heavy and boring.'

'Oh.'

'And what the hell is wrong with KT Tunstall?'

'Um, nothing, it's just . . .'

'What?'

'Um . . . what she represents.'

'Oh, do yourself a favour, Clive, take a load off.' Gathering up her bag now.

'You going?' I asked, downcast.

She shrugged. 'You tell me.'

And then for some reason I still can't really understand, maybe because I correctly figured that the evening couldn't get much worse, I did this:

'I'm writing a book about Lance Webster. I'm trying to interview him. That's why I volunteered to work at the vet's for the day.'

Now here's the interesting thing, if you're interested in atmospheric shifts. Instead of storming out, hurling abuse ('How dare you deceive me!', etc.) – she sat down in one of the kitchen chairs with her bag on her knee, her facial expression flattened, and she nodded, bidding me to continue. But from that split second onwards, it permanently ceased to be a romantic evening.

'I discovered he lives on this street, so I followed him on Saturday.'

'Why do you want to write a book about him?'

'Vindication. Among other things.'

'For you, or him?'

I smiled at this. 'Him, really.'

'Why does he need to be vindicated?'

I sighed. 'Because everyone's forgotten who he is.'

'How do you know he's not pleased about that?'

'Well, I don't. But that's what I want to find out. Do you remember . . . well, maybe you won't, but . . . he had a bit of trouble, just before the band split up . . . he got drunk onstage at a festival, had a fight, got arrested . . .'

'Actually, yeah . . . I've a vague memory of something.'

'Well, after that, the Magpies were forgotten within six months. Virtually erased from the rock history books, as though Lance had been arrested for child molesting rather than simply having a pissed punch-up.'

'What was the fight about?'

'No one knows. There are all sorts of rumours.'

'Like?'

'This friend of his had vanished a few months previously. People reckon he was told she'd been found dead that night, or something. The guy he punched was just a security guard. It's pretty clear he was just . . . you know.'

'In the line of fire?'

'Yeah.'

'Did he go to jail?'

'No, but I think he got fined or something. But that was basically the end of his career.'

She shrugged again, and stood up. 'Well, I don't know . . . but if I were you I'd be careful. People don't usually enjoy reliving shit like that.'

'Do you want another glass of wine?' I asked, aware of the fact that I'd enjoyed the last minute or two more than I had the rest of the evening.

'No, I'd better be going, Clive. It's really late.'

As I let her out, she gave me a look such as you might give someone who's about to climb a skyscraper without a rope.

'Take it easy, will you?'

'I'll try. Oh . . . and sorry.'

'Yeah,' she nodded, and was gone.

So there we are. Yes, I am alone on my bed – no night of hot passion for me – but at least I told the truth. In the end. And I don't have to pretend not to be disgusted by some turgid musical bollocks that, in truth, would have been liable to seriously affect my performance anyway.

But I'm still wound up. If tonight has done one thing, it's helped to crystallise my feelings regarding the Magpies – and all their ilk, as a matter of fact – having been effectively wiped from the parlance and playlist of the musically savvy, and the knock-on effect this seems to have on people like The Other Vet. It really is remarkable. I plonk my wine glass on my bedside table and turn to my much maligned piles of CDs, eventually locating another battered jewel case with a familiar picture of an empty hospital bed in an empty room, above which the handwritten statement 'THIEVING MAGPIES/ BRUISE UNIT' is crudely but unmistakably scrawled. Lance's voice leaps out of my speakers: '*I'm ready for the tears . . . I'm ready for the nausea*' – and we're off.

It's never been difficult for me to understand why, back in 1992, this record was outselling its nearest British rivals by something like two-to-one. The reviews at the time say it all, with unanimous word-processor ejaculation ('the sound of a band who have REM, Nirvana, U2 and Guns N' Roses firmly in their sights, and are ready to fire', decided *Q* magazine). But looking closely, there's always been a difference with the Thieving Magpies. A subtle difference – practically invisible in 1992 and barely noticeable in 1993 – but a contradiction nonetheless existed that would become crucial to their survival, or lack of it, in music lovers' hearts and minds beyond their eventual demise. The fact was: they had little or no influence over any other groups. There was a small clutch of imitators just after their debut album, as there always would be, but from about 1990 onwards you'd be hard pushed to find Thieving Magpies listed as a reference in any 'musicians wanted' advert, let alone quoted as an inspiration by a hotly tipped newcomer. Of course, this doesn't always matter; in fact, U2 have been the biggest band in the world for more than twenty years, and aside from a few losers doing impersonations of *The Unforgettable Fire* in 1986 they've hardly influenced a soul. But it doesn't matter, because U2 are just so damn successful and so damn good at being U2 that no one cares.

And it didn't really matter either with the Magpies, until Lance's colourful evening at the Aylesbury Festival. The world-straddling *Bruise Unit* tour rolled on into 1993, they had a bit of a break, Lance rather ill-advisedly tried his hand at acting (a small role in the television adaptation of Stephen Fry's *The Liar*), the band reconvened in the autumn of 1994 ('back for the Christmas term', as Lance put it) to record what would be their final album, *The Social Trap*. It was released in May 1995 – and it simply didn't matter that, in the meantime, Kurt Cobain had died, pulling the carpet from under every other alternative rock band's feet; it was of no concern that Britpop had arrived, that everyone was suddenly singing in cockney accents about making tea or cleaning their teeth, or that the major cultural concern was what Noel would say about Damon next, or vice versa; it didn't matter – not when the music was as good as it was on *The Social Trap*, with its healthy pair of singles, 'Retro Hetero' and 'Contribution'. The album entered the UK charts at number one and lingered within the top forty for the following three months. The singles easily graced the top ten. The tours sold out. Aylesbury, a three-day bash in only its third year, shifted most of its weekend tickets immediately after Thieving Magpies were confirmed as Saturday-night headliners. In short, there was nothing to worry about.

Then Lance got drunk, and the rest is . . . well, tragedy.

All right – so fifty thousand loyal fans were cheated out of a gig and insulted, but that goes no way towards explaining the speed at which *The Social Trap* flew out of the world's album charts and into its charity shops. The few onlookers who have since bothered to apply rational thought to the deletion of the Magpies from the world's musical hard drive have argued, with some substance, that while Britpop was unable to harm a popular band, it was certainly capable of inflicting lethal damage on an ailing one; but they offer no reason for why, a decade later, the Thieving Magpies are still pretty much absent from any retrospective compilations, pop cultural histories, 'best album' polls or 'classic indie' club nights (and I think I've heard 'Look Who's Laughing' *once* on the radio in eight years).

My own rather meagre explanation is that as they were merely *popular*, rather than having any real *influence*, it's been very easy for the Magpies to be completely forgotten, because hardly any bands have had to alter anything about themselves in order to do so. Looking at it another way, it would be impossible even to *attempt* to forget a band like Joy Division, because so many musicians would instantly lose their entire careers.

Not that the Magpies are the only group in this predicament.

There's a whole crop of them. A lot of these bands were listed by that cretin Tony Gloster during the final, fateful Magpies press conference at Aylesbury: Carter USM, Jesus Jones, Pop Will Eat Itself, The Wonder Stuff, The Mission (he also mentioned The Cure, who now seem to have been vindicated thanks to the undeniable length and quality of their career, and some recent namechecks from the young and hip). To Gloster's list I'll also throw in the Levellers, EMF and – fuck it – Ned's Atomic Dustbin. Let's analyse them all for a moment. Between 1988 and 1994, all these bands had large fanbases, big indie hits, albums that sold respectably, extensive tours abroad and high-billing (in some cases headlining) festival appearances.

Okay. Here we go.

But so did: The Stone Roses, Happy Mondays, The La's, Primal Scream, Inspiral Carpets, The Charlatans. In some cases, these bands were *less* commercially successful than those in the above paragraph. But the highbrow alternative pop fraternity still, more than ten years after they played their final, off-key note, go *potty* over The Stone Roses. They still call Shaun Ryder a 'genius' or a 'poet'. They refer to The La's sole album as 'the greatest debut ever made'. They cite *Screamadelica* as 'a pivotal moment in the history of popular music'. They constantly request 'This Is How It Feels' and 'Saturn 5' in indie clubs and on radio shows. And there's a nice little comfy chair set aside for dear little Tim Burgess at the right hand of Noel Gallagher, even though The Charlatans haven't made a convincing album in a decade.

So – why? Well, I will venture two possible reasons. Both of which combine to form one big, fat, intangible and thoroughly irritating reason.

Reason Number One. If you think of Britain as a country of two latitudinal halves, with its 'equator' bisecting the island at a point roughly in line with Nottingham, all the bands in the first group – with the exception of The Mission – were from *the South*.

All the bands in the second group were – or are – from *the North*.

The North, we are taught, is traditionally grittier, harder, more industrial, somehow more *real*, and – due to its widely alleged and lamented habit of being forgotten by the southern jessies in Whitehall – is the perennial underdog. That very British preoccupation. Therefore the idea of gritty, hard and *real* rock music coming from the North is an infinitely more attractive and sexy proposition than having it performed by someone from Wiltshire. And if there's any remaining doubt, the North is, I need hardly remind you, where The Beatles came from.

Reason Number Two. If you think of British rock music as an art form bisected by the two types of refreshment that fuel it, i.e. drugs and alcohol, then all the bands in the second group made music that is inseparably – in some cases heavily – linked with taking drugs. Most of these bands make you think of acid, ecstasy, being 'blissed out' or at the very least stoned off your nuts, sometimes more. Indeed, the histories of two of the bands – Happy Mondays and The La's – have been almost entirely *dictated* by the presence of drugs.

But all the bands in the first group, with the possible exception of EMF, had no such association. They were booze bands. They make you think of cider, snakebite and black, a few pints of cheap lager at the very least, sometimes of being violently sick outside the student disco. How dreadfully *gauche*.

There you are. Two reasons.

And the one big, fat, intangible and thoroughly irritating reason that they join forces to create?

The bands from the second group . . . are *COOLER* than those from the first.

That's it.

I've said it.

It doesn't make it any better, but I've said it. That's what I reckon.

What does it mean? I don't know. Perhaps nothing. But I've said it.

And having said it, and having had a pretty rancid day, and

being finally pissed from the cocktail of beer, wine and no dinner inside me, and not having the single fuckingest clue what to do next with the whole Lance Webster debacle, I'm going to bed, probably for the rest of the week, so goodnight and fuck off.

THAT'S A BLOODY SILLY NAME FOR A FANZINE, MAN

Alan William Potter – thirty-four, slightly padded around his middle and hanging on for dear life on top, wearing a beige sweatshirt he wouldn't have been seen standing next to at a bus stop six years ago – finishes his bacon cheeseburger with a wince (it's probably the cheapest meat he's eaten in months), takes a long drag on his Kronenbourg and reclines, his eyes following the path of one of the prettier bar staff as she saunters round the pub collecting pint glasses. Clive Beresford (my parents mysteriously neglected to bestow me with a middle name) – thirty-three, just a touch more portly than a garden rake, lanky hair with a generous sprinkling of salt and pepper and in need of a cut, the same competition winner's XFM T-shirt I've worn for years in the hope that someone will think I work there – gathers up the remaining peas on his plate with a dollop of mashed potato and wishes, not for the first time, that he'd ordered the steak. You'd think I'd have mastered the strategy by now: if Alan is paying, order big.

'Nice?'

'Yeah,' I splutter. 'Thanks.'

'Where the fuck's she gone with my card?'

I watch my old friend's beady eyes as they try to make sense of the developing debate behind the bar. I finished recounting the Webster/day-at-the-vet's saga some forty minutes ago and, while it'll hardly win prizes for the most gripping story of the year, I'm still rather dismayed that Alan has yet to ask me a single question about it, much less give any advice on how to proceed. Instead I've been treated to a brace of mundane details about the fortunes of his business and an update on Jocasta's latest cute-toddler antics, which today I'm not really in the mood for.

'Gotta go back in soon,' I sigh, eyeing the clock as it nears half past one.

'How's it going in that dump, then?'

'Same-old, same-old. Moving offices on Friday.'

'They making any money?'

I start to reply but his attention wavers after less than a syllable, the barmaid hurrying past with an order of nachos.

'Love, sorry . . . any chance of getting my debit card back before this evening?'

She blushes and apologises; I decide my lunch hour is over.

'I'm going. Thanks for the meal.'

'Shit, man, I never asked – what are you gonna do next with Webster?'

'Fuck knows. See you.'

'Vorsprung Durch Peanut?' he calls, with a gratifying hint of guilt.

'Vorsprung Durch Peanut,' I reply, adding a little twist of misery and dejection to the final word. Ha. He deserves it, anyway. Even if he did pay for lunch.

Vorsprung Durch Peanut.

So what does it mean? It means nothing.

It was the first term of A-level history, you understand. Bored out of my mind after the euphoria of doing relatively okay in my

GCSEs, I was sitting next to Billy Flushing – who was an incredible saddo really, but could be quite good value – and we'd been to see Carter the Unstoppable Sex Machine, a band who I'd decided to check out (as hundreds of others did) purely on the strength of their name. Despite Billy's lingering love for all things Genesis, Marillion and Rush, he'd taken a passing interest in the new tangent my music taste had taken, and over that long, hot, final summer of the eighties we'd attended a handful of shows together (The Primitives, REM, um . . . Simple Minds), my parents recognising in Billy an adequately reliable companion (my mum knew his mum from Conservative Party functions). Billy remained largely unimpressed by these fairly standard rock outings, dwelling as he did in a world of comics and graphic novels (every trip I took with him to central London included a torturous thirty-minute section when I would wait outside the Forbidden Planet shop while Billy did . . . well, Christ knows what, really), but the slightly less obvious stuff I placed in front of Billy he loved. Carter – two punkist, anti-Thatcherite late twenty-somethings with their cheapo drum machine, Rottweiler guitars and pun-tastic lyrics – turned out to be right up his street. A more compelling draw for me was that Alan Potter, who I was still desperately trying to impress, appeared to have little idea who they were.

'Who's that, man?' he asked, when I sauntered across the school playing field wearing one of their T-shirts (that one with the baby on it).

'Oh, Carter,' I replied, with all the nonchalance I could summon.

'Right . . . yeah . . . saw 'em once, supporting someone. Can't remember who . . .'

'I saw them last week at the Powerhaus.'

'Any good?'

'Fantastic. The ruck was brilliant. Stage-dived, too [this bit was a lie].'

'Hmm,' Alan murmured, idly watching some girls limbering up across the pitch. 'I remember their drummer being great.'

I was delighted at this gaping hole in Alan's usually spotless knowledge, though it presented a dilemma. Should I reply truthfully or, in the name of harmony, let his clumping error lie – but potentially leave myself open to looking similarly ignorant later on? Just as I was deciding, Billy showed up.

'Good grief, Charlie Brown,' he blethered, with his rather awkward chuckle.

I shrugged at Alan apologetically.

'That's, um, one of Carter's song titles.'

'That's our favourite one,' Billy continued, beaming, his forehead bearing its usual sheen of sweat. He twitched, pulling his rucksack further onto his shoulder – an endlessly uncool manoeuvre. 'The other good one is [and here he fully broke into song, head bobbing and everything] *"Pump it up, Jack, pump it up, Jack – pump it up!"'*

Again, I sighed and explained to Alan, 'That's, um, this song, on my T-shirt.' But it was too late.

'Laters,' Alan muttered, and wandered off.

'Billy!' I snapped, once Alan was out of earshot.

'What?'

'Couldn't you be a bit more . . . ?'

I regarded him, his confused expression, his mum-cut hair, his relentless habit of pushing his glasses back up his nose. No, he probably couldn't. Oh well.

'Want to go for a milkshake?' he enquired excitedly. I pondered my wealth of more attractive options.

'Yeah, all right.'

Anyway. Summer came and went, GCSE results arrived and suddenly we were sixth formers. Thinking this might mean a marked improvement in Alan's at-school attitude towards me, I bowled up to him outside the assembly hall on the first day back and asked him how Reading Festival was.

'Um, yeah, it was wicked, man,' he responded, then frowned,

played with his floppy hair and wandered off towards a group of people from his own year.

So there we were, Billy Flushing and me, halfway through an interest-free ninety minutes during which some old teacher, the identity of whom unsurprisingly escapes me, furnished us with riveting details of Bismarck's progress up the Prussian power ladder. We started mumbling things to each other in stupid German accents, certain phrases from our life at the time: *'I've got my spine, I've got my orange crush'*; *'Don't ask any more stupid questions'*; *'Take me down to the paradise city'* (all hilarious, I assure you), eventually coming across *'Ich bin ein Berliner'*, which Billy tried to convince me actually translated to 'I am a jam doughnut' (which is kind of true, but I'll let someone else explain that one). Finding this vastly entertaining, I shortly uttered those fateful words 'vorsprung durch peanut'. And why? On account, obviously, of *'vorsprung durch technik'*, that nifty piece of eighties sloganeering, but also the aforementioned track 'Good Grief Charlie Brown', which had led Billy and me to decide, just as fans of the Grateful Dead were known as 'Deadheads', that Carter USM fans should be known as 'Peanuts' (it didn't catch on).

Gawd. Sorry. It's like describing an episode of a bad sitcom to someone.

And what, you may quite reasonably demand, was the earthly point of telling you all that?

Well, over the summer I had decided to start a fanzine. Apart from the fact I enjoyed writing, it seemed the only way of arranging my various ideas and opinions regarding this peculiar music whose trickle towards my eardrums had rapidly turned into a torrent, with all the attendant phrases, attitudes, subgenres and items of merchandise. What I wanted to achieve was something indie laymen could read and feel comforted by, reassured that they had a sane companion on this journey into the wide alternative yonder. As I knew comparatively little myself at this point, there would be a strong atmosphere of mutual discovery in my fanzine's pages, with irreverent explanations of the various acts

I encountered (Pop Will Eat Itself: 'they're white, they're from Birmingham, but they rap! No one knows why.' The Pixies: 'completely barmy, the band all seem to be playing different songs to each other, apart from "Here Comes Your Man", which sounds like The Archies' "Sugar, Sugar" after a few pints.' The Stone Roses: 'I thought they would be really good. They're not'). The name of this nascent publication was originally going to be something to do with the Thieving Magpies, but I correctly figured it was likely to be taken more seriously by Alan Potter if it wasn't. I had toyed with *Info Freako* but this also seemed too obvious. After that history lesson with Billy Flushing there was little doubt it should be called *Vorsprung Durch Peanut.* Billy had offered to be involved, and despite some reservations, I agreed.

The thing with Billy – and I think we've all had a friend like him at some point in our youth – was that you could have real, childish, eccentric *fun* with him, without caring for a second about how *cool* you ended up appearing. When I was with him, I sank (depending on one's perspective, of course) to his level, and became a super, hyper, fucking *supernova* geekboy, a nerd incarnate, laughing at things that weren't funny, entertaining possibilities that a four-year-old would dismiss as immature, and crucially, because I was slightly higher up on the school food chain, could temporarily feel as cool as a bastard by comparison. But the problem was, should anyone arrive on the scene who displaced *me* from this little hierarchy – one of the 'hard lads', or Alan Potter, or any member of the opposite sex – I instantly wanted Billy Flushing to be swallowed up by the floorboards or to spontaneously vaporise. This facet of our friendship eventually gave rise to One of the Nastiest Things I Have Ever Done Ever – but we'll come to that.

Alan Potter himself was a big part of the fanzine strategy, though he was presently unaware of this. You may wonder why on earth I was still set on the idea of befriending the graceless sod when he was so blatantly uninterested in acknowledging my existence; here I must hold up my hands and utter two words of explanation, two timeless teenage preoccupations which, as we streak into the iPod-filled, MySpace, my-arse, your-Facebook latter half of the first decade of the twenty-first century, show absolutely no sign of waning: Girls, and Music. Alan seemed to know a lot of both. Billy Flushing, for all his entertaining observations and ability to make double history pass more quickly, had precious little of either commodity. My plan, then, was to get the first issue of the fanzine out as quickly as possible, making it so exciting that Alan Potter wouldn't be able to resist getting involved with the next one. Cue: doors opened to a wealth of newly discovered bands, easy access to gigs (Alan had many friends who drove), respect from the sixth form at large, with particular focus on the female half. At least, that was the theory.

Work began in earnest, Billy on the design, me on the actual content. I had spoken to one of the trainee teachers – a lacklustre undergraduate known as Mr Eversmith, who looked a good deal younger than us – and he had agreed to sneakily let us use the art-room photocopier as long as we provided the paper. Here Billy once again proved his worth: his elder brother worked for a stationery company. A tentative date in December was set for our first issue's launch, but it quickly became clear that an extra ingredient was required. We couldn't very well fill an entire organ of twenty (or even ten) pages simply with my ramblings on whoever ignited my interest from the pages of *Melody Maker* (which I'd recently abandoned *Smash Hits* for). Original material was necessary, and not just my ham-fisted attempts at album and single reviews. We needed a proper interview feature.

The most impressive coup for me would obviously have been an interview with Lance Webster, but superficial enquiries confirmed this was way out of our league. Further brainstorming boiled down to an unnatural selection of the acts Billy considered 'not boring', those whom I naïvely felt were within our grasp, and people we'd actually heard of: All About Eve's Julianne Regan, Jesus Jones' Mike Edwards, New Model Army's Justin Sullivan and The Sugarcubes'

Björk were all mentioned, among a very few others. We wrote to their record companies and were greeted, predictably, by deafening silence. After waiting vainly until half-term, I agreed to an idea Billy had suggested ages ago but for some daft reason I had rejected: try Carter USM.

Carter were a completely different matter. Slated as 'ones to watch' (their anthem 'Sheriff Fatman' had begun to work its magic on the more adventurous of the country's indie clubs, and I'd noticed one of their badges had by now appeared on Alan Potter's school jacket) but still hardly significant players even in the alternative sector, theirs was the only record sleeve I owned which bore a residential address. We fired off another letter and forgot about it. A week or so later I got home from school to a frosty reception from my mum, furious to report that someone from 'one of those dreadful sex companies' had been on the phone for me.

'What did they actually say?' I demanded.

'Oh, it's just too awful for words . . .'

'No, no, Mum – what did they *actually say*?'

'He said he was the boss of a sex machine,' she moaned, extracting the leftovers of a roast chicken from the fridge. 'I can't bear it, I never thought you'd get involved in anything like that . . .'

'Adrian *Boss* . . . and he manages Carter the Unstoppable Sex Machine!' I exclaimed, as if this would improve matters. My mum blinked at me for a few seconds, then sat down and started angrily pulling bits of chicken off the carcass.

Of course she'd refused to take a number, but directory enquiries were useful for once and I was soon nervously speaking to the manager himself. Carter had a show at the Marquee the following Tuesday, he explained; there was a gap in their schedule after soundcheck, around seven-ish, when I was welcome to join them for a pint at a pub called the Blue Posts, 'just north of Oxford Street'.

'Excellent!' exclaimed Billy, when I phoned him straight afterwards. 'I think I know where that is.'

I had been so breathlessly excited about the whole thing, I'd forgotten to get a more detailed address.

'It's not far from Forbidden Planet.'

'I don't like Forbidden Planet,' I reminded him.

'Yeah, but I do. I can nip in there before we meet them.'

Oh dear.

'Um, Billy . . . I was thinking . . . I'm not really sure we both need to go?'

'Eh?'

'Well, I reckon it would, you know . . . look a bit more professional if it was just one of us – otherwise it'll just sort of look like two mates who want to meet their favourite band.'

'Which it sort of is,' Billy pointed out.

'Well, I don't really see it that way. I mean, this is a big deal for us!'

'I agree. But as it was my idea, perhaps it should be me who goes.'

Strange thing about Billy: as awkward and difficult to take seriously as he was in person, he was actually very good on the phone, almost businesslike.

'But the whole fanzine idea was mine in the first place,' I countered, 'so it should really be me who goes.'

'All right, how about you do the interview, I come along and take some photos?'

The thought of Billy bumbling around with his camera while I attempted to interrogate the duo was more than I could deal with.

'Billy, sorry – no. Next time. Once we get going. There's just a bit too much riding on this first one. Please let me do it by myself. I'm sorry.'

'Oh.'

I felt pretty rotten. But sod it. I had an interview with Carter! How many other sixteen-year-olds could claim that? And the fact that they were on the cusp of some serious cult stardom (I knew this;

I'd read it somewhere) meant I was officially going to be one of the hippest guys in my year. School-wide fame, popularity and gaggles of previously unobtainable girls were surely just the other side of the carol service. A state of affairs I sadly found too thrilling to keep to myself.

'You're gonna do what?'

Guess who.

'Interview Carter,' I breezed, ladling some custard onto my sponge pudding. 'Tomorrow evening.'

'Where?'

'Oh, up in town. Before their Marquee show.'

'What for?'

I grabbed some cutlery and mooched off with my lunch to an empty table near the back of the dinner hall. I didn't even need to look back. As if I was pulling him by a string attached to his nose, Alan Potter followed, and put his tray opposite mine. Oh, the power.

'What for?' he repeated.

'Oh, for this fanzine I'm starting next month.'

'You're starting a fanzine?'

'Yeah. Carter are going to be the first cover stars.'

I tucked into my curried something-or-other while Alan looked helplessly around him, frowning with the bewilderment of a dog who'd just had its ball taken away.

'What's the fanzine called?' he asked, finally.

'*Vorsprung Durch Peanut*,' I enunciated, after swallowing what I had in my mouth.

'That's a bloody silly name for a fanzine, man.'

'All fanzines have bloody silly names. That's the deal.'

He stared down at his suddenly unappetising plate of chips.

'We wrote them a letter, the manager phoned back,' I continued. 'They like doing fanzine interviews, apparently. More than they do for the proper music press.'

'Who's we?' Alan enquired, with a suspicious glint in his eye.

'Me and . . . you know, the others involved.'

'You're not doing it with that dweeb, are you?'

'Who d'you mean?'

'That knob in your year, with the glasses and the hunchback.'

'He's not got a hunchback,' I protested.

'Yeah, he has. Quasi-Flushing. Billy-modo. So he's doing it with you, yeah?'

'No. He's helping out a bit, you know, providing some of the paper. But he's not *part* of it.'

The shame of it. It gets worse, unfortunately.

'So, what are you going to ask them?'

'Well, a few things. About the album. About, you know . . . how far they want to go. About the lyrics. And stuff.'

'You must have a list of questions,' Alan improvised, forking some chips into his mouth, his appetite regained. 'You've got to have your strategy worked out, man.'

'Strategy?' This was a concept that hadn't occurred to me. I was interviewing them, not trying to beat them at chess.

'Yeah, sure,' Alan rambled, like the expert he wasn't. 'If they smell a rat, if they think you're not for real, they'll be out of there.'

'Really?'

'Of course, man.'

'But this is Carter. They're, you know . . .'

'One of us?' Alan laughed.

'Yeah!'

'Don't believe it. That's how they come across, but if those guys want to get anywhere they'll be complete bastards like everyone else. Especially to the press.'

It was my turn to look confused, as my mental picture of two chummy, wacky-haired men-of-the-kids drifted down the gutter.

'Don't let that put you off, though, man!' Alan beamed, slapping me on the shoulder. 'I'll come along if you like, give you a hand.'

Without a second's hesitation, I nodded vigorously.

'Okay, yeah! That'd be great.'

Hmm.

Well, the next day and a half passed with agonising lack of speed until, at last, we were alighting from the train at Euston. At this point in my life central London was a relatively unknown quantity to me. I fancied that I possessed passable awareness of its rough shape and contents, but in reality this consisted of little more than Trafalgar Square, Harrods, Piccadilly Circus, Regent Street, Oxford Street and whatever other snippets had engraved themselves on my cranium from the occasional half-term shopping and 'culture' trip with members of my family. Plus, as I acknowledged to myself with a hefty slab of guilt when Alan and I emerged from the tube at Tottenham Court Road, the bit of New Oxford Street that was then home to Billy's beloved Forbidden Planet. It was a mildish November evening, which I was glad about; I was dressed in a black, long-sleeved Thieving Magpies T-shirt but had forgone any sort of jacket as none of mine was remotely what one would wear to meet a pair of fledgling alternative superstars. Alan, on the other hand, looked irritatingly cool in a Red Hot Chili Peppers' *Mother's Milk* T-shirt and a black leather jacket (which I later discovered was actually his brother's). We sauntered down the rapidly emptying shopping strip and came to a halt at the corner of Newman Street, on which, Alan had assured me, resided the boozer in question.

'We're a bit early, man – let's walk round the block a bit.'

Alan's stand-offishness towards me had thawed considerably on the journey up (just as it had materialised on the way back from the first Magpies show). Rather than being pleased about this, I was actually pretty pissed off. Was he so surgically attached to school etiquette that he felt unable to communicate with me in a civil manner within a ten-mile radius of the place? How 'alternative', then, did that really make him? I planned to firmly ask him so, as soon as the interview was behind us. But for now we nattered amiably about the musical concerns of the day.

'When's it out?'

'Monday.'

'You gonna get it?'

'Dunno, man. I'm not really that keen on it.'

'Me neither. I prefer the other side.'

'You heard it?'

'Yeah, Janice Long played it.'

'I was thinking of just buying it on seven-inch so it gets a good chart placing.'

'Ian Brown reckons it'll be number one.'

'He would. He's full of it, that guy.'

'So what d'you reckon it'll get to?'

'Top ten? Maybe.'

'Really?'

'Yeah. Pisses me off, though, man. They'll beat the Magpies to it.'

We rounded the corner and found ourselves outside the pub itself. Two minutes to seven. There was a moment's awkward silence; I was feeling pretty wretched with nerves, and it wasn't easy to tell whether I felt better or worse for Alan's presence. On balance I think I probably felt worse. I was certainly going to be even more self-conscious with his seemingly unflappable confidence next to me, and was foreseeing all sorts of horrific tripping-over-word scenarios. So you can imagine how much better I felt when, just before we entered, Alan was the one to say it.

'I'm shitting it, man. I hope they're nice to us.'

'We'll be fine,' I smiled, and pushed open the door.

The first thing we noticed was the pub did not contain Carter. The second was that it was fairly hard to imagine it ever doing so. The youngest person there was about fifty-five. The barman looked about seventy, and more importantly, far from the sort of guy who'd be relaxed about the drinking age. Most people in the room looked up as we entered, then returned expressionlessly to their pints. A

raddled old mess in the corner nursing half a stout looked like he'd
recently died.

'You sure this is the place?' Alan whispered.

'What are you asking me for?' I hissed back. 'You led us here.'

'But they definitely said the Blue Posts, right?'

'Yes!'

The decor was plain, unadorned dark wooden panelling, and
probably hadn't changed since the war. It was a good few years before
the benefits (and the irony) of visiting such an establishment would
occur to younger folk, and as we gingerly approached the bar the
landlord smiled dubiously at us.

'Looking for McDonald's?' he gruffed.

Alan coughed anxiously.

'Um . . . can we have a couple of pints of cider and black, please?'

'And you are, of course . . .'

'Eighteen,' we chanted.

He gave us a long, hard stare, then to our amazement started to
pour our pints.

My drinking career still being in its infancy, there was quite a
kick to be had from sitting in a pub with a pint. I hadn't much
affection for the bittersweet red liquid which I now sipped; it was
simply a relatively palatable way of ingesting alcohol. (Lager made
me gag after a few gulps, wine was considered far from appropriate
and the only other drink I could tolerate was Southern Comfort
and lemonade – although this was solely reserved for the purpose
of getting pissed.) Still, I felt pretty pleased with myself as we occupied our table in the corner, and I almost forgot what we were
really there for. After ten minutes or so, the novelty for Alan was
clearly wearing a bit thin.

'Dunno, man . . .'

He took a large swig of his drink and frowned around the room.
Everyone seemed engaged in dull conversations about work or sport.
The pair of men nearest us were discussing the trials and tribulations

of being employed by the Royal Mail, who had a large sorting office across the road; it's likely this pub was the *de facto* company bar.

'I'm not convinced, y'know . . .'

'They'll be along in a minute,' I asserted.

'It's just that . . . I can't think why they'd want to come and drink in a place like this.'

'Maybe they like the prices?' I mused. 'That was a bloody cheap round . . .'

'Yeah, but . . .'

'. . . and there's nothing wrong with it,' I continued, lowering my voice. 'It's not unpleasant. Just a bit . . . you know, old.'

'Yeah, but I've seen the sort of joints these people go for, man. Are you sure he said the Blue Posts?'

'Yes!'

'And you don't think he was winding you up?'

'No!' I exclaimed, starting to get a bit irritated. 'I had a long conversation with him. He was totally genuine. He went on and on about fanzines being the backbone of the independent music industry, all that stuff. Carter are a bit different, you know. We're not dealing with Bon Jovi here.'

'Hmm. Maybe it's something else, then.'

'What do you mean?'

'Maybe they've forgotten, or something better came up.'

'Bollocks,' I stated, quite enjoying bossing him around a bit. 'It's only twenty past seven. The soundcheck might be overrunning. It could be anything. Just relax. Shall we have another pint?'

Of course the answer was yes, but as the bottom of that next glass came into view even I was beginning to have my doubts. Fifty minutes seemed pushing it. I stood up and fished around in my pocket for some change.

'What you doing?'

'Thought I'd give my folks a quick ring,' I replied. 'See if they've phoned to cancel or something. I dunno. Just an idea.'

I didn't let on, but I'd also allowed myself to slip into the unfortunate habit of speaking to my parents halfway through an evening out to tell them I was okay; a policy I vowed to discontinue as soon as I hit seventeen. I ambled over to the payphone at the end of the bar, recognising the still relatively uncommon feeling of booze kicking in, my legs feeling a bit light and my eyesight blurring a little around the edges. I dialled and pushed in a coin at the sound of the pips. Although the ensuing exchange with my mother was unremarkable, the ancient landlord started to eye me strangely towards the end.

'Yeah, I will . . . No, I promise . . . Well, I can't have much more anyway, I've only got two pounds left . . . No, I've no idea . . . We'll just wait a bit longer I suppose, and then I dunno . . . come home or something . . . No, the Blue Posts . . . as in signposts . . . What was that? . . . What did he ask? . . . Of course there isn't another one. How could there be another one? . . . Well, maybe, but not in the same area . . . I know . . . Well, they're not pop stars yet, but . . . Yeah, okay, I will . . . See you later . . .'

I replaced the receiver and started back towards Alan when the landlord stopped me.

'Just a minute, my lad. I couldn't help overhearing your conversation.'

'Uh . . . yeah?'

He'd finally twigged my real age, I was certain.

'Your father's right.'

'My what? . . . Ah, yes. I was just, er . . .'

'There is another Blue Posts around here.'

I gaped at him.

'Is there?'

'Yes,' he laughed. 'We call it the Teenage Posts, although it's actually older than this pub, strange as it seems. But full of teenagers, y'see. Snotty little place, in my opinion, but I guess you'd prefer it.'

'What? Oh, shit!'

This met with a stern frown.

'Sorry, sorry! I don't suppose you could tell us how to get there . . . Alan!'

A minute later we were sprinting back the way we'd come, veering left and left again into the alley-like Hanway Street, where we slowed to a fast walk. There was a palpable shift in ambience as we hurried past a few unnamed drinking dens and characters of questionable occupation. A skinny woman lighting a cigarette in a doorway asked us if we wanted to come in and play with her Lego.

'Fucking patronising cow,' Alan growled under his breath. 'I've been going out round here for ages.'

But not, as it turned out, long enough to be aware of the funny-looking pub at the Tottenham Court Road end of the street, with a wonky Courage brewery sign bearing its name. It didn't look like many London boozers I'd ever seen, the outside resembling a narrow shop or funeral parlour rather than a pub. But it did look suitably old and tatty, and the colourful movement we could detect through the frosted glass suggested a place considerably livelier than the one we'd just left. It was also infuriatingly close to the tube exit we'd surfaced from a little over an hour ago.

'Hang on, let's get our breath back,' I commanded, leaning on a lamp post. Alan was frowning, looking up and down the street.

'Shit, you know . . . I think I have been to this place.'

'Yeah,' I replied, unconvinced.

'D'you reckon they're still in there?'

'I guess we're about to find out.'

'Fuck, man. What are we going to say?'

'The truth,' I shrugged. 'That you got the wrong pub.'

Alan drew breath to protest but I was already heading through the door.

It was as obvious that Carter would frequent this Blue Posts as it was doubtful they'd ever darken the threshold of the other one. Crunchy indie music was merrily careering out of a copious-looking jukebox; young alternative-esque people of various shapes, sizes, hairdos and T-shirts were lounging around smoking and notching up empty pint glasses; and the bar staff looked tame. It was clearly a place we'd want to spend time in, Carter or no Carter. Which was just as well.

'Throwing Muses, man,' commented Alan, nodding at the jukebox speakers.

'Never mind all that. Where the fuck are Carter?'

Not there. The pub was small enough to ascertain this within seconds. They might have both been in the loo, but this seemed unlikely. All the more galling was the distinct impression that they *had* been there; I could see several Carter T-shirts in the room, most tables had more empty glasses than seemed possible for the amount of drinkers present, and the general atmosphere was laced with antici- pation. This was indubitably the pre-gig drinking hole, and Carter weren't really big enough yet for there to be several of them. I locked onto an appropriate-looking group of folk and, fortified by the pair of pints inside me, stepped forward.

'Er . . . excuse me, this may seem like a silly question, but . . .'

A girl with cropped bleached hair and slightly mad eyes looked up.

'Hahaha! How silly?'

'Er . . . pretty silly,' I admitted. 'You know the band Carter?'

'Yes?'

'You just missed them actually, mate,' volunteered a bespectacled bloke sat next to her.

'They were here?'

'They were,' confirmed the girl, pointing to a couple of empty chairs. 'Right here. And now they've gone. Haha!'

'Fuck,' I gasped, turning to Alan.

'Do you know them?' Alan asked the girl.

'Sort of,' she smiled.

'Did they say anything about being interviewed?'

A long-haired guy in a Mega City Four T-shirt across the table suddenly wagged his finger.

'Oi! Are you the fanzine?'

Gingerly, I raised my hand.

'I am the fanzine.'

The whole table erupted with laughter and suddenly everyone seemed to be pointing at us. Alan and I stole a quick glance at each other for support.

'You knobs!' screeched the girl. 'They've just been sitting here slagging you off for the last half an hour!'

'Really?'

'Yes! Hahahaa! "These bloody fanzines," they kept saying, "they always stand you up."'

'Are you serious?' frowned Alan.

'Yeah!'

'Shit. We were in the wrong pub,' I explained. 'It was his fault.'

This heralded another volley of mirth. ('Oh noo, it was *his* fault!') Alan looked like he was ready to punch someone, probably me.

'It's all right,' laughed Mega City Four bloke. 'They weren't proper narked off, just taking the piss, y'know.'

'You can apologise to them at the gig if you like,' suggested the girl.

'Ah . . .' I began. 'The problem is, we're not actually going, um, to the gig . . .'

'Why not? Come on, it's only three quid.'

I turned to Alan again. If I'd spent much of the evening feeling relatively grown up, I now felt about twelve.

'I haven't enough cash . . . have you?'

'Um, yeah . . . but . . .'

'We're on the guestlist,' the girl continued. 'We could try sneaking you in too if you like?'

Once again, all faces seemed to be on us. Alan was clearly finding the situation very tricky to deal with.

'Um . . . I think we need a private meeting for a moment, man.'

'Okay,' I nodded, and followed him to the door.

'I can't go,' he hissed into my ear.

'Why not?'

'I promised my mum I'd be back by ten. I've got a mock tomorrow.'

'A mock?'

'Mock A-level, dumbo.'

Blimey. First the wrong pub, and now this. The famous Alan Potter was seriously starting to ruin my week. I suddenly caught a mental image of Billy Flushing, grinning stupidly as he always did – but also leading me to the correct pub and then on to the gig, chuckling like a lunatic, arm in arm with the mad blonde girl. I shook my head and he vanished.

'Sorry,' Alan murmured. 'I'll make it up to you. We don't have to leave just yet anyway. I'll buy you another pint.'

The Carter guestlist crowd had finished their drinks and were now gathering by the door to leave.

'What's the verdict, then?' beamed the girl. 'Are you there, or are you square? Hahahaha!'

The final nail in Alan's coffin of credibility was still to come. After we'd made our excuses to the group I sat back in one of the pub's well-worn seats, contemplating this impressive start to my career as a music journalist while Alan went to buy another round. A minute later he was back.

'Cunts wouldn't serve me,' he announced, flopping down on the seat opposite.

We stared at each other for a moment, swirling the incalculable futility of the evening around our heads like a vintage cider. But I had a plan.

'Shall I have a go?'

'No,' Alan stated firmly.

'No, really. It might be all right for me. You're taller, but I've got an older face.'

'That's utter bollocks.'

'Just give me the money. What have we got to lose?'

I didn't tell him I'd suddenly remembered I had a dog-eared photocopy of Billy Flushing's brother's driving licence lurking in one of the pockets of my bag. Billy had made one for each of us (with little thought for what would happen if we presented both at the same time). He used his regularly to buy certain extreme items of literature; I had never tried using mine. It put me, if memory served, just a few days shy of nineteen, but was worth a go.

'Two pints of cider and black, please.'

This particular girl behind the bar had a permanent frown, a fierce-looking nose ring and a GBH T-shirt, none of which assisted my acting skills.

'Got any ID?'

'Yeah,' I replied, scrabbling around in my bag and hoping the thing was in one piece. Just about. I presented it to the barmaid.

'You're almost nineteen,' she noted, scrutinising the threadbare document.

'Yup.'

She shrugged and handed it back.

'Okay, whatever.'

The thrill of having trounced Alan Potter at the booze-buying game sent a flood of confidence through me. I looked over at him (he was flicking through the jukebox selection) and winked. He mouthed 'fuck off' and turned away.

'Did you put something on?' I asked, as I returned with the drinks and a packet of Quavers.

'Yeah.'

'What?'

'You'll see,' he grumbled, taking a gulp, as the intro to something I didn't recognise started up. We sat and listened in silence. 'Did I get any change?'

'Yeah,' I replied, handing him a few coppers.

'Fuck's sake.'

More silence.

'Fucking hate not getting served, man.'

'That's okay, I did!'

'That's not the point,' he glared.

I was starting to get the distinct impression Alan was slipping back into school mode. The guy on the record seemed to be singing '*why can't I get just one fuck*', but I was sure I'd misheard.

'So who is this, then?'

'Violent Femmes.'

'Ah.'

I pulled open the bag of Quavers and grabbed a handful.

'So I was wondering,' I began, between crunches, 'whether I should just go ahead and pretend we actually met them, for the purposes of the fanzine.'

'Could do.'

'I could make up a few answers, y'know . . . what I think they would say, study a few of their interviews, that sort of thing. It wouldn't be too naughty really. This first edition's gonna be too small to really get noticed anyway.'

Silence.

'Are you all right?'

'Sorry, man. I'm just in a wig. Hate not getting served. Hate the fact that we fucked it up this evening [I decided not to suggest he change the 'we' to 'I' at this juncture]. Hate being at school. Hate the fact that people in my year are all wankers. Hate having to work at bloody Sainsbury's. Hate looking seventeen. Hate being seventeen. No one ever told you it was this shit. They say going through puberty and stuff is bad, but that was a fucking breeze. I didn't even notice it happening.'

I kept quiet for a moment, considering his points.

'Right,' I finally said, encouragingly. 'Anything else?'

He looked up.

'Failed my fucking driving test yesterday.'

'Sorry. That's a pain.'

'Yep.'

(*'Don't shoot, shoot, shoot that thing at me, you know you've got my sympathy, but don't shoot, shoot, shoot that thing at me . . .'*)

'I thought a few people in your year were all right, though? Simon Goodfellow? Eric Bastow? He's a good bloke, isn't he?'

Alan looked at me like I'd just suggested he eat the contents of the ashtray.

'What gave you that impression, man?'

'What about some of the girls? They seem human. Claire Batey?'

'Slapper.'

'Joanna Clerk?'

'Rich bitch.'

'Gemma Holdingford? I see you hanging out with her a bit.'

'Only so I can copy her biology.'

(*'. . . oh my my, my my mother, I would love to love you lover . . .'*)

'Nicola Cartwright?'

Alan said nothing and sipped his drink. I let the Violent Femmes complete their strange rant and waited for the next song to kick in. Another unfamiliar introduction, but different this time, less quirky, a one-note guitar riff backed by some jangling, mid-tempo pop. Then the words started and I almost spat out my drink with mirth.

'I don't know why I love you . . .'

'Ah, I see,' I chuckled. 'Nicola Cartwright.'

'Fuck off, man.'

'No; that's fine . . . I mean, she's nice! I would.'

'Don't fucking tell anyone.'

'I promise,' I smiled.

(*'How can I get close to you, when you got no mercy, no you got no mercy . . .'*)

'Has anything happened so far, then?'

Alan frowned and took a Quaver.

'Almost, Sunday night before last. We were at the Three Crowns with some others.'

'And?'

'I chickened out.'

He looked so genuinely heartbroken that I decided to stop taking the piss.

'How long have you liked her?'

'Fucking ages, man. I mean, you know, she's always been pretty and stuff, but there was this nice warm day in September, I bumped into her in the park . . . she was sitting by herself, wearing . . . fuck, man, you better promise not to tell anyone this shit!'

'Honestly, I won't.'

'She was wearing this summer dress and she had her hair in pigtails, totally different to how she looks in school, and some eye make-up, almost . . . gothic, you could say. But she hadn't overdone it. So I said hello and she took off her headphones, asked me to join her . . . She showed me this compilation tape she was listening to, and man . . . I just had no idea. You know what I mean? Some of the stuff on there . . .'

He sipped his drink, overcome with the romance of it all. He nodded up to the speakers.

'There was these guys . . .'

'Sorry, who are these guys?'

'House of Love, man . . . and The Cure . . . and I'm not talking about the pop shit, she had "Fascination Street" and "A Night Like This" on there . . . "Birthday" by The Sugarcubes . . . "Shelter from the Rain" by All About Eve . . . some Pixies and that Violent Femmes one . . . some Smiths, I think . . . "April Skies" by the Mary Chain . . . even that Primal Scream one "Please Stop Crying", or whatever it's called . . .'

The House of Love finished their ditty and another, more abrasive track started up.

'This one wasn't on there. I just stuck it on 'cos I like it.'

I shook my head ignorantly. Shit. Third song in a row I didn't know. I may have won the getting-served match, but Alan had won the music game hands down. That was probably the idea.

'Wedding Present,' he obliged. 'So anyway, she offered me one of the earphones, and we just sat there listening while the sun went down . . . I know, man, it's corny as fuck, but . . . by the end we were holding hands.'

'Why didn't you just go for it there and then?' I asked (like I'd have had the guts to do such a thing).

'I was just about to . . . but then she stood up and said she had to get home.'

'Damn!'

'Yeah. Since then I've kind of been in limbo. She says hello briefly at school, smiles occasionally, but . . . it's like I discovered a different person that day.'

'Maybe you did. Maybe she has a twin.'

'Anyway, I had this plan to invite her to see All About Eve, but that got fucked up 'cos of my mocks.'

I pondered Alan's predicament for a moment.

'So . . . would you say all this has made you a little . . . er . . . preoccupied around school?'

'Yeah, course.'

'So is that why you've been bloody blanking me all over the place?' Alan looked up, frowning.

'Nah, man, there's other reasons for that.'

'Which are?'

'Well, you know how it is, with the whole different-year thing, for a start . . .'

'Bloody hell. Isn't that a little bit childish?'

'Well, yeah, but it still makes a difference, man. Girls have a memory for that sort of thing.'

'What, they won't talk to you 'cos you're friends with a lower-sixth-former? Bullshit.'

'Some wouldn't.'

'Not the ones worth knowing,' I countered, enjoying myself again. 'I bet you Nicola wouldn't mind.'

'Well, she doesn't talk to me anyway, so it doesn't matter.'

'So is this really all about girls?'

Alan looked down sheepishly. I swigged my pint, looking away with calculated indignation.

'It's also about that cock you hang out with, man,' Alan admitted suddenly.

'Billy?'

'Yeah. He's a total loser.'

I found myself jumping to my much maligned acquaintance's defence.

'He's a lot more intelligent and fun than you might imagine, actually.'

'Don't care, man. He's off the scale. You want me to talk to you when we're at school, ditch the dweeb.'

Ditch the dweeb.

This phrase has festered in my head and formed a little guilt-edged frame around my conscience ever since that night, over seventeen years ago. Alan and I debated this topic until the end of our drinks and part of the way home, but that was essentially what we agreed: I ditched the dweeb, and Alan became my friend.

Although obviously, school being school, I couldn't completely cut Billy off just like that. I still sat next to him during history, where we enjoyed a muted form of our previous capery, and I still oh-so-graciously allowed him to help with the first issue of the *Peanut*, but he only once again accompanied me to a gig (the less said about that episode, the better), and I kept contact with him outside the confines of a classroom to a minimum. After a month or two he got the message and, quite understandably, stopped bothering with me alto-gether. The only reminder of our former bond came from my mum (who, incidentally, disliked Alan from the moment she first heard his name) when she occasionally returned from a Conservative Party do and asked why Billy never came round any more.

Ho-hum. There's still a part of me that wants to go back in time and give the sixteen-year-old me a good kicking, tell the seventeen-year-old Alan Potter to piss off and stop being so ridiculous, and politely suggest to Billy Flushing that he simply get a decent haircut and perhaps some contact lenses. But what can I say? Other than: I have always had a vague feeling that my actions of winter 1989 will catch up with me one day.

Alan never did get hold of Nicola, by the way. A week or two later we beheld the sight of the delectable Miss Cartwright strolling arm in arm with one of the biggest, meanest rugby players our school possessed, with whom she was also seen dancing at the Christmas ball to – among other things – a Jive Bunny record. Whether she privately exposed this chap to the delights of The House of Love, All About Eve or the Violent Femmes was never clear, but we certainly never saw that side of her again.

Not that it mattered much to Alan, however. For within a month, he (and I, whenever the chance presented itself) was happily shagging anything in a tie-dyed skirt that drew breath.

YOU'RE COMPLETELY MENTAL

Come on – you know how tricky life can be.

It's a Friday. You've had a bloody hard week at work. Hard in the sense that it's been hard to maintain your enthusiasm for something as monotonous as arranging insurance for nine hours each day. A minor stab of variety has invaded the tedium today, as the firm has spent the whole day packing for the office move tomorrow. For reasons you've not bothered to contemplate – though cost-cutting must be somewhere fairly close to the centre – the bosses have put you in charge of picking up a hire van the next morning, entrusting you with their driving licences and appropriate hard currency. You plough through the afternoon, shifting boxes of lever-arch files, finding to your surprise that something approaching physical labour feels oddly pleasant after months, nay years, of sitting on your arse making phone calls, drinking too much coffee, eating endless packets of sandwiches and downloading crap off the Internet.

Evening arrives. At seven the phones and computers are switched off and, unusually, everyone hits the pub together. Something about the camaraderie of the day has made the collection of motleys who've ended up working for this small but perfectly dysfunctional organisation behave, for once, in a normal, even wholesome manner.

Someone fires in the first round and you nail your pint quickly, partly because you're damn thirsty, but also it's your favourite little trick: neck the first and immediately buy the second round, so it's only you and that fat dude from accounts who need a refill. Six quid, and your round-reputation is still spotless. Needs must when Satan vomits into your bank account. You kick back, quite content for the moment to play the part of the Friday-night office drinker in the rowdy Friday-night pub. Some show-off from customer service decides to get everyone a shot of sambuca. Well, why not? That boring girl who sits next to the shredder doesn't want hers, but would you like it? Of course you would. Coffee bean and all.

Third pint, and by now it's all getting nicely merry and the banter flows. You remember you've got Ron and Michael's driving licences in your bag. You dig them out and hold a small contest with everyone: who can guess their year of birth? Everyone aims too low for Michael, but too high for Ron, miserable git that he is. Then you pass round the licences so everyone can laugh at the photographs.

Remember that, Clive? Shall we say it again?

You pass round the licences so everyone can laugh at the photographs.

Got it.

You're fully aware that you have to be up at the crack of arse tomorrow morning and off to some fucking cheapo van-hire place near the Holloway Road, but hell, it's only eight-thirty, most of the crew are still out and that fourth pint is sorting you right out.

Right out.

Right . . . out.

Finally you're on the bus. Going home at what must be a nice sensible time. You even manage to read a bit of your book. Strange how most of the books you've read have entire chapters you don't recall, characters that materialise without adequate explanation as to who they are, plot points that are somehow missing. Bizarre, because you're certainly taking everything in right now. A text message bleeps. Who could it be? Polly, of course. 'Fancy lasties?' Well, why not? 'Wot u having, the bar's about to close.' The bar's about to close? It can't be midnight already. But it is. Where did those hours go? Shit. Well . . . you'll be okay. It's not like you have to do *real* work tomorrow, just, erm . . . driving.

You barge into the pub. Polly laughs heartily at your predicament. She's obviously been swigging red wine all night as her teeth are black. You listen to her latest disastrous date encounter – 'a surgeon from Durham, for God's sake' – with wavering attention, your lubricated mind now beginning to float back towards a certain ex-alternative-rock star you've been trying to meet. Let's be brutally frank: it's not going terribly well, is it? Three weeks and all you've had is a two-minute exchange in a vet's waiting room about hormones that stop cats pissing on the bed. You've soundly failed to pinpoint any of the man's other haunts, and any other sparks of genius are sadly unforthcoming. Alan's scrapbook remains on top of your record player, unbothered by any of its central players, still wrapped in its industrial-plastic legal sheath. Sod it. You have to do something. This is fast turning into one of those painfully unsurprising Ideas of Clive's that amount to absolutely fuck all.

'. . . so in the end,' Polly blethers, sloshing red wine into the ashtray as you briefly tune in, 'I just told him it simply wasn't going anywhere. I had no interest in surgery, or Durham, or any of his opinions really . . . I was honest with him . . . and he was fine about it, really . . . even paid for dinner . . . It's amazing what you can achieve when you're just honest with someone . . .'

Suddenly a cartoon light bulb appears above your head. You're only halfway through your pint but something compels you to rise, apologise to your companion and lurch off in the direction of your flat. With a certainty that only vast quantities of beer can provide, you've rarely been more sure of what you need to do. Be honest. Enough of this tomfoolery, skirting around the issue. Just be honest.

You stop off at the Turkish shop for a couple of beers (you're not sure how long this will take, after all), pass by the abode of the man himself (no lights are on, but that doesn't matter), descend the steps to your own flat, let yourself in, crack open a beer and settle at the kitchen table. This is the right thing. It has to be. The magic solution. The key to the lock, the long-sought combination code. The turning point, frankly. The pivot on which everything else swivels. That Zane Lowe moment. 'It was really that simple, you see, Zane . . . all I had to do was be honest.'

And now you're outside again.

And now you're standing in front of a large black door.

And now you're walking.

And now you've forgotten your keys.

And now you're looking at the moon.

And now . . . Polly. In her dressing gown.

'Clive, what the fuck are you doing?'

'Sorry. Left my keys.'

'Why'd you leave me in the pub like that?'

'Sorry, just needed to . . . you know.'

'You're completely mental. And I thought *I* was drunk. Where've you been? What time you gotta be up?'

You manage to focus on your watch. Someone must be mucking around with it. Why the hell is time going so quickly?

'In about five hours.'

'Ouch.'

'Sorry, Polly. Better go to bed.'

Bed. Now there's a bit of rational, reasonable thinking. Bed. See, there's still sense somewhere in that brain of yours. Amazing. It continues to operate, even at this drunken juncture. The last thought it processes before you fall into a leaden, exhausting sleep, is that you're somehow missing something – but you can't imagine what it could be.

Never mind.

You're sure it'll come to you in the morning.

TWO TOTALLY SEPARATE BUT EQUALLY FUCKING DISASTROUS OUTCOMES OF ME GETTING WANKERED

There's an old *Peanuts* cartoon; I'm not sure if you remember it but bear with me: Snoopy wakes up one winter's morning, he's been sleeping on top of his kennel in the usual way, he starts reflecting on how nice it is to wake up with a feeling of well-being, a cosy sensation that, although not perfect, life is generally fine and dandy. Only then does he spot this bloody great icicle with a huge razor-sharp edge, hanging precariously over his doghouse. One move and it'll fall off, slicing him and his abode clean in two.

Well, that's essentially how I feel when my clock radio prods me out of slumber around seven. I have no headache. I'm warm. I had a nice dream about cooking barbecue sausages on a Norfolk beach. It's a Saturday. Even the song playing (that stupid Libertines one about the Likely Lads) doesn't irritate me too much. I lie there feeling pleased with myself for twenty seconds or so. But then I see the icicle. Except, in my case, there are two of the fuckers. I only see one of them right now. But don't you worry – I'll be seeing the other one soon enough.

I leap out of bed and grab my bag. After a superficial look in the main section I simply unzip all the other pockets and tip it upside down. Lots of rubbish, bank statements, foreign coins, my diary, a couple of bills, but nothing else. I blunder over to where yesterday's trousers have been unceremoniously dumped and check the pockets. Nothing. Then my coat. Fuck all. Then I try to find my phone. I need my bloody phone. *Now.*

I find it under my socks and call directory enquiries while running to the kitchen for a glass of water.

'Yes, it's a pub, the Schooner, Old Street . . . London . . . Uh, I dunno. N1? EC1? Or 2? Not sure . . . Right, got it . . . Yes please, thanks . . .'

I glug the water and frantically search the kitchen top – loads of papers and bills, mainly Polly's – while the pub's number rings and rings. There's plainly no one there at seven in the bloody morning, what was I thinking? I slam the phone down on the kitchen table.

Which is when I see the second icicle.

My notebook, open, pages ripped out, a few scrunched-up sheets lying loose. Blue biro hanging about nearby. Empty can of beer.

A horrible, dim memory surfaces.

'Polly!'

Still wearing only yesterday's underpants, I look bloody every-where. All over the kitchen. Out in the stairwell. Up the steps. The bathroom. My bedroom again. A cold sweat emerges from my brow, as does Polly from her bedroom: a splendour of smudged mascara, light-blue dressing gown and those damn slippers with toothpaste stains.

'Clive, what the hell are you doing *now*? Jesus, it's seven o'fucking clock.'

'I've lost it,' I splutter, turning my bedroom upside down.

'Dare I ask?'

'No. Everything. What the fuck was I doing last night?'

'What?'

'What was I doing? Last night. After I saw you.'

My phone rings. I push Polly out of the way before she can answer and stumble to the kitchen.

Withheld number.

'Hello?'

'Yes,' responds a male voice. 'You call this number.'

'Are you the pub?'

'Yes.'

'The Schooner?'

'Yes. I am cleaner.'

'Look – I was in the pub last night. I left something there.'

'Yes.'

'A plastic wallet. Two driving licences. And ... um ... five hundred quid in cash.'

I realise how hopeless this sounds as soon as it leaves my lips. I half expect the bloke to laugh.

'I check,' he says.

'Thanks.'

'Oh, Clive,' murmurs Polly, leaning on the kitchen door.

'Never mind all that. What was I doing?'

'You left me in the pub.'

'Sorry. But when you came home?'

'You were writing at the kitchen table.'

'What was I writing?'

'How should I know? Looked like a letter.'

'Fuck!' I yell, unscrunching one of the sheets of paper.

'What?'

'I think I wrote to Lance Webster.'

The unscrunched piece of paper has nothing written on it. Lord knows why I scrunched it up. Another merely has the date. Which I'd got wrong.

'So?'

'So . . . I was drunk. So it was probably nonsense. So it was probably hysterical, with my stupid name at the bottom, possibly even my address.'

'So?'

My voice allows a bit more exasperation past the flood barrier.

'So, Polly – he has a history of stalkers! So – I've probably completely sodded up my chances of ever getting within a hundred yards of him! Let alone interviewing him!'

'Right . . . so what's that got to do with you leaving money in a pub?'

'Nothing! They're merely two totally separate but equally fucking disastrous outcomes of me getting wankered, as bloody usual!'

'Well, if you ask me I'd say the money thing is slightly worse, but . . .'

'Shhh!'

At the other end of the line I'm hearing steps coming back towards the phone. Steps that my entire bank balance and probably my job hang from.

'Hello,' he says.

'Hi. Any luck?'

'No, sorry. Nothing. I can ask manager when he come, he come nine-thirty.'

'Fuck. Thanks anyway, I'll ring back.'

I sit down uneasily in one of the kitchen chairs and think for a moment. My one advantage is that I'm awake. It's five past seven. Time is on my side. Polly, who has a nice habit of going into maternal-style overdrive at times like this (at complete odds with the total shambles of her own life), puts the kettle on and fetches her laptop, which she places in front of me.

'Right. Go online and check your bank balance. Work out how

much you can afford to blow on this, then I'll lend you the rest. The important thing is that you show up, on time, with a van. Then at least they can see you're trying.'

I discover I can physically withdraw two hundred, and God knows what I'll do for the rest of the month. Polly, bless her, lends me the other three. I phone and wake various other people as I dress and jump on a bus to Holloway: a couple of people from work ('Was there cash in the packet as it was being passed round? Are you sure? Yes, yes, I know Ron's going to crucify me', etc.), the Turkish shop, the other pub, the bus company, none of whom reveals anything useful, while the perpetual question of what the hell I put in that letter rattles around at the back of my mind like a broken exhaust pipe. Incredibly, all this frantic activity manages to cancel out the vicious hangover I certainly deserve, although that probably says more about the general level of alcohol present in my body these days than any psychosomatic theory one could consider.

I pick up the van – a suitably knackered-looking Luton – and clatter back down the Holloway Road without further mishap. It's eight-thirty when I pull up outside our grey office building. I'm greeted by a few tired and grumpy faces from last night; everyone cheers up considerably when I inform them of my impressive blunder. Ron hasn't appeared yet so we retire to the café round the corner, where I drink coffee like a man possessed and interrogate my colleagues. No one seems to remember anything. One of them suggests the bar staff pilfered it when collecting glasses. Further speculation seems pretty futile. The unanimous view is that I'm fucked. I groan and order another coffee. I picture Lance Webster opening and reading my letter. It's nice to have another self-made catastrophe to focus on. It's times like this that I thank the gods I never started smoking.

My mobile rings at nine. It's Ron.

'Good morning, Clive.'

'Morning, Ron. We're just having a coffee.'

'I see the vehicle is currently parked in a car-parking space that ceases to be free at nine-thirty. Now, what I propose is that you give me the keys, and while you commence shifting some of the objects downstairs I'll familiarise myself with the van and find a free car-parking space.'

'Ah, yes – um, good idea, Ron, but I need to just quickly have a word with you about something, if you just wait there . . .'

I run round the corner. He's standing by the van wearing an absurd pink and purple fleece and jeans that look like they've just come out of a packet. Bright white unbranded trainers. His glasses are held on by a yellow elastic band. None of which makes him look any less scary. Gingerly, I tell him the news. His reaction is interesting.

'Oh, fuck!' he exclaims.

Ron is not a man who says this word very often. He looks genuinely gutted, and stares at an unspecified object halfway down the road for what seems like the next ten minutes while I stand there stupidly.

Finally he sighs and says, 'Well, these things happen, I suppose, but I can't believe you couldn't have been more careful.'

And that, it seems, is that. I actually think he's far more upset at not being able to drive the van than he is about the money. Of course, that could very well mean that in his view, the money is not his problem.

The rest of the day passes at an unbearable crawl. The van now being solely my charge, I spend most of the time either sitting in it, driving it or standing next to it, wondering if my parents will lend me some money, if my bank will extend my overdraft limit, if there's any space left on one of my credit cards. And when I'm tired of thinking about those things there's always the rich worry-seam of the Webster letter for me to relentlessly mine. It's amazing how my brain has recorded none of the contents whatsoever, although – crazily – I somehow recall the *shape* of the text on the page. For some baffling reason I balanced it all in the centre, starting with the greeting, the sentences spreading out below, line by line, wider and wider like a Christmas tree; a design decision that will certainly lend currency to the argument that he's being addressed by a gibbering lunatic. Mercifully, I don't think I went beyond one page. I hope to buggery I didn't mention I was the guy working in the vet's.

We continue shifting and packing the rickety truck with endless loads of paraphernalia, Ron in his element, presiding over the process with mathematical precision. One wonders why he became an accountant at all and not the boss of a removal firm. Only after every cubic centimetre of space is filled and the van's arse begins to sag dangerously am I permitted to trundle round to our new premises: an even more depressing sixties block behind Brick Lane. There I find a second team of weirdos, who reluctantly extinguish cigarettes and get busy hauling the stuff inside every time I appear. Towards three o'clock, when the old office finally starts looking emptier than the new one, Ron accompanies me on one of the trips to find four of his employees relaxing in the car park with pints from the pub round the corner.

'I find it improbable that you have moved all the furniture to its correct place, and completed setting up the electronic equipment,' he reflects, shortly before going inside to discover his hunch is correct.

Typically, Michael doesn't appear until around six. He strides about in his suit, concentrating on the less essential aspects of the undertaking: finding a place for the coffee machine, putting up the pictures, the calendar and various statistical charts, instructing a few chaps to instal his orthopaedic chair. Just before seven, after I've swung the van into the new yard for the last time, Michael does that annoying thing of beckoning me over with his little finger.

'So, Clive. Sounds like you had a colourful evening last night. Has someone reimbursed you?'

I'm agog.

'Er . . . no?'

He extracts ten fifty-pound notes from his wallet as if he's giving me change for milk. I swallow hard, fighting to remain dignified, although frankly I feel like kneeling down and kissing his brogues.

'Oh, Michael, that's really good of you ... I wasn't expecting that, to be honest.'

'Well, that's the kind of company we are, Clive. We give our staff money and they go off and lose it.'

He smirks and strides off towards Ron, who is happily changing a strip-light bulb in the foyer.

The phrase 'more money than sense' has regularly been bandied around in the region of Michael, but never before has it been of such miraculous benefit to me. Thank God for the upper classes. Whether Ron will approve of Michael's munificence is another matter but, for the time being, I have the luxury of unrivalled worry-time devoted to the Webster letter.

The plan is that I take the van home tonight and return tomorrow for some final bits and pieces, which effectively means I have my own set of wheels for the evening. I phone Alan and, not going into too much detail, request an emergency meeting. His expert knowledge of Webster's brief spell as the object of a nutter's desire will hopefully inform me a little of the reaction I might expect. I set the van's controls for the heart of Crouch End – but never get that far. I'm just crossing Essex Road when my mobile rings. *Home*.

'Polly,' I answer.

'Clive, where are you?'

'Um ... Islington, near Canonbury. I'm driving. I'd better be quick.'

'Are you coming home?'

'Yeah, eventually. Just having a quick beer with Alan first. You all right?'

'Look, there are some men here to see you.'

'Men? Which men?'

'They say they're associates of ...' I hear someone say 'Mr Webster' in the background. 'Did you hear that? Mr Webster.'

A swarm of butterflies lets rip in my digestive region. This is my life, ladies and gentlemen. Jesus O'Fuckwit, how do I get into these things?

'Ah. Um . . . okay. Don't . . . don't let them in.'

'They *are* in.'

'Shit. Okay – don't let them further in. I'll be home in ten minutes.'

Instantly I'm picturing a few plug-uglies from *The Sopranos*, or the Kray twins, or at the very least some Vinnie Jones figure accompanied by, perhaps, Ken Stott, standing in our hallway giving poor Polly intimidating stares. So, after I've broken all the speed limits back up the Essex Road, buggered the suspension on the speed bumps and found somewhere to dump the van, I am somewhat surprised and relieved to find two middle-aged crusties who I instantly recognise as former members of the Thieving Magpies road crew, sitting at our kitchen table sipping tea. In fact, I think I've an even more involved recollection of them, although I can't presently place it. They rise as I enter, politely introduce themselves as Stan and Malcolm, and for the moment seem fairly reasonable and unthreatening. Nonetheless, their smart, dark jackets, chunky no-nonsense raver's jewellery, thick tattooed arms and hardy complexions suggest they are not to be fucked with. Malcolm, the slimmer and probably older of the two, asks the questions while Polly lurks supportively in the doorway.

'So. You know why we're here?'

'Erm . . . I think so, yes.'

'Why?'

Damn! Why did I say yes? What the hell do I say now?

'Why?'

'Yes, why?' he repeats, quietly.

'Erm . . . because I wrote a letter to Lance Webster.'

'That's one way o' describing it,' remarks Stan. Glaswegian accent.

'Erm . . . how else could you describe it?'

Stan sniggers and shakes his head disparagingly.

'Mr Beresford,' continues Malcolm, 'we are here because our associate Mr Webster wishes to illustrate to you how seriously he views his privacy and safety.'

'Okay.'

'Given the contents of your communication to Mr Webster, am I to understand that you have some knowledge of his life, and his former musical career?'

'Um . . . yes.'

'You may therefore remember a couple of incidents, ten or so years ago, where the attentions of certain . . . ah . . .'

'Fans?' I suggest.

'Tha's a polite way o' putting it,' remarks Stan again. I'm already getting a little tired of his useless interjections.

'The attentions of certain members of the public,' Malcolm resumes, 'reached the point where the police had to be involved.'

'Yes, I remember.'

'Good. You will therefore understand, I hope, that Mr Webster never wishes matters to escalate to that point again.'

I exhale, thinking hard. Are they really so worried about *me*? What the hell could *I* do?

'We wish you to know that, if he feels that his privacy and safety are being threatened, Mr Webster will not hesitate to take immediate action.'

I hold up my hands in submission. 'Listen, guys – I wasn't planning to threaten either of those things. You really don't need to worry about me.'

'Tha's not the impression we got,' Stan comments.

'But . . . come on, the guy is an ex-internationally famous rock star! He must get letters from fans? Occasionally?'

Malcolm nods slowly.

'Letters from fans, yes. Hand-delivered letters that say what yours did, no. Well, not any more.'

'What the hell did it say?'

Both men gape at me for a good few seconds.

'You wrote the fuckin' thing!'

'Yes,' I concur desperately, 'but . . . um . . . what particular part are you referring to?'

'Fuck's sake, which bit de y' think?'

'Well, I . . .'

'It's fuckin' obvious what sorta shite he mighta felt just a bit threatened by, don't ye think? Ya wee wanker.'

Polly leaps across the room.

'Right – I'm sorry, but you have absolutely no right to talk to Clive like that.'

'Oh yeah? Ah'm not the one doin' the fuckin' stalkin', love.'

'Ah, I think you'll find there's a very specific legal definition of stalking,' improvises Polly, 'one that whatever Clive is supposed to have done, or written, he still lies some considerable distance from.'

'And ya think we give a fuck about that, do ye?'

'All right, calm it down,' instructs Malcolm. 'We're not accusing anyone of anything. We're here on a purely preventative mission. This situation is really very simple, Mr Beresford. Whatever you're doing, or are trying to do, that concerns Mr Webster – cease it. With immediate effect.'

There is silence. I'm hoping Polly doesn't say 'or what?', or similar. She doesn't. Perhaps because, like me, she doesn't really want to know. I'm not sure what they do to miscreants in the crustie-verse. Tie them to a chair and play them Ozric Tentacles records for twelve hours, maybe. Either way, I realise that it's probably over. All of it.

I show them out. As I shut the front door, it finally hits me.

'I knew it,' I smile, as I turn back to Polly. 'Me and Alan beat them at pool. Ninety-one, in that pub next to the Dome in Tufnell Park. The Magpies were playing a secret gig there. I knew it! We fucking slaughtered them as well.'

Polly glares at me from behind weary eyes.

'Clive, I never thought you'd hear me say this . . .'

'What?'

'For God's sake, will you *grow up*!'

She storms off to her bedroom.

I agree. I should. But how?

I WAS KIND OF FAMOUS, I GUESS

So, you might be wondering whether my Visit from the Roadies has successfully thwarted my Webster-based ambitions. To answer this, let me quote a few minutes from a phone conversation I had with Alan sometime on Monday morning. I was at work, balanced on the edge of a desk in our new office (crap still all over the place, Internet not yet working, not enough chairs to go round); Alan was somewhere on the A505 between Baldock and Royston (Bluetooth headset, BP garage coffee, suit jacket hanging in the back).

'You're out of your fucking mind,' Alan noted.

'Thank you.'

'I'm fucking deadly serious, man. You're heading for a major catastrophe. Except . . . you quite enjoy all this, don't you? It's like a game. It makes your life more interesting.'

'Maybe,' I mumbled, watching one of the plainer secretaries feed a wodge of paper into the shredder.

'But it won't be a game when these cunts end up putting you in hospital. Where I shall not be visiting you.'

'Oh, Alan, I'm not entirely sure that they'll . . .'

'I am! Of *course* they will! He's not going to just call the police, Clive – he *hates* the police. By sending these berks round he's fucking . . . *blatantly* demonstrating that he does not intend to involve the law.'

I grunted vague acknowledgement.

'For God's sake, mate – just do as they say.'

He's right, of course. There's something terribly exciting about being perceived as a threat. Particularly being someone only ever viewed as threatening by the pint he's about to consume. Nonetheless, I have no desire for a lengthy and painful visit to the Homerton Hospital, so I agree, for the time being, to shelve my plans; although it must be said, these currently consist of very little.

My world rumbles along in its uneventful way until Wednesday, when an appreciably more peculiar afternoon commences with the arrival of a text message while *en route* for the two-till-ten shift. Despite being something of a text-message sceptic (try saying that with a mouthful of porridge), I must admit they are occasionally quite useful. For example, to inform someone that you're running late. Or to tell your mum something really quick when you don't want the inconvenience of actually speaking to her. Or so that, more than a week afterward, a vet you have dated can send you the following:

Hi Clive, hope u r good. Just 2 say ur friend's cat died yesterday. Maybe u should find another way of communicating with him. See u around X

I'm not entirely sure why she's chosen to do this. It must be against all sorts of vet-to-customer privacy ethics and suchlike. Naturally I wasn't expecting to ever hear from her again, so it's a relatively nice surprise, despite the news being bad. I'm pretty certain the message has no hidden depths, but I pause for a moment before replying. See, the thing about texting is there's no way of gauging humour, or sarcasm, or warmth, or anything, because everyone's so concerned about fitting it all into a single 160-character message. But then, what else could be said about the situation? There's an X – which is something, I suppose. My bus has reached Spitalfields by the time I decide on a response, then I dice with blunder by attempting to write the thing while walking along the busy lunchtime streets. I get halfway through ('Thanks, good of u 2 let me know! Hope u r well, sorry again about the oth—'), when I am confronted by the sight of Michael, my boss, charging down the opposite side of the road, people frantically darting out of his way. The strange thing is, this will actually be the last time I see him. Although I don't realise it until two minutes later, when I arrive at the office to be informed by Ron that my services are no longer required.

'Your performance has sunk to an intolerable level,' he states impassively.

We are standing by the entrance to the room which houses the electricity generator, for God's sake; I mean, it's an open-plan office, finding a private place is hard, but I'd like to think my three years with the company deserve slightly better than *this*.

'Your monthly figures are the second poorest in the firm,' he continues, proffering a coloured spreadsheet. 'The only employee below you is Natasha Reynolds, and she's only here two days per week. Robert Warren and Suzie Oakley are both above you, and they left the company two weeks ago.'

I remain silent, wondering how I can possibly fight back, or if it's even worth it. I know for a fact Rob Warren used to mess around with the figures, but now may not be the time to open that particular can of worms.

'These statistics in isolation would warrant a warning but, combined with Saturday's vehicle debacle, I can no longer support your presence in this organisation.'

I frown and play with my fingernails. He's using 'I' a lot. Ron has always disliked me, you see – I'm not quite sure why – while Michael, absence of emotion aside, has occasionally divulged that he considers my genial presence 'good for morale'. A naïve thought enters my head: that Ron could be seizing the opportunity to give me the boot while Michael's off at a meeting (a bit like in *Schindler's List* when Ben Kingsley gets carted off while Liam Neeson is shagging some floozy – well, sort of).

'And what about Michael?' I enquire.

Ron widens his eyes. 'What do you mean, "What about Michael"?'

'What does Michael think about my, um, presence in this organisation?'

'Michael and I have agreed that the example you set, as a senior member of staff, has become detrimental to the fortunes of the company.'

Wow. Threatening *and* detrimental, all in the same week.

I could say a lot of things. I could tell him I spend almost half my time fixing the phone network when it fucks up, or ordering stationery when the secretaries have (again) forgotten, or showing new staff how the credit checks are done. I could mention Rob Warren's statistical adjustments, or John Barrow swearing at customers on the evening shifts, or Anita Stopford running her mail-order clothing business from the office at the weekends. Or I could go all sentimental, remind him I've been with them from almost the begin-ning, that I once went without wages for three weeks when a big payment didn't come through, assure him I'll pull my socks up if he gives me one last chance. But I don't. Partly because I know it won't make any difference, partly because I no longer give a shit. But mostly because he's given me a month's notice, a month they'll pay me for, which I don't have to work. In fact, I can go now.

In spite of this pleasing detail, Ron's news leaves me in some-thing of a daze. I shuffle out the door, not stopping to say goodbye to anyone, and wander back towards Liverpool Street in the sunshine.

It's times like this when I like to pretend I'm acting in the film of my own life; things always seem better that way. I grab a coffee from a roadside vendor, just as Dustin Hoffman might do in New York, before drifting back home across Central Park. I amble along Bishopsgate, smiling at all the City workers as they hurry back from lunch, knowing I am on my way home, like Kevin Spacey, never to return to his coma-inducing, soul-destroying excuse for a job. And then I gaze out at the various landmarks and skyscrapers as my train weaves its way through the rough, northern part of the city – as perhaps Leonardo DiCaprio would do, while trying to avoid phone calls from the police or the Irish mafia. That's the thing about films. The romance of these images is uncomplicated, compelling. What you never see is Hoffman being asked for change as he comes out of the litter-strewn station, or Spacey getting home and opening his gargantuan credit-card bill, or DiCaprio finding a teetering pile of washing-up, no washing-up liquid, and no change in his pocket to buy more. It's at this point that I start to worry. And when I start to worry, there's only one place to go.

As you may have surmised by now, I have the most appalling will power when it comes to drinking. Sometimes it borders on the ludicrous. I remember one Sunday I woke up feeling pretty miserable, and as the day progressed it struck me that I could attempt to make myself feel happier by *not* having a drink that day – give the liver and brain a break. This notion instantly cheered me up, lifting the proverbial dark cloud. I suddenly felt free from the, shall we say, shackles of alcohol. In fact, I felt so elated that I decided to celebrate by having a few beers.

So it comes as no particular surprise that the first thing I decide to do after today's blow – no, let's be optimistic: today's *life challenge* – is go to the pub. Most of my life is one long search for an excuse to go to the pub. Not to get drunk, you understand, not to drown my sorrows in an irrational pool of nasty lager, but often to simply give myself a few quiet moments to ponder this crazy series of balls-ups we call an existence. As Billy Idol once sang, '*Let's sink another drink, 'cos it'll give me time to think.*'

On these occasions there's always a particular boozer I choose. It's the nearest one to the flat. It's carpeted, generally old-fashioned and *plays no music*, thus ensuring maximum mental concentration. I love it. My ex-girlfriend detested it. Oh well. She doesn't need to put up with *that* one any longer.

I wander in and settle myself at the bar. It's quarter to three in the afternoon. There's an elderly bloke in the corner nursing a bitter. There's a younger guy a few stools up from me, reading a paper. That's it. Apart from the pub's spaniel, who is flat out on the hearth. Oh, and the barman. From whom I order a London Pride.

I take a sip.

Silence.

It feels good.

I feel good.

Strangely okay.

There may be trouble ahead . . . but while there's—

'Oh, hello.'

Someone's addressing me.

'Hi. You're the guy from the vet's. Right?'

Please don't be Lance Webster. Please don't be Lance Webster.

'Sorry, don't mean to disturb.'

It's Lance Webster.

He's having a Guinness and reading the *Independent*.

In my local.

His local.

Ah.

'No, that's . . . fine,' I manage to articulate, eyeing him unsteadily. The Square, Harlow, 1990, shorter hair now, etc.

'Still working there?'

'Where?'

'At the vet's?'

'Me? Uh . . . no. Not any more. It was only . . . you know. Temporary.'

'Ah. Right.'

Conversation. Conversation might be an idea at this point.

'Your, um . . .'

He raises his eyebrows.

'Your cat. I was sorry to hear . . .'

'Oh,' he shrugs. 'She was old.'

'Yeah.'

'So where are you working now?'

Me. He's asking me.

'Well . . . actually . . . nowhere, really. I lost it. My main job. This morning.'

Here we go with his goddam narrowing-the-eyes thing again. Mouth slightly open. Puts me right off what I'm saying. One day I'm going to figure it out. It's as though I'm saying something a bit odd, or as if a fly's landed on my forehead.

'This morning?' he repeats.

'Yeah!' I grin, barely able to believe it myself.

'Shit,' he says. 'That's a nuisance.'

'Yeah. Well – no, actually. I hated it.'

'Okay,' he laughs. 'So what are you going to do now?'

This is too odd. *He's* interviewing *me*.

I sigh. 'Dunno. That's why I'm in here, I suppose. Give it some thought.'

'What are you interested in?'

It's weird; although the man asking me this question is certainly one of my top ten human beings in the known universe – the name I still immediately offer in answer to those stupid 'if you could be stuck in a lift with anyone' things – I have a strong desire to say, 'Why on earth do you want to know?' or even, 'What are you, a bloody careers advisor?'

But I resist.

'Um . . . well,' I ponder. What *am* I interested in? Not music. Can't say music. Then he'll know that I know who he is. Which I don't want.

'Writing,' I settle on.

'You a writer?'

'Well . . . yeah. I have been. I mean, I am. Sort of.'

Christ, this is sounding believable.

'What sort of thing do you write about?'

Ah. Another obstacle approaching. Can't say music. Then *he* might figure out who *I* am. Which I want even less.

'Well, I er . . . I write novels. Or I try to. Don't always finish.'

'Funny that. I tried to write a novel once. Didn't finish either,' he smiles.

Ha. You tried to act too, and that was also a dismal failure.

'So . . . er,' I begin, 'what was yours about?'

He grins and takes a sip of his Guinness. I've done it. Ladies and gentlemen, I've asked Lance Webster my first question. Is it about the night of 12 August 1995? No. Is it about Gloria Feathers? No. Does it have anything to do with bloody music *at all*? No.

But it's a start.

So he tells me.

He tells me this story about four people who wake up one morning with a magical power, like they can move objects around with their minds. None of them has the foggiest where it's come from. One freaks out and hides. One goes out and robs banks. One destroys stuff. One ignores it and hopes it goes away. They've got it because these aliens have come to earth to try and acquire fuel for their dying planet, but they've fucked up and accidentally given their special power to these morons. It's really a social comedy, he says, but for some reason people always think it sounds like science fiction. I can't imagine why that would be. I think it sounds utterly preposterous. But I don't tell him that. Instead I feign interest.

'How come you stopped writing it?'

'Because I'm lazy. I got as far as I could get without having to do a load of research.'

'Did you try to get it published?'

He purses his lips and looks down. Almost sheepish. It's quite a sight.

'I, um . . .'

He laughs nervously. Good God, I do believe I've hit a nerve. This man has commanded audiences of sixty thousand. But stop. Stop it. He's just a bloke. A bloke in your local pub.

'I didn't because I . . .'

He tails off again and takes another glug of his drink – but then fixes me with a frown. I freeze. He looks like he's about to turn on me.

'I'm not sure if you *know*, but . . . I, um . . . used to be a musician.'

I'm already shaking my head. Maybe too quickly.

'Don't really follow music.'

Oh, Clive. Of all the shamefaced, unconvincing, downright, whopping great big porkers. I take a quick glance down at my attire. Ha. That would've been funny, saying I'm not into music while wearing a Young Knives T-shirt or something. But Webster exhales, relieved – as if I've just been approved by the Criminal Records Bureau.

'Right. Well, I was in a position where it would have been relatively easy for me to get someone to publish it.'

'You had connections,' I suggest.

He twists his face and becomes busy with the beer mat.

'Well, sort of. I was . . . I was kind of famous, I guess.'

And I'm kind of enjoying this. I say nothing and sip my beer.

'So it would have probably sold a bit anyway, even if it was rubbish. Which,' he laughs into his pint, 'it very well might have been.'

He pauses, thinking.

'But if I got a publisher I would've had to finish the damn thing and, I don't know . . . I was worried about it. I might not have had the time – lots of research; it could have been shit, which then could have affected the . . . well, my other career.'

I'm still saying nothing. It's proving rather successful.

'But I did enjoy doing it. Writing. In a room, just me. Making my own decisions. Without having to check with three other bastards first.'

He looks at me and sniggers.

'There you go. That's the long version. So how about yours?'

'Mine?'

'Your novel.'

Oh shit. I've been so wrapped up listening to him witter on, it hasn't occurred to me that he might ask this.

'Oh, there are a few,' I blether. 'Funnily enough I, er, have a similar problem – that is, never enough time to research, to really get down to it, you know . . .'

He shakes his head, still chuckling. 'Come on, tell me. You ain't getting out of it that easily.'

'Oh . . . well . . . the main one I had was . . .'

'Uh-huh?'

I take a deep breath, and, from fuck knows where, out comes this:

'Well, I quite like the idea of flawed genius, so I had this idea for, like, a scientist-type inventor bloke, still in his twenties, super intelligent, works for NASA and all that sort of thing, but he's this incredible misanthrope, fucking hates everyone, lives on his own in the middle of a field in East Anglia or somewhere with his dog. Spends all day in his lab trying to build a time machine, but he's a borderline alcoholic, so he keeps buggering it up. Meanwhile these people try to steal his idea. The whole story is seen through the eyes of a journalist who tries to interview him for a Sunday paper.'

I finally run out of bullshit. Webster has spent my entire speech, you guessed it, narrowing his eyes at me with his mouth slightly open.

'You wrote that?' he gasps, finally.

'Erm . . . yeah! Well, I got about halfway through.'

'Wow!'

'Or maybe a bit less.'

'Wow. You should finish it.'

'Yeah, but . . .'

'But what?' he insists. 'You've got the time now!'

'True,' I nod.

'Did you get any publishing interest?'

'No.'

'Did you try?'

'Erm, no.'

He drains the last of his Guinness, extracts a fiver from his wallet and bangs it down on the counter.

'What are you having?'

And, just like that, we are talking. Not about anything linked to the Lance Webster I know, of course, but chatting nonetheless, enthusiastically, about jotting these silly ideas of ours down on paper. I feel like I'm with someone else – quite literally, a random bloke in my local pub – and for that reason of course it's easier to relax. Although when he comes back from a loo visit (during which I fire off a frantic text to Alan) I do have to pinch myself as the familiar grinning figure appears round the corner. But the closest he comes to saying anything about himself personally is when I express my dislike of the inevitable love interest in a story.

'Yeah, me too,' he nods. 'I was actually going through a pretty horrible break-up at the time, so there was none of that shit in my one, I assure you. It would've all been soaked with venom, dripping with hate! No one would've got through the fucker.'

We continue in this manner for another quarter of an hour, then he glances at his watch.

'Shit! Didn't realise what the time was. Gotta get going.'

'That's cool. Thanks for the pint.'

Again, he fixes me with one of his stares.

'I don't suppose you'd, erm . . .'

I stare back.

'Do you wanna do this again?' he asks. 'I mean, maybe I could have a look at some of your stuff, you know, and you mine. Bat a few more ideas around, that kinda thing.'

'Er, well – yeah?'

Fuck! And what, exactly, would I be showing him?

'Maybe go and have a coffee sometime, something like that?'

'Yeah, sure! Good idea.'

He smiles. 'Great. In fact . . . hope you don't think this too weird, but do you wanna put a date in right now?'

So he doesn't have to give out his telephone number. Clever bastard.

With the suddenly wide-open weekday time I have at my disposal, we agree to meet on Friday at three in that café opposite the park. Which means I have . . . ooh, just under forty-eight hours to write a hell of a lot of nonsense. I feel like I've enrolled in the world's strangest creative-writing class.

He puts his jacket on and gathers up his newspaper.

'Well, it was nice . . . shit, man, I'm so sorry, I don't even know your name! Nor you mine,' he laughs, shaking his head.

'No!' I concur, holding myself back one last time.

'Geoff,' he grins, holding out his (surprisingly small) hand. 'Geoff Webster.'

I shake as firmly as I can manage.

'Alan,' I tell him. 'Alan Potter.'

PART

TWO

Little man
with no clue and no plan
your head's in a whirl
over the funny words of a funny girl.
It's a confusing dream
just like it was when you were seventeen
but you're learning how to laugh
in your little house on the flight path.

Thieving Magpies, 'Little House on the Flight Path'

I'M GLORIA BLOODY FEATHERS

The initial rise of the Thieving Magpies was unremarkable enough. Bunch of mates from school form band, learn a load of covers (Clash, XTC, Echo and The Bunnymen, Psychedelic Furs), start writing own songs, play first gig (Reading School Summer Bash, June 1984), get spotted by loud-mouthed eccentric from nearby public school (Webster) who promptly forces his way into band and demotes previous singer to rhythm guitar; more gigs, disgruntled previous singer departs, Webster takes over rhythm guitar duties, more original material appears, ditto bigger local bookings (Reading After Dark Club, Windsor Old Trout, Brunel University Union), first London gig (West Hampstead Moonlight Club), fledgling entrepreneur Bob Grant attends show by chance and offers his services as manager, record first demo, tout it round to record companies, they show some interest . . . so far, so normal.

But what really set the Magpies apart from every other band of the time was their strange, and still largely unexplained, relationship with one Gloria Feathers.

Few would deny that Feathers (née Rosamund Amhurst) was

the unofficial figurehead of the late-eighties/early nineties British alternative scene: she was an individual so regularly and easily viewable, one almost imagined her to be on the payroll of various venues, promoters and labels (as, indeed, she may have been). Not a film-star beauty by any means, but oddly beguiling, due in part to her mesmerising almond-shaped brown eyes, and characterised by a loud upper-class accent and a selection of attention-grabbing hair creations, tattoos and piercings. She was one of those people who simply seemed to be *everywhere*: every important gig, every club night, every festival, every party, in a multitude of different cities, often on the same evening (one Feathers legend tells of her happily jumping around at a Wedding Present gig in Salisbury, only to be spotted later that evening in the hotel where Therapy? were staying in Dublin); and she also seemed to know everyone, every band, tour manager, roadie, bouncer, barman. Sometimes she was drunk (she famously favoured lethal half-pints of cider, vodka and blackcurrant, a drink still known as a Gloria Feathers in some music venues), sometimes sober; sometimes doing nothing, other than regaling the world with her latest exploits; sometimes doing everything, from selling merchandise to busily darting about with a walkie-talkie. And yet no one claims to have actually employed her or given her any official role as such, nor did she ever appear to be simply a 'groupie'; in fact, several prominent indie stars are known to have pursued her, with little success.

She was also at school with Lance Webster.

There have always been assumptions that they were lovers, either at first, at the end or all along, but there has never been any proof of this. What is undisputed is that they were very close friends. She arrived at Webster's school in the sixth form, part of the dubious English boys' school arrangement wherein females are admitted at sixteen to gently introduce the poor innocent lads to the concept of a dual-gender world. By this point Webster was a loner and quite breathtakingly pretentious, a pretty-boy scholarship kid spending most of his days seated on a bench in the school kitchen garden gently strumming a classical guitar, apparently modelling himself on some bizarre crossbreed of Nick Drake, Robert Smith and Hamlet. Feathers, despite her unusual appearance and tendency to trouble her school house with the sounds of The Sisters of Mercy and Killing Joke, was universally popular with the rest of the clean-cut boys and girls, but naturally drawn towards Webster's individualism. Together they missed lessons, experimented with drugs, attended gigs, played impressive practical jokes (they once managed to enliven a parents' evening by spiking teachers' drinks with LSD) and also dabbled with spiritualism; it was during this period that she adopted her new name, bestowed upon her by a medium she and Webster met in East Grinstead. Webster too swapped 'Geoffrey' for 'Lance' around this time – a decision reportedly reached at the 1984 Glastonbury Festival. Feathers encouraged the singer to simplify his image and toughen up his songwriting, and it was with her blessing that Webster invaded the newly formed Thieving Magpies and began to follow his rock calling in earnest.

Physical distance was briefly put between the pair when they left the school in July 1985; Webster and his band began their steady ascent of the alternative-rock mountain, while Feathers, in a final attempt by the exasperated Amhurst family to civilise their increasingly madcap daughter, was packed off to a finishing school in Switzerland. She made sure her time there was as colourful as possible – she cultivated a habit of luring boys from the local village back to the premises in the dead of night, photographing them in various uncompromising positions, developing the pictures in the school's darkroom and delivering them to the boys' families in one of the school's embossed envelopes – but somehow she failed to achieve expulsion. By the time Feathers returned to Britain in the summer of 1986, Webster had already become a serviceable candidate for the title of Next Big Thing, the Magpies having contributed a song – 'A Month of Mondays' – to the legendary flexidisc compilation

Indie-duction. What followed was to establish a pattern for Feathers' approach to her friend's group and their career choices.

Suddenly finding themselves on the receiving end of not just one but two potential record deals, the Magpies opted, with Bob Grant's not unreasonable guidance, for a modest arrangement presented by a major label, rather than an even more humble offering from Abandon, an independent outfit based in Gerrards Cross. A few days before the contract was to be signed, Feathers summoned Webster to her Bloomsbury bedsit, where she made her thoughts on the matter perfectly plain: the Magpies should reject the major and go with the indie. Webster, then nineteen and hardly *au courant* with the arcane ways of the music industry, was baffled, and after a blazing row departed for Bob Grant's office in Kilburn. By the time he got there Feathers had already phoned the manager to declare she would not be eating or drinking again until the band took her advice. Webster feigned nonchalance for the next seventy-two hours but caved in on the way to the label's headquarters, bolting through the closing doors of the tube train as the band passed Russell Square. Horrified to find Feathers prostrate on her bed and in a state of some delirium, Webster glumly phoned the record company to inform all concerned that the deal was off.

Unsurprisingly, several weeks of heated debate and recrimination ensued, but once these had given way to fresh talks with Abandon for a level-headed agreement that would eventually spawn two high-profile indie hits ('Monument' and 'Siamese Burn'), the logic of Feathers' directive became more clear. By remaining, for the time being, on the independent side of the rock fence, without the relentless attention to sales figures on which a major would surely have insisted, the band would be allowed to develop their sound and build their audience properly, as the following eighteen months were to prove. A fervent following was already baying for the Thieving Magpies when they took to the various festival stages in the summer of 1987, new material displayed the refined lyrical venom and melodic clout that was to become their trademark, and the band topped the 'best newcomer' category of just about every poll in the country at the end of the year. As 1988 dawned, the flapping sound of major labels' chequebooks was little short of deafening. Bob Grant, now fully in control, steered the Magpies towards a generous but workable deal with BFM, Abandon received a handsome payout and an appreciable percentage of the first album's takings; everyone was a winner.

Except, of course, the major record company who originally offered them a deal. But six months after Gloria Feathers' tactical hunger strike, missing out on the Magpies had become the very least of that label's worries. The failure of a year-long campaign to break a very expensive band had meant dipping shares, staff cuts and ailing confidence, followed by – inevitably – new signings being dropped. It is a mathematical certainty that the Magpies would have suffered this fate. And yet Feathers never claimed to have any insider knowledge of the company's potential difficulties; in fact, she displayed very little interest at all in the business side of her beloved music. 'She just had an inkling,' shrugged Webster in a March 1989 interview. 'Must have been a fucking strong inkling, I grant you – but that's all she says. We'll probably listen next time she has one.'

Little did he know that another of 'Gloria's inklings' was brewing even as he spoke. Having extracted as much mileage as possible from *Shoot the Fish*, the Magpies had decided to quickly record a four-track EP to cash in on the upcoming festival season, before embarking on their second album in the autumn. A typically abrasive high-speed pop song entitled 'Something About Him' was chosen as the lead track; the green light was duly given by the label; the release date was set for 28 May; the master and artwork were poised to be sent off to the manufacturers – and Lance Webster's phone rang.

'I knew something was up by the tone of her voice,' he told *Melody Maker* later that year. 'As everyone knows, Gloria hardly ever speaks calmly, or slowly. She's usually so excited about what she has to say that it all comes out in this mad torrent of words, and there's almost always some gag or some hilarious situation she's got herself into. But now she was deathly serious . . . like, eerily calm and deliberate. I'd only ever heard her speak like that once before, and two days later she was bloody starving herself to death.'

This time, Feathers solemnly instructed her old friend to demote 'Something About Him' to side B of the EP, and make something else the lead track. When asked why, she had even less reasoning to offer than on the previous occasion. Despite his earlier pledge to pay more attention if this happened again, the arbitrary nature of the request led Webster to dismiss her once more. Just as she did in 1986, Feathers countered by laying a hefty threat on the line, the details of which have never been disclosed. One assumes it was pretty compelling, as twenty-four hours later Webster was hurriedly persuading his exasperated band and manager that the more funky and atmospheric 'What If Everyone Goes Mad?' would really be a far better radio song. 'Thank fuck Gloria phoned me on the Saturday,' he commented afterwards. 'If she'd left it 'til Sunday, it would've been too late.'

Indeed. The amended EP was despatched to the pressing plant at lunchtime on the Monday, and soon the earlier plan was all but forgotten. 'What If Everyone Goes Mad?' did the usual rounds of pluggers, journalists and DJs, a video was made – and everyone agreed that it was a nice shift in direction, something a little more laid back, but retaining the now familiar Magpies bite. More fortuitously, the song slipped neatly into an embryonic movement that was currently being stirred by the likes of The Stone Roses, Happy Mondays and Jesus Jones: the heyday of indie dance was just around the corner and the Thieving Magpies knew it. Of *course* they did. A few forward-thinking producers offered to remix the track. Well, why not? Get played in a few nightclubs for a change. The release date neared, Radio One put the track on their B-list (not bad for an alternative-rock single in 1989), the band went on an eight-date hike around the UK (climaxing with a sell-out show at London's Brixton Academy), the record hit the shops – and on Sunday 4 June, Bruno Brookes announced to the nation that Thieving Magpies had a new entry at number nineteen. It was the highest position a single of theirs had reached to date. Webster, receiving the news from the record company that afternoon, allowed himself a mild whoop and then rang Feathers to congratulate her on another successful 'inkling'. Of course, there was no way of knowing how well 'Something About Him' might have done, but everyone agreed 'What If Everyone Goes Mad?' had done the business.

That afternoon, band, entourage and friends gathered at Bob Grant's house in Cricklewood for a small celebration in his back garden. But it was an odd sort of day for a party. The world was reeling from reports that hundreds, if not thousands, of demonstrators had been killed in and around Tiananmen Square, Peking, at the hands of the Chinese army. Aside from sheer horror at the extent of the bloodshed, the political implications of the news hit the Magpies' camp pretty hard; being a liberal, nouveau-hippy sort of bunch, there were certainly a few doom-and-gloom merchants giving the gathering an anxious edge. 'Gloria was pretty frantic,' Webster recounted in a 1992 interview. 'She'd been to some acid-house parties that year which the police had shut down in a rather heavy-handed way, so she was wandering around saying, "This is now the yardstick for the planet. They'll get away with anything after this." I thought the connection was a bit tenuous at the time – I guess now with the whole Criminal Justice Bill thing you can sort of see what she was worried about. Anyway, she and a few others were just sat in Bob's lounge, smoking and watching the footage of the massacre, then rewinding it and watching it again. I told them to stop it and try to enjoy themselves. It got pretty weird.'

Unfortunately, things were about to get a whole lot weirder. Around seven, once the chart rundown had finished, Grant attempted to enliven slightly damp spirits by loudly playing the EP that had brought them all there in the first place. The opening track pumped out, eliciting the usual head noddings, critical comments ('I still reckon that backing vocal could've been louder') and eye-rollings that emerge when a song is played in the company of the band that created it. Then it started to rain. The second track, a thrashy workout entitled 'The Bitch Is Still Around', was almost completely ignored as everyone relocated to the living room, where Feathers and her cronies were still studying the Tiananmen video, endlessly conspiracy theorising. By the time former lead track 'Something About Him' kicked in, the EP had become nothing more than mildly irritating background noise. A minute and a half later, things were substantially different.

'We hadn't heard that song in over a month,' drummer Craig Spalding told the *NME*, 'it being track three now. For some reason we'd even stopped playing it live. I'd almost forgotten what it sounded like. Then the middle eight kicked in and everyone in the room just *died*.'

The lyrics of 'Something About Him' were basically a bitter rant about Webster's ex-girlfriend's current boyfriend: an individual whose sole redeeming feature, if the song was to be believed, was his bank balance. The middle eight in question – and the entire outro, for that matter – contained merely one phrase, repeated over and over, in a tone that boiled with tongue-in-cheek rage at the dullness of the man's job, clothes, hair and personality: *'death to the square'*.

'Gloria instantly burst into tears,' continued Spalding. 'There she was, repeatedly watching this bloody massacre on the telly, and then her best mate starts singing *'death to the square'* over and over, right in her earhole. Plus the thought of what might have been, of course.'

It didn't take long for the 'what might have been' to sink in. The debacle that the Magpies had escaped would have done inestimable damage to their budding career. The original EP, with 'Something About Him' as the lead track, would have charted on the same day; radios around the country would have reverberated with the sound of this young alternative upstart from Reading yelling *'death to the square*' amid the aftermath of one of the worst peacetime massacres in modern history, which had taken place in – of all the ludicrous coincidences – a square; a *Top of the Pops* appearance (which had already been scheduled to air on the coming Thursday) would have beheld the macabre spectacle of Webster stomping around the stage in his customary manner, looping the unfortunate statement like some crazed despot or sick lunatic. Cue: record dropping without trace from the chart, ruin of the band's mainstream profile, record-company unease. At the very least, it would all have been acutely embarrassing.

But it may not have got even that far, as Webster himself acknowledged the following year. 'That shit in China had been brewing for a month or so. No one knew it was going to end like that, but towards the end of May if you'd heard me singing that line I reckon you'd have made the connection. It'd be like I was egging them on. The record would've probably been withdrawn. The whole thing would have been a God-awful, expensive mess.' As it turned out, the controversy-free EP managed to climb even further, to number fifteen, the following Sunday; again, a very respectable feat in a chart topped by Jason Donovan and with a Cliff Richard record in the top five.

In spite of palpable relief at the offending phrase being comfortably buried at track three, shock and the general feeling of oddness ensured that Bob Grant's party never became the swinging affair he had perhaps envisaged. What, though, of Feathers herself?

'Once she'd calmed down, she totally downplayed it,' Webster commented in a 1995 *Q* interview. 'As usual. I remember her saying "I never thought much of that song," or something. She still just called it an "inkling". But God knows what she was thinking privately. I do remember that was the start of everything going a bit wrong.'

When the saga eventually found its way into the music press – bearing in mind that Feathers' roots, omnipresence and outspoken behaviour had found her a fair amount of enemies – a few figures in the industry tried to stir up trouble, spreading rumours of her apparent clairvoyance, nicknaming her 'the white witch' (which fitted rather too neatly with her peroxide blonde dreadlocks) or 'Webster's witch'. While Feathers was perfectly capable of dealing with any snide comment herself (she famously punched *Melody Maker* journalist Kenny Mann at a Northside gig in 1991), the band decided to keep any further 'inklings' of hers private; although Webster let it slip to *Q* that there had subsequently been 'three or four at least'.

Whilst the Thieving Magpies were the sole recipient of these rather unusual pieces of advice, they were by no means the only band to whom Feathers spread her unique brand of love. A child of the trust fund, she was fortunate enough to have few concerns other than which gig she'd be going to next, what she would wear, what she would drink, and sometimes what drugs she would take. She was loudly opinionated about her music but cast her net fairly widely: she was as happy at a Levitation gig as she was at a Stereo MCs show, as content to be stage-diving in front of Thousand Yard Stare as tripping her head off to The Orb. Success, too, was no measure – you'd just as easily spy her at a Wembley Arena backstage party as you might watching an unsigned troupe of spotty teens at the Red Eye on Copenhagen Street. No one, however, meant as much to her as the Thieving Magpies: a band for whom she had quite literally laid her life on the line. As the nineties progressed and the band's popularity rose to giddying heights, Feathers' protective instinct began to take on a more physical shade.

If 1990's *Lovely Youth* confirmed Webster's status as a British alternative pop hero – a caustic but approachable elder-brother type with a twinkle in his eye – the release of 1992's globe-straddling *Bruise Unit* converted him into something altogether more celestial. Things that fans did in order to be near him became more outlandish, the desire to capture his undivided attention more intense. At Denmark's Roskilde Festival in 1992, this characteristic of Webster's success reached an unwelcome zenith. He had mooched off by himself and was happily watching Danish band Innocent Blood in one of the smaller tents when a girl next to him struck up conversation. All was fine until Webster tried to leave for another stage where The Wonder Stuff were scheduled to play, only to discover the girl had somehow managed to manacle their ankles together with a pair of handcuffs.

'It was a variation on what had happened to Mike [Patton, of Faith No More] the previous year,' recalled Craig Spalding, 'though the fact she'd chosen the ankles made him much more vulnerable. She suddenly turned into this total nutter, yanking Lance's leg and making him trip over, then forcing herself on him. She was a fucking big girl as well. But Gloria came from out of *nowhere* – she grabbed the girl and just went *mental*, had her up against this massive tent pole, sent someone off to get the police and kept her right there until they arrived.'

Despite Feathers' impressive emergency response, the incident caused Webster considerable distress and he has never discussed it in public. It was also the last time he wandered about on his own at such an event. Sadly, it was not the final occasion on which he was subject to obsessive behaviour; in fact, worse was to come.

In the summer of 1993 the Magpies staged their own large-scale event at Langley Park, near Slough. For supporting attractions they filled the early evening with a few ascendant bands of the moment: The Frank and Walters, Terrorvision and a promising outfit from London named Elastica, while the afternoon had been reserved for the unsigned winners of a demo scramble. During a break from the mammoth *Bruise Unit* tour the Magpies themselves sat down in Bob Grant's office and listened to some four hundred demo tapes, selecting a list of three lucky winners: a funk-metal troupe from Kensington by the name of Fabric Flesh, a gloomy quartet from Middlesbrough known as They Say He Jumped and a solo artist from Luton who identified herself simply as Lesley. As anyone who remembers the day will attest, the first two acts were deeply unmemorable. The third was the precise opposite – but it had nothing to do with the music.

Although her demo contained passable angst-driven pop-rock

(not a million miles from the noise Alanis Morissette began to peddle a year or so later), Lesley surprised the Magpies' sound crew by showing up with just her acoustic guitar and a videotape. When quizzed as to the whereabouts of her backing musicians, she embarked on a lengthy but plausible tale of woe: her bass player had attempted to smuggle incriminating quantities of cannabis on the way back from a short European tour, and the band had been stopped at Hook of Holland, where all the gear, both musical and narcotic, had been impounded, and what a nightmare it all was, and thank God she came back separately or she'd have missed this amazing opportunity, and 'I promise to still put on a brilliant show', and 'Can your lighting guy project these visuals during my set', blah blah. The crew thus persuaded, Lesley strolled onto the large stage at half past four and, in front of some twenty thousand people, began to play.

The first thing onlookers noticed was that she wasn't very good. She had the moves, for sure, throwing back her long brown hair while she bashed away at her low-slung instrument, her apparent lack of concern at playing for such a large audience suggesting an amount of experience, but the sound that emerged was far from accomplished: a scratchy, slightly out-of-tune guitar with approximated chords accompanied by a voice that was all expression and no skill. It wasn't totally unlistenable, however, which ensured that people continued to pay attention long enough to notice the second, more startling ingredient. Her lyrics were composed entirely of Thieving Magpies song titles.

'*It's* War on the Floor,' she sang, '*and it's* Arguably the Last Time *I'll be riding your* Pit Pony.' Other lines were less grammatically successful, such as '*I'm going to sleep with* The Cool and the Crooks *while the* Inappropriate Girlfriend *sleeps with* The Ballad That Never Ends' – while some ('*I want you to fuck my* Squarehole *with your* Roundpeg') left little to the imagination. Towards the end of the first 'song' she'd garnered more attention than she deserved on account of this feature; in fact, a collection of pissed blokes down the front were merrily listening out for the titles and cheering each time they spotted one. But most observers had started paying more mind to the increasingly peculiar moving images projected behind her.

Some reports suggest Gloria Feathers was already calling for Lesley to be removed by this point, aggressively bending the ear of the stage manager next to the monitor desk (the Magpies' crew were quite used to fielding – and usually ignoring – Gloria's requests). But when the figure wandering about on the dimly lit home video became more recognisable, there is little doubt that she instantly made a beeline for the main sound desk. There were problems, however. The first was that Gloria's route – from the side of the stage, down the steps, across the crowded backstage enclosure, through the section where all the trucks were parked, past security into the main arena, around the bustling inner ring of fast-food stalls and bars, across the field strewn with happy punters and finally right up to the sound tower – took the best part of five minutes to navigate. When she arrived she encountered a fresh difficulty: no one would let her in. Feathers was so well known on the scene that sometimes promoters didn't bother to give her a security pass; or even if they did, she rarely condescended to wear it. Usually this wasn't a problem, but on this occasion a brand-new security firm, LiveTime, was being used and none of the staff knew who the hell she was. One can imagine the bemusement of the sound-desk guard, confronted by this frightsome woman with multicoloured dreadlocks, demanding to be let in, hurling various indignances ('How *dare* you *not* recognise me! I'm Gloria bloody Feathers! They should hand round photos of me at your fucking induction sessions!') while Lesley played on, her lyrics becoming more twisted ('Look Who's Laughing – *me when I Lose It, kill you and feast on your* Chopped Heart'), the visuals more worrying.

Actually Webster himself was watching the whole thing, but was too paralysed by shock to do much about it. For in front of his, and now close to forty thousand other disbelieving eyes, played what could effectively pass for a filmed summary of his recent activities. Starting, tentatively, with a few dark and grainy sequences of Webster wandering around a record shop, then following him along a few quiet streets, sometimes alone, sometimes with his girlfriend (who at this point was an Australian drama student named Camilla McBriar), the film then started to gain a bit more confidence and featured long shots of Webster having lunch in a restaurant, zooming in on his mouth as he ate, drank and spoke; then a series of shots that pursued him on a car journey along a dual carriageway, stopping next to him at some lights, tracking him through an industrial estate and watching him pull up next to a large brown factory, get out of the car with his guitar and enter an unremarkable building (this was the Magpies' rehearsal space near the Guinness brewery in Acton); then it changed scene entirely, following him round a supermarket (Sainsbury's in Camden, as closer examination would prove) and again closing in on his mouth, hands, eyes and belongings, even to the point of focusing on the contents of his trolley (this prompted the film's one and only laugh from the audience, presumably due to the extra-ordinary number of Ambrosia creamed desserts you could see); then there came a montage of assorted situations: Lance relaxing in his garden, drinking with the rest of the band in a pub, driving again (this time filmed from a motorway bridge, under which a shaded Webster passed), hurrying along streets in various parts of London (Kilburn, Soho, Putney) and concluded with – unbelievably – some similar footage of him in Amsterdam, Paris and what was almost certainly New York (the Magpies had recently played summer festivals in these various countries). But if the sequence had so far been, from a legal point of view, inoffensive – while certainly devious and creepy (not to mention well-funded) – here was where it became downright nasty and felonious. Via a method one finds difficult to fathom, the remainder of the film consisted of Webster and McBriar mooching around at home, cooking in the kitchen, canoodling in front of the television and ultimately, just before the video was at last removed from the player, having sex in the bedroom.

Again, reports differ as to how Feathers was eventually admitted into the sound tower. The probable story is that she was spotted by one of the chaps inside and ushered in; a more colourful tale is that she punched out the hapless security guy. Either way, it was certainly Feathers that pressed the eject button. She then promptly sacked all the crew. Clutching the video tape, she stormed back to the main backstage area, sacked pretty much everyone else (it is assumed that, like Webster, they were all too transfixed by the film's sheer audacity to put an immediate stop to it), then grabbed Lesley by the scruff of the neck (she had finally been booed off by the crowd after the film stopped) and dragged her off to the nearest police van, where the officers simply cautioned her and advised that she should leave the site immediately.

The rest of the day passed without further drama and was, if truth be told, a trifle dull. Even the Thieving Magpies themselves were a little under par, knackered from close to eighteen months of playing virtually the same set. Webster did not, as had been hoped, make some witty remark about Lesley's video, which perhaps demonstrated how freaked out he really was by the whole thing. Gloria Feathers angrily left the site around eight, after Bob Grant calmly reminded her that she was not in a position to go round dismissing Thieving Magpies employees when she was not even one herself.

In fact, as the autumn of 1993 approached, you didn't have to be within the Magpies' inner-circle to surmise that Feathers' reign as their closest confidante was nearing its end. The band, although road-weary and in desperate need of the impending break, were bigger than ever, their mushrooming popularity now seemingly invincible to any hitch or bad move that Gloria may or may not foresee. Her arrogance, at one time laughed off by all as a charming quirk of her multilayered character, had now reached alarming proportions, and become insufferable to everyone from hotel porters to other rock stars; not helped in the slightest by her excessive drinking. The 'last semi-useful thing she did', to employ Craig Spalding's expression, was to spot the infamous Lesley, camcorder in hand, following Webster around while he was on holiday with Camilla McBriar in Barcelona, and to again cart her off to the authorities (the Spanish police took a rather more serious view of Lesley's antics and kept her in a cell overnight) – but even this had its downside: one may reasonably ask what the hell Feathers was doing in Barcelona anyway. It was supposedly a coincidence, although by now you were beginning to wonder. Whatever the explanation, Feathers' almost constant presence was causing noticeable strain between Webster and McBriar, and they eventually split just before Christmas of that year.

1994 dawned and progressed, with all its attendant cultural gear changes, and Feathers was seen less and less in public. For the most part she was unwelcome in Britpop circles (Liam Gallagher allegedly described her as a 'punk-rock Miss Piggy'), but the feeling was usually mutual. She still ventured out to see some of her favourites: Swervedriver, Cranes, Senser, Eat Static – and even managed to fly to Seattle for the public vigil that followed Kurt Cobain's death ('Gloria would go to the funeral of an envelope,' one music journalist quipped) – but her omniscience and popularity had long since waned. Even her indestructible friendship with Lance Webster was showing visible signs of wear and tear; they were seen having a rather large argument over dinner at Quo Vadis, leaving separately, Webster looking close to tears. In an interview conducted to coincide with the television screening of *The Liar*, he both acknowledged and denied that something was amiss with his chum: 'Off the rails? Naah. Listen, you don't become someone like Gloria by having lots of early nights and drinking orange squash. And I've been friends with her through worse than this.' Worse than what, exactly, he did not articulate; but it wasn't difficult to take a few wild guesses.

The last undisputed public sighting of Feathers was at the February 1995 Brit Awards, where Blur won in a record-breaking four categories. Britpop aside, the band had been indie staples since 1990 and were therefore known and liked by Feathers, who seemed very much her old self as she delightedly applauded their many trips up to the podium. She looked well and, unusually, in possession of a slight suntan – she didn't even appear to be drinking quite so much. Apart from her dreadlocks' new colour scheme (red, white and blue: perhaps a nod to the new obsession with all things British), the rest of her appearance could have been the Gloria Feathers of any point in the previous eight or nine years: short red PVC skirt, fishnets, thick studded belt, threatening boots and a heavily ripped Head of David T-shirt. She remained at the event until Sting took to the stage to present Elton John with his Outstanding Contribution award, perhaps deciding that this was a step too far into the land of the mainstream. Skipping off through the vast hall, kissing goodbye to a few friends, stopping to retrieve her fake-fur coat from the cloak-room, jumping into a taxi and heading south: that was the last the world at large was to see of Gloria Feathers.

Unlike history's other disappearees (not least Richey Manic, who had only been missing for a few weeks by this point), there was relatively little hue and cry about Feathers' vanishing act, the funda-mental reason for which being that her next of kin, father Donald Amhurst, decided not to report her as a missing person following a farewell note he received. In her legendary and incredibly well-researched feature 'Where the Fuck Is Gloria Feathers?' (published in the 1996 edition of the fanzine *Things That Make Me Go Moo*), Alison O'Bawd quoted from this message (although how she managed to be privy to its contents also remains something of a mystery). 'Fate united us,' it purportedly read, 'and now please accept that fate has separated us. You may wish to find me; perhaps you may not. If any love for me remains within you, please understand that I wish to be left alone.' It is difficult to say whether Amhurst took his daughter's elegantly Garbo-esque advice as a result of any remaining love, or simply because he was sick to the back teeth of her. Either way, no official moves were made towards tracing her whereabouts, and the Feathers-spotter must rely on the few friends and family members who conducted their own independent investigations. Based on slight contributions from this group of people (which, conspicuously, did not include Lance Webster) and noting other independent sightings heard through the indie grapevine, O'Bawd's feature makes an admirable stab at constructing a possible passage, thus: having shaved her head and donned unremarkable clothing, Feathers travelled to Switzerland, where she met with an old schoolfriend, acquired a fake Swiss passport and became Rosamund von Feder; she lived in the small town of Dietikon, near Zürich, for the next four months (among Feathers' few academic successes was her proficiency in German), after which she travelled by car to Moscow, where she ditched the vehicle with a hitchhiker (and Thieving Magpies fan) she happened to meet at a petrol station near Minsk, boarded the Trans-Siberian Railway and headed for Vladivostok on the far-eastern coast of Russia. Here her voyage apparently drew to a halt.

Two Feathers-related visits to Vladivostok were made that year: the first by her elder sister, Persephone, who after a few weeks of fruitless searching was told by some locals on the outskirts of the city of a strange young Swiss woman fitting Feathers' description, living alone in a remote apartment block, calling herself Slava Pero ('Glory Feather'). Unfortunately this character was nowhere to be found at the time of Persephone's visit. Shortly before Christmas, Alison O'Bawd herself made the trip with her boyfriend, fellow writer Sam Northam, managing to locate Pero having lunch in a nearby café:

She has short, scruffy black hair, a thick, baggy black jumper that easily hides any tattoos, a brown skirt, and a blank, stoned expression. A lot of people look like that around here. Must be the vodka. But one look at her eyes and she is unmistakably Gloria. She might as well be wearing a name badge. She's abandoned all her face jewellery, but you can see the little piercing holes from right across the room. Sam is initially not so certain – but after a minute or two Slava Pero glares at us, leaps up, frantically throws a few roubles at the waitress and darts out the door. We've not spoken a word since we walked in, and we're wearing purposefully neutral clothing, but she must just *know*. Sam shakes his head and says, 'That was *blatantly* Gloria.'

And that is the last we see of her.

Or, indeed, that anyone saw of her.

Naturally, rumours abounded that Lance Webster was somehow involved in her vanishing act; stories that he had ordered her to leave the country, to take on a new identity, even that he had paid for her to be kidnapped, finally tired of her wild instructions and intrusions to both his personal and professional life. A particular advocate of this explanation was Persephone Amhurst herself, who had reportedly never cared much for the singer, believing he and his band had kept her Rosamund at perpetual odds with the rest of reality. When Webster's own world collapsed six months after the disappearance, Persephone made sure her opinions were heard in any media that listened: 'This drunken, hostile lout has finally shown the world his true colours – a streak that our family have experienced at close quarters for too many years. It is our hope that he receives a custodial sentence and hefty fine for his violence and disregard for those who have given him a career.' O'Bawd, however, saw it differently, as her exhaustive article – referencing a 1993 letter Feathers wrote to her friend, *NME* journalist Alan Leader – concludes:

She was the life and soul of the party, the first to arrive, the last to leave, with a stamina few could match. Something had to give eventually. No one removed Gloria but herself. 'I'm tired,' her letter continued, 'and feel older than I should. I long for far-off places, where no one knows me, where I can be myself, whoever that is. I had a dream, just the other day, of a distant city, with trees, and rain, and dramatic seas, and wilderness I can explore, unfettered by complication and all these silly, trivial things. Do you ever feel that way?' Her curiosity perhaps finally got the better of her. The choice of city is a bit dubious: a dirty, dark, cold, bleak and depressing sort of place, with an infeasibly healthy organised-crime ingredient – but maybe that is the whole point. Perhaps she has to sink right down in order to rise back up. And few can deny there is a typical ring of eccentricity to it: at the eastern end of the former Soviet Union, a mere thousand miles from Peking and Tokyo, and just five hundred miles from Seoul, but in what is still to all intents and purposes a European country, Gloria Feathers has finally found a place in which to unfetter herself.

Cynics also trumpeted that Vladivostok was one of the cheapest places in the world to buy heroin – but who really knew the truth. By the end of 1996, the question, 'Where the fuck is Gloria Feathers?' – rather like, 'Whatever happened to the fat bloke who introduced Carter USM?' or even, 'Is the singer from Placebo a boy or a girl?' – seemed to be a question only losers would ask.

But the mystery remains. And there are still some losers out there who intend to solve it.

EVERYTHING THAT'S HAPPENED TO ME FROM THAT MOMENT ONWARDS HAS BEEN VAGUELY DISAPPOINTING

I press save, and shut the creaking lid of the almighty laptop. The dark-grey laptop I bought in 1997, when I inherited a grand from that great aunt who met her end in a nursing home in Leighton Buzzard; the laptop that had seemed so slick and ultramodern back then with its groovy navigation keys and Windows 95, but now looks as ancient as my mum's typewriter when side by side with Polly's spanking Mac on the kitchen table. I've ridden it hard, like a faithful old workhorse (does one ride a workhorse?) – I've had parts replaced, upgraded the memory and processor two or three times, dropped it down umpteen flights of steps, allowed friends to skin up on it, almost set fire to it (it has no power switch thanks to this particular incident), spilled tea on it, nearly lost it completely when Heathrow decided to send it to Frankfurt while I was on the way to

Copenhagen – but it still works. Granted, it takes two or three minutes to open up a Word document, and navigating to certain web pages is often an excuse to pop out for another can of beer, but it's been a reliable old thing and I'll be quite sad to see it go. I say that as if I've got a spare eight hundred quid for a new one, which as you've probably figured is something of an untruth, but I imagine it'll happen one day when I get a windfall or it finally kicks the bucket and goes to the big IT department in the sky.

Like a shirking schoolboy, I've been studiously avoiding what I'm meant to be doing. It's now eleven o'clock at night, but the frantic scribbling of likely-looking plot outlines, sample chapters and character explorations for the alleged novel I'm supposed to show Mr Webster tomorrow afternoon has not yet commenced. You may wonder what the arse I've been doing for the last twenty-four hours. Funny, I've been thinking the same.

You see, being unemployed is not simply a situation one puts up with for a while. It's actually a full-time job in itself; a wholly absorbing occupation that commences the second you leave the building of your outgoing employer and doesn't stop until you arrive at the door of your next, however many days, weeks, months or years that takes. There is never, in my fairly comprehensive experience, a period of grace when one cheerfully thinks, 'Ooh, I'll catch up on my reading/tidy my papers/go to a museum/learn to make curry/take advantage of the cheap afternoon cinema tickets', etc. From minute number one there is a massive, ugly, concrete prehistoric mammoth of guilt and worry standing in the useful bit of whatever room you're in, trumpeting loudly whenever you try to concentrate, butting you with its tusks if you attempt to do something normal like have sex or eat in a restaurant. A small number of unemployed people – chiefly dependent on their bank balance and/or mental state – manage to give the mammoth its marching orders at five-thirty every day and at weekends, enabling them to coexist with partners and friends in a relatively civil and functional manner until nine o'clock the following morning; but alas, the majority continue to mope around like grumpy, directionless dickheads until they're either too drunk to care or asleep. You can guess which group I belong to.

That said, a few hours spent on the life of Gloria Feathers is hardly time wasted, and will be handy for my eventual masterpiece. Even Alan might give it a quick read. He went through a period of unnatural obsession with Gloria; oddly, it was long after what might be described as her 'heyday', by which point she looked extra emaciated and white as a Tudor. Alan, nearing the end of a degree at Manchester University, had heard the song '4st 7lb' from the Manics' *Holy Bible*, decided Gloria was anorexic (he wasn't entirely alone in this opinion) and made it his mission to 'save' her, as recounted in this charming scrapbook entry:

WEDNESDAY 5 OCTOBER [1994]
S*M*A*S*H, Manc Union
Went with Gavin Walker and Dave Smith cos everyone else was revising, turned out to be a fucking nightmare, never going near either of them again. They had loads of speed before then drank about five pints and just got really obnoxious, support band unknown think they were local, then GLORIA appeared. Can't believe it, what's she doing up here. Haven't seen her in time and she's even worse than before but she's so delicate, beautiful, why didn't I notice this years ago, she's ill though, sure of it now, waited til band came on (don't know what all the fuss is about really) then went up to try and say hello . . . she ignored me at first then I said 'would you like a drink' and she said 'yes, but don't expect me to talk to you'. I got her a vodka and she smiled when I passed it to her, my God her eyes are so gorgeous, they look into your soul, I was just going to ask her something about her health when those PRICKS came up and

asked if she wanted a cheeseburger. I kept telling them to piss off then Gloria moved away. Was so gutted bought myself three bottles of Mad Dog and had them all while walking back down Wilmslow Road then puked, phoned Clive

It cuts off just like that. I remember my university years being peppered with these late-night phone calls from Alan, which became more drunken at both ends of the line as the years went by and our student debts soared. The discussions usually involved either a band he'd just seen and felt the need to gush or rant about (Miranda Sex Garden and Suede, respectively, seem to stand out in my memory), or a girl he'd just been wounded by. '*Why* won't she go out with me, man?' he'd whimper, while I'd try to work out which one of the many he'd recently mentioned had spurned him and why I was suddenly considered an expert. I'm straining to remember the contents of that specific night's discussion, shivering as I probably was in one of the long corridors of my hall of residence near Marylebone, hanging on the incoming-calls-only intercollegiate phone, wearing my boxer shorts and Power of Dreams '100 Ways to Kill a Love' T-shirt (I kept my rarest shirts for pretend-nonchalant use around the hall in the hope that some girl would notice). It was around this time I turned down the job at the *NME* (oh yes) so maybe we were talking about that, in between bouts of Alan's ongoing Gloria-related misery and Mad Dog-fuelled blethering.

I place Alan's fragile scrapbook carefully on my desk and make the usual trip past Polly's bedroom (she's in there with someone, judging by the wrestling noises) towards the kitchen in general and the fridge in particular, where I find my habitual can of liquid refreshment. I hold the funny, cold metal tube in front of my eyes for a moment, pondering its ingredients and precisely how I'll benefit from them. Looking at it logically, I'm not drunk, nor do I need to be, but there's the general buzz of half a dozen units of alcohol inside me; if I increase that buzz, is it *really* likely do anything for the creativity which must occur at some point between now and 3 p.m. tomorrow? It's doubtful. I'm thirsty, but there's water in the tap, tea or coffee in the cupboard, milk in the fridge, even some orange juice. I could have any or all of these things. Polly, in a fit of health consciousness, has even bought some echinacea tea, which I also could sample.

I stop being so silly and crack open the beer.

Returning to my room, I decide – inspiration now being somewhat thin on the ground – to take a look in my Important Box. This is a wooden chest I inherited from a university friend who'd been at boarding school, in which I have stored my most valuable and noteworthy items: my passport and birth certificate, my twenty-first-birthday cufflinks, my signed copy of *Casual Sex in the Cineplex* by The Sultans of Ping FC, my university dissertation (some rambling bollocks about Arthur Miller), my letter from Stephen Fry ('I am delighted you so hugely enjoyed *The Hippopotamus*'), my Letter of the Week in *Melody Maker* ('you are an important and usually excellent newspaper; STOP abusing your position!'), other assorted paraphernalia and some of the more superior copies of *Vorsprung Durch Peanut* and its Britpop-era successor, *Definitely Not*. Although I'm supposed to be writing about anything but music, I can't resist a quick leaf through these. The first issue that reaches my hand is from autumn 1991, by which time the *Peanut* had evolved from a bedroom concern to a bedroom concern with slightly faultier equipment (I'd managed to buy one of my ex-school's old photocopiers at a knock-down price). It primarily consists of a report on the 'Great Summer Indiethon' – an insane, forty-two-band slog designed to take in various Reading Festival warm-up gigs, in-store performances, the festival itself and, coincidentally, the secret Thieving Magpies appearance before which Alan and I thrashed those two roadies of theirs at pool in the pub next door to the venue. Throughout, we're referred to by our fanzine nicknames, Clive Pop and Anal Alan; there's a cast of other occasionals (including Alan's university chums Steve the Swede and Emily from East Anglia), loads of banter, in-joking and far less cider than one might imagine. Reading Thursday of that year was my eighteenth birthday, in fact.

A happy memory.

Now, I'm not normally the kind of bloke who mopes around wondering where it all went turnip-shaped, but there's an irony to all of this that's making me wince. Unless the rose-tinted specs are messing with me, it goes something like this – eighteen: contented, not a lot to worry about except how much indie the human body can physically absorb, indulging in cheeky snogs and fumbles with whichever female permits it, my weakness for alcohol still in its infancy, trouncing two hardy, dreadlocked Thieving Magpie roadies at pool. Fast-forward to thirty-three: frustrated, no job, next-to-zero money, recovering from a six-year relationship which probably lasted five years too long, my weakness for alcohol well into its senility, being scolded by two hardy, shorn-headed, former Thieving Magpie roadies for writing foolish, bunny-boiling letters to an ex-alternative superstar. I wouldn't say things were improving with age, would you?

And yet, they tell me to grow up.

All right, so I've had a few drinks and Thursday is rapidly turning into Friday, but I'm deathly serious: how many problems, arguments, insecurities, guilt complexes and overdrafts are a direct result of this 'growing up'? The demon adulthood, and what's expected of you, or what you expect of it?

'Grow up,' they say. My ex-girlfriend said it. Alan says it. My mum says it. My sister once said it (then my five-year-old nephew repeated it all afternoon). My bank manager says it, albeit in a style owing slightly more to interest rates and loan top-up policies than models of emotional development. Geoffrey 'Lance' Webster says it; for what was the sending round of his pair of amplifier-lugging stooges, if not a big, unwashed crustie fist with the words 'GROW UP' tattooed in that hideous, faded greeny-blue colour? And now even fucking Polly – Polly the neurotic, nymphomaniac disaster, who somehow manages to hold down a legal job in-between crazed nights of mainlining red wine, tying pizza-delivery men to her bed and getting taxis from London to Bristol, Polly who can't even sit still through a film at the cinema without nipping out for a fag and a gin and tonic – *she* has decided to start saying it. Why? Why are all these people trying to convince me that life would somehow improve if I started behaving like a textbook version of a thirty-three-year-old?

For my small amount of money anyway, most people on this paltry little island are actually trying to be *younger*, at least cosmetically speaking. Or *feel* younger. They want the body, face, libido and spontaneous spirit of a twenty-year-old, welded seamlessly onto the carcass of an individual with a forty-year-old's level of experience, discipline and knowledge of the property market. I spend a substantial amount of my time trying to squeeze forth the tiniest drop of enthusiasm for any of that stuff. But in truth, I'd rather drink dishwater than glance in an estate agent's window; would sooner chat to a dead pigeon than with someone who's about to renovate their loft.

I find it fascinating, this differing view of 'growing up'. For me, it was nothing more than the process of becoming physically larger, less interested in getting extra track for my Scalextric and more interested in what lay behind women's clothing. Maybe I'm deeply lacking something, but that was pretty much it; apart from being able to buy certain items and go to certain places without pretending to be Billy Flushing's elder brother. From then on, the improvements of ageing ceased. My first eighteen years were spent looking forward to the age of eighteen, while – if I call upon the sort of brutal honesty only five cans of lager can summon – the last fifteen have basically consisted of looking back.

Blimey.

I sit unhappily in my chair, staring through my bedroom window at the funny little yardy bit we never use ('Why don't you try growing veg out there, man?' Alan once asked), nagging on my beverage, wondering if there was ever a period around the turn of my twenties (the 'happy gap'?) when I was satisfied with the status quo, and if so, how long did it last? Or was it more like some deranged Venn diagram of life, the middle loop representing a period when I was both looking back and forth with equal levels of dissatisfaction?

Being in the fortunate possession of what amounts to a diary covering the days following my arrival in adultland, I leaf through the *Peanut* – looking so impossibly dated now with its thin, typed white pages, slightly thicker blue paper serving as a cover, and near pitch-black photographs (Jane Stokes from Beef, 'surely the most underrated and undervalued indie group to currently grace the circuit', is virtually unrecognisable as that season's cover star) – to see if there are any clues. There's indeed much evidence of a fun and carefree time: 'the *Peanut* team do their best to ruck among the retail racks like it's a real gig, but Clive Pop knocks over a huge stack of Blue Aeroplanes CDs'; 'Clive Pop is back at his *Peanut* "stall" trying to flog last season's fanzine as people leave the club – the only one he sells is to a passing elderly Indian chap who walks off studying the Scorpio Rising feature intently'; 'the official *Vorsprung Durch Peanut* Clive Pop eighteenth-birthday celebration takes place on the way back from Camden Palace at four in the morning outside 7-Eleven in Hendon, with packets of Jelly Babies and (Clive Pop's favourite) pork scratchings, plus various cans of soft drink which the assembled "crack" open, champagne-style. Anal Alan has his second mini-snog of the day (different girl, obviously . . . shhh!)' – and so on. My eyes skim past antics we'd never get away with, nor even attempt, these days: a penniless Steve the Swede had bought a dodgy Reading wristband which came off in the Five Thirty ruck on the second night, so he snuck into the arena at daybreak, while the toilets were open for the campers, hid under a catering lorry for the next four hours with only a bottle of Mendip Magic and a bacon sarnie for company, finally emerging when the gates opened properly at noon. What strikes me most, though, is how little we actually drank. Sure, we had a few, but it was more a case of 'let's pass this bottle of apple schnapps round, get a bit tiddly, dance our arses off to De La Soul and then sober up', rather than the emphasis on pint after pint of lager that took over by about 1994, when we had access to comparatively large reserves of borrowed cash. This change in approach also had a big effect on the *end* of our festival day – again, from twenty-one onwards I would ingest as much beer as anatomically possible and pass out by one o'clock at the latest (even if drugs were involved), whereas in the old days we sat around the campfire, ours or anyone else's, singing, talking bollocks, perhaps going for strolls around the moonlit arena, not considering hitting the sack until either the smoke became too much for our eyes or we'd finally tired of endlessly debating which of the two Ned's Atomic Dustbin bassists was better.

But I clutch on to my can of beer and refuse to entertain the thought that this malaise is entirely down to booze. No – it must be something else.

It doesn't take me long to find it. Cast your eye over the snippet below – and bear in mind that this is August 1991 we're talking about.

4.15 p.m. [Friday] Another mini-debate over the *Peanut* team's next move. Clive Pop is off to meet and greet The Family Cat, but Anal Alan and Steve the Swede decide to see Nirvana on the main stage ('they're meant to be pretty good, man'). Clive Pop sticks around for a few minutes, the first song is energetic but pretty metallist (plus they've got some really irritating bloke with a Mohican doing a Bez) so he sticks to plan A and heads for the signing tent.

4.25 p.m. It's a big queue for the Cat! They're not playing until Sunday, but the fans are already out in force. Good for them.

4.30 p.m. Still queuing for the Cat. A song Clive Pop faintly recognises drifts over from the main stage – must have heard it in a club. Not bad. Never mind, we'll soon hear all about it from Anal Alan.

4.40 p.m. Swizz! Who should walk past Clive Pop but all five members of The Family Cat! The cheeky so-and-sos have *only just arrived*!

4.50 p.m. Clive Pop reaches the front of the queue, his copy of the *Peanut* is cheerily autographed by the band. 'Nice of you to turn up,' Clive laughs. 'Sorry,' they all chorus. 'Watching Nirvana,' admits the singer, shaking his head. 'Jaw-dropping.'

4.55 p.m. The *Peanut* team reconvene by the Pennine Pizza bus. For a minute or two it looks like Anal Alan and Steve the Swede have just been told a relative has died, they look so shocked. After a while Steve manages to blurt 'that was the greatest of my life' – but this is his standard post-gig proclamation (he even said it recently about a Cud show), so there's no need for Clive Pop to worry.

Except, of course, there was.

For the rest of the bloody day, as I now recall, I heard nothing other than how unbelievably brilliant Nirvana had been, sprinkled with general mirth that I had missed them in favour of 'The Family Shat' as Alan and Steve immediately christened them. My usual comeback to such garbage (which I very successfully employed when Alan made similar noises about Underneath What and The Atom Seed) was to calmly state that we'd see how big they were in six months' time. But on this occasion, fate was stacked so heavily against me that I get a toothache just thinking about it. I don't need to tell you (but I'm going to anyway) that by the time those six months were up, not only were Nirvana the biggest alternative-rock band in the world, but they'd also unwittingly set the plan for nineties popular culture firmly in stone. I had missed what is widely regarded, at least in Britain, as the pivotal moment – by about two hundred metres. Of course, I saw Nirvana headlining the following year, as everyone and his dog did, but by then it was far too late.

Call me melodramatic but this recollection hits me square in the emotional goolies. I grab Alan's scrapbook again to cross-reference. There it is, plain as day, in Alan's usual blend of hyperbole and questionable grammar:

> Thank fuck I ignored Clive going to get signatures from the fucking family shat cos instead I saw NIRVANA, okay they started a bit metallist but by song 4 they were bloody revalation. Amazing then I remembered it was them that do the q. good 'gramma take me home' one we dance to at that shitty club on Oxford Street but man, they made everyone else look shit. Singer dived into kit. Could be big. Poor old Clive we took the piss a bit he spent the rest of his birthday money getting drunk, had to wake him up for the poppies.

Yeah, poor old Clive. Now I think about it, I do have a faint sense of the rest of the weekend feeling entirely different, like I'd become another person.

My God.

Panicking slightly (God knows why, it's sixteen years too late to do anything about it), I quickly nip to the kitchen for another beer, pick up my phone and speed-dial number three.

'Yeah?'

'Alan, it's Clive.'

'I know,' he growls. 'I meant "yeah" as in, "what can you possibly want at this time of night?"'

I glance at my watch. Bugger. Twenty past midnight.

'Sorry, did I wake you up? Need to ask you something.'

He does that maddening trick of not replying, leaving the phone line a silent void which only I am required to fill.

'Err . . . you know when we saw Nirvana at Reading in '91?'

'Uh-huh.'

'Were they really that good or were you guys just winding me up?'

His usual scoffing-burp sound comes speeding down the wire from Crouch End. 'Doesn't it say anything about this in my scrapbook?'

'Yeah, it—'

'Because part of the reason I gave you the damn thing was so I didn't have to answer daft questions at times like this. I've got to be in Cardiff by eight-thirty.'

'Sorry. It says they were a "bloody revalation".'

'Well, there you go.'

'Yes, but was it, like, life-changing?'

'Oh, probably not.'

'Do you think it changed me?'

'Changed you?'

'Yeah.'

'You missed them, didn't you?'

'Yeah – I mean, do you think *not* seeing them changed me?'

'How the hell should I know?'

'Sorry, it's just that . . . I've suddenly realised, everything that's happened to me from that moment onwards has been vaguely disappointing . . .'

'Oh, for God's sake.'

'And that it might have been the start of me . . . you know . . . losing it slightly.'

Unexpectedly, this heralds a laugh.

'Losing your edge,' Alan chuckles. 'And you were there, off your tits at Spike Island, 1990. "It'll never catch on," you said.'

'Did I say that?'

'Something along those lines. Forget it. Listen, put that crap away for the night, finish your can of beer [how'd he know I was drinking one?], get some sleep and stop being so bloody hysterical.'

But Alan is an expert at the slick closure of a phone call, even agreeing to a swift morally supportive coffee tomorrow afternoon before I meet Webster. I can't say I feel an awful lot better, though. I ignore his advice, return to the fanzine, and yes: the post-Nirvana results are quite remarkable. According to our reporter, Pop Will Eat Itself and Ned's were both 'a disappointment'. The Fat Lady Sings 'didn't deserve an encore'. The Sisters of Mercy were 'ridiculous'. Flowered Up and Teenage Fanclub were 'boringly similar' (which seems unlikely), while Blur 'only have one good song'. The Family Cat's actual performance on the Sunday doesn't even garner a review. Only De La Soul sparkle – watched, as we know, with the assistance of Steve the Swede's apple schnapps – but this judgement is accompanied by a sophisticated observation that 'drinking at a festival is actually quite fun, all the bands sound great when you're a bit pissed, and no one cares about the weather; this could be the way forward.'

Fuck.

I drain the last of my can, pull on my hooded top, grab my keys, stumble through the kitchen and just go, out into the north-east-London night. I know from experience that feelings like these are only soothed by walking. It doesn't really matter where I go, but naturally I always end up heading in a south-westerly direction, as if magnetically drawn towards London's centre. I don't really spend much time there these days, but its pull remains compelling. It's a dry, windless night, and after an initial stiffness (I haven't left the house since yesterday evening) I'm soon up to speed, hurrying out of my locality, past a few stragglers contemplating a kebab after leaving one of the later-shutting pubs, beyond the church, past the final bus stop and out onto the road bordering the park. There was a time when I would leap over the fence and cut across but nowadays even I – naïvety and slightly disposable attitude to life aside – take the long route round. Not that I've ever had the problems with muggers and nutters some of my friends have had. I put this down to perpetually marching at breakneck speed, pulling my woolly hat down to my eyes and doing my best to look more barmy than anyone else.

There are two things I always see on these small-hour jaunts. Indeed, both appear with such clockwork regularity I think I'd be concerned for the state of the universe if I didn't see them. One is a collection of elderly African ladies with huge multicoloured shopping bags. Doesn't matter what time it is. Once I saw them at three in the morning. It's extraordinary. They always look perfectly happy, gossiping away, never in the same place (tonight they're ambling along Green Lanes; another time they were coming out of a house in Finsbury Park; once they were even as far away as King's Cross). When I spy them this evening I almost feel like saying hello. The second thing I habitually encounter is an old chap walking his dog. Again, time seems to make little difference — one o'clock, two o'clock, even around six on one occasion. Both man and dog always look totally miserable. The bloke's probably got one of those jobs with crazy shifts, like Alan's tenure a few years back in a certain banking department that required him to be there from 11.30 p.m. until 8 a.m., Friday to Tuesday; the bizarre upshot being that his working week kicked off just as everyone else was getting plastered at the end of theirs, and his 'weekend' began first thing on a Wednesday morning. Typically, Alan made damn sure he didn't miss out on a proper 'Friday night', rooting out some meatpacker's boozer near Smithfield Market where he would sup away happily until lunchtime and then drunkenly retire to bed. 'Saturday-morning hangovers are so much nicer on Wednesday evenings,' he would tell people, 'plus there's better telly on.'

Tonight dog-walking man is looking extra pissed off, tramping past Canonbury station as his dog feigns enthusiasm for a clutch of weeds.

'Ivan!' he shouts. 'Git a bladdy move on!'

Loosely following that stupid bus route that doesn't go anywhere useful, I enter the no-man's-land between Canonbury and Highbury, my mind frantically sifting through a multitude of topics – my bank balance, Nirvana, Alan's continued indifference to my plight, Spike Island (why did he have to bring *that* one up?), the ubiquitous Mr Webster, my ubiquitous ex-girlfriend – although my anxiety is beginning to recede thanks to my ferociously marching along. It works every time. The gaunt, alert figure of a fox appears from behind the council block a few hundred metres ahead, then vanishes up that posh tree-lined road I always turn down by mistake when waywardly returning from nights at the Garage. I wince as I pass the school where I vomited after one tequila too many on Alan's thirtieth birthday. I round the corner where I had that huge row with the Ex (I wanted to walk, she wanted to get a cab: a recurring theme) and stride past those silly-looking cafés that precede Highbury Corner, finally shooting straight down the strip of overpriced shops and restaurants that is Upper Street.

Given that I've never been overly attached to this particular thoroughfare, it's remarkable how effectively it hoards memories and unleashes them as I walk, like one of those slow-release vitamin-pill things. That's the problem with living in one corner of a city for too long, I suppose, and this top mile of the main Islington drag is all about (again) The Ex. No wonder she moved to Camberwell. Example: when I look at the Hope and Anchor, I don't see a semi-decent music pub with a creditable punk heritage, I see the place I first met the friend of a friend who joined us for a pint after we'd seen Arab Strap at the Union Chapel. When I see that petrol station on the left, I see the first packet of sandwiches we shared while waiting for a cab to take the two of us and a paralytically drunk Polly home. The King's Head pub is the place I spilled my first pint over her. The Turkish restaurant is where I took her for a date on that first Valentine's Day and my debit card got rejected. The Bull is where I used to listlessly wait for her to finish cackling with her work colleagues on a Thursday evening. Then the cinema, where I realised once and for all that she'd never fancy me as much as she did Ralph Fiennes. The Slug and Lettuce, where I got into that huge argument with a male friend of hers about his method of getting to work (he used to *drive* from Hackney to Willesden every morning; had he never *heard* of the Silverlink train line?) – the argument which finally precipitated The Conversation.

Which I'm not going to bore you with.

As I reach the southern end of the street the memories are older, often of an Islington that no longer exists. The Camden Head pub, once the second-best jukebox in London, now replaced by the questionable music taste of the bar staff. The old pizza restaurant, long since replaced by something trendier, where Alan and I used to do the all-you-can-eat buffet thing for about three quid, scoffing vast amounts of stodgy, nutritionless mush before going to gigs at the Powerhaus. The old tube station, pre-renovation, without ticket barrier, an essential bolthole for every discerning student fare-evader. And then: the Powerhaus itself.

Today, the idea of an impossibly dingy, dirty, sick-smelling indie hole parked squarely on the frontline of Islington's retail paradise is as incongruous as ordering a snakebite in Starbucks, but exist it did, and we fucking loved the place; the scene of some of our crunchiest, scummiest gigs: Extreme Noise Terror, Die Cheerleader, Tad, Cardiacs (I've also heard Alan boast to people that we saw a very early Radiohead show there, which I regret to say is bollocks). It was the perfect alternative venue, a fabulous, feedback-drenched sin bin of head-crushingly loud musical chaos; you could smell the clientele as they rolled across Islington High Street, particularly after the gig, when the cider, beer, sweat and patchouli oil had blended to form a now sadly extinct compound we christened Powergunge, caking the boots, leather jackets and hair of the faithful as they headed home. That the Powerhaus was replaced in the mid-nineties by an All Bar One tells you all you need to know about London's descent into chain-driven consumer nonsense. That the All Bar One subsequently became a branch of the Halifax is where social commentary and I go separate ways.

By this stage in my thoughts I'm standing right opposite our former glory hole, getting my breath back. It's just hit me how knackered I am and how many beers I've had, and considering it's now quarter past one in the morning and I've still not put finger to laptop for the Webster project, I probably ought to start thinking about home. But an unseen force is drawing me across the wide road. I skip across to the central reservation and wait for a half-empty police riot van to pass, its passengers eyeing me suspiciously as I itch the back of my legs. I hurriedly take off my woolly hat and tidy my hair – my typical, feeble knee-jerk attempt at looking innocent – and the van switches on its siren and speeds off in search of real criminals, leaving me to stroll over to our old haunt with its unchanged mock-tudor front. I stare through the sterile windows, now advertising tax-free savings and personal loans rather than appearances by The Fall or Huggy Bear, and wonder if customers ever feel the Ghost of Indie Past as they fill in their deposit slips, whether the staff realise their quiet, carpeted office is exactly the room in which three hundred unwashed lunatics rucked to Crazyhead, spat at The Damned, gaped at Polly Harvey or blissed out to Orbital, or if they know they're interviewing new mortgage customers in the very same space of air from which Wayne Hussey once breathed to serenade his eskimos. It's doubtful.

I linger awhile, not entirely sure what I'm trying to find. Perhaps nothing. I suppose it would be enough to think that, very occasionally, an office junior shifts some file boxes in a back room and wonders what that foul smell is, or speculates the origin of the awful substance clinging to the bottom of the filing cabinet, or asks why his suit always reeks of patchouli oil after working late. Satisfied by this notion, I'm taking a deep breath and turning to go when something odd – no, make that bloody extraordinary – catches my eye.

On an otherwise standard-issue black signpost between the Halifax and Snappy Snaps are the remnants of a sticker: a black, triangular sticker that somehow resisted the efforts of the graffiti removal teams. Although faint, I can still make out an unmistakable red and yellow comic-book-style emblem, formed from the letters A and H; an emblem I first beheld about sixteen years ago, not ten yards from this very spot, emblazoned on the cover of a fanzine entitled *Alternative Heroes*. The geeky bloke enthusiastically peddling the fanzine to the gathering pre-gig crowd was none other than Mr Billy Flushing.

My face is now so close to the signpost I'm practically licking it, but I still can't believe what I'm seeing. When did the Powerhaus close down? 1995? 1996? I'm pretty sure Billy wasn't still doing his fanzine right up until that point, but even if he was, a sticker like this couldn't have remained on a signpost for the eleven years since. Stuff like this gets blasted off almost immediately these days, even in Camden. No, this sticker must have been slapped on recently. What's more, unless there's another oddball out there with a job lot of *Alternative Heroes* promotional stickers, it's Billy himself who's been doing the slapping.

This established, I don't hang about. I turn and run back up the street, frantically hailing a passing bus. I whip out my mobile and call my own number, leaving one of those ridiculous aural notes-to-self as I pelt down the Essex Road, after which I sit down for a moment and ransack my memory.

The Powerhaus gig Billy showed up at with his stack of fanzines was a fan-club-only Thieving Magpies show to launch the single 'Roundpeg Squarehole' in June 1991. By this point our once enthu-siastic friendship had completely evaporated, but I nodded at him outside the venue and strolled over to look at his creation while Alan scoffed and went inside.

I must confess my heart sank when I examined it. Evidently using Billy's brother's stationery resources to the full, *Alternative Heroes* had a glossy cover and proper, newspaper-style pages. Inside, Billy had combined his knowledge of music with his deeper love of comics, creating double-page strips featuring some of the alternative world's current stars: a wacky, *Beano*-style battle between Faith No More and the Red Hot Chili Peppers, a ghostly drama concerning The Cure's

Robert Smith, a seaside caper involving The Wonder Stuff, a sitcom with the Pixies as a dysfunctional American family, and on the front page a swashbuckling adventure story starring all four members of the Thieving Magpies. It was imaginative, original, witty, frequently surreal and decidedly well-constructed. In those terms at least, it was streets ahead of *Vorsprung Durch Peanut* – and Billy, of course, knew it.

'Nice 'zine, Billy,' I offered.

'Thanks!' he replied, neglecting to look me in the eye, instead eagerly rooting out potential punters. He was still wearing his school shirt and trousers but had removed his glasses for the occasion, which must have made life a little tricky. 'Come on, don't be shy!' he yelled, eliciting a cringe from me. '*Alternative Heroes*, only forty pence.'

'Forty pence!' I exclaimed. He was mad. It must have cost at least seventy to produce.

'Opening offer,' he commented.

I flicked through the pages again.

'It's odd though, Billy – aren't these bands a bit too, um . . . *normal* for you?'

'Of course,' he shrugged, 'but business is business.'

Except it wasn't. Although a few people stopped to look, no one was buying; *Alternative Heroes* went straight over everyone's head. In the time I stood next to him I managed to sell four copies of the *Peanut* without even trying. The indie-verse simply wasn't ready for Billy's comic-book/music-press crossover.

'Well, see you in there,' I said after a few minutes.

'Don't be silly!' Billy frowned, his eyes meeting mine for the first time. 'I'm not *going* to the gig. I don't even *like* the Thieving Magpies.'

I made my excuses and shuffled inside.

The final time I saw him was a year later at a pointless, premature school-reunion lunch my parents forced me to attend. Again, the conversation was stilted and we made no move to remain in contact, but I remember thinking he'd become an altogether more confident presence. Tellingly, he spent much of the afternoon chatting to a girl from our year who wouldn't have even acknowledged he belonged to the same species a year previously.

I sit back in my bus seat, strangely calmed by my latest plan. It's always good to occasionally know what you're doing. Soon I'm marching down my own street, past Lance Webster's house, which I acknowledge with a two-fingered salute that wouldn't look out of place in a primary school. I jump down the steps to our flat and burst into the kitchen, where Polly's latest conquest (a tall, curly-haired posh bloke) leaps up and grabs the nearest dishcloth as Polly calmly butters some toast. They are both unavoidably naked.

'Sorry, Clive,' Polly murmurs, while the chap smiles awkwardly – but I am out the other side of the room before further discussion can ensue. Seen it all before anyway.

I barge into my bedroom, open up the almighty, creaking laptop again, jam my finger firmly into the hole where the on button once was and retire for a tactical loo break while the dear old thing boots up. Ten minutes later, I'm excitedly awaiting the results of a Google search. I'm not entirely sure what I'm expecting: a few cursory references to the man perhaps (I've even got a few of my own if you look hard enough), maybe a MySpace page. I'm starting simply with 'Billy Flushing'. What I don't realise is it's the last search I'll need to bother with.

Welcome to **BillyFlushing**.com – home of visual artist, graphic novelist and publisher
Join the mailing list.
www.billyflushing.com/welcome.htm – 3k – Cached – Similar pages – Note this
[more results from www.**billyflushing**.com]

Billy Flushing - Wikipedia, the free encyclopedia
Billy Flushing aka 'RoyaleB', 'Fsycho Bill' (born Watford, England on 23 January 1973) is an internationally recognised

comic artist, graphic novelist and critic. He founded the XCarto . . .

en.wikipedia.org/wiki/**Billy_Flushing** – 43k – <u>Cached</u> – <u>Similar pages</u> – <u>Note this</u>

Billy Flushing

Billy Flushing in my opinion is the king of modern comics. Having read his stuff as RoyaleB I didn't think anyone could beat it, then I discovered he was also Fsycho Bill! Amazing, he . . .

www.graphixchat.com/board/forumdisplay.php?f=42 – 94k – <u>Cached</u> – <u>Similar pages</u> – <u>Note this</u>

<u>Xcarto corporation</u> – **Billy Flushing** <u>CEO</u> <u>founded Xcarto after leaving univ</u> . . .

21/12/2006. Xcarto Webshop Spring Offers 10/1/2007. **Billy Flushing** in Comic Zone Magazine (issue 120) – Fsycho Bill – new hardback retrospective with DVD extra OUT NOW . . .

www.xcarto.com/ – 13k – <u>Cached</u> – <u>Similar pages</u> – <u>Note this</u>

<u>Graphic Novel Art @ Forbidden Planet – The Online Entertainment</u> . . .

Forbidden Planet feature. For the first time, we interview graphic God of our time **Billy** 'RoyaleB' **Flushing** on the eve of his retrospective interactive hardback Fsycho Bi . . .

www.forbiddenplanet.co.uk/ . . .

/Fmag/Features/**Billyflushing**.htm – 19k – <u>Cached</u> – <u>Similar pages</u> – <u>Note this</u>

And that's just the first five.

With a movement straight out of *Fawlty Towers*, I slam the lid of my laptop and wait for a second, then reopen it and look again,

desperately hoping all the references will have magically disappeared.
They haven't. Resisting the temptation to instantly phone Alan, I
delve a little further, first checking Google Images for proof that
this world-beating graphic icon really is my gormless former school-
mate (it is – he wears funky, white space-age spex and his hair is a
bit spiky, but otherwise seems quite unchanged), then reading some
of the articles just to check he hasn't written them all himself (he
hasn't – there are simply dozens of the damn things, in online newspapers, magazines, on the BBC, art-gallery websites, publishing
briefings – the list goes on). In addition to his artistic prowess, the
Xcarto company he founded some ten years back appears to have
acquired most things worth bothering with in the comics world,
providing proof that the embryonic business acumen I suspected all
those years ago grew into something formidable and produced –
most surely – a hefty bank balance. He's had his own exhibition at
the Tate Modern and even warrants a compendious page on the
Internet Movie Database, thanks to an abundance of technical and
artistic-consultant credits, some stretching back as far as 1998, and
a story of his – *Dawn of Zfly* (I mean, really) – being turned into a
2004 Paramount film starring Crispin Glover, Brittany Murphy and
Michael Gambon; the existence of which has somehow *completely*
eluded me.

As my mother would say: *hell's teeth*.

Two questions immediately spring to mind.

Not, you may be surprised to hear, 'how the hell has that total
dweebhead loser boy managed to become such a super-successful,
globally inspirational graphics megabloke?' – which is certainly
the first thing that would emerge from Alan's lips. In fact, I can
totally see how the Billy I knew became the high-achieving eccentric guru who stares at me from his homepage. It was all there
from the very start. All he needed was to *not be at school*. No – the
question I really want an answer to is 'how the hell did I manage
to miss it?' Granted, I pay about as much attention to the ins and

outs of the comics industry as I do the history of agriculture in Lithuania, but you'd think I'd have spotted his (far from common) name at least somewhere.

The other question I'm now pacing up and down my room mumbling to myself is the following: if he's this successful, this busy and this artistically satisfied, what on earth is he doing plastering stickers of his long-forgotten indie fanzine on a signpost outside a former scuzz-rock venue in Islington?

And the immediate explanation my dazed, confused and self-centred brain settles for? That Billy Flushing – wherever he is now – is trying to communicate with *me*.

I click on his website's 'contact' page – annoyingly, it's just one of those mailing-list forms, and there's no actual address. Returning to my original Google search I get myself to the Xcarto website and do the same. There are two addresses – one in New York (but of course) and one in London. A glance at the postcode – EC1V – tells me the London office can't be more than a few streets away from my old work. Who knows, I could have been buying my lunch from the very same Tesco Metro as Billy – when he wasn't having his caviar 'coptered in and carried to his drawing board on a velvet cushion by a team of trained meerkats.

(A quick aside to this fascinating stuff: in all seriousness, I sometimes wish there was a website that could tell you other people's movements throughout their life in relation to yours, so you could type in their name and see a kind of joint route map; how many times have people said, 'Oh, I was at that gig too' or something. With this site you could see how close you actually got; perhaps you were unwittingly waiting next to each other at the bar or some such . . . but then I also wish there was a device that could magically tell you all sorts of random facts and figures about your life, e.g. how many Jaffa Cakes you've eaten, which is the bus you've taken most often, how many times you've been through East Croydon station, which is the person you've had sex with the most. Like a sort of itemised phone bill of existence . . . a universal statistics engine . . . hmm . . .)

The Xcarto site's contact page displays a few email addresses – the standard 'info@' one, a few named entries for the sales and marketing people, but nothing for their exalted CEO. However, I notice the format is pretty standard, 'firstname.surname@' – so, it being too late at night for procrastination, I take a wild stab in the dark and quickly bash out this:

From:	CLIVE BERESFORD(cliveberesford@hotmail.com)
Sent:	27 April 2007 01:57:04
To:	billy.flushing@xcarto.com
Subject:	the geeks shall inherit the earth

Dear Billy

I hope this has reached the correct destination! Blast-from-the-past time. Yes, it really is **that** Clive Beresford. Sorry. Imagine my surprise when I passed the old Powerhaus on Liverpool Road this evening and saw an *Alternative Heroes* sticker on the signpost. Can't imagine it's been there for over a decade, so I figured maybe you'd been feeling nostalgic?

You seem to be one of the few people from school doing something slightly interesting with their lives. Glad to hear it. It's amazing what dull jobs people have ended up with! I've actually lost touch with almost everyone, apart from Alan Potter, who you probably remember. You may shudder at the name, but Ben Simons sent me an email recently (maybe he did the same to you?), which I have to admit I completely ignored. If the photo on his MySpace page is anything to go by, he's exactly the same – slightly over-weight and perpetually angry.

Despite my cynical tone I haven't become some completely
bitter 33-year-old drunken mess. I'm actually quite happy
with life, doing what I want (most of the time). Hope you
are too – it appears so.
Drop me a line if you get a sec – take it easy
Clive

p.s. sorry about Spike Island

Okay, so there's a couple of fibs in there to give it a bit of sparkle.
I refresh my inbox page a couple of times and nothing comes hurtling
back at me saying the email address doesn't exist, so it seems to have
gone somewhere. Well then, we'll see.

Having accomplished this task of dubious benefit, I'm just about
to shut down and finally make a move towards bed when I remember
bloody Webster and this fabled novel I'm meant to have started.
Satan's arse. As I'm meant to be seeing a job agency tomorrow
morning, I really need to have a go at the bloody thing now.

Wearily, I open up a new Word document and – risking a second
encounter with my naked, toast-eating flatmate and her bit of equally
naked posh totty – return to the kitchen to put the kettle on.

ALAN, MY EDITOR

[From the *Sunday Times Magazine*, Sunday 4 May 2025.]

A Life in the Day of GAVIN SMITH

Gavin Smith, 32, has been an inventor since the age of 4. In 2015 he became the youngest scientist selected by NASA to work on the Martian element Quartaneum, which led to the invention of the Universal Statistics Engine (USE) in 2017. He lives in Cambridgeshire with his dog, Ivan.

Ivan wakes me up by licking my face at around 6 a.m. He's been a lot happier since we moved out of London, as have I – the media attention was starting to get on our tits. I make some toast for Ivan (with butter and honey, spoilt son of a bitch, quite literally, ha ha) but just a coffee for me. I've normally got a raging hangover, so I can't think about eating anything until I've had my oxygen hit. I might also plug in for some saline if I'm feeling extra rough. Then I check my emails: the usual boring crap, although there might be something from one of my collaborators in the States. I choose the people I work with extremely carefully – especially since the USE was stolen.

I take Ivan for a quick walk and then it's time to start working. I mainly work in a little back room, just as I've always done. It's cheaper than renting a lab, and it means I don't have to travel or talk to anyone, unless I really want to. Ivan's all the company I need. I've had better conversations with him than with any human being.

People ask me why I started to invent things, and the answer is simple: I wanted to perform a certain task, so I invented the tool I needed to do it. For some reason this came naturally to me. The first thing I invented was an intruder alarm for my bedroom when I was four years old. I made it out of a couple of shoelaces and my sister's old mobile phone. I did it so that my mother would stop going in there and wrecking the bloody place with her so-called 'tidying'.

At around midday I stop and go to the pub to have something to eat. The Prince Albert round the corner, usually – Ivan's allowed in, the landlord is bearable and the regulars leave me alone. I might read the paper if I'm bored, not because I want to know what's going on in the world, but because I find it so hilarious how stupid people are. A newspaper to me is just like one big joke book.

I have a few pints and then it's back to my room. Sometimes I listen to music while I work, depending on how menial my current task is. I'm not really fond of modern music – I'm one of those people who reckon that nothing good's been recorded since about 2007.

I've been working on the same invention since I was 18. Everything I've invented in the meantime has been accidental – or because I needed the money. That's why I invented the USE. I never had any personal interest in it, but I knew it would be lucrative. Which of course it has been – although not for me.

I'll probably crack open the first beer at about three, but I usually carry on working until at least six o'clock, when my mind starts to wander and Ivan begins to get restless. That's when he gets his long walk – perhaps along the disused railway line and across one of the smaller fens, or sometimes just along the river. Ivan doesn't care, there are always new pieces of shit to smell and birds to hassle. Then I grab a take-away from somewhere and head home.

Most of my evenings are spent drinking and flinging stuff around the house for Ivan to chase. Why do I drink so much? Because it helps me forget that I'm human, and that I exist in 2025. That's why I'm trying to build a time machine. One day I'll finish it and fuck off to another dimension, where I'll stay. If those cunts hadn't stolen the USE I'd have enough money to build it by now, but I don't care – I'll do it eventually.

I pass out at around midnight. Hopefully I'll have managed to get myself into bed by then, but it's not unusual for me to wake up anywhere in the house – sometimes even the garden. It doesn't matter, I sleep anywhere. I never dream.

Alan does his best sceptical belch-scoff, casts the sheaf of papers aside and takes a sip of his organic coffee.

'What do you think?' I ask.

'What do *I* think?'

'No,' I reply, rolling my eyes. 'All the other people I'm currently talking to.'

'I don't know?' he shrugs.

'Is that a question or a statement?'

'Both, I guess. I mean, I'm not really sure what you want me to say, Clive. You know I never read, for a start.'

'Sure, but that doesn't matter. Did you enjoy it?'

'Um . . . yeah?'

'What did you think of the character?'

'Um . . .'

He looks frantically around the café, as if he's going to see the word he's looking for emblazoned on one of the posters. Then he gives up and takes a bite of his vegan brownie.

'Did you like him?'

'Er . . . he's a bit . . . um . . . odd.'

'Odd, yes,' I nod. Adjective. Houston, we have an adjective. I pop the last piece of free-range garlic and birdseed flapjack into my mouth and sit back, hoping for further commentary. Instead, he fiddles with his tie and looks at his watch.

'Gotta go in a sec.'

'Okay . . . but did anything else strike you? I mean, did you think it was . . . you know . . . funny?'

'Yeah, it was funny.'

Christ on a bike.

'Okay – well, thanks for all of that, Alan. This is what I'm going to show him when he appears anyway. It should be enough, I guess.'

'Enough . . . yeah, I s'pose.'

Amazing how such a high-flying, over-achieving entrepreneur can be so alarmingly useless sometimes. He stands to leave, then sighs.

'Sorry I haven't been much help, man. I'm finding it all a bit strange really.'

'Strange?'

He frowns.

'Clive, you're about to meet our biggest teenage musical hero for coffee, pretend you don't know who he really is while you show him highlights from a book you haven't written, after being warned by his bodyguards about your stalking, which you're also going to pretend hasn't happened.'

I can't resist raising my eyes in mock astonishment.

'And what, may I ask, is so strange about that?'

'Nutter,' Alan concludes, striding off.

'Vorsprung Durch Peanut,' I shout after him.

'Up yours.'

As he vanishes through the door I grab my handiwork for a final study. But half a minute later, he is back.

'Hey man, I've just thought of something.'

'What?'

'Are you gonna give him this stuff to keep?'

'Might do. Dunno.'

'There's no copyright notice on there.'

'Eh?'

'You can't give it to him unless it's got a copyright notice. He might try to nick it.'

'Oh, I don't really think that he . . .'

'Clive, at least follow this one piece of advice on a subject I *do* know something about,' he instructs, taking a pen from his bag. 'Just write "copyright, two thousand and seven, Clive Beresford".'

'Okay, I will.'

'Well, do it now,' he commands, pushing his biro at me.

'Uh, I'll do it when you've gone.'

'Why? He'll be here any minute.'

'Uh, I need the loo.'

'Well, fuck it, don't bother,' he gruffs, stomping off again. 'If your stuff gets pinched I don't give a toss.'

I wait until he's out of sight, fish my own pen out of my pocket and quickly scrawl 'Copyright © 2007 Alan Potter' on each of the pages.

Lance Webster – sorry, fuck – *Geoff* Webster slurps his apple and ginger herbal tea and carefully reads my paltry creation. I'm trying not to watch him, but it's nigh-on impossible. Particularly because (by accident, he alleges) I have nothing of his to read. He's had a haircut since we last met, and he's wearing black-rimmed reading glasses and a dark grey polo-necked sweater. None of which helps to dispel the unsettling realisation that he looks slightly like Matthew Broderick. Claiming to have eaten nothing today (it's about quarter past three), he's ordered the vegetarian all-day breakfast (organic duck eggs, dolphin-friendly mushrooms, plywood and nutmeg sausage), which hasn't yet arrived, and toast, which has. He clearly knows the place, not needing to look at the menu, addressing the female proprietor (perhaps of Dutch origin?) as 'Marzy'.

'This is seriously good stuff,' he frowns.

'Thanks,' I mumble, assuming he's talking about my writing and not his toast.

'You immediately get a sense of the character.'

'I'm glad about that.'

He reads on. I sip my third coffee – which is starting to make me feel sick – and wait for him to finish, but once he does (he reads the 'I never dream' bit out loud, with a laugh) he shuffles the papers and starts all over again. When he reaches the second page he adjusts his seating position and kicks his legs out so they rest heavily against mine. I freeze, then cough, and he looks up.

'That line "a newspaper to me is just like one big joke book" is awesome,' he comments, smiling. 'Funny thing is, I actually know people like that.' Then his head goes back down and he continues reading. There's nothing frivolous or ambiguous in the way he spoke, so I move my legs away from his and try to forget about it.

Then his breakfast arrives. To my carnivorous eyes it looks as appetising as a plate of wooden clothes pegs, a load of fibre in search of a hefty percentage of obliging porker, but Webster is close to ecstasy. I have more empathy with the large splattering of ketchup he administers, and things really start to look more like Christmas when he generously covers his toast with butter and asks the waitress for a black coffee. Suddenly, Lance is back again.

'Hope you don't mind,' he grins, tucking in. 'Had a really late one last night. I've got a friend in New Zealand and we were Skype-ing 'til about four, then I had these remixes to finish off.'

'Remixes?' I enquire, treading carefully.

'Yeah, I've got a little studio in the flat. I do a bit of stuff for people, radio-edits and so on.'

Strange. I didn't know that. I wonder what name he uses?

'Never really lost that whole musician's nocturnal-timetable thing . . . you an early riser?'

I give him a brief but nonetheless uninteresting description of my sleeping habits while he continues to shovel nosh into his mouth, and then, astonishingly, his legs come careering back over to my side of the table again, booting mine out the way. I pause mid-sentence and frown at him. His eyes rise above his glasses from a cruelty-free tomato.

'You okay?' he asks.

'Um . . . yeah,' I murmur, shrug and continue. Amazing. I honestly don't think he's aware of it.

We chatter on about this and that while he puts away his breakfast. The fact that he's looking about as different as it's possible to look from the long-haired alternative rock star I used to worship is helping me immensely to maintain my composure, but that doesn't stop it from being pretty damn odd. In a way, we're both pretending we know each other more than we do, while at the same time I'm pretending I know him less than I do. If you follow. Now I know what one of those double agents feels like. I'm also getting increasingly cross that he didn't bring any of his writing with him, for it means the discussion is focused almost entirely on me, which is at best boring, at worst damn difficult.

'Were you always good at writing, then?'

'Um, well . . . English was my best subject at school.'

'But did you try to get stuff published? Like short stories in magazines, or anything like that?'

'Um . . . not exactly. I really kept stuff to myself.'

He nods vigorously.

'Confidence issues. Yeah, I had that. Never thought anyone would care about my silly little tales when there was other shit going on in the world.'

'But . . . the um . . . with your music thing. I mean, you'd've had to . . .'

He makes a face like he's just sat on a drawing pin.

'Yeah, but that's different. So, did you carry on writing through your twenties?'

And that's how the afternoon proceeds. He's delighted to hear about me, and relatively comfortable talking about himself in the strict context of writing these 'funny stories' (one of a few excessively quaint phrases he employs), but all my tentative turns down the musical avenue end abruptly in a series of cul-de-sacs. After a while I stop bothering and just try to keep him talking about anything, in the hope some nuggets will drop out.

'What made you think of having characters with superpowers?'

'They're not really superpowers,' he states. 'It's one particular power, telekinesis.'

'Why that?'

'It's the most inconspicuous one. If you find one day you're able to fly, everyone's gonna see you and notice it – same with super-strength. With telekinesis, particularly this long-range one they've all got, they're not necessarily gonna be found out. You could stand in a crowd and control, say, a flying car, but as everyone's gonna be watching it, what's to say you're the one doing it? I reckon there's more comic potential. Invisibility didn't seem as much fun. Mind-reading's cool but a bit too eerie. I didn't want it to be eerie, like some scary horror book or graphic novel.'

'You don't like graphic novels.'

He shakes his head vigorously, munching his last mouthful of toast.

'Me neither,' I concur, the spectre of Billy Flushing's gurning mug momentarily appearing.

'So why does your guy need to be such a pisshead?' he asks, scooping up and scanning my papers again.

Ah. A nugget could be approaching. I take a large gulp of coffee and begin slowly.

'Well . . . partly because I thought it'd be amusing to have an inventor who's always drunk, and either invents things that don't work, or work differently to how they're meant to. I once went to these brandy cellars in France. The spiders down there are actually drunk on the booze fumes so they build these crazy spiderwebs. Maybe he'd be the inventor equivalent of that . . . perhaps he builds a time machine that ends up being a nuclear vacuum cleaner or something, I dunno.'

'Wouldn't that be funnier if it was drugs?'

'Yeah, but . . . drugs don't really fit with him being a pissed old misanthropic bastard. I quite like him just hating the world and drinking himself into a void every night.'

'Your kind of character?'

'Um . . . yeah,' I reply, not too sure what he's driving at.

'Do you drink a lot?'

Time for a strategic fib.

'No. I used to, but then it started affecting my life too much . . . it almost messed things up for me at work.'

'And then they sacked you anyway,' he laughs.

'Yeah . . . but it used to be pretty bad. I'd come back from lunch drunk and so on. What, um . . . what about you?'

'Nah,' he frowns. 'I like a pint from time to time, but my hard-drinking days are long gone.'

'You used to drink, um, hard?'

Then his fucking mobile phone rings. Damn. Two more questions and we'd have been at the Aylesbury Festival, I'm sure of it. He chats for a minute (some dull talk about the remixes), then dashes off to the loo. Just to make sure I can't repeat my question when he returns, he brings Marzy over to our table, smilingly introduces her as 'my caterer' and me as 'Alan, my editor'. Two minutes of mindless banter follow, during which I grin like a moron and marvel at how strange it is to be addressed by a name that isn't my own. By the time we're alone again my nugget has long since disappeared.

'So, what exactly is this Universal Statistics Engine?' he beams, glugging the remnants of his coffee.

And on it goes, me babbling more claptrap about stupid, non-existent Gavin Smith and his stupid, non-existent invention; Webster asking more and more but revealing less and less, then ordering some cake and another coffee (I settle for a gluten-free lemonade, but in truth I'm having murderous thoughts about a beer), frequently parking his damn legs where mine are, and often agreeing so enthusiastically with all my useless, dreamed-up-on-the-spot philosophies about writing that organic cake crumbs come flying out of his mouth in my direction.

Finally, when I'm really beginning to wish I hadn't bothered and start to wonder what imaginary pressing engagement I could hurry off to, he sits back, smiles in a businesslike manner and exhales.

'Well, okay,' he nods. 'I really enjoyed that, Alan. How about another one of these next week? And I promise, I will *not* forget to bring my stuff this time.'

It's only then that it hits me. This has actually been an interview. No, an audition. For the role of Lord Highest Looker-at-Writing-Material to Grand Emperor Webster. And I appear to have got the part.

Great.

YOU CAN'T JUST WANDER AROUND WITH A DRUNKEN GRIN ON YOUR FACE

[From Geoff Webster's writing ideas notebook.]

SAINSBURY SID

'Oh, drat it!'

Sid the fly sighed and moved quietly around the milk bottles and yoghurt. Here he was, at ten o'clock, shut in Sainsbury's. This was all he needed. He was just flying at full pelt towards the door when the manager closed and locked it. Sid was shut in, left for a whole night to ramble among the Fairy Liquid bottles and the oven-ready chickens. But hang on! This thought hadn't yet occurred to him.

'Food!' exclaimed Sid excitedly.

He pulled himself together, took off from the yoghurt pot and flew up to the roof of the supermarket. There he could see the full scale of his lucky find. He looked at the signs. Biscuits. Crisps. Cakes. Fruit. Delicatessen. Fly swats. Fly swats? He had a sudden moment of panic, then he thought: hang on! There was nobody there to use them. Suddenly, with a burst of excitement, he dived like a plane and soared into a packet of Dairylea.

'Delicious!'

He had a few huge bites and moved onto the finer taste of a packet of French Brie. This was the life! He flew back up to the ceiling and looked at more signs. Meat. Frozen vegetables. Bags of soup. Off-licence. Then he took a look behind him, across the sea of Persil Automatic. What a huge shop! As he looked at all the words, one of them hit him smack across the eyes and stayed there for five seconds before he could see normally again.

HONEY.

He shot like Concorde towards the Jam and Chutney section and rammed straight into a jar of honey with a paper lid. There he was, slurping and gulping his way through a huge pot of the sweet, sticky, glorious gunk.

After a while, he got tired and squeezed his way out through the hole and flew in the direction of the fresh-bread counter. But he could only get as far as the cash registers, and then flopped out; tired, full, but happy.

At about five o'clock in the morning Sid woke up, but not naturally. A baker had come in to make fresh bread for the day's customers. Sid quickly rose from the cash register and flew as quietly as he could towards the bread section to get a better look. But the baker instantly heard Sid buzzing around and, to Sid's horror, walked over to the fly-swat counter! Without further ado, Sid soared high into the air and zoomed over to the other end of the shop, far away from the fly-swat-waving baker. He spotted the pot of honey he had opened the night before, swooped down and soared into his breakfast.

He was just about to leave the pot when he saw the huge face of the baker through the glass! But hang on! Sid had an idea. Where the baker had come in, he must go out. He shot out of the jar, making another hole, and zoomed towards the bakery, where he saw an open door. Just as the baker was about to smash down the fly swat, Sid flew out into the morning air.

'Phew!' he gasped, heading towards his nest in the gutter of the train station. But he would be back soon, for some more of that delicious food.

I stare at the lined page for a few moments longer. It's not the first time in my life I've had no idea what to say. But it is, perhaps, the first time I've had a grinning, former hero of mine merely two feet away, his face practically bursting off its hinges in anticipation of my considered opinion. I've got, ooh, probably four more seconds to think of an opening comment, so I buy myself an extra two by taking a large gulp of tea. This, unfortunately, is the wrong thing to do.

'You didn't like it,' Webster moans.

Shit. Now I have to do *double-strength* lying.

'No!' I begin. 'No, not at all. It's . . . sorry, it's just not, um . . . not what I was expecting.'

'What were you expecting?'

'Well, a . . . for a start, something for . . .'

He frowns. Time's up.

'I didn't think it was going be a children's story,' I admit.

He frowns some more. Oh God. Please say it *is* meant to be a children's story.

'I love children's stories,' he mutters at last, in a tone an East

End gangster might use to describe a favourite cuddly toy. 'Roald Dahl, Enid Blyton, Michael Bond.'

'Right.'

'Penelope Lively, Astrid Lindgren.'

I'm completely lost, and my face must be saying it rather loudly.

'Pippi Longstocking,' he continues.

'Blimey, some of these pen names,' I smile desperately.

'No, that's a character – one of Astrid Lindgren's characters.'

'Ah.' Glad he cleared that one up for me.

'Jill Murphy, Helen Cresswell.'

'JK Rowling?' I suggest hopefully.

'Not my cup of tea,' he shrugs. 'Norman Hunter?'

'Sorry . . . who?'

'You know . . . Professor Branestawm?'

'Oh yeah, him! Fantastic!'

'Then you must also like Spike Milligan?'

'Yes!' I bark. 'Genius!'

I'm so relieved, I bang my mug down and tea escapes all over the table. Everyone in the café looks round and Marzy comes running over with a cloth.

'Exciting stuff, this editing process,' Webster quips as she wipes up the mess. He smiles at her, and for the first time I see a drop of the rock-star charisma that must have worked wonders with the ladies back in the day. Marzy goes all gooey for a second and it strikes me she may be doing more for him than just making his lunch.

'Thanks . . . sorry,' I mumble uselessly.

'Not a problem, Alan,' Marzy replies, departing. Ugh! I'm sure people don't remember my name so readily when I'm using the real one. Perhaps 'Clive' is eminently forgettable.

'Anyway,' Webster resumes, 'for some reason I've been reading nothing but children's stories lately. And when I wrote the other thing – the one about the people with the power – one of the publishers said it might actually make a cracking children's book. So I thought I'd have a go at a kid's yarn.'

'Why not just make that other one into a . . . um . . . a kid's thing?'

'Wanted to do something new.'

'Okay,' I nod. 'Well, in that case, it's . . .'

'Go on. You can be honest. That's what we're here for.'

So I launch into a timid examination of his piece, concentrating heavily on the few bits I thought were good ('slurping and gulping his way through a huge pot of the sweet, sticky, glorious gunk'; 'across the sea of Persil Automatic'), and some harmless criticism about repeating words too often. I steer well clear of my true thoughts, i.e. that it's as exciting as a maths lesson and would bore the bib off any self-respecting child within three sentences. My jaw is already hurting from all the fake smiling, and the temptation to blurt out, 'Fuck all this, let's talk about rock!' is daunting.

'Oh, and of course – it'll be accompanied by illustrations,' Webster declares, fishing around in his bag. 'Sorry, I should have shown you these already. One of my friends has done some mock-ups.'

He passes over some decent pencil sketches of a smiling housefly in various states of honey-related bliss, and a fly-swat-brandishing baker who bears more than a passing resemblance to a career-peak Webster himself, goatee and all.

'Wow, these are great!' I enthuse. 'It'll make *so* much more sense with pictures.'

Webster glares at me.

'Better than the story, then, huh?'

'Well, er . . .'

'Come on, Alan. It's obvious you don't like it. There's no point in us sitting here unless you tell me why.'

'Uh . . . well, it's just not really my thing . . . it's a little bit . . . um . . .'

There's the glimmer of a smile on his face and it occurs to me he's actually enjoying making me squirm.

'A little bit what?'

'Unbelievable.'

'What, a fly buzzing round a supermarket eating food is unbelievable?'

'No, but . . . you know, the things he thinks, and the fact that he's able to read . . .'

Webster almost spits his coffee out with incredulity.

'It's for kids! It's *make-believe!*'

'And there's a whole section of the shop devoted to fly swats.'

'It's supposed to be funny!'

'And who says "drat it!" these days?'

'Yeah, well, you may have a point there,' he concedes, grabbing his notebook and scribbling in the margin.

'And is "hang on" meant to be his catchphrase?'

'Hang on?'

'Yeah. He says "hang on" about six times.'

'Three times,' corrects Webster.

'Well, maybe he should say it more often – turn it into a catchphrase.'

'Okay,' he shrugs, jotting it down. 'Fair enough. [BBC announcer voice] "*Hang on, with Sid the fly.*" Anything else? You see – this is more like it!'

'Right,' I reply dubiously. 'Um . . . well, there's heaps of product placement – Dairylea, Persil, Sainsbury's of course . . .'

'Which could be an advantage.'

'What, get some of them on board?'

'Yeah,' he smiles craftily. 'In fact, my illustrator knows some of the Sainsbury's marketing team – they're interested in taking a look.'

'Blimey.'

'Ha,' Webster snaps. 'Gonna start taking it seriously now?'

I pick up the notebook again. This potential interest seems to be nothing to do with his being Lance Webster, so maybe he's genuinely got something. I still think it's bollocks, though. And I can't imagine Sainsbury's wanting to advertise that their shops are crawling with insects.

'Um . . . Concorde doesn't exist any more,' I volunteer, spotting another glitch. Webster waves this away.

'Doesn't matter. Kids still know what it is.'

I sigh and have a final scan, running out of straws to clutch at.

'I guess you're really not into kids' stuff.'

'Not really,' I admit, 'not since I was . . . you know.'

'A kid?'

'Yeah.'

'Not enough beer involved, perhaps?'

'I'm sorry?'

'Ever think about having kids?'

Uh-oh. Here comes his 'life coach' act again.

'Well, I probably would do, but . . .'

'I understand. There's an essential ingredient missing.'

'Yup.'

'Did you enjoy your own childhood?'

Who is he now? Freud?

'Yeah, well enough,' I grumble. 'You?'

Suddenly the café has gone very quiet, and I'm certain the five or so people present, Marzy included, are hanging on our every word. How I long to be elsewhere.

'Tell you what,' says Webster. 'Are you doing anything tomorrow afternoon?'

'Saturday?' I reply, mentally flicking through my packed diary. 'Not a lot. Why?'

*   *   *

One thing that can be said for all this: at least it gives Alan (the real one) a kick up the arse. I'm on the bus when he rings me, about halfway down Mare Street.

'Clive-ist!'

This is Alan's new thing, putting '-ist' on the end of everything. Much like a few years ago when he added '-ster' to everyone's name: I became 'the Clivester', Polly 'the Pollster'. For a short time Liz was 'the wifester', which was where the craze abruptly met its end.

'Meet me for a jar!' he trumpets. 'Liz went to her mum's for the avo with Jocasta – I got let off 'cos of my sore throat.'

'I can't,' I tell him, reluctant to go into too much detail.

'What you up to?'

'I'm meeting someone.'

'Who?'

'Just someone.'

'You're meeting Webster *again*? Didn't you meet him yesterday?'

'Yeah.'

'Aren't you guys getting a little friendly?'

'Piss off. It's actually all getting a bit annoying. He's taking me on a "mystery tour". Says he wants to reacquaint me with my childhood.'

'Wow. Can I come?'

'No.'

The line goes a little quiet; when Alan speaks again his voice has lost its edge of mockery.

'What's he like?'

'Alan, I can't really talk about this when I'm on the bus. I'll meet you later if you like.'

'How long you gonna be?'

'Dunno. Depends what he's got in mind.'

'It must be quite cool to hang out with him, though?'

I groan, and take a quick look round the bus to see who's listening.

No one looks remotely interested, but I turn back and lower my voice to just above a whisper.

'He is cool to hang out with – as long as you can stand the way he continually asks you probing questions about your life, kicks his legs over to your side of the table, keeps banging on about children's books, eats the most boring food known to man, never suggests meeting in a pub . . .'

'Why don't you suggest it, then?'

'He says he's on the wagon at the moment. I've also got to keep up the act of not knowing virtually everything there is to know about his life and career, and not having been his biggest fan for the past seventeen years, and not even knowing very much about bloody music at all.'

'You seem to be managing okay so far, man.'

'Yeah, but it's bloody hard work! I feel so . . . suppressed when I'm talking to him. I'm not me. I trip over my words. My face aches from this perpetual grin. I spilt my tea . . .'

'Well, that does sound a little bit like you.'

'And I keep wanting to say stuff about his songs. He . . . when . . .' – I lower my voice still further – 'when we were paying in the caff yesterday he handed me a fiver and said, "There's my contribution," and I swear I was within fucking *molecules* of saying—'

'"... *to this pretend revolution*"?'

'Yeah.'

'Fair enough, man, but look . . . just think, you're in the presence of the bloke who gave you all that stuff. He got you through some tough times . . .'

'Oh, please.'

'He did! I don't mean to be cheesy, man, but this guy wrote the soundtrack to your fucking youth . . . and he genuinely wants to hang out with you!'

'Well, I can't think why.'

'Well, whatever! The fact is, he does. Just try and enjoy it for what it is. Be a bit grateful.'

'Uh.'

'And . . . honestly, man, if the opportunity arises . . . I wouldn't mind saying hello.'

'Ah! I see.'

'Yeah, well. Like I said, if the opportunity arises.'

'Right. I'll keep you posted.'

'Have a good one. Later.'

'Yeah.'

I've been instructed to meet him outside Bethnal Green tube station, although as it turns out neither of us arrives by tube. I've been waiting a couple of minutes on the busy corner of Roman Road when a black cab pulls up, from which Webster leaps, again suggesting the reserve accounts haven't completely dwindled.

'Morning!' he beams. It is two o'clock.

'Hi,' I wave, receiving that day's frisson at the appearance of my companion. He's looking more like Lance than ever – jeans, chunky trainers, a dark-blue suit jacket and shades. His hair even looks relatively funky. He pays the driver then gives my hand a squeeze.

'Let's go back in time,' he announces, in a deep-throated American accent.

'Sorry?'

'Oh, cheer up you miserable fucker!' he yells, slapping my back. 'Christ, dunno why I bother.' He propels me briskly up the street, runs up the steps to a large, red, factory-looking building on the right, bursts through the double doors and two seconds later I find myself inside the Museum of Childhood.

'Now,' he informs me, 'this is just about the best fucking thing in London.'

From that point onwards, my presence is purely incidental.

Webster, with an enthusiasm more animated than *anything* I ever saw him do onstage, is truly besotted with the place. He bounds around, from toy exhibit to doll's house, from antique pram to puppet show, whooping with joyous recognition ('Oh, man! My neighbour had one of these! I stole it one weekend and busted it. Got grounded for a month'), sobbing with painful memories ('My first girlfriend had this doll . . . when she moved away she gave me its cardigan to remember her by . . . I was heart-broken . . . was only five'), pointing out vintage remote-control cars and video games to any hapless kids that pass ('You see this? It was brilliant. You could programme it to go anywhere, up stairs, the works. Better than your "wee" or whatever it's called') and almost, before I step in and calm him down, jumps into the indoor sandpit with a collection of toddlers. While fairly enter-taining in itself, the downside of this absurd behaviour is that I can't, as I had hoped, furtively try to spot if anyone recognises him, because just about everyone in the building is gaping at him anyway.

Compared with Webster's larking about, the actual contents of the museum are of mild interest to me: the train set is pretty cool, some of the old video games raise a smile (*Astro Wars!*), but the Scalextric and Lego collections are underwhelming and I reckon it's a bit of a swizz that you can't actually play with most of the stuff. After half an hour I'm starting to eye the downstairs coffee bar hopefully – until I spy something out the corner of my eye and proceed to make a *total* tit of myself.

'Alan! Alan, man! You okay?'

What's come over me is anyone's guess. I'm standing staring through one of the glass cases, sobbing uncontrollably. I can count the number of times I've cried in the last decade on one finger, so it's really a rather bizarre sensation, made even stranger by the man comforting me – who is, funnily enough, the bloke responsible for me crying the previous time.

'Alan, dude! Shit, what's the matter? Can I get you anything?'

I feel like saying, 'For a start, you can stop calling me Alan' – but stop myself.

'No, no, I'm fine,' I splutter. 'Thanks.'

'Jesus, man,' he laughs, 'you should've just told me you were bored and wanted a coffee, no need to do this!'

I break into a smile. 'You know . . . actually, a cup of tea would be great.'

We descend the stairs and Webster sits me down at one of the large tables. He dashes off while I wipe my eyes and continue to feel pretty bloody silly. A minute later he returns with a pot of tea and two pieces of cake.

'Bloody hell, I'm sorry,' I tell him. 'No idea where that came from.'

'No worries,' he replies. 'This place tends to bring odd emotions out.'

'It was the toy.'

'Well, I'm pleased to hear that. I'd be slightly concerned if you were crying because of the design of the carpet.'

'It was my dad's favourite toy.'

'Right,' he nods solemnly. 'Your dad is . . .'

'Oh, no!' I laugh, catching his drift. 'He's alive and well and living in Elstree.'

'Well, we can't have everything.'

'Ha. It's just . . . oh, it's so stupid.'

'No, not at all. Please carry on. That is, if you want to.'

'Yeah . . . well, that wind-up Pinocchio-on-a-donkey, he had it since he was a kid and . . . well, my dad wasn't really much fun when we were kids. He worked loads, came home late. He was very much a "kids should be in bed already so I can have my sherry in peace" kind of guy . . . not unpleasant at all, just . . . I dunno . . . distant . . .'

'Got it.'

'And when I was about eight, I was a right little brat . . .'

'As we all were.'

'Yeah, I s'pose . . . but I was really stressing my mum out this one weekend, wanting this, wanting that, arguing with my sister and stuff . . . I dunno what happened, my mum probably had a word with my dad and told him to try and chill me out or something . . . He came into my bedroom with this toy. He'd never done anything like this before. He knelt down and said something like "Well, son, here's a toy I had when I was a boy," and he showed me how it worked – and bless his cotton socks, it's a toy for four-year-olds probably, but it obviously meant loads to him . . . but all I could fucking say was, "Dad, it's rubbish! It's wooden and crap and . . ." – I dunno, probably that it hadn't got any Space Invaders on it or something . . . and he just looked so heartbroken and picked up his toy and stomped off out the room . . . He never tried to do anything like that again . . . I can't help thinking he was never really arsed with trying to get close to me after that, he'd reached out to me once and I basically told him to fuck off . . .'

Poor old Webster is just gazing down into his tea, probably doesn't know where the hell to look.

'Anyway,' I conclude, 'that was his toy up there.'

Webster does a bit more of his solemn nodding, then:

'I understand . . . wish I could help, y'know? But the truth is we must've all done stuff to our folks that we regret.'

'You have, then?'

'You're kidding, aren't you?' he gasps. 'Come on, mate, I was a pop star. None of my family wanted to be anywhere near me for the best part of ten years, I was such a stuck-up, inconsiderate wanker.'

'Really?'

'Of course! I was a total knob.'

I keep quiet, hoping he'll elaborate. Unfortunately, he doesn't.

'No,' he sighs, 'the only thing we can do is just hope they

forgive, or forget. Preferably both. And for you – to be honest I wouldn't worry about it. If you don't mind my saying so, your old man sounds exactly like mine was: well-meaning, responsible and respectable, but totally set in his ways. Not changing for no one. He probably put that toy straight back in its cupboard and hasn't given the incident a second's thought since.'

I study my cake and think this over. Then I think about Webster's dad. He died of cancer in the late nineties: another blow in what must have been a chain of nightmares for Lance. Or Geoff. Or whoever.

We're silent for a good half a minute. A group of French people on the next table suddenly erupt with laughter at something. Makes me feel even worse, being this picture of misery in a such a fun-oriented place.

'God, this is ridiculous,' I sigh, breaking off a piece of cake. 'What a way for you to spend your Saturday afternoon.'

'Hey,' he counters, 'I'm the one who suggested it. And don't forget, my idea was to put you back in touch with your childhood – so, in fact, I've *completely* succeeded.'

'That's right. You've over-performed!'

We laugh for a moment, then Webster ruins it by getting serious again.

'But it's good to feel these things, y'know, get 'em out there in the open. Don't you feel a little bit better?'

'Not really.'

He frowns and looks straight at my forehead in his customary way. I'm kind of used to it now. But suddenly his eyebrows shoot up again.

'Hang on a sec! I've got an idea.'

He leaps up and skips over to the French table whom he addresses in perfect-sounding French, prompting much surprised laughter and delighted smiles. One of the girls hands him their copy of *Time Out*. He glances at his watch and flicks through the magazine for a second, then hands it back, accompanied by yet more francophone witticisms and eyelash-fluttering. The man really is a charm machine.

Eventually he returns to boring old me.

'One of my favourite artists has a new exhibition nearby,' he announces. 'D'you fancy popping in? The works are to do with music, apparently – which I know you're not that keen on – but it's bound to cheer you up 'cos it won't remind you of anything!'

Oh joy. More lying. My favourite.

By the end of the next hour, I've told so many lies that it's actually starting to affect my digestive system. I lurch into the loo of the little gallery, pale-faced and breaking into an unhealthy sweat, bolt the door and settle myself on the crapper, where I bury my head between my legs and try to breathe evenly. This is all getting far too much for me: first an emotional breakdown in a public museum, combined now with this ridiculous performance of perpetual musical ignorance, which I'm certain Webster is seeing through like cling film. I've had enough of being someone I'm not, pretending to know nothing about the thing I love most. I feel an unadulterated charlatan with this watery, featureless persona I've adopted, and I'm minutes away from jacking the whole thing in, coming out of the men's room with my hands up: 'Hey, Lance – it was fun while it lasted, tell your roadies I said hi . . . Oh, and by the way, that saxophone part at the end of "Bad Little Secret" *sucks*.'

When Webster told me the exhibition was 'to do with music', it could have meant *anything*: it could have been a sound installation featuring recordings of an assortment of buskers from Vancouver, or a collection of classical composers' portraits done in the style of Banksy, or an exploration of the design similarities between Scottish bagpipes and Mongolian nose-flutes. But no. It was none of those things, nor the several billion other things it might have been. It was, in fact – ta-daaa! – seven multicoloured, densely decorated 'shrines', each one complete with garlands, effigies, trinkets, various memorabilia, and the idol itself: an oil painting of a deceased, usually alternative, pop star.

Each of these wretched items presented a new and woefully dicey challenge for me. It ended up like playing some crazy reverse pub quiz where you try to get as many questions wrong as possible, but are then required to justify why you don't know the correct answer. To make matters sizeably worse, Webster insisted on helpfully guiding me round the place, making sure I appreciated the finer points of each work, and, of course, who the featured musical icon was. In truth, I probably massively overdid it, as the majority have wormed their way into mainstream popular culture anyway – but I had my reasons, which I present for your inspection as follows:

1.   Ian Curtis (teacups, return train tickets to Macclesfield, a couple of old radios, a seven-inch of 'Transmission' broken in two, etc.). I suppose this was the 'flagship' work of the exhibition, positioned right by the desk at the entrance. In retrospect it would have been totally safe for me to know who this was, but Webster caught me off guard by asking, 'You heard of this guy?' – and I actually thought he was referring to the artist, so I said no, heralding the first of Webster's unbearably playpen descriptions ('Well, at the end of the seventies, there was a band called Joy Division' – oh, the humiliation!)

2.   Kurt Cobain (cut-up plaid shirts, broken guitar strings, dollar bills on hooks, etc.). A no-brainer, you might say. But the bastard has based his painting on that photo session from summer '92, when a short-haired Cobain had taken to wearing black-rimmed glasses, thus rendering himself near-unrecognisable to anyone but a music-press reader, so I mumbled some twaddle about him 'ringing a bell'. 'It's Kurt Cobain!' exclaimed

Webster, with a hint of exasperation. 'Met him once, nice bloke,' he added breezily, as if discussing Dennis Waterman.

3. Syd Barrett. Remembering his appearance in the dream I had at the beginning of this sorry saga, I greeted this 'shrine' with a gasp – which Webster interpreted as appreciation of the predictable psychedelic bunting which accompanied the image of the man. 'Amazing, isn't it?' he sighed, and thankfully moved on to the next piece without further enquiry.

4. Richey Manic (ripped-up pages from philosophy readers, various *Holy Bible*-era military-chic clothing items, '4 REAL' carved in red across the top of his portrait, etc.). 'Ah, the odd one out,' smiled Webster as he approached. 'Why's that?' replied bonehead over here without really thinking properly, prompting yet another punchable explanation: 'Well, there's a rock band from Wales called the Manic Street Preachers, and before they became really popular they had a fourth member called Richey, who disappeared one day.' Argghh! The frustration! Perhaps he *should* write children's books.

5. Nick Drake (five large, pressed autumn leaves, various cannabis-related paraphernalia, a sepia-tinted photograph of a – presumably fruit – tree, etc.). Too obscure, I calculated, for a non-music enthusiast to know about; then I remembered that Webster is a massive fan. Too late. The ensuing rundown of facts I was already aware of took almost ten minutes, during which the only words I spoke were 'oh, right' and 'ah'. Just two more to go, thank God.

6. Layne Staley shouldn't really have been a problem. It would be perfectly possible for even the most respectable

music fan to be stumped by this shade-wearing, pink-haired B-list grunge-rocker, although by now I was so bored of saying no that I was tempted to say yes, giving some improvised explanation that an ex-girlfriend ran the UK branch of the Alice in Chains fanclub or something – but my brain was numb, I needed water and the rather gory syringe-related decoration had already kick-started my descent into the land of nausea.

7. Michael Hutchence. Another no-brainer; but again, greeted by this lurid concoction of blond wigs, empty cans of Victoria beer and photos of the Charles Bridge in Prague (all surrounded, pretty tastelessly I thought, by a thick leather belt), I was tempted to go against the grain and shake my head again. Sense prevailed, however. 'Oh, that's the bloke from INXS,' I chirped, to a frown from Webster. 'Can't believe he's the only one you knew,' he despaired. 'Just going to the toilet,' I replied.

So here I am. I must confess, I really have no idea how this ridiculous afternoon is going to finish. I'm sorely tempted to either tell all and bugger the consequences, or try to climb out this back window and leg it. There'd be little lost from doing that, and not much chance of comeback from Webster – he doesn't even have my phone number. But after coughing up a small amount of bile, I summon my final reserves of patience and strength, and stride back into the main room where I see, through the large front windows, an interesting little scene taking place on the street outside. Webster is being asked for an autograph.

The two girls who've accosted him don't look English – perhaps Spanish? – and they weren't in the gallery beforehand, so perhaps they've followed us here from the museum; this being a little side street in the East End's former industrial area, random passers-by are few. They certainly look suitably flustered and adoring. Unable to resist, I venture outside to catch a bit of the conversation.

'Oh, yeah?' Webster is saying. 'Which one was that?'

'Feile, in Cork,' one of the girls answers (Irish – I was close). 'Must have been '94, or '95?'

'Ah,' comes the response. 'Our third from last gig.'

Wow. Ladies and gentlemen, we are now two gigs away from Aylesbury. This could be interesting.

'No kidding?'

'Yep,' he smiles sheepishly. 'Just one in Amsterdam, then it was all over bar the drinking.'

They all roar with laughter. I'm madly studying Webster's face for any signs of . . . anything. But there are only smiles, as he autographs a little notebook, then a dog-eared copy of the Lonely Planet guide to London belonging to the shyer, prettier one of the pair.

'It was a deadly gig,' she offers, blushing as he hands the book back.

'Yeah? Well, thanks. We'd been going ten years at that point, so we were probably quite good by then.'

More laughter at the mock-modesty of the man. Then – as simple as a sunny day in August:

'Why d'y'all jack it in?'

Oh, you Irish beauty. You direct, perfectly charming asker of blissfully baggage-less questions. I'll meet you in a parallel universe and buy you a crate of Guinness.

I settle back in my metaphorical armchair and prepare myself for Webster's answer.

'Oh, we ran out of steam,' he breezes. 'Ah, Alan! Girls, this is my friend Alan. We're collaborating on a writing project.'

I rise again from my metaphorical armchair, put on my best smile and step forward to shake their hands.

* * *

Despite Webster's wagon claims, I convince him we should close our afternoon with a quick visit to a particularly nice nearby boozer with an awesome selection of Belgian beers. He's never been to the place and is duly impressed, ordering himself something dark and strong. We settle in. Feeling much more comfortable on this familiar turf and having witnessed a pop-star incident first hand, I decide to risk a pop-star question.

'Does it happen often, then, being recognised?'

He bites his lip and flashes a quick look around the pub.

'Y'know, it's odd. For years it didn't happen at all in this country. Recently, it's happening more again – dunno why. It's the cycle of things, I guess. But it's always happened abroad. Never stopped.'

'Yeah?'

He nods.

'What was the name of the band you were in?'

He grins and rolls his eyes, but doesn't answer.

'What?'

He takes a sip of his drink and looks away, shaking his head.

'Have I said something wrong?'

He exhales.

'No . . . nothing.'

He looks, for about thirty seconds, like he's about to confess to a particularly sordid crime from a past life. Then, finally:

'Thieving Magpies. Or "the" Thieving Magpies, depending on how much of a hurry you're in.'

'You don't like talking about it?'

Another sip.

'Sorry,' he says, 'I reckoned you would have Googled it by now, or something.'

I shake my head, taking my own sip.

'It's funny,' he muses, 'how I seem to turn to my computer for everything these days, every single thing I want to know. I lost my keys the other day, and I swear I got halfway to the computer to Google "my keys". How bloody ridiculous is that?'

We laugh, then stop.

'But no,' he continues, perhaps realising he can't avoid 'it' for ever. 'You're right, I don't always like talking about it. Sometimes I do. I'll bang on and on about it like you wouldn't believe. Depends who's asking, a lot of the time. But you and I . . . no offence, but we've always talked about other things, so it just seems . . . wrong.'

'Okay.'

'But there are things you don't like talking about as well, I suppose? Like earlier.'

'Er . . . yeah.'

'Emotions don't seem to be your favourite.'

I shrug. 'Good ones are okay.'

'They're all good, though. Feeling sad, feeling angry, it's all completely necessary. Especially if you're gonna be a writer. You can't just wander around with a drunken grin on your face. I mean, when I write songs, they're not all happy. It'd be duller than fuck if they were.'

I nod, trying to ignore the four hundred questions instantly racked up in my mental outbox. I feel like I'm studying the eating habits of a particularly rare bird, and that it's standing in front of me right now, chomping away. One move and I'll scare it off.

'And the best stuff I ever wrote,' he concludes, 'was when I was feeling like utter shit every day. It's horrible at the time, I wouldn't recommend it, but you know – you gotta go through it.'

This nugget digested, we move onto other topics. Yes, I could try to press him more. But frankly, I'm exhausted. And the unavoidable fact is we're getting on well, but every time the talk goes anywhere near his music we take a nosedive into a steaming heap of conversational manure. 'Just try and enjoy it for what it is,' instructed Alan (the real one) on the phone earlier. 'Be a bit grateful.' So, in one of my rare instances of following Alan's advice, I do. And in fact, miraculously, I start to enjoy myself. We finish that drink, then have another. We talk some more about *Sainsbury Sid*. We talk about my 'project' and how it could perhaps develop. We talk about each other's parents, a bit more about childhood, a little about school and teenage years. Then, finally, we return to *Sid*.

'Well, I think you should go for it,' I state confidently. 'Don't worry about what I say. I'm just a miserable git who reads a lot of Iain Banks.'

'He's fantastic,' comments Webster.

'Of course,' I concur, 'but hardly the type of thing that would put you in the mood for a kid's book. No, I reckon you're onto a good thing, and with those illustrations I think it'll be a lot of fun.'

'Wow, Alan. You're actually starting to sound relatively optimistic.'

'Thanks,' I reply, with a guilty smile. 'But it needs some work still, I think . . . to bring it up to the standard of the illustrations.'

'All right then, Mr Expert. How about this? I'm going away in a week's time. Until then I've got quite a bit of production work to do, so what if . . . we reserved an entire afternoon of mucking about, properly, at my computer, on my stuff – and some of yours, if you want – get it into a shape where I think it's fun and you don't think it's crap. Then we'll go have some nosh in a pub.'

The pair of trappist ales I've consumed leave me so delighted with this idea, which I assume means a visit to his flat, that in my rush to accept I don't think to ask him where he's going. But then, I suppose it doesn't really matter.

After we've drained our beers and said goodbye (he's going onwards to town in another taxi), I board the bus and feel something approaching contentment. It's perhaps on the same rugby pitch as that rush of pleasure I received all those years ago, at the Harlow Square, frugging away, not five yards from Lance Webster, feeling that you're genuinely where the action is; that the best of life is occurring right there, and that you're not merely looking at it through a frosty window, vicariously trying to catch whatever scraps you can. I may not have my award-winning story of the last days of the Thieving Magpies, but in a funny, roundabout sort of way, I have become good friends with their lead singer.

All in all, quite a good thing.

And that's not all, folks.

When I finally return home – via, of course, the off-licence (well, I've got something to be happy about now, haven't I?) – I treat myself to a round of the 'Best of' game. This is a game where you close your eyes and stand in front of your CDs or records, letting your index finger search freely, and whatever album it eventually arrives at, you have to play the best song – in the picker's opinion – of that artist or band. Playing this game at Alan's is amazing because of the size of both his speakers and music collection; at my place it's a bit limited, but I crack open a beer and shortly find myself listening blissfully to Beck's 'Sissyneck', the Foo Fighters' 'For All the Cows', REM's 'Orange Crush' (their best song is actually 'Sweetness Follows' but I decided to bend the rules a bit in the interests of keeping things happy), The Cardigans' 'Been It', Senseless Things' 'Easy to Smile', Radiohead's 'Talk Show Host', Thieving Magpies' 'Little House on the Flight Path', Blur's 'Blue Jeans', ABBA's 'Hole in Your Soul', Drugstore's 'El President', Beef's 'Lazen Hags', The Beatles' 'Lady Madonna', The Mission's 'Tower of Strength', Pop Will Eat Itself's 'Inside You' and finally 'Walk-In Disaster' from Lance Webster's solo album. After this I get Magpies-centric and also play 'A Good Time Was Had by None' and the live version of 'Zeitgeist Man' – a relentless, charging stomp of a number, which finds me leaping around my room as if at the gig itself. I catch my reflection in the window and wonder what on earth Lance would think if he could see me now, merely hours after asking which band he once belonged to, bouncing to his records with such verve that I actually whack my head on my standard lamp and spill some beer on my laptop.

I notch the volume down a tad and mop my long-suffering computer with an old T-shirt, then decide to make sure everything's still working by checking my emails. Imagine my surprise when there's one sitting there from a certain 'William F' – which turns out to be this:

From: WILLIAM F (wroyalebf3791@billyflushing.com)
Sent: 5 May 2007 09:54:34 -0500
To: cliveberesford@hotmail.com
Subject: RE: the geeks shall inherit the earth

Dear Clive
What?? I can't believe you're not a completely bitter 33-year-old drunken mess. You should know that's the minimum pre-requisite for anyone who went to our school. Have you gone the route of obese and balding? I'm working on it.
So, **that** Clive Beresford, eh? I'm mentally flicking through all the Clive Beresfords I know. If you're writing to me about *Alternative Heroes* then you must be – wait! The former editor of *Vorsprung Durch Peanut*! Well, well. Sorry about Spike Island, eh? You bloody well should be. It may be seventeen (fuck!) years ago, but you'll still be hearing from my solicitors. Yes, I remember Alan Potter. Tell you the truth, I always thought he was a bit of a dullard, but there you go.
If you're thinking about that incident you must be feeling nostalgic yourself. Yes, that was me sticking the sticker up. How amazing that you saw it! I sold a flat in Farringdon recently and when I cleared out one of the

bedrooms I found a whole load of stuff like that. After a few drinks I decided to have a bit of a trip down memory lane, got a friend to drive me up there, and to the Garage and even past Camden Palace (nice to see they've changed its name to something sensible . . . what the fuck is Koko??!!), while listening to this brill compilation tape I also found (Carter, New FADs, Cardiacs, Kitchens of Distinction, Sandkings, Eat). A lot of it sounds much better than I thought it would.

So what are you doing nowadays? Still writing? I found a lot of stuff on forum pages that seems to be written by you, and your Amazon review section is awesome, they should start paying you. Yes, life's rumbling on for me and there's a lot to be happy about, I must admit. I got passable A-levels before ending up at Bristol University, which was a riot (come to think of it, I think I caused a few). After Bristol I did some commercial graphic design, screwed that up and worked for a bank (similar to working with zombies, but with better pay), and then finally packed it all in to do my own art and comic stuff. Haven't looked back since and am having a ball writing and drawing, running a little company and even occasionally being a newspaper and magazine critic – I can't believe people trust the opinion of a lunatic like me!

I've lost contact too with just about everyone from school. I did get a mail from Ben Simons actually – surprisingly I didn't immediately write back with, 'Ah, my old friend!!'

So, want to meet up for a beer soon to thrash out the highs and lows of the last sixteen years? Let me know and I'll give you a shout when I'm next in London, probably in a couple of weeks.

Cheers

Billy

Thoughts that immediately strike me:

1. There appear to be no hard feelings. Or maybe life is just too damn good now for him to care.
2. Clearly he no longer lives in London; I wonder if he works out of his firm's New York office?
3. He 'sold a flat in Farringdon'? The 'a' would suggest it's one of many. Hmm. How the other half live.
4. Seems to be a funny blend of modesty about his business and artistic achievements with a David Brent-style pretend modesty regarding his personality (the comments about the riots and being a lunatic). Generally he sounds level-headed, though.
5. He's right. Amazon *should* start paying me.
6. He's also right about Alan. I love him dearly, but a dullard he certainly is.

But really – how interesting. I wonder what he's like in person. I know it shouldn't affect the way I think, but it seems funny that someone so obviously successful could be . . . normal. I suppose I'll be finding out in a few weeks when he jets in,

Billy Flushing. Good grief, Charlie Brown.

And after that, something quite strange happens. Although it's just past ten o'clock on a Saturday night, and I've had no more than three drinks today, a bizarre wave of tiredness engulfs me and I decide to go to bed. I stick on something mellow (Elliott Smith's *XO*) and settle down to an unusually satisfied and worry-free sleep from which I don't stir for the entire night, apart from when Polly crashes in around three to ask if I've got any spare condoms.

For once, a chapter ends on a happy note.

But don't you worry.

I'm sure I'll fuck it all up somehow.

LANCE!

You know what it's like on one of *those* days.

One of those days when it's like you've got a million things to do. So many things that you actually make a list, as your mother used to tell you to do, although her lists are more likely to consist of things like 'pick up beef from butcher's, have hair done, order flowers' rather than the fascinating contents of the following:

get suit from dry-cleaners
buy laces
buy stain remover for Polly
iron shirt
(breakfast!!)
pay council tax
ring housing-benefit office
ring bank re: extending overdraft limit
Put more credit on phone!! – charge battery
ring sister re: lunch on sunday
finish application form
finish JSA report

check shoes – if dirty polish
take:
(job centre) JSA book
(job meeting) passport, NI number, pen/paper
(webster meeting) laptop, printouts, polly's mr men books
take out cash
money on oystercard
10 a.m. sign on
11 a.m. new fetter lane EC4 (james brandish)
1 p.m. geoff W, no. 3A

So, you're up on time, jeans and T-shirt, cup of tea and straight outside, cursing at the pissing rain, leg it to the dry-cleaners to collect your suit, grab the laces and Polly's stain remover (don't ask), and belt back home before everything gets drenched. You're the world's worst shirt-ironer but it starts to look wearable after about ten minutes, so you sling in some toast and settle down at the kitchen table for the first of your phone calls.

The council tax one is without hitch, but when you ring the housing-benefit office you get put in a calling queue for about twenty minutes. You clutch your mobile between your ear and shoulder and continue with your tasks: buttering and eating toast, cleaning and polishing shoes. Halfway through relacing them you finally reach the front of the queue and a wonderfully circular conversation ensues:

'We don't seem to have your claim on our system.'

'I sent the form in ten days ago.'

'Sometimes it takes up to three weeks to be put onto our claiming system.'

'So where is it now?'

'In our queuing system.'

'How do I know it's definitely been received?'

'You could speak to the queuing department, but you'll need a claim number for them to be able to find your form.'

'Can I get a claim number?'

'Not until the form gets put onto our claiming system.'

And so on. You hang up and proceed to what should be a more straightforward experience: ringing your bank. Wrong. Straight onto another queuing system, and with the clock nearing quarter past nine there's no choice but to continue your chores with your phone still wedged under your ear, your head cocked at a neck-cricking angle. Finally you speak to a human being and – after surprisingly little persuasion – your wish of a few extra hundred quid is granted. You're just reaching for your to-do list to get the next item, when one of the items decides to get you.

'Hello?'

'Clive! It's Maggie!'

You dispense with your sister as swiftly as you can without having an argument, then continue your way down the list. Pretty good idea, really, this list. Those parents, eh? Occasionally they have a point.

Quarter to ten and you're on the bus, one of those disorienting rainy bus journeys where you can never see where the hell you are. Finally the Job Centre appears through the steamed-up and splattered windows; you dash through the rain to catch your ten minutes of hearing about all the exciting data-entry vacancies north London has to offer. Then it's back on the bus for more wet public travel, and this time you're not so lucky: there's something happening at Angel so the bus has to go some crazy route which not only takes you miles in the wrong direction, but the added traffic is horrendous. Ten minutes of trying to circulate the Old Street roundabout and you're getting your sweat on in your woollen suit, toying with the idea of bus hopping, but it's so hard when you can't see where the fuck you are – and would a different bus necessarily be any quicker? Suddenly a picture appears in your head of Mr James Brandish (a City recruitment consultant you've been hooked up with via an old university friend) tapping his watch as it nears five past eleven, mentally crossing off the many human-resources departments who simply wouldn't accept this lateness. You stand up and stumble to the back of the bus, leaning over to wipe a peephole in the condensation so you can see if any potential connecting bus is behind. A glance at your watch (10.46), a final flash of James Brandish – and you belt down the stairs, beg the driver to let you off and race through the rain to catch another bus just as its doors are closing.

10.58 and you're pelting down Hatton Garden (past the jewellery shop where you considered buying an engagement ring five years ago), nearly enjoying a collision with a bike as you hurtle round Holborn Circus and finally coming to a halt outside the office in question. You're dripping with sweat and your hair's all over the place, but you decide this can be more easily explained than lateness of even a minute, so you tuck in your shirt and firmly press the intercom.

It's important to reflect on the circumstances which sometimes guide us in a slightly curious direction. London is not an easy city: its size, expense, weather and transport system are often enough to drive one potty, and this has so far been, in a number of ways, a fairly typical London morning. The next fifty minutes, in a very different way, are also highly representative of the kind of minutes one can experience in London when knowing the right people. An old university friend is often the best of references; the sort of connection which can turn 'sorry', 'nothing at the moment', 'not the sort of skill-set we can place' and 'goodbye' – into 'excellent', 'inundated with opportunities', 'should find you something by the end of the week' and 'see you soon'. Certainly, they will not be the sort of jobs you crave, but needs must when Satan gobs in your wallet and blows his nose on your career-development plan. A brisk handshake, a promise of a phone call on Thursday morning, a last glug of Marks & Spencer's organic coffee later and you are back on New Fetter Lane in the drizzle.

You stroll as casually as you can back up Hatton Garden, chewing over the prospect of health and colour returning to your bank balance, but lamenting the immediate shrinkage of your free daytime. It's been a while since you've had a real nine-to-five; you gallingly recall how deadening a schedule it is, week in, week out. But hey. It's only Tuesday. You've got almost a week before any potential job could start, and an hour before you're due at Webster's. It's been a tough morning, but you've achieved everything on your list. And there, across Clerkenwell Road, as if by magic, is the Duke Of York. And what's the time? Midday.

On the dot.

Now, you're fully aware that you've an afternoon of work, as defined by Mr Geoffrey Webster, to get through: a collaborative and inventive burst of brainstorming for which full alertness and flowing creative juices are mandatory. But a quick pint won't do any harm. On the contrary, given your previous record of being over-analytical, nervous and prone to weeping in public places, it'll probably be just the ticket. You march in, order yourself a Stella and settle down by the window to watch the rainy traffic. They're playing the first Killers album, so you cast aside the disappointing memory of seeing them live at Reading and enjoy the album for what it is.

The first few gulps are just as refreshing as you expect them to be, and by the time a text message appears at five past twelve you've had a whole half. Never mind, always the way: the second half will be slower. You glance at your phone. Alan, of course: 'HOWD IT GO' (no punctuation as usual). You hammer out the good news; then, already feeling a positive rush from the alcohol (and 'Everything Will Be Alright' is the Killers song currently playing), you take a chance on adding the following:

> Meeting Webster later, prob going to 3 Kings after, turn up
> later if you want but make it look accidental

You've decided this won't be a problem. After all, how would Webster know Alan had driven from four suburbs away to accidentally bump into him? And Alan will hopefully behave himself – but even if he doesn't, your brief friendship with Webster has just about run its course, with his impending departure to God knows where, so it won't make an awful lot of difference if he thinks Alan's a leering goon or, as Billy Flushing would have it, a dullard.

You take a few more gulps. Everything will be all right. You're just wondering to what sort of horrendous job Mr Brandish will send you when another text arrives.

Except it isn't a text. It's your phone telling you the battery's running out. Shit! That was on the list too, giving it ten minutes on the charger! How could you have missed it? And this silly new phone of yours has a rubbish battery – two more of these alerts and it's curtains. Pondering what to do about this, you drain your pint. Gah. The first pint is always so fast. But never mind.

The second pint will be slower.

By the time you've ordered it and returned to the window seat, your phone has spoken again. This time it really is a text.

GREAT WILL DO WHAT TIME ROUGHLY

No sooner has this appeared, it's the low-battery noise once more. There's no shutting this phone up. For the second time that day, beads of sweat appear on your brow. It's vital that Alan should know what time to arrive; you don't want him getting there just as you're ordering food 'cos he'll have nothing to do for the next forty minutes, and it *will* look like the whole thing was planned. But right now you've no way of knowing what time to tell him. Damn! Why the hell didn't you charge the battery? Angrily, you snatch your to-do list from the bottom of your bag. How in God's name did you . . . sister. Sister! It's all the fault of your sister! You were meant to ring her *after* you put your phone on charge, but she rang you and jumped the queue! So you missed the bit about checking your battery and . . .

. . . putting credit on your phone.

Now this is getting stupid. You were down to your last couple of quid last night, and since then you've made those stupid long phone calls. Never having grasped the finer points of your phone's tariff system, you've no clue how much credit will be left, only that it won't be much. You could call the service that tells you how much is left, but then the battery will instantly die.

Arse!

But there must be something good in this pint, for after your next sip comes a brainwave: the sort of thought that simply doesn't occur very often in 2007, although ten years ago it would be obvious. You drain your pint, gather up your belongings, bid farewell to the barman and, feeling that usual extra bright daylight after a daytime pub-stop, look up and down the road for a payphone.

It's years since you've had reason to be inside one of these things, and you haven't missed them. Forty-pence minimum! You shove your pair of coins in the slot and wait as Alan's phone rings . . . and rings. Voicemail. Actually, that's better; you don't have to waste time talking to him.

'Alan, it's Clive. Um . . . listen, I'm not sure what time's gonna be best for later, and my bloody phone's running low on credit and battery, so what I'll do is . . . I think I'm gonna have enough juice for [*bleep! bleep! bleep! bleep!* announces the accursed mobile as its final power courses through the circuit] . . . well, I'll hopefully have enough juice for, like, a one-word message . . . y'know, after it's had a rest, so I'll just write the time you should get there. I should think it'll be seven-ish, but we'll see. All right? Later.'

Yet another rescue mission accomplished, you trot back over the road just in time to catch your bus. You climb to the top deck, where, apart from feeling a little dazed, prematurely knackered and slightly in need of a piss, you manage to enjoy the half-hour ride back to your home turf. You scoot round to your own street, ring the buzzer of 3A and shake the hand of the beaming former indie-rock icon who energetically swishes open his front door – but only then do you recall another, infinitely more important thing Alan should know before bowling happily into the boozer this evening.

'Hey!' exclaims Webster, chuckling slightly. 'What's with the suit, Alan?'

Bugger.

Considering the pair of pints (you realise that 'have lunch' might also have been a good thing to write on the to-do list) and the maelstrom of worries churning around inside you all afternoon, you do pretty well at the Webster children's-book workshop. Having bonded over toys, shrines and Belgian beer three days previously, frankness is forthcoming and ideas surprisingly plentiful. But every time Webster leaves the room to do anything – put the kettle on, visit the loo, make a phone call – you're frantically working out how you can say what you need to say in the shortest possible text message before your phone bleeps its last:

> 7 pm Web thinks my name is Alan please don't call me clive sorry explain later
>
> 7 my name is alan will explain later
>
> 7 my names alan explain l8r

Other lines of communication haven't been written off: it's a possibility that you could open up your email page on Webster's computer, compose the appropriate message to Alan and send it before he reappears, but it's risky. If the page locks up, he could return to find the name Clive Beresford slapped all over his screen, shortly before showing you the colour of his front door and reacquainting you with his roadie pals. Just about the only safe option is to announce you must suddenly pop home for something, giving you the chance to run to another payphone – but what for, and why is it so urgent? You'd need an excuse – but imaginative resources run dangerously low when you've spent the last few hours trying to dream up catchphrases for a talking fly.

Inevitably, because of all this mental turmoil, you haven't had much chance to properly take in your surroundings. You are, after all, inside Lance Webster's flat; notes should be made, searching questions should be asked, a small amount of emotion should even be felt. But in truth, there's not an awful lot to see. You're working on a laptop in a comfortable but sparsely furnished front room; the kitchen is functional but hardly top of the range; there's a paucity of gold discs, musical instruments or any other memorabilia that might suggest the abode of a pop star; there's a flash-looking stereo but only a small rack of CDs. An indifferent ginger cat you've been warned not to approach – evidently the more vicious colleague of the recently departed Jessica – periodically prowls through the room. You haven't been offered 'the grand tour' and you're not completely comfortable asking for it, but the hospitality has been reasonable enough: tea, biscuits and even, at around four, a round of cheese and pickle sandwiches. But the distinct impression remains that you've purposely not been allowed into the real inner sanctum, the studio, where Geoff still occasionally becomes Lance. The only item you've seen that's worthy of a second thought is a framed photograph, on the mantelpiece, of a male toddler.

The session starts winding down at around half past six. Webster is beside himself with joy at the afternoon's achievements and you feign suitable amounts of enthusiasm and satisfaction, but you're close to exhaustion, regretting every last millilitre of beer you consumed earlier in the day for both its mental and physical effects (you've had a pounding headache for the last two hours). Delightedly, Webster asks if you're still up for 'some grub', to which you nod and smile. He dashes upstairs to 'freshen up', leaving you to contemplate your mobile phone and whether, in your hour of greatest need, it will be there for you.

You hold down the power button gingerly just as the ginger cat strolls into the room. You eye each other warily as the phone boots up. The first thing that happens is it makes the low-battery noise again. The cat doesn't like this noise, flips back its ears and jumps onto the window sill: an area Webster has spent a considerable portion of the afternoon trying to stop the cat reaching. You do your best to ignore its behaviour, racing to your 'write message' function, but the cat is poking its nose through the open crack in the window. You quickly write your pre-rehearsed message (you've risked expanding it to '745 Web thinks my name is Alan sorry explain l8r'), scroll to Alan's number (thank fuck his name begins with 'A') and press send just as the cat wins its grip on the bottom of the window and pushes it upwards to make good its escape.

'Lance!' you shout, running into the hall and halfway up the stairs. 'Lance! Your cat's trying to get out of the lounge window!'

In the silence that follows – as the name you have chosen to shout reverberates around your bewildered head – your phone bleeps to merrily announce its own untimely death and an upstairs door creaks open.

'Sorry,' Webster's voice slowly articulates, 'what was that you said?'

'I, er . . . I said . . . that your cat . . . Is trying to escape . . . From the lounge window.'

Webster runs wordlessly past you down the stairs and rushes out the front door. Mercifully he appears a moment later holding the wretched animal, which he carries into the kitchen. He throws a handful of cat food into a bowl and leaves the room, shutting the door. He grabs a jacket from one of the coat hooks in the hall and then stops, looking straight at you with a hard, featureless stare that could mean a number of things. You reasonably decide it's probably 'what fucking name did you just call me, and why?' – so you respond with a look one might give a girlfriend if caught trying on her clothes.

After a few incredibly long seconds, your companion shakes himself out of his brief trance, announces brightly, 'Come on, then – let's do it,' grabs a batch of printouts from the day's travails ('just in case we want to talk about it in the pub') and you're off towards the drinking hole of choice as if nothing has happened. You decide he's either convinced himself he heard wrong, or surmised that you did indeed Google him after he told you the band name the other night. Either way, the banter is soon back up to speed, or as speedy as you can manage. Christ knows whether Alan received your text.

You feel slightly better as soon as the first drink is placed in front of you, your brain and body probably in limbo since the last one some six and a half hours ago. The two of you chat about this and that, consider ordering food but decide to wait a while. Webster is in his usual good mood but your own brain wanders easily; on more than one occasion in the next half an hour Webster asks you if you're okay. The final time he asks, you apologise and slope off to the toilet.

Once inside, you splash some cold water on the gaunt, ill-looking face reflected in the mirror and decide, not for the first time, that enough is enough. You simply cannot keep doing this: living your life via a string of grey lies, all of which cascade into one another, leaving you with a perpetually impossible clean-up task. You must shape up, turn the leaf, cease the 'harmless' lunchtime pints, get your shit together, be honest. Possibly even right now. With the much lied-to alternative hero of yours, who waits on the other side of the wall.

But sadly none of this will be possible. Exactly as you initially felt his presence about a month ago, when you leave the gents' and return to the pub's main room you just *know* that Webster has vanished. You know, even before you see his jacket missing from the back of his chair, the pile of papers gone from the little table. The room simply feels Webster-less, before you've even rounded the corner. You approach the table, your new pint waiting (at least he had the decency to deliver it) – no trace of a drink for him. He's not at the bar. Then you spot the thing. Your bag is slightly open. You look inside: perhaps a note? But nothing. Apart from your wallet, not zipped shut properly, one of the credit cards sticking out. A card that of course bears the name 'Mr C Beresford'. Not 'Mr A Potter': that innocent, sensible name of a man who doesn't go putting crazed, drunken notes through ex-pop stars' front doors at two in the morning.

You sit down and instinctively clutch the pint glass in front of you. You consider crying, but no tears come (which isn't an altogether bad thing – it would start to become a habit). You look up, frowning hard, your eyes coming to rest on the clock behind the bar. Quarter to eight. Punctual as ever, Alan comes bursting through the door, swinging his car keys, glancing around the pub. He meets your eyes and comes bowling over. Nice that he's tried to make it look accidental, just as you asked him to.

'Where is he? Is he in the loo? Am I too late?'

You look up at your old friend wearily, and shake your head.

'He's gone.'

'Gone? Whadya mean? You said seven forty-five, didn't you? And what did you mean, he thinks your name is Alan?'

'Alan – get yourself a drink, and I'll explain everything.'

He waits a second, then mopes off to the bar.

So.

That's how it happens.

You know how it is.

Given the chance to do it all again, perhaps you'd do things differently.

But that chance is probably not going to come.

Is it.

THREE

This is what you wanted,
now throw it away.

Thieving Magpies, 'This Is What You Wanted'

FAREWELL, ZEITGEIST MAN

At around 3 p.m. on Wednesday 8 April 1998, Lance Webster walked into BFM's headquarters on London's Mortimer Street, ostensibly for a meeting with his former label's product and marketing team about a planned Thieving Magpies 'greatest hits' release. He signed in with security, settled himself down cross-legged by the lifts, hoisted a large hand-painted sign bearing the legend 'SAY NO TO POINTLESS RECORDS' and remained there until removed by police at around four.

During his one-hour, one-man demonstration, a wave of gossip swept through the London offices of the British music industry. From record company to management office, rock venue to promoter, press agency to music paper – the telephone-propelled whispers of derision streaked across the city until a small crowd of highly amused and merrily intoxicated industry representatives gathered on the pavement outside to catch a glimpse of the fallen indie idol and his latest madcap blunder. I myself was halfway through my first – and, as it happened, last – week working as a staff writer for the dying Britpop rag *Craze*; I shelved my workload and jumped in a taxi, arriving on Mortimer Street to find I was Webster's sole supporter.

To add stinging insult to considerable injury, Webster had dressed from head to toe in white (a reference point woefully displaying his inflated opinion of his intentions) and had printed a stack of information leaflets, which he handed to anyone entering or exiting the lifts, painstakingly listing BFM's crimes against the campaigner himself, his erstwhile group and British music fans in general. The rambling and frequently repetitive copy boiled down to three main points:

- that BFM had effectively 'assassinated' the Thieving Magpies via a sustained policy of underspend, forcing them to embark on a massively overlong tour to promote *The Social Trap*, accompanied by a level of financial support fit for a 'recently signed band on their first outing' rather than an act who'd just sold four million albums. 'But we were an "old school" alternative band,' harped the leaflet, 'so *obviously* we were used to slumming it.'

- that the same label 'blackmailed' Webster into swiftly releasing a 'substandard' solo album (1997's *Commercial Suicide*) to fulfil his contractual obligations.

- that 'greatest hits' albums are an utter swindle and merely a quick, cheap, easy way for record companies to make pots of cash out of their old catalogue. BFM's decision to release such an album by a band they themselves had 'destroyed' proved they had neither respect for their artists nor the listening public.

While there may have lurked a grain of truth in all three charges, the fact it was Lance Webster who chose to bring them, and in such a public and pathetic manner, struck a distinctly incongruous note. In the weeks and months following the Magpies' infamous final performance in August 1995, Webster appeared to do everything in his power to sabotage attempts at salvaging the band's career: prohibiting further single releases, refusing requests to record new material, rubbishing their output whenever the opportunity arose, even blocking plans to stage a special free gig for those who'd been present at the abortive Aylesbury show. When the entity known as Thieving Magpies officially ceased to exist in March 1996, Webster redirected his bile towards the record industry itself, calling it a 'coke-addled circus of pointless, peripheral morons', adding petulantly that 'everything was fine before Britpop came along and fucked everything up'.

The typewriters of the music press duly veered between ignoring the man completely (*NME*), encouraging hot debate as to whether he was right or plain bonkers (*Melody Maker*) and merciless mockery (*Craze, Select, Vox*). A number of publications mentioned the continued absence of Gloria Feathers, musing that Webster seemed a very lost and unfortunate soul without her apparently 'cosmic' guidance. For my own part, still scribbling as hard as I could for my fanzine *Definitely Not* (which aimed to give space to anything but Britpop), I went as far off the scale as you could imagine:

The behaviour of the man is admittedly perplexing, but how can anyone be surprised? He's spent the last ten years giving us precisely what we wanted: consistently brilliant, inventive alternative rock, endlessly witty and thought-provoking lyrics, exhilarating live shows and entertaining interviews. But he made one mistake; and now you've all decided you don't want him any more. You're either too drunk, too stupid or you've shoved too much white shit up your nose to realise that Lance Webster, and a few others like him, are the reason you're able to do what you do today. None of these Britpop bands, none of your shitty little magazines, would be selling *anything* if he hadn't done the groundwork. If you sat down and examined your rock history for one second, you'd realise he's the closest thing Britain's ever had to its own Cobain. And who are you clueless pricks worshipping instead? The Gallagher brothers: a pair of charmless, primeval fools who've somehow learned to use a microphone and string a few chords together. They're the kings of your pitiable little world, and you lap it up like the weak, brain-dead, sycophantic little cunts that you are.

But irrespective of your opinion on the man, it came to everyone's surprise in the summer of that year when it emerged that Lance Webster would be appearing at a brand new festival, V96, to road-test material for an upcoming solo tour and album. Odder still, he had agreed to a mid-afternoon slot on the weekend's Britpop-heavy second stage, sandwiched between Space and Kula Shaker. Even the choice of festival itself was puzzling; as quickly became clear, everything about the clean, well-ordered V was emphatically 'new school', from the wooden walkways of the inner arena to the ticketed method of purchasing drinks. Still, a couple of thousand faithful dragged themselves away from the delights of Mike Flowers Pops on the main stage and waited with bated breath or (in my case) bitten-down-almost-to-the-cuticle fingernails for Webster's appearance, hoping that this time he would be sober.

In retrospect, it probably would have been better if he'd been drunk. Accompanied by nothing more than an acoustic guitar and an expressionless male piano player barely into his teens, he slouched on, uttered no word of greeting and proceeded to play six of the most dismal ballad-style numbers imaginable; none of them bearing even the faintest hallmark of the man's former prowess. His voice retained its range and power, but the material it warbled was of such a bewilderingly low standard that half the audience were gone by the end of the first song. The remainder clapped politely (I remember thanking the gods he hadn't tried doing this at Reading) and steeled themselves for the next intake of bilge. Webster spoke only once, before the final track, informing us that 'this is David over here; he's doing music A-level' – far from the expected, bitter slagging of all things Britpop which might at least have been worth watching. The few onlookers who'd bothered to stick around sighed and gradually sloped off to see . . . well, anything.

Although in its own way as derisory as the Magpies' Aylesbury show, Webster's V96 performance had the unexpected result of temporarily killing the Lance-bashing; why bother, when he'd done such a good job of it himself? Consequently, by the time reports of a completed debut solo album circulated the following spring, Webster had as good a chance as ever of redeeming himself. Frustratingly, he both did and didn't.

On the one hand, no one could deny he'd made a decent record. It was mercifully bereft of any material debuted at V96 and featured a lean combination of conventional rock and electronics, not a million miles from the sound of certain tracks on *Blur* and *OK Computer*, two of 1997's biggest releases. Most of the songs matched the quality of those on *The Social Trap* ('The Bad Life', 'Blissful Indignance'), a few of them ('Walk-In Disaster', 'His Fax Beats Out the Blues') as convincing as anything the Magpies had ever recorded. All in all, Webster could hardly claim BFM forced him to put a 'substandard' record out.

So much for the good news. Sadly, his behaviour throughout the summer of 1997 capably supplied the bad. For a start, the album was mixed, mastered and ready by April, but for reasons best known to himself a managerless Webster insisted on holding the release back, employing various delaying tactics: unexpectedly lengthy publishing negotiations, dissatisfaction with artwork, sudden loss of confidence with the final mix, illness, disappearing abroad, even alleged jury service. At last, a firm date of 18 August was agreed upon: later than BFM would have liked, but thank God they were finally getting the thing out there. They even grudgingly agreed to the rather portentous title. Only after the date had been set in stone did they realise Oasis's highly anticipated third album *Be Here Now* was scheduled to arrive – unusually – on the Thursday of the same week, and not the following Monday as originally planned. Evidently having acquired this information via the few industry contacts he had left, Lance Webster was quietly ensuring his album would receive as little attention as possible.

In addition, Webster refused almost all interviews, only agreeing to a handful of continental publications, a few in the States and a short chat with the *Big Issue*, in which his monosyllabic grunts were so worthless the feature was ultimately abandoned. A UK tour was arranged, then scrapped – again, the phantom jury service cited – Webster honouring only a one-off date at London's Borderline, where he enraged punters by starting his set ten minutes before the doors opened and ordering his support band to play after he'd finished.

Looking back, it's amazing any of his fans continued to bother with him at all. But I recall hearing the strong, reassuring sound of 'Walk-In Disaster' emerge from my radio that summer, and with it the promise of similar things to come; I remember finally getting my hands on *Commercial Suicide* and grinning like an idiot for practically its whole length, such was the cocktail of relief and joy. However, I hadn't been one of the poor bastards at the Borderline show. In the end, it was people like me who ensured the album entered the UK chart at twenty-five; far from the heights scaled by even *The Social Trap*, but also far from disastrous. In Europe the record fared even better, scoring a top-five showing in the charts of both Denmark and the Netherlands; although the likelihood of a hit in these territories was significantly boosted by Webster actually bothering to grace them with his presence, even dispensing that rarest of Webster commodities: a proper gig. It was for the Danish one of these that I decided *Definitely Not*'s shoestring budget could stretch to a Copenhagen plane ticket.

Digressing for a moment, it's one of the ironies in what might generously be described as my career in music journalism that both of my 'breaks' – one that I allowed to slip away unfulfilled, the other so short-lived as to render it almost irrelevant – came from publications I despised. For years I had tried to interest my beloved *Melody Maker* in bits and pieces, but met with zero response (apart from the editor of the letters page). In the autumn of 1994 a friend who worked at the *NME* whispered to me that a recruitment drive could be taking place, advising me to send in some material, which I did; a week later I got a message to call the apparently interested editor. Over half a dozen phone conversations with Alan in the days that followed, we examined my position. Aside from the knee-jerk dislike of *NME* proudly held by all *Maker* devotees, we genuinely couldn't bear the writers, the layout, the music it championed, even the paper it was printed on. But, unsurprisingly, the greatest portion of our disgust was generated by their own hatred for the Thieving Magpies. All their albums, with the strange exception of *The Social Trap*, received terrible *NME* reviews, and interviews were always peppered with bitchy asides from the writer. Webster himself was philosophical about the situation: 'It's healthy to have enemies,' he bragged. 'You can't have *everyone* liking you. Christ, we'd be even *more* popular then . . . I'd have to buy a bigger house! It'd be a nightmare.' Still, to us, this represented the organ's greatest crime. Unable to decide, I caught the train to Manchester that weekend so Alan and I could thrash out the pros and cons of any potential employment at the *NME* together. Just before I left on the Sunday afternoon, we finally reached a decision, over which Alan's rational business head reigned: as a purely 'foot in the door' exercise my pride could temporarily be swallowed, so I would call Stamford Street the following morning and feign enthusiasm for whatever was being offered. I bade Alan farewell and settled back on the London train with a two-litre bottle of cider and Soundgarden on my stereo. By the time the train hit Rugby I'd finished all the drink, permanently reversed the decision – and *Definitely Not* was born.

As you've probably gathered, I never really *got* Britpop. I fully agreed with Webster's thesis that it was a fairly decent little scene with some fairly decent music. It was not, as rock historians often desperately scribble, the most important and influential movement in British music over the last twenty-five years. For a start, that's a claim to a pretty weak accolade; there've only really been two of the damn things, and even then Britpop lost by some distance to its one competitor, acid house, whose musical influence remains almost omnipresent, registering (albeit sometimes unwittingly) on the dial of every current artist from John Lydon to Shirley Bassey. All that Britpop has given us is some faintly memorable pub songs and an opportunity for a band like the Kaiser Chiefs to exist: a group in every way inferior to the Barron Knights.

But then, Britpop never really got *me* either. Everything about the effect it had on me was wrong, or at least at odds with what everyone else seemed to be feeling. I detested Oasis, from the moment I heard the opening chords of 'Shakermaker' to the first time I listened in disbelief as Liam Gallagher twattily yelled 'Good evening Great Britain!' on a BBC session. I loved Blur's *Modern Life Is Rubbish* but considered *Parklife* a motley collection of disjointed ditties which sagged badly in the middle (*The Great Escape* was far better, but now everyone else hates it). I didn't like the way all the indie fans in England suddenly cut their hair. My favourite bands of the era (Longpigs, Dubstar, Marion) were the ones who seemed to die immediately afterwards. My favourite songs (Sleeper's 'What Do I Do Now', My Life Story's '12 Reasons Why I Love Her', Supernaturals' 'The Day Before Yesterday's Man', Bennett's 'Mum's Gone to Iceland') were far from the biggest hits of the period. It was all very much like a jolly good party which someone had forgotten to send me an invitation to. When the Magpies returned in 1995 I felt vindicated that their success still remained, but when the tidal wave of backlash began after the Aylesbury debacle, I experienced, as you've seen, fury such as I hadn't felt since a day in 1981 when my sister melted all my Easter chocolate on a radiator. All of this bile flowed straight into *Definitely Not*, which found a gratifyingly large circulation despite my heaping praise on the unlikeliest of people in my determination to crush the Britpop hyperbole:

I had the most marvellous argument at the weekend over a few drinks in the Jeremy Bentham. Unfortunately someone brought along a friend who I'd already earmarked as a goon on account of his Oasis T-shirt. However this was tolerated until a Phil Collins song ('Sussudio') randomly came on the pub's stereo.

'Aw, what the fuck are they playing this shit for?' began the goon. 'I thought we'd seen the last of this bollocks.'

'What d'you mean?' I enquired innocently.

'I mean,' he replied, a smug tone creeping into his voice, 'now the revolution has come we shouldn't have to sit in a pub listening to Phil Collins.'

'You don't like Phil Collins.'

'Whether I like him or not isn't the point. We have real music now, real honest British pop played on real instruments . . . by the people, for the people . . . created by real characters living real life, not hiding away in their Surrey mansions staring at their gold discs.'

'I've always quite liked old Phil,' I muttered, biding my time.

'Yeah,' scoffed the goon, 'the same way I like putting my fucking head in the oven.'

'There's nothing wrong with Phil Collins.'

'No, other than he's a complete cock. You don't honestly like him?'

'Yeah, I do actually. He's got an ounce of intelligence,

which is more than those knobs combined,' I concluded, gesturing at his T-shirt.

'Oh, come on, Clive,' joined in one of the others. 'If it was a choice between having Liam Gallagher or Phil Collins round for dinner, you'd definitely go for—'

'Phil Collins,' I insisted. 'He'd be a perfectly charming, courteous, entertaining guest. You could quiz him about twenty-five years in the music business as opposed to two crappy little years. Plus there's the added bonus that he can actually use cutlery.'

'He's the devil,' said the goon, shaking his head and sipping his vodka tonic.

'Oh, yeah? And how much good has Liam fucking Gallagher done? I don't see him doing charity work. That's the trouble with this fucking Britpop shit, everyone thinks the sun shines out of the Gallaghers' arses, when all they're doing is shoving royalties straight up their noses. People like Phil Collins get completely pissed on now, even though he's probably done more for "the people", as you put it, than all the fucking Britpop twats put together.'

Meant every bloody last word of it, as well. I don't remember seeing the goon again after that.

So, another deeply ironic note struck when, in the autumn of 1997, I received a call (on my first-ever mobile phone) from Stuart Harris, editor of *Craze* – the most defiantly, laddishly Britpop of all the new 'music' magazines. Harris had finally realised the musical foundation on which his magazine was built had long since passed its sell-by date, and that diversification would be essential for *Craze*'s survival. He'd been aware of *Definitely Not* for a while, he explained, but had been struck by – of all things – the passionate review I had written for Lance Webster's show at Copenhagen's Christiania Grey Hall:

No apologies will be made for the liberal use of super-
latives and melodrama in this review. No explanation will
be given for how *glorious* is the sight of Webster, his head
thrown back, his face frozen in that familiar but long-missed
plateau of exhilaration. I refuse to hold back when I say
that tonight a lost lover is welcomed home, a long-dreamed-
of kiss has been returned, a brutal husband has finally
chosen to be kind. The bittersweet passion of 'More Than
Ever', the adrenalin rush of 'Walk-In Disaster', the bite of
'Disposal' – it's all here, and more. And the acoustic encore
of 'This Is What You Wanted' is almost too much to bear;
the years of disappointment, the hurt and the yearning, the
purple, the blue and the red. The wounds. They're all healed.
The silver and gold return. It's all better now.

Yeah, I know. What can I say? I was probably stoned. For some
reason, Harris saw this and thought a slice of my old-fashioned
Maker-style gothic waxings would be a good antidote to the tire-
somely thuggish scrawlings of people like deputy editor Tony
Gloster, who was still snarling from our run-in during The Boo
Radleys at Aylesbury. Over the next six months Harris kept an eye
on my work, all the while arguing with Gloster about my potential involvement, as I discovered later. Finally, a week before Webster
pulled his Lennon-style stunt at BFM's headquarters, Harris offered
me a position to belatedly develop the magazine's 'non-Britpop
wing'. Believing (rightly, as it turned out) that it would be my last
chance to write for a real publication, rather than one I had to
staple together myself, I cast my principles aside and accepted.

Meanwhile, Lance Webster's future was also looking slightly more
rosy. Following his European dates and the lacklustre release of single
'Blissful Indignance', Webster was without a record deal for the first
time since 1986. This state of affairs appeared to revitalise him: he
reunited with manager Bob Grant, returned to the studio and started

hunting for a new label, with *Music Week* reporting in March '98 that negotiations had commenced with a 'prominent indie'. How those chickens must have been counted at the beginning of that April: by the label, whoever they were, by Bob Grant, by me.

Then the 'madness' returned.

I remember sitting at my desk in *Craze*'s poky little Camden Town office, wrestling with a pile of paperwork, trying to eavesdrop on the new Massive Attack album which Stuart Harris was reviewing next door, when my arch-enemy Gloster (still dressing like a cut-price Graham Coxon) slithered into the room and sardonically informed me of my hero's antics across town.

'Isn't it time someone sectioned him?' he laughed, sliding out again.

It was three-thirty. Two hours of official work time to go, but the monthly issue deadline was looming and people normally seemed to stay until at least seven. But I felt so nervous, fidgety, unable to relax or concentrate – as if I was needed, somehow. The bastard Gloster had done it on purpose to torture me. I pushed papers around my desk pathetically for the next five minutes before calculating that if I cabbed it over there for a quick half an hour I could be back by five; then I could continue working until the building was locked, if need be. I dashed out onto Pratt Street and was in a taxi two minutes later.

What good I imagined I'd be able to do was debatable. There was a crowd of knobs on the pavement outside the BFM building, some holding pints from the nearby pub, some who I recognised from rival publications or record labels. Unfortunately one of them also recognised me.

'Eh! It's "definitely never" bloke.'

'Hi,' I greeted him abruptly, and pushed my way through the doors.

Inside the foyer the scene was grimly familiar. The receptionists were attempting to continue as normal while four security guards, plus a few members of label staff and poor old Bob Grant, surrounded the white-shrouded figure. I could see his ridiculous sign, still held aloft, and after a few seconds I spied that the fool had shaved all his hair off. It was apparent that no one had yet tried any force; perhaps they remembered what had happened at Aylesbury.

From that moment, 'madness' also took hold of me. A receptionist had already asked me what my business was but I was too preoccupied to answer, so a fifth security guard, clearly given the marginally less exciting job of keeping the building free from further undesirables, now approached to usher me back outside.

'Lance!' I screamed, suddenly. 'Lance! Get a hold of yourself! You don't *need* to do this!'

'Right,' snapped the guard, grabbing my forearm. 'Out! *Now!*'

'It's *okay*, Lance! You've done enough! Thousands of people still love you! *We* understand!'

'Get *out!*' continued the guard, increasing his grip to Chinese-burn level and yanking me towards the door. 'Or I'll throw you out!'

My arm hurt so much that I obeyed and stepped back; but I continued to shout.

'Don't listen to those cocks! It'll come around – it'll all come around! You don't need to fight any more!'

And with that I was back out on the pavement, facing the astonished crowd. After a few seconds they started to snigger so I moved a little way down the street.

'Twat,' I heard one of them say, as a distant police siren started to become louder.

The next few minutes I only hazily recall. I know a police van must have arrived, out of which some policemen must have emerged, but only because they came out of the building some minutes later with a handcuffed Webster. I remember him looking relatively calm and resigned; a far cry from the ball of wrath that raged in August 1995. He no longer had his sign (I later saw one of the beery knobs carrying it off as a souvenir). The police were firm but gentle, perhaps because he looked like a monk – and few people would be rough with a monk. The industry representatives were amused, but didn't seem to jeer or shout. No – the most animated, wild and enraged person on the scene, by a country mile, was me.

I wept. I howled. I shouted all manner of terrible things ('Why are you cunts *doing* this? He's done nothing *wrong*!), I almost took a running kick at the side of the police van but stopped myself, thankfully. Once Webster was inside, most of my monologue was directed at him: 'We won't forget you' – 'You've done so much' – probably, I fear, 'We love you' – and other desperate garbage. You'd think he was being put away for twenty-five years on a false murder charge, I was making such a bloody fuss. My final utterance I remember being '*farewell, Zeitgeist man*', to which a suddenly teacher-like Bob Grant turned and said, 'Oh, for God's sake, will you be *quiet.*'

By the end of that day, three things had happened:

1. George Michael had been arrested in a Los Angeles public toilet for a supposedly lewd act with an under-cover policeman, thus snatching every inch of enter-tainment-related news space available. To the best of my knowledge, the Webster incident didn't make it into the national press; it barely even made it into the music press.

2. Lance Webster was released from Marylebone Police Station without charges, but with an instruction to seek psychiatric help. Whether he did or not is unknown. He never signed the rumoured record deal and, apart from a small solo gig in Bergen, Norway, the following year, effectively retired from the music business.

3. I was summarily sacked from *Craze* magazine. In addi-tion to leaving crucial items of work undone for two hours on the week of an issue deadline, eyewitnesses

had recounted my embarrassing hysterics to Stuart
Harris, who had finally been convinced by Gloster that
I was a non-starter. In any case, the beleaguered *Craze*
folded within months.

And why, I hear you desperately wail, am I telling you all this?
Well.

Partly because it's now just under a month since the Artist
Formerly Known As Lance disappeared from both the pub, and my
life – after discovering that nice, boring, timid and interest-free 'Alan
Potter' was actually nasty, opinionated, threatening and borderline-
alcoholic Clive Beresford – and I've got fuck all else to write about.

But mainly because I'm plundering my memory banks, wracking
my brains and scouring the very bottom of my soul with a Brillo
pad, trying to work out why the *hell* he would choose to send me
this:

From:	GEOFF WEBSTER (geoff@gwebmusic.com)
Sent:	1 June 2007 07:23:46
To:	cliveberesford@hotmail.com
Subject:	(no subject)

Dear Clive
I've spent a fuckload of time and money trying to escape
the person I was ten years ago, and I've no desire to meet
him or be him again. I don't like being lied to, either. But I
suppose I never got around to thanking you for all you did,
so here I am. Also, now the past has been dug up, I might
need your help sometime burying it again. Be ready.
Geoff

This arrived two days ago. Since then I've done very little but stare
at it and wonder what the hell he could possibly be on about. I

haven't shown anyone. Even Alan. Actually, make that *particularly* Alan. The tone of deathly seriousness makes me feel very peculiar every time I look at it, like someone's thrown a handful of rice down the back of my T-shirt. Yesterday, the reason why occurred to me: it's like Lance himself is speaking to me, Clive, for the very first time. Today I realised it's not *like* at all. It *is*.

Other things have changed since Webster's departure: some good, some bad, some significant, some irrelevant. It's become summer (good). I've started a temporary job of quite breathtaking banality (bad), but the pay is decent (good), so there is a tiny shaft of light at the end of the overdraft tunnel. Alan, awkward bastard that he is, has suddenly decided to take an avid interest in the whole Webster thing, ringing me up on a twice-daily basis with a new theory ('You know what, man, I reckon he *knew* it was you all along and was just winding you up'), or to ask if there've been any 'updates'. The only update I know of is that Webster's flat has been put on the market. Occasionally I see an estate agent taking people in there. Last weekend I saw the smaller of the two roadies (was it Malcolm?) coming down the outside steps with a large cardboard box; he glared at me, so I glared back. No sign of Webster himself.

Until the arrival of Webster's email, the most significant thing that's happened – although not directly connected to the Webster saga – is that Billy Flushing has been in touch again. He sent me a breezy text message earlier this week saying he was in town, and would I like to go for 'brunch on Sunday'? Picturing a sunny, pleasantly busy pub, Bloody Marys, a stout fry-up and some fit waitresses, I immediately replied in the affirmative; but then was a little perturbed to receive a call from his PA on Friday giving me details of a members' club in Soho where the dress code is 'smart casual' (ye gods). So now I am in my work trousers, black trainers, an acceptable-looking pink shirt I found in a charity shop yesterday, and a blue jacket I'd forgotten I owned. I look pretty absurd and I've got the faintest notion that Billy is perhaps slyly punishing me for being such a dick at school.

You know about most of this. You know about me 'ditching the dweeb', letting Alan steal Billy's role both as my friend and as assistant editor of the *Peanut*. You do not yet know about Spike Island.

Perhaps it's time you did.

WHY YOU'RE SITTING HERE STILL THINKING ABOUT ALL THIS SHIT IS BEYOND ME

Well, for a start, I've sort of misled you about something. Two things, actually. One is that the teenage Alan and I didn't take any drugs. The second is that we didn't go a bundle on any of the Manchester bands. Both these things are slightly untrue. Not that I am suddenly revealing we spent all the early nineties off our tits, wearing flares and fishing hats, listening to Northside and informing all and sundry we were 'havin' it' – but we did indulge in the occasional smoke and, increasingly, as the nineties wore on, pill. It all started at Spike Island.

Not at the gig, you understand. On the way home.

Having spent an underwhelming New Year's Eve in the local pub vainly trying to convince some girls that our tonsils would be worth investigating, we spent the first few hours of 1990 stretched out in Alan's parents' copious lounge, where – having initially dismissed it as drippy, tuneless mush – we finally 'got' *The Stone Roses*.

'This stuff isn't so bad, man.'

'Yeah,' I replied. 'You just have to chill out to it.'

We listened on, getting appropriately excited when everything goes doolally at the end of 'Resurrection', then flipped over the disc and started again.

'What do you think about drugs?' Alan mused, munching a cream cracker.

'Not sure, really. Smoking doesn't really appeal to me. I physically can't do it.'

'Takes practice, man. But I was really thinking about the more chemical stuff. Speed . . . trips and so on. Ecstasy. I wouldn't mind trying it sometime.'

'Yeah, maybe,' I replied. 'It'd have to be the right occasion, I think.'

The right occasion presented itself when a month or so later The Stone Roses announced plans for their Spike Island gig. We ordered our tickets and spent the spring wondering how on earth we were going to get there. Despite the trouble we had getting back from The Heart Throbs gig in Harlow that April, we decided our budgets were too meagre for anything other than hitching. Alan's dad gave us a lift to junction five of the M1 (the ridiculous sight of two indie oiks getting out of a spotless top-of-the-range Mercedes, then holding up a cardboard sign saying 'YOUNG AND SKINT, IN SEARCH OF PARADISE – BUT SPIKE ISLAND, CHESHIRE WILL DO' must have been a treat to anyone driving north at that moment). And there we waited, at eight o'clock on a thankfully dry May morning . . . for around two hours. At last an unmarked lorry stopped half a mile up the road and stuck its hazards on.

'Yer want Runcorn?' the driver yelled, once we'd reached earshot.

'Yeah, thereabouts!' I shouted back.

'Better check he means Runcorn, Cheshire, and not Runcorn, fucking Scotland,' Alan grumbled as we trotted the final few yards.

I opened the passenger door and smiled uneasily at our driver. He was a short, stocky bloke in his fifties with grey hair and a red beard. He frowned at me and spoke in a breathless, prematurely irritated way.

'Yer getting in or not?'

'Er, yes, thanks, can I just check . . . you do mean Runcorn, Cheshire?'

'Yer know another one?'

'Ah, no. Thank you.'

It took us half an hour to fully realise he was drunk. Initially we just thought his truck was a bit dodgy – something about the wheel balance that kept sending us veering into the adjacent lanes – but soon the truck's cab became sickly with booze fumes and he started taking large, obvious swigs from a hip flask. Finally he started to nod off. Alan and I exchanged worried glances, silently wondering if we'd live to see Birmingham, but just as we were passing Northampton a miracle occurred.

'I need a slash,' the driver spat, steering his lorry across two lanes to join the service station's slip road. No indicators were involved in this action.

'Aw, shut the fuck up!' he bawled at the resulting fanfare of horns.

He parked in the services' lorry zone and wordlessly dismounted. We waited until he'd rounded the corner, then scarpered across the picnic area into some bushes.

'Fuck,' I spluttered. 'What a total nutter.'

'I knew it,' Alan stated, in his usual worldly tone. 'As soon as he stopped so far up the motorway, I knew it was a bad idea.'

'Yeah, sure,' I nodded sarcastically.

We hung out in the bush for a few minutes then saw him in the distance, staggering back. He jumped back into the cabin, manoeuvred the truck out of the space and drove off. The memory of picking us up had simply ceased to exist, consumed by cheap gin.

'Mad old bastard,' summarised Alan as we brushed ourselves off. 'He'll be dead soon.'

Temporarily putting the problem of onward transport to one

side, we grabbed a burger. We were sitting on the wall outside the services' shoddy main building, silently chewing in the sunshine, when I spied a familiar figure making his way through the car park.

Even from this distance we could see Billy Flushing had committed not one but two style crimes: he was wearing a Stone Roses T-shirt (never, *ever* wear the T-shirt of the band you're actually going to see), and his hair was slightly longer at the back than it was at the front. Alan and I were dressed in black jeans and carefully selected Thieving Magpies T-shirts (mine from a recent tour, Alan's from much earlier in their career, which I was naggingly jealous of), our hair shorn around the edges but deceptively floppy on top. We considered ourselves the epitome of alternative cool, which Billy fell some considerable distance from. That said, I didn't think he looked quite as horrendous as usual (he had at least traded his black school shoes for some DMs) – a view Alan was unlikely to share.

'All right, guys?' he beamed.

'Hi Billy,' I murmured. Alan looked away and began to moodily study one of the picnic tables.

'You're not going to Spike Island too?' he gushed.

'Uh . . . yeah, we are,' I admitted, feeling there was no point in lying.

'Silly! You should'a told me; we could'a shared the petrol. Ah, well. See you there,' he remarked, bobbing off into the cafeteria.

Alan and I remained silent for another minute, after which – very gently – I cleared my throat.

'Don't even *think* about it,' Alan snapped.

'Oh, come on.'

'No.'

'Alan, it is already eleven o'clock . . .'

'I don't care.'

'Even if we drove straight there, we wouldn't be there before two.'

'I don't care!'

'And for all we know, we might have to wait another couple of hours for someone to—'

'I don't give a shit. I'm not arriving with that knob.'

'Well, we can drop you off and you can walk the last mile or something.'

'I'm amazed he can even fucking drive, man.' This, of course, was sour grapes.

'Yes, what was it you failed on?' I leered. 'Parallel parking, was it?'

'Piss off.'

'Well, I think it's bloody silly – he's going *exactly* where we're going. We don't even need to hang around with him once we get there.'

'Too fucking right we don't.'

Billy came bouncing out at this point, happily slurping a milkshake.

'Still here? Not hitching, are you?'

And so, two hours later – Alan sulking in the back of Billy's orange Vauxhall Chevette, me chatting to the driver but keeping the conversation free of our former lunacy – we finally approached our destination in a queue of like-minded vehicles on the M56. Billy was impossible to shut up; so much so that I began to agree that Alan and I should cover the last few miles on foot ('I'd better get in there early, if you don't mind, Billy – to set up my fanzine stall'). He was commendably frank about his reasons for attending the gig: 'I'm not too keen on the band, but I've heard girls are easy when they're on ecstasy' – which proved the only sentence of Billy's to prompt the slightest response from Alan (his then embryonic but now infamous sceptical belch-scoff).

The gig itself wasn't up to much. That may seem something of a cop-out for what, in some circles, is seen as the crowning moment of Madchester, one nation under a groove, the pre-Britpop benchmark for what indie could achieve, and all that bollocks, but it just seemed like a lot of people hanging around to me. The weather was all right but the 'support acts' consisted solely of tedious DJs; no one was remotely interested in the second issue of the *Peanut* (the five black splodges on the front were meant to be the Inspiral Carpets); and we couldn't find any cider. Billy understandably assumed he'd be spending the rest of the day with us, which meant having to tolerate a grumpy, uncommunicative Alan. Even the famed ecstasy was unexpectedly hard to come by. When we finally found a suitable character bearing the inoffensive-looking beige pills at around half past seven, we painfully handed over thirty quid and waited for something to happen (Billy decided not to partake, knowing he'd be driving later). After an hour and a half the only detectable difference was I'd developed a headache and Alan claimed to be 'hearing the bass more'.

The Roses came onstage at long last; we tried to push forward with our usual blend of rucking and going along with the 'Mass Forward Movement', but there really didn't seem to *be* one. People were dancing but the only frenzied jumping up and down appeared to be taking place about half a mile in front of us. The sound kept getting blown around and was woefully quiet compared to the passable sound systems of earlier. During 'Sally Cinnamon' I looked around at the darkening sky and reflected that this wasn't really my scene. I longed to be back where the cider flowed freely and the bands crunched where the Roses drifted; the audience leapt, kicked and punched where this lot swayed and waved their hands noncommittally. Everyone seemed relatively happy, but I couldn't really tell why. The band cantered to the end of their set and everything got slightly more exciting during an extended 'Resurrection', then a semi-decent firework display was unleashed and the show was all over, bar thirty thousand sweaty kids squeezing back over the bridge to the mainland. Alan, in an interesting turnaround, started to make noises about finding Billy (we'd lost him just before the band came on).

'Oh, so you like him now, do you?' I joked.

'Don't be daft, man, I just can't be arsed to hitch.'

We stepped out of the stream of exiting punters and waited by a fence to see if we could spot Billy. An older guy was already standing there holding a large camera and sucking on a cigarette. After standing there for a minute, Alan sighed loudly.

'Well, those tablets were a fucking success, weren't they.'

I nodded. 'Thirty quid down the drain.'

'Did you think the band were any good, man?'

'Nah,' I frowned. 'Couldn't hear a thing.'

'I'm gonna see if I can find some chips,' Alan announced, stomping off.

The camera guy turned round to me and smiled.

'Had a dud?' he asked.

'What?'

'Just heard your mate say you'd taken a "tablet". Hasn't done you any fuckin' good, has it?'

'I don't think it's my thing, really.'

'Bollocks,' he pronounced, puffing smoke in my face. 'How long ago d'you take it?'

I looked at my watch.

'About three hours ago?'

'Rubbish. You've been conned.'

'You mean they were . . . ?'

'Duds, yeah. Fuckin' cornflour or summat. Here, try these.'

He handed me another couple of pills, white this time.

'Oh, no – that's okay, thanks,' I told him politely, as if he was offering me some sponge cake.

'Go on! Take 'em. Don't want you kids goin' back down south saying our drugs are shite up here.'

And that appeared to be the end of the conversation. The bloke ambled off, leaving me to study my gifts. When Alan returned with his snack a few minutes later I recounted the episode; he immediately grabbed one of the pills and knocked it back with a mouthful of water, so I did the same.

'When in Rome,' Alan shrugged.

A minute after that, Billy appeared.

'Hi guys, wasn't that amazing?'

As we pushed through the partying throng back to the car, we discovered why Billy's experience differed so dramatically from ours: he'd somehow managed to achieve his aim of accosting a loved-up female, with whom he'd had a 'fiddle' behind one of the burger vans. Alan still refused all direct communication with Billy, but instead repeatedly murmured, 'It's all bullshit,' in my ears. Occasionally he'd offer Billy the packet of chips, but withdrew them when he tried to take one. By the time we reached the car I was getting pretty sick of this, but I was a little distracted by a strange tickling feeling I had behind my ears. As we started our long wait to leave the car park this tickling had spread to the joints of my mouth, and had also started to develop in my gut. Then my slightly frustrated mood lightened up a tonne-load, and before I really knew what was going on Alan and I were leaning out of the car windows, hollering back to the other cars in the queue, dancing to other people's music, telling each other it was a great gig and ordering Billy to drive faster.

'How can I drive faster?' muttered Billy, still creeping along behind the other vehicles. 'You guys are so weird.'

It must have taken us ages to get to the motorway, but I didn't care. I was too busy telling Alan that I wanted to go back in time, and asking Billy to change lanes because 'it feels nice'. Finally addressing him, Alan asked Billy whether he had any dance music. Billy responded by putting on his tape of *The Stone Roses*. This was greeted with a roar of approval; and so, travelling at probably no more than twenty miles an hour back down the M56, Alan and I relived the Spike Island gig, the way it should've been: screaming out the lyrics to 'Waterfall', aping Brown's crazy backwards-style warbling on 'Don't Stop' and waving frantically to other revellers during 'This Is the One' as we all gradually sped up. We didn't even mind when some geezer shouted 'Thieving Wankpies!' in the direction of Alan's T-shirt.

If only my memories of the evening could end there. If only we drove all the way back to Hertfordshire in those blissful spirits, Alan finally talking to Billy as another human being, perhaps even saying hello to him in school on the Monday. But no. As soon as we turned onto the southbound M6, Billy's car started to make worrying noises. As we approached Knutsford Services these noises worsened: horrid, grinding sounds that seemed to emanate from the entire lower body of the car. In Alan's and my heightened state of – shall we say – alertness, these struck us as variously hilarious ('Billy, man, d'you give your car curry instead of petrol?') and scary ('Fuck, man, this is getting a bit hectic'). Finally the car started to lose power; we were doing a maximum of ten miles an hour as the car crawled up the services' slip road.

'This is bad,' frowned Billy, remaining admirably calm as we limped into the petrol station. 'Are either of you guys members of the AA?'

Of course the answer was no.

I've relived the contents of the following ten minutes countless times in my head, praying for them to turn out differently; like watching a disaster film when someone's already spoiled the ending for you. But I'm always forced to endure the same grim details: Billy going inside the garage to be told there's no mechanic around at this hour to look at his dying car; Billy phoning his dad to discover the AA policy doesn't cover any other members of the family; Billy looking vainly inside his bonnet; Billy looking vainly inside his wallet. And Alan, oblivious to any of this, still pilling his nuts off, delightedly chatting and flirting with a pair of bubbly female Spike Islanders whose blue Fiat Uno had just pulled into the forecourt, their stereo pounding out the sound of Jesus Jones as they filled up the little car for their journey back to London. In truth, I too was still very much all over the place with the effects of the drug, and I can't deny that the thought of a joyful ride home with these two sweet-smelling indie chicks was quite breathtakingly attractive, but I knew full well: this would be *wrong*.

'Come on, man,' Alan was blethering. 'They're giving us a lift!'

'We can't!' I spluttered. 'We can't leave Billy here!'

Alan shrugged nonchalantly.

'It's not your problem, man.'

It's not your problem. Of course. It's never your problem. I'd been proper friends with Alan for about six months now, and was familiar with his overdeveloped sense of self-preservation – but this was pushing it even beyond his usual standards.

Billy was agog at the gathering atrocity.

'You can't just fuck off!' he yelped. I was standing in the centre of the forecourt, equidistant to the two vehicles. The girl driver had paid for her fuel and was skipping back to the car. Alan was already inside, leaning out of the window.

'Clive, stop being a knob! Come on!'

I looked helplessly over at Billy, who looked like he was going to cry.

'Billy, I . . .'

'Well, at least give me some fucking petrol money, then.'

I pulled my wallet from my pocket and tried to focus on the contents. There was nothing. It had all been spent on useless drugs. The girls' car beeped its horn.

'Sorry, Billy,' I muttered, and ran off.

Ouch.

As you know, this wasn't the last time I saw Billy, but that final glimpse of him from the Fiat's back windscreen – tired, alone, penniless, accompanied only by a useless hunk of orange metal, stranded two hundred miles from home at two in the morning – has always lingered with me, like a massive glob of chewing gum on my shoe of conscience. To this day, I have no idea how he got home. When I next spied him in school the following week I was too guilt-ridden to go anywhere near him. Alan, of course, reverted to his standard behaviour of denying Billy's existence. Yes, I allowed it all to happen. Yes, I went along with it, didn't protest. But what can I say, your honour? It was all about the girls and the music. You know how it is.

Girls and music.

Having relived that sorry escapade on this pleasant Sunday morning as the bus trundles along towards Soho, I'm finding myself quite gut-wrenchingly nervous. I keep telling myself it's only Billy Flushing I'm going to meet – Billy 'Quasi' Flushing, who once managed to trip over his own arm in the school computer room – but it doesn't help. It occurs to me that Billy's the second famous person I've had drinks with in less than a month, and for some stupid reason this thought makes me feel a bit unusual. As I'm a bit early, I slip into Bar Italia to steady myself with a quick coffee.

I sit there in my silly smart trousers and silly shirt and even sillier jacket, and reflect that perhaps it's not the fame that's making me nervous. Perhaps I'm just subconsciously preparing for the paltry little achievements of my life to be hurled into Billy's bottomless swimming pool of global success; even more so than with Lance Webster.

But what nonsense. It's Billy fucking Flushing. The dweeb I ditched. I neck my coffee, march across the road to the unmarked door and buzz the intercom.

'Forsyth's.'

'Oh, hi, I've an appointment with . . . Billy Flushing.'

'Certainly, sir,' replies the female voice. 'Come upstairs.'

This is one of those private members' clubs that are so private you don't even know you're in a club. You just feel like you're in some very rich person's house. I trot up the carpeted steps and emerge into a dark, slickly furnished sitting room, with some more stairs ascending to my right. An extremely pretty girl (dressed, to my bemusement, in a cropped T-shirt and jeans) leaps up from behind her laptop and shakes my hand.

'You must be Clive,' she beams.

'Er, yes.'

'Have a seat. Billy will be with you in just a moment.'

I sink deeply into one of the black velvet sofas while the girl summons a colleague on a tiny CB radio.

'Leona, please tell Billy his brunch has arrived.'

She gives me a melting smile and settles back behind her computer. 'Smart casual', my arse. I feel like sprinting to Oxford Street and buying some proper clothes.

'Oh my *God*!' says a voice suddenly. I turn to where the sound comes from, and there he is, Billy Flushing himself, coming down the stairs. 'Who the hell is *that*?' he laughs, bounding over to me and grabbing my hand before I've even had time to raise myself from the incredible sinking sofa. Our handshake morphs awkwardly into a strange sort of hug as I stand up; not that Billy looks remotely awkward himself.

'Clive Beresford, Clive bloody Beresford.'

'Billy Flushing,' I respond, trying to sound as natural as I can. I want the world to pause for a minute so I can study his appearance properly, but Billy has never been the sort of guy that *does* pauses. Now with his mantle of authority, he does them even less.

'What the fuck do you look like, you lunatic? You look like you're going to a boat race! Come on up,' he commands, turning back where he came from.

'Your PA said it was "smart casual",' I protest. He glances round and shakes his head.

'Oh God, sorry. Emily is so bloody by-the-book with people. I need to have a word . . .'

There's a distinctly transatlantic edge to his voice, I notice – you can hear it in the way he says his Ls. 'Emily' is 'Eh-mul-y'. – 'Bloody' is 'Bul-uddy'. Plus there's a little roll on the Rs. I follow him upstairs and we come into a plush bar, where another stunning girl is opening wine.

'Kate, can we have some drinks on the roof? Bloody Marys? Clive, you wanna Mary?'

'Er, yeah . . .'

'Two Marys, and menus.'

Kate nods and grabs two tall glasses.

I only get a proper look at Billy once we're on the roof terrace (a disappointing view, but the sun is shining; a man and a woman are already out here, drinking coffee). His face is certainly the face of Billy Flushing, not a lot has changed; but his skin looks healthy and taut, his big, chunky glasses look incredibly pricey, his black hair is scruffy but perfect and there's no trace of the clumsiness or bad posture which engulfed him as a youth. He's wearing rich, dark-green combats and a perfectly fitting white T-shirt, a chunky silver bracelet and trainers that look like they've been biked over to the club just a few minutes ago. Although he probably wouldn't be recognised if he walked across Leicester Square on a Saturday night, everyone he passed would know he was *someone*; it's that kind of look. He's also trim, muscular, and generally exudes health and vitality. The bastard. We settle ourselves at a table near the ledge and get started.

'So, Clive Beresford,' he smiles. 'Clive Beresford. The highs – and indeed the lows – of the last sixteen years, if you please.'

You don't require full details of the autobiography I embark on, but it's important you should know that I manage to tell the truth. Though I also refrain from mentioning Lance Webster. At first. Towards the last five or six years of my dull story, when less and less of any conceivable merit took place, his face noticeably drops.

'So . . . who are you writing for now?' he asks.

'I'm . . . not. Myself, really.'

'You're *not*? Clive, come on! What's your job, then?'

'I'm temping. For a bank.'

'For a *bank*? Oh, Clive, no! We gotta sort that out, for a start. Have you got a girl?'

'Nah, split up eight months ago.'

'Well, I can't help you with that one, my friend.'

'So, what about you?' I enquire, to which Billy grins and launches into his own rundown. Predictably it's a lot more interesting than mine: aside from the success story you already know (which he continues to be appreciably modest about), the following facts emerge:

1. He moved permanently to New York a year ago, but still has a house in Rickmansworth and a flat round the corner from the club ('I'd invite you for brunch there, but I've forgotten where all the supermarkets are').

2. He moved permanently to heterosexuality (as he describes it) two years ago, when he met his current girlfriend Clara, but has essentially been bisexual since leaving school.

3. He runs a fledgling indie label in London called Civilian Flush, one of the reasons he's over here this week.

Chatting to Billy produces a predictable blend of pleasure and misery. Obviously it's great to see him doing so well and, encouragingly, he keeps saying stuff like, 'I can put you in touch with the right guys, easy. You're a good writer, man! I could get you writing in New York within a week. I assume you still fucking hate comics, else I would have you working for *me*!' But throughout most of the conversation an enormous, vulgar-pink neon sign is flashing at me from behind Billy's head, complete with accompanying music, asking the obvious question: WHAT THE FUCK HAVE I BEEN DOING WITH MY LIFE?

After a while, naturally, Billy asks me about one of my current 'writing' projects, so I take the plunge and tell him about the recent Webster escapades. I tell him *everything* – or, at least, the first part: seeing Webster in the street, following him, working at the vet's and then putting that stupid letter through his door. Billy is almost on the floor with laughter.

'Noo!' he hoots. 'Clive, you fucking nutter, man! You weirdo! That's actually quite *dark*! I *like* that! And you've *no* idea what you wrote in the letter?'

I shake my head, glugging my drink.

'All I know is it had my email address in it.'

'How d'you know that?'

But of course, I can't tell him. Not without telling him all of the next bit: bumping into Webster in the pub, not being able to say it's me 'cos he sent the roadies round; calling myself Alan 'cos it's the only name that pops into my head; having to pretend I don't know who he is; looking at each other's writing; him finally realising who I am and running off, blah blah. By the end of this saga Billy almost needs an ambulance he's laughing so much, and the other people on the terrace have turned to look, perhaps thinking we're engaged in a tickling contest.

'Oh, my *God*, Clive! You *freak*! This is too much! What have you turned *into*, man?'

'I know,' I sigh, chuckling sadly. 'It's ridiculous.'

'It's *desperate*, that's what it is, mate. We need to sort you out! Cheryl, two more here,' he instructs a passing waitress. 'So, anyway – are you saying he's emailed you since then?'

'Yeah.'

'What'd it say?'

'It was weird. It said he didn't like being lied to, and he'd spent lots of time and money escaping from what he used to be . . .'

'So he was in therapy, basically.'

'Was he?'

'I dunno, I'm guessing,' Billy shrugs.

'Right. Then it said something about the past being dug up, and now he wants me to help him bury it, and to "be ready".'

'Oooooh!' screams Billy, his campest utterance yet. 'Wow! This is great! Why don't things like this happen to me? That sounds spoo-*ooky*!'

'Yeah. But there were no further instructions.'

'Aw, come on. Sounds like he wants you to get back in touch with him.'

'No.'

'He must do, man! It's obvious! Why would this guy, after all that's happened, give you his own fucking email address?'

'Dunno.'

The next round of drinks arrives. Billy busies himself with the straw, and I get a brief flash of what he used to be like with a milkshake.

'Hmmm,' he ponders. 'Lance Webster. Did they ever find out what happened to that crazy bitch?'

'Gloria?'

'Yeah! The one he was shagging.'

'They were *never* shagging,' I state firmly, to a stern look from Billy.

'Oh, Clive. Wake up, man! *Everyone* knows that! Even *I* know that, and I was never into the bloody band!'

'Well, *I* don't believe they were.'

'You'd defend their honour to the death, wouldn't you?' he sniggers. 'Christ, Thieving Magpies, eh? I remember you guys . . . you and that cock Potter, in your little indie uniforms. Sorry, dude, but you guys were so *sad*. I mean, you probably thought *I* was a total loser at school, but you were like fucking football supporters with that band . . .'

'Yeah, I s'pose,' I grumble. 'I was never into football, so they were like my surrogate football team.'

'So, are you gonna reply to him?'

'I dunno yet. There was something else he wrote, a weird bit about thanking me for all I'd done.'

'For looking at his writing?'

'No,' I frown. 'This was written to Clive, not the other guy.'

'But you *are* the other guy.'

'Yeah, but this was . . . different. I can't quite describe it, but it was blatantly written to Clive, and not "Alan".'

'And *did* you ever do anything for him?'

'Well . . . not really. Apart from writing a load of stuff in my fanzine, back when he was freaking out, and some letters in *Melody Maker* and so on. Y'know, supporting him. Telling everyone to leave him alone. Nothing he'd have known about, though.'

Billy giggles and shakes his head.

'Clive, I don't mean to belittle you, man . . . but I do feel kind of sorry for you. Christ, I mean . . . you're such a nice bloke, you always were, but you do end up sticking your neck out for people who probably don't deserve it. Isn't it time you put yourself first?'

'Well, I kind of am, really.'

'How so?'

So I spin him my usual yarn about Webster being forgotten, and how vindication for him would be equal vindication for me. I try Billy with my theory that all those druggie northern bands continue to bask in reverence while all the southern 'booze' bands – particularly my beloved Magpies – are quietly swept under the carpet, and how I want to redress the balance. Billy waves all this away.

'What can I say? Sorry, Clive. Thieving Magpies were *boring*. Everyone knows that. Lance Webster's one of the most boring men to sell a million records.'

'He's not!' I argue hopelessly. 'He's got mystery. Who else had such a public fall from grace that's never been explained?'

'Where's the mystery in that? He was just pissed off his career was going down the pan.'

'But that's the point,' I insist. 'It wasn't. Not yet.'

'Well, I dunno. He always seemed pretty dull to me.'

'He wasn't dull in interviews,' I point out.

'Who remembers interviews? It's all *words*. People only remember actions – visual stuff.'

'I don't agree.'

'Yeah, well . . . no offence, Clive, but you're not the sort of person that counts. Yes, you love Lance Webster's witticisms, Carter's puns, but God, how far down the food chain d'you think that shit goes? Do you know why I don't get too involved in movie adaptations of my stuff? Because I can't bear how much they have to cut *out*. So I just leave 'em to it. At the end of the day, audiences don't wanna think. People like songs for the choruses and catchphrases. They like films for a cracking good story with some laughs, a few bangs and crashes and a bonking scene. They like interviews for quick soundbites, and rudeness. Not intelligence.'

'What about Morrissey?'

'Morrissey was in The Smiths,' he shrugs, indicating no further explanation is necessary.

Something about Billy's directness is both appalling and refreshing. I expect I'll come away from this experience feeling rather like I did the few times I've ever been to a gym: that I enjoyed little of it, but it was precisely what I needed.

'You hate Liam and Noel for being mouthy, arrogant assholes,' he continues, 'but they're loved by a billion people for precisely the same reason. Yes, Ian Brown says fucking homophobic stuff in interviews and gets away with it, gets arrested for plane rage, and people still love him. But what do you want? Everyone loves a bad guy. I know it's not fair. *You* know it's not fair. But fuck it, that's life.'

He takes a fortifying swig of his Bloody Mary.

'But don't think you're the only one. I fucking love heaps of stuff – music, comics, films – which doesn't get anywhere *near* the sort of recognition it deserves, even from the "alternative mainstream". But I ain't crying. You talk as though you're the only person who still likes Thieving Magpies, or any of those bands. That's bullshit! I'll give you two scenarios, right? One: an alternative radio station, tomorrow lunchtime, plays 'Wonderwall'. Or 'I Wanna Be Adored'. Or, I dunno, that fucking Verve song. What happens? Nothing. Scenario two: the same station plays 'Look Who's Laughing'. Or 'Sheriff Fatman'. Or 'The Size of a Cow'. What happens? Twenty, thirty people phone up and say, 'oh, that song's so amazing, haven't heard it in years, reminds me of going to the fucking student bar' or whatever. They're *loved*, man. Rather than just part of the fucking wallpaper. And in the States? Let me tell you. If Thieving Magpies reformed tomorrow – God forbid, but let's just say – where would they play? Madison Square Garden.'

'No . . .'

'Madison fucking Square Garden! Guaran-*teed*. People in the States, and in Europe, they *remember*. But I'm telling you, the British press sends out a warped fucking viewpoint on culture, man. What's big and what isn't. Particularly for music. Dunno why. And when I say Britain, I really mean England, and perhaps Wales. Scotland and Ireland, they're fucking on the continent by comparison. You've no idea. England's a weirdhole. Thank fuck I left.'

I remember the Irish girls who accosted Lance outside the art gallery. Goddammit, the man might be right.

'But Clive . . . this is all just the gravy. Why you're sitting here still thinking about all this shit is beyond me. You're thirty-three years old, boy. The only way *you* can get ahead in your life is to forget all that shit, and get on with what *you* want to do. You want to meet this guy? You want to finally get that story out of him? You've fucking got to *go* for it. You email him back, *demand* he tells you what you want to hear. Make sure you lay it on really thick, all the guilt tactics, tell him you stuck your neck out for him, back in the day, tell him he *owes* you, then *drag* those fucking sordid details out, whatever the hell they are . . . and then you *move* . . . *the* . . . *fuck* . . . *on*! You want to write for somebody? Come to New York, I'll hook you up. You

want to sit around on your arse dreaming of 1990? Stay right
here.'

Stay right here.

We stay right there for another hour, blethering about this and that,
returning to our main subject every so often. We put away a delicious
brunch, have a few more drinks, then the natural time to go approaches
and Billy calls for the bill. I'm not quite sure why, but I'm a little taken
aback when it arrives and, having captained the entire experience –
drinks, conversation and meal, right down to ordering my own food
for me ('I know the best stuff they have here, dude') – Billy announces,
'So we'll split it, yeah? It's eighty-two quid, so that's forty-one each,
plus tip is forty-five . . . forty-five pounds and ten pence each.'

'Er . . . sorry,' I splutter. 'I haven't . . . um, I've only brought twenty
along with me . . .'

'Oh,' he frowns. 'Damn. Well, there's a cash machine up the street.'

'Ah, right,' I nod, and put my jacket on. 'Well, I'll be back in
five minutes, then.'

'Yeah,' he grunts, already starting to text somebody.

Billy waits until I'm almost through the terrace door, then howls
with laughter.

'Ha ha *haaa*!! You *goon*! Of *course* I'm paying for the whole thing!'

'Wha . . . uh?'

'This isn't even a proper bill,' he continues, scrunching it up. 'I
don't *get* bills here, man! I *own* half the bloody club. Ha ha *haa*!! Your
face was so *classic*!'

'Okay,' I smile, dripping with embarrassment. 'You got me.'

Suddenly Billy's smile vanishes, he reaches out and shakes my
hand with startling firmness.

'Now *that* was for Spike fucking Island.'

Fair enough.

And so I leave the cosseted world of the extremely successful and
mooch off into the warm, sleepy Soho Sunday afternoon. As usual

at these junctures, the temptation to instal myself at a nearby pub, phone a friend and let the rest of the day take its long, boozy course, is compelling. But Billy's proactive words are ringing loudly in my ears and I'm driven by some invisible energy back up to Oxford Street and straight onto the bus. By the time we hit King's Cross I've mentally composed three quarters of my missive to Webster, and even consider jumping off somewhere to get it done in an Internet café before I forget. But I stay on, repeating 'you *owe* me' like a mantra as we lurch up the Essex Road.

Once at the flat, I storm through the kitchen (where Polly is drinking Pimm's, wearing a bikini and midway through a jigsaw), settle myself down and begin to write what feels like the email of my life. And oh, it's a good one. It's beautifully written, sincere but not too cheesy, impassioned but steering clear of the stalkerish vernacular which doubtless screwed up my previous effort, well-argued, well-intentioned (I only say 'you owe me' once, and make plenty of references to it being for his own good), there are even a few laughs (I think) and, crucially – for this is a bad habit of mine – not too long. I finish it, step outside for some air, come back and edit thoroughly, remembering to add appropriate heartfelt apologies for having misled and repeatedly lied to him. It takes me the better part of four hours, no further alcohol touches my lips (but our kettle works overtime), and then, just when I'm scanning one last time before guiding my mouse to the send button, my computer dies.

No. It *really* dies.

It quite literally does *nothing*. It's like it has suddenly refused to accept electricity into any of its circuits any longer.

'Polly!'

I am so pissed off, so knackered, so unable to even *consider* writing the whole thing out again from memory, that I grab Polly's laptop, open up my email page, hit reply to Webster's original message and simply type this:

From: CLIVE BERESFORD
(cliveberesford@hotmail.com)
Sent: 3 June 2007 20:02:31
To: geoff@gwebmusic.com
Subject: (no subject)

Dear Lance
I'll gladly help you bury the past as long as you tell me
everything about the night of 12 August 1995. I think you
owe me.
Clive

p.s. sorry I lied to you

I add my mobile number to the bottom of the email, hit send and watch the little dial go round and round in the corner of the screen, counting down the milliseconds I have to stop the thing from leaving. I exhale as the confirmation page appears, shut the machine down and join Polly in the kitchen for a large Pimm's. The email vacates my head for the rest of the evening, not returning until I'm halfway to work next morning, at which point I chuckle heartily at life, with all the funny twists and turns that propel one to send abrupt emails to ex-pop stars on random Sunday evenings in June.

But the even funnier thing is – it works.

IT'S MY LIFE, SO I'VE NEVER FOUND ANY OF IT PARTICULARLY ENTHRALLING

It happens on a Thursday morning.

Thankfully, as it turns out. For several reasons.

But we'll get to that.

It's the usually underwhelming arrival of a text message that kicks it all off, while I'm engaged in that noblest of activities: taking my recycling to the recycling bank (I say 'my' and not 'our' because Polly decided some months back it was all claptrap and now throws everything rather ostentatiously into the council litter bins). I ping the last of the green bottles through the black plastic brush thingies, wipe the remnants of stale beer on the back of my suit trousers and stride over to the bus stop feeling rather pleased with myself. Then the phone bleeps and my world, frankly, stops.

> Ok you little shit you win. I'm at Heathrow terminal 3 for the
> next 4 hours, after that I won't be in the country for a very
> long time. Come and get it. L

Not acquainted with anyone else whose name begins with L and who'd send me something like this, my heart starts thumping and I frantically review my options. There aren't any. I make a breathless phone call to my office (despite being a crap liar I am the world heavyweight champion at pulling sickies) and race over to the other bus stop, the one that goes to the tube station. I'm still panting with anticipation, pinching myself and, more cynically, congratulating Webster on abandoning this 'Geoff' nonsense (though that *is* his real name, the poor man), when the karma comes hurtling back at me and my phone bleeps again.

> P.s. I'm beyond security so you'll have to buy a ticket some-
> where

'Buy a ticket somewhere? What the fuck do you mean, "buy a ticket somewhere"? Are you fucking out of your *mind*? Where? Where does terminal three *go*? Do you think I actually have *money*?'

I'm so incensed, all of the above is said out loud to the assorted bods gathered around the stop. With beer on my suit and profanities on my tongue, I'm one can of Carlsberg Special Brew away from the kind of nutter everyone moves away from. Lacking further bright ideas, I hurry off in the direction of home.

'I don't understand,' ponders Polly five minutes later, in between drags of her cigarette. 'Why would he be the other side of security?'

'God knows! He's fucking with me!'

'Mmm . . . maybe he's on a massive stopover?'

'From where?'

'I dunno,' she frowns. 'Like he's flying from Mexico City to . . . um, Warsaw?'

'Ah, yes. That commonly travelled route.'

'Well, anywhere you have to change in London, really.'

'Why would he be doing that? He's *from* London.'

'Clive, I really don't know. Sometimes people make odd trips. Might be work-related.'

'But he'd be able to *leave* security . . . wouldn't he? I mean, he's British.'

'I don't suppose you fancy texting back to ask why?'

I consider this for a second, but any of the phrases I might use ('Is there any particular reason you can't meet me in the public area?') sound pretty pathetic in the face of what he's offering me. Polly pulls her dressing gown around her and exhales elegantly, producing a plume of smoke that hovers above our kitchen table for almost half a minute. We both stare, as if it's about to morph into a genie. Which would be quite useful, in fact. Instead, Polly bangs her coffee cup down on the fridge and strides off to fetch the next best thing: her laptop. She plonks it on the table and starts looking at the Heathrow website.

'What are you doing?'

'You've expended too much energy on this bilge to bugger it up now,' she mutters.

'And?'

'So I'm finding out where terminal three goes, and we're going to get you in there.'

'But Polly, I haven't got any—'

'Clive, be silent. I've had quite enough of this cocking about.'

'But you can't seriously be suggesting we buy a whole airline ticket just to get me the other side of—'

'Shush! Here we go. Terminal three. Canada. China. Air India. American Airlines. Mauritius.'

'Nice of him to pick the budget one.'

'New Zealand, Emirates, Egypt, Japan . . .'

'Maybe we could just do it over the phone?'

'Balls,' Polly counters. 'Malaysia . . . lots of Middle Eastern places . . . Korea . . . ah, here you are . . . Turkey . . . Scandinavia. That's better.'

But the day-of-travel ticket prices are all astronomical. A couple of one-way tickets to Stockholm and Copenhagen for seventy-ish look promising, until we notice they go at ten o'clock (just over ninety minutes away, and I'm still at the wrong end of the Piccadilly line). Later this afternoon the fares shoot up to two-sixty.

'This is fucking ridiculous,' Polly yells at her machine. 'Why isn't there a flight to Guernsey or somewhere?'

Time is racing on and I'm pacing up and down the kitchen; the best bet seems to be Stavanger in Norway for two twenty-five, but then Polly has a brainwave.

'Air India fly to JFK,' she remembers, hammering on her keyboard. 'I bet they're . . . yes! Look! Two hundred!'

'You mean New York?'

'What other fucking JFKs do you know?' she snaps, pulling her purse from her handbag.

'Um . . . New York's a bit far, isn't it?'

'You're not bloody *going* there, Clive, you moron. There you go, two hundred including everything. Not bad. Who'd have thought?'

'Okay,' I sigh. 'Let's do it.'

Polly whips out her credit card and a few moments later I am heading back out the door. I turn round and give her a smile. She's a mad old fish but she has her moments. On Thursday she works from home, you see. At least, that's what she tells her employers.

'Any plans for today, then?' I ask.

'Jamie's coming round in an hour, there's a bottle of Stoli in the freezer and my legs need waxing,' she shrugs.

'Sounds like fun. Thanks, Polly.'

'Go on,' she nods. 'Fuck off.'

Of course, going to Heathrow on the tube is a journey longer than most flights, so there's plenty of time to review this incredibly odd place at which I've arrived. Exactly what's come over the man, I really cannot guess. As the train trundles past the familiar stops – King's Cross, Green Park, South Kensington, Earl's Court, Hammersmith, Acton Town – I become more confused and more nervous. It's pretty far from how I imagined I'd feel, on the way to receive this most precious of explanations. At Northfields I start worrying it'll be the anticlimax Billy Flushing suspected: simply a bad day, too much booze and the distinct impression his career was heading toiletwards. I require nothing short of Armageddon: at least four deaths of close family members, perhaps the revelation that Gloria Feathers had been male all along, and an alien visiting him in his dressing room before the show. Deep inside, I know I'm going to be disappointed. I'm also wondering how much of this 'burying the past' I'm obliged to help him with in return, and what it could possibly entail in a Heathrow departure lounge. As the train halts between Boston Manor and Osterley I look at my watch and realise that, whatever it is, we haven't got long to do it: a little less than two and a half hours.

At Hounslow East I'm starting to sweat, and another text arrives.

Are you fucking coming or not?

It's funny, his swear-count has gone zooming up since becoming Lance again. I fire an optimistic one back ('Yes, am ten minutes away') and wonder what sort of moody ex-rock star awaits at the other end. As we creep through Hatton Cross I find myself worrying that perhaps this is all an elaborate and expensive wind-up (which I may well deserve); a punishment for stringing him along with the whole 'Alan the writing coach' charade. At the very least, I suspect he'll be a little cold and uncooperative. Finally we roll up at Heathrow 123. I pelt down the long corridor (the travolator is conveniently broken), sprint into the packed departure hall, a nice lady checks me in . . . and then I discover the most likely reason for Webster's reluctance to come back out to the public area.

The queue for security is of *biblical* proportions. It's an epic. They've made entire Hollywood films about it. First I think it's a joke, or they're actually waiting for Richard Branson's autograph, or something. But no. It starts from a point irritatingly close to the barriers, then loops around the entire building, presided over by incongruously smiley airport staff, until it returns to its original source. It winds past three airport information desks, several bureaux de change, countless check-in areas, umpteen shops and no less than twenty-five branches of Costa. Occasionally an announcement is made, along the lines of 'if you're on such-and-such a shortly departing flight, go to the front of the queue', but as it's only ten past ten and my flight doesn't leave until after one, I'm not going *anywhere*. Once again my woollen suit is providing me with my own private sauna, and I'd kill for a coffee. Something must be done.

I leave the queue (I've moved a whole two feet since joining it) and wander over to the barriers. It's the usual bedlam of various airline employees ordering people about, arguments over the rules about carrying liquid, folks trying to push in and then being told to sod off by fluorescent-yellow-waistcoat-wearing Heathrow bods. I stick around for a moment to see exactly what occurs when passengers are legitimately allowed to barge through. A soon-to-leave Dubai flight is called, prompting a flurry of people flocking to the barrier from whatever distant corner of the terminal they'd reached. I watch carefully: a female airport official looks at the boarding pass of the first person, then unhooks part of the metal fence which holds the line of punters together, allowing the lucky few to walk down the side and straight past the hundreds of passengers shuffling along in the amusement-park-style internal queuing system until they reach the short line of people waiting their turn to put bags and jackets on the X-ray belt. The official at the gate only bothers to look at about one in three passes, whereas the bloke by the X-ray belt itself will look at every one of them, but by that stage in the process all he'll care about is that your boarding pass is valid, not how soon your flight leaves. I glance at my watch, then at the terminal-straddling queue. By the time I reach the front, it's certain that Lance Webster will be gone, up in the sky, off to wherever the hell he's going, leaving me with no story, no two hundred pounds and, as Alan would probably say, no *closure*. It's blatantly obvious what I should do.

I nonchalantly amble away from the gate, pretending to be on the phone. The further away I get, the slower I walk. I've travelled fifty metres or so when a new announcement is made.

A Virgin flight. To JFK.

One out of two ain't bad.

I turn around. All along the queue, people are ducking out and marching up to the barrier. I dash up the outside and spy a suitably chaotic family by the gate: a dad, a mum, a teenage boy, a nine- or ten-year-old girl and a toddler of indeterminate gender. I take a deep breath and sandwich myself between the woman and the teenager, smiling cheerily.

'Thank God for that, eh? Thought we were gonna miss it.'

'Oh, it's just madness,' replies the mum. 'Daniel, look after your sister. Jason, stop pulling on that gentleman's jacket!'

'Flying with kids, eh?' I smile at the dad. 'Nightmare.'

'We tried to leave 'em at home,' he winks. 'Rumbled at the last minute.'

'Been to New York before?'

And so, chatting away, we push our way along. As regular as clockwork, the airport official looks at mum and dad's boarding pass. Then everyone gets distracted by the toddler. The mum rushes back to fetch him. The teenager shows his own pass, then the girl and I walk through together. Finally the mum returns carrying the toddler, apologising profusely to the official. I'm just a slightly older cousin, or maybe the mum's much younger brother. But suddenly:

'Sorry, where are you going?' the official asks, pointing at me.

The whole terminal seems to screech to a halt.

'New York!' I beam, waving my boarding pass and risking a familial hand on the toddler's head. 'With this lot!'

'Okay,' she smiles.

Phew! Good old Uncle Clive. We're all one big, crazy holidaying family. We rush past the poor bastards snaking round the queuing fences and reach the X-ray belt in no time, where the nice man studies my passport and boarding pass and rods me through. My shoulder bag goes onto the belt, jacket goes in the tray. I skip through the metal detector and . . . I've done it. Three minutes. Fuck. It worked. I can breathe again.

And not before bloody time, because my phone is ringing. It's him.

'All right, all right, I'm here,' I puff. 'Where are you?'

'The Bistro, at the back.'

'Do they serve coffee?'

'Of course. Get your arse over here – I'm leaving in an hour.'

'An hour!' I yell, but he's hung up already.

Okay. So he's an impatient rock star again. Fun lies ahead.

I worm my way through the quagmire of shops, overpriced fooderies, tables, chairs and people, finally spotting the place he's at. I can see him in there, face wrapped in his damn shades, sitting at a table next to a frosted window. I'm sure he's seen me, but he's not smiling. I clear my throat, put my phone on silent and stride over.

'That was a very long ten minutes,' he begins.

'Have you seen the bloody queue?'

'No,' he says. 'I'm in first class.'

'Of course you are.'

'Hey. That doesn't stop my flight from being delayed by five fucking hours.'

'Five hours? Who the hell are you flying with?'

'Don't ask.'

He puts his newspaper away while I order my coffee. Once the waitress has departed he sits back, folding his arms.

'So.'

'So,' I reply, in a slightly more hesitant, questioning tone. His next statement is a curve ball.

'You've been dreaming about me.'

'I'm sorry?'

'That's what it says here,' he explains, extracting a wrinkled piece of paper from his pocket. '"Dear Lance, I've been dreaming about you."'

'Oh, God,' I gasp, the penny dropping.

'"I feel you are looking for vindication,"' he continues, one of his crafty smiles forming, '"and I can help you."'

'Just give me that bloody thing, will you?'

'Ah, na-na-na-na . . . not so fast, writer boy,' he commands, whipping the note out of my reach as I try to grab it. Bastard. He *is* enjoying this.

'So you kept it, then,' I blush.

'Course I kept it. I keep everything. What do you think "Disposal" is all about?'

'Hmm, yeah,' I nod, trawling through the lyric section of the old cranium. '"*I've got expanding cupboard space, for every word, every kiss, every punch in the face . . .*"'

'Well done,' he says, either impressed or being sarcastic, I can't really tell with his shades on.

'I'm afraid I'm a bit of a fan,' I venture, rather pitifully.

'Oh, I know *that*,' he smiles, looking at the wretched letter again. '"Thieving Magpies ruled my life and I hung on your every note but then you left. I need to know why, then I can move on." I've got to say, Mr Clive, after all your harping about grammar and sentence structure, yours is simply *appalling* in this letter.'

'I was very drunk.'

'I should hope so. You've even misspelled Thieving Magpies. Didn't they teach you, I before E?'

'Sorry.'

'Oh, please. The one thing I will not tolerate from you today is pathetic apology. You did what you did, and it got you here.'

'Uh, yes. Via two hundred quid for a single to New York.'

'New York? Bloody hell, was that the cheapest ticket you could get?'

'Yeah, but don't worry. I'm assuming it's all going to be worth it.'

'Dunno,' he muses, playing with the salt cellar. 'It's my life, so I've never found any of it particularly enthralling.'

'Right,' I consider, dredging up another lyric. '"*When the blinds are drawn and you can't see me, secretly engaged in some boring activity.*"'

'Aw, man . . . stop it! You're freaking me out now.'

'Sorry.'

'You know the bloody solo album well, don't you?'

'Yeah. Underrated.'

'Underrated, overrated?'

I prick up my ears at the title of a feature from *Definitely Not.* He can't know about that, surely? Must be a coincidence. I study his face, but I can't interpret anything with those stupid glasses he's got on.

'Sorry, could you take your shades off, please?'

'No.'

'Ah.'

'You never know,' he deadpans, leaning in, 'I might get recognised. Come on, time's ticking by. We'd better get on with it.'

'Yep. Well, I'm ready to listen.'

'Oh, are you, indeed? Well, I'm sorry, Mr Beresford. Before I tell you a damn thing, I want you to tell *me* something.'

'Uh?'

He brandishes my letter again.

'What on earth do you mean by this? "I know of the unspoken

love between you and Gloria. It's there—" spelt T-H-E-I-R, by the way – "in your lyrics."'

'I wrote that?'

'You did.'

Holy poo. I buy myself a few seconds by glancing around the restaurant.

'Please take note,' he comments politely, peering above his sunglasses for a moment, 'a response along the lines of "dunno, I was pissed" will result in immediate termination of this interview.'

'Which one, mine or yours?'

'Ha!' he laughs, genuinely. 'Both.'

With majestically good timing, my coffee arrives. Lance gazes up at the waitress while she pours, grinning at her in a slightly peculiar manner. She leaves without looking at him.

'No, she doesn't know I was a rock star,' he sighs. 'This country has gone to ruin, eh, Clive? Oh, sorry . . . you were telling me about Gloria.'

'Uh, yeah. Well . . . I always had a theory about you and Gloria. Everyone always said that you were shagging. Or, I mean, that you were romantically . . .'

'Romantically shagging. Yeah, I get it.'

'Yeah. But me and Alan . . . that's Alan my friend, the one I sort of named myself after . . . we knew you weren't. Dunno how. Just a feeling. But we also knew you wanted to, or at least, that *one* of you wanted to.'

'Hmm . . . right?'

'But that for whatever reason, it never happened. You had . . . um . . . other girlfriends, and she, well . . . she did whatever.'

He's frowning. I can tell that much, through the thick black plastic.

'It's funny,' he says, '*I* always had a theory that you'd be more eloquent than this, in person.'

'Sorry. I get a bit tongue-tied when I'm talking . . . *you* know this.'

'I meant you as Clive.'

'It's the same. I only write well. I had a dreadful stammer 'til I was thirteen.'

'Ha. That makes two of us.'

'Really?'

'Yes. Anyway, you were saying. So, what made you think all this? My lyrics?'

'Yeah. I mean the obvious one is "This Is What You Wanted" . . . "*The animals are fighting. They race around the building site, pretending it's exciting*" – that's the building site opposite Gloria's flat in Belsize Park. "*The candles and balloons are out, but it is not my birthday*" – that's Camden Palace decorating the venue for Gloria's birthday, but getting the wrong date. Then there's—'

'Wait, stop. How do you *know* all this?'

'We were *there*!'

'At her flat?'

'No, I mean . . . Alan and I were indie fans for years, which basically meant we hung out in Camden for years. You get to know where people live eventually. I knew where *you* lived . . . uh, not in a stalkerish way, of course.'

'Of course not,' he glares, tapping my letter.

'Er . . . anyway. Then that line "*another silent victory, but I'm still uninvited . . . I'll fight it out another year, convince myself I like it*" – That's Gloria, sort of lurking in the background, but never being . . . um . . . invited into your life, kinda thing, and fighting it out, as in, she'll keep being friends with you and the band but she's not really enjoying herself and it starts affecting her, in quite a bad way, which is what you meant in that interview when you said, "That was the start of everything going a bit wrong."'

He's silent. I stand and look over his glasses, just to check he's not fallen asleep.

'And there's others . . . um . . .' I delve into my bag and pull out Alan's scrapbook. 'There was this one time we went to a Pearl Jam show at Brixton, and Gloria was there in the bar looking pretty ill, really . . . She had one of her punk T-shirts on. We remember all this 'cos Alan managed to get a photo of me with her in the background. Might even still be in here . . .'

I'm flicking through the scrapbook for the particular date. Lance leans forward to look.

'Quite a piece of work,' he offers.

'Ha, yes. Alan's, not mine, I'm afraid. Here we are.'

A double-page spread devoted to the gig in question has a small coloured photo glued to the right-hand side. A smiling, long-haired me in a Flaming Lips top fills most of the frame, but Gloria's impossibly skinny figure is unmistakable amid a crowd by the bar. Her white ripped T-shirt bears the characters 'F=W+M'. Lance sees this, then gasps and sits back, his hand in front of his mouth.

'We thought about what the letters meant for ages, after the photo was developed,' I explain, 'but the only conclusion we could make was "Fuck Webster and McBriar". Then you wrote that "Bells Around the Ankles" song and we knew we'd got it right.'

Webster looks shocked and I consider stopping, but hell – he asked for it. 'Make sure you lay it on really thick,' as Billy Flushing said.

'Those lyrics: "*there in your white uniform, cursing him and cursing her*".'

'Okay, that'll do,' he snaps.

'Sorry. I told you I was a fan.'

At last, he takes his sunglasses off. There are tears in his eyes.

'Remember when we were sitting in the café of that toy museum, and I told you I was a selfish bastard, or something?'

'Uh, yes. I think you said you were a stuck-up, inconsiderate wanker.'

'Oh, even better, thank you. Well, I wasn't exaggerating. I dunno . . . it took me a while, but I now realise that it's hard, when you're that young, to be famous. It ain't natural. It all goes to your head. Even if you seem to be one of those people who handle it well . . . you're not really. Something's going to give somewhere, sometime. If it's not drugs, it's booze, and if it's not booze, it's . . . well.'

'Well . . . what?'

He exhales and looks at his watch.

'I suppose I'd better tell you the whole thing. Hadn't I.'

I CAN'T REACH YOU ANY MORE

You know how it is sometimes.

When you're headlining a festival. Not Reading or Glastonbury, like any normal band would; they'd been bagsed already by a couple of Beatles cover bands, some hairy old grungers from way back and (I mean, really) the singer from The Sugarcubes. So you're left with Aylesbury. Doesn't trip off the tongue, does it? Aylesbury. 'We're headlining Aylesbury,' you mention to people. 'Oh, yeah?' you half expect them to reply. 'Who's doing the other nights? Steeleye Span? Wishbone Ash? Landscape? Racey?'

But anyway. You wake to the sound of the phone ringing, climb across what you initially think is your guitar but actually turns out to be your girlfriend, and answer.

'Yeah?'

'Lance.'

'What?'

'Fancy coming for some breakfast?'

It's Martin, your unpredictable guitarist.

'What time is it?'

'Eight.'

'Fuck's sake. What time are we being picked up?'

'Ten.'

You ponder the breakfast option for a moment. It's a good Dutch hotel: strong coffee, cheese, cold meats, fruit salad, maybe a bit of smoked fish, scrambled egg, crispy bacon and those crazy little frankfurters. All of which you normally enjoy . . . in bed.

'Nah, I'm gonna ring for it.'

'No, but I need to talk to you.'

'Can't it wait?'

'No.'

You glumly climb into some jeans. Predictably unpredictable. But last time Martin wanted to 'talk' it was nothing more than him suddenly deciding he wanted to swap guitar parts in the bridge of 'The Cool and the Crooks' – so it comes as some surprise a few minutes later to find yourself being told, while he calmly spoons yoghurt and banana into his gob, that he wishes to leave the band.

'When?'

'Soon as this leg of the tour's over.'

Although you've often rehearsed receiving this particular bombshell from one of the others, and even considered dropping it yourself once or twice, hearing it for real is a totally different barrel of ale and your stomach is instantly bombarded by a blast of the most ferocious adrenalin.

'Who else have you told?'

'No one.'

'Really no one, or Bob no one?'

'Really no one. And I'd appreciate if you'd keep it that way, for now.'

'Uh . . . yeah, sure,' you reply breathlessly, gazing around the grand hotel dining hall. A few groups of business people. Some week-ending couples. A girl who's been giving you the eye and obviously knows who you are. You picture strolling up to her, sitting down and announcing, 'Hi. Do you know, you've just been watching Thieving Magpies split up?' As chat-up lines go, it'd be quite a winner.

Because ultimately, that's what it will mean. Yes, Martin could be replaced for live work, but the prospect of producing new material without his calming influence over the frequently squabbling Dan and Craig is unattractive in the extreme.

'Shit,' is all you can say, followed by a very long pause. Martin painstakingly clears up every last drop of yoghurt from his bowl, then wipes his mouth thoroughly on the starched white napkin. He's always loved his hotel breakfasts, has Martin. Especially in the early days. With no food in his fridge at home, arriving at a foreign hotel with breakfast included was almost better than getting paid.

'Aren't you going to ask me the obvious?' he enquires, raising you from memories of rosier times.

'I can't think of anything obvious.'

'I'll give you a clue,' he frowns, leaning in. 'It's one word. It begins with W, ends in Y and has an H in the middle.'

'All right, less of the fucking sarcasm, man. I'm in slight shock here.'

'No, but it's just *like* you to not even care.'

'Hang on. Is this about me?'

'That's part of it. I can't reach you any more, Lance. Neither can Dan and Craig.'

'What's the other part?'

'I wanna move abroad. It's . . . it's getting too much. In England. I need a break. I don't want to raise my kids in London.'

You're doing your best to consider the now ex-guitarist's words, but you can't keep your eyes off the girl across the room. She's a peach. She's also poured a glass of champagne for herself, and appears to have placed an empty glass opposite her, suggestively. Nice breakfast. She winks . . . or was that just your imagination.

'Lance? Are you even fucking listening to me?'

'Yes, yes. You're moving abroad.'

'I can't take another cycle of this shit. Album, tour, album, tour. It's driving me insane.'

'You don't mind the cash, though.'

'I knew you'd say that.'

The girl has now been joined by her man. What a little tease.

'I haven't been happy in *time*,' Martin continues. 'Not that you've noticed.'

'Well, I have been kinda busy . . .'

'That's right, you have. In your bedroom.'

'No, Martin. I've been writing the fucking songs that keep us afloat, in case it's passed you by.'

'As we all have.'

'Yeah, but . . .' God damn it. You drum your fingers on the tablecloth, thrilled to be having this conversation *again*. You should have taken Bob's advice years ago, insisted on a greater share of the songwriting credit; make the others realise how small their input actually is. But that would only mean more arguments.

'And I've been dealing with the Gloria thing,' you venture.

'The Gloria thing,' Martin leers, 'is mainly your fault.'

'Fuck you, wanker!' you shout, suddenly jumping up. 'You can fucking go anytime you like; we'll cope.'

You storm out of the dining room, everyone's gaze following you. Then, just for the hell of it, you walk back to the girl's table and smile at her boyfriend.

'Oh, sorry to disturb. Before you arrived just now? Your woman was *fully* flirting with me.'

You stride out, chuckling at the protestations and threats that ensue.

Back in your room, Katie has risen. She's doing her make-up, a time she always looks her best: her long, dark hair cascading over her tanned shoulders.

'You okay?' she asks, and you consider telling her the news. Instead, you open the minibar, knock back two Jack Daniel's miniatures in a row and artlessly fuck her on the hotel-room floor.

It doesn't matter how much money you're being paid; travelling with the band is always a dreadful experience. It was fun when you were eighteen, but now your late twenties are kicking in you'd prefer a method of getting about better suited to a man of your standing. Like: private plane. Or helicopter. Or even a nice, big, private car – anything that doesn't entail smelling Dan Winston's farts or pretending to laugh at the road crew's interminable 'humour'. It's enough to drive you to drink – which, funnily enough, it has. Anyone wanting reasons for why *any* rock star flew off the rails need only spend a couple of days on the road with a band. Of course, it would be a lot better if BFM were providing adequate tour support – but that's a conversation for another day.

You're met at Heathrow by Petra, Bob's relatively new assistant, who ushers you into the minibus. There's the usual frisson between her and Katie, but that settles down once Petra produces some lunch for everyone, and for once she's remembered Katie's veggie stuff. Petra's very excited as it's her first big festival headliner, bless her. You remember the morning back in May when Bob phoned to confirm you'd got the gig: Petra had just come out of the shower, all white towel and wet blonde bob, and she squealed so delightedly that you decided it was only fair to make her squeal again. Ah well, happy days.

Dan and Craig munch away; it's been a cordial morning with them, as usual, but who knows what they're really thinking after Martin's earlier suggestions of growing dissent. Martin himself has been maddeningly *over*nice; by the time the bus reaches the A41 turn-off you feel like punching him. You instead decide to ask Petra if the sun is over the yardarm.

'Of course it is, Lance honey,' she beams, producing a bottle of bubbly and some glasses from a cooler. 'You want to be mother?'

'Nah, Martin can be mother,' you smile, handing him the bottle. 'What do you say, Mart?'

He pops the cork and pours it out. You hold up your glass, look Martin straight in the eye and announce: 'To the Magpies, summer '95. And to the future.'

'The future,' everyone chants. Martin dawdles a second, wiping some mayonnaise off his trousers. When he takes his swig of bubbly, the minibus swerves slightly and he spills it all over his T-shirt. Ha. Screw him.

You've never been to Aylesbury before, but all British festivals look the same from behind. Same assortment of trucks, vans, tents, people with radios trying to look important, other people on mobile phones trying to look even more important, portable huts for a multitude of uses, security guards, bars, cordoned-off areas, even-more-cordoned-off areas, TV cameras, TV presenters running around with bowling-ball-sized microphones – and the laminates. The amount of different laminate passes always bewilders you. All you ever care about is that the one *you* have can get you in anywhere. So long as you've got that one, you don't give a fuck. If you approach an area – any area – and get stopped by a guard, then you've been given the wrong pass. Simple as that.

Petra doesn't seem to have the passes today. That's another thing that occasionally concerns you, but you try not to let it. Sometimes the passes come from a promoter, sometimes the festival organiser, sometimes from BFM (these are most frequently the wrong ones), sometimes your press agency, sometimes Bob. Sometimes from none of these people. Today is one of those days. The van parks up, the usual flurry of people start hovering nearby, and you wait.

'Best not get out yet,' advises Petra. 'We haven't got the passes.'

'And why is that?' asks Katie. Petra ignores her.

After a few minutes a man called Jonas, 'from the local crew', appears at the window and hands over some purple passes. They are all warm from the laminator. You are the headline band.

'Are you telling me you forgot to *make* our passes?' shrieks Dan, who's become a right little prima donna ever since he shaved his hair off.

'Uh, no, there's been a mix-up,' shrugs Jonas.

'Too right,' frowns Katie.

But you decide not to let this bother you. Besides, there's half that bottle of champagne left, and you're sure you spied another in the coolbox. Good old Petra. Bob always hires good girls.

Then comes the long walk from the van to your dressing room. You stick on your shades, grit your teeth and get on with it.

'Lance, hi! Delighted to have you here. I'm Rod Blunt from Aylesbury Festival, this is Siobhan who'll be looking after you today . . .'

'Lance, good to see you again. Vijay Shah from BBC Radio One. We're looking forward to the interview later . . .'

'Lance, how ya doin'? Mari Wechter, MTV Europe. Hoping to have a few words with you later . . .'

'L, ah dohn't noo if Malcolm's told ya yet, but the Gretsch's dead.'

'The Gretsch is dead?' you reply, feeling this is the only thing so far worth responding to. 'How did that happen?'

'Er . . . ah dohn't noo, musta happened in the truck somehoe. We're gonna have ta get one in for later . . . unless ya just wanna stick with the Gibson . . .'

'Stan, why the fuck would I want to stick with the Gibson?'

'Ah, ooh-kay, ah'll sort it out.'

'Hi Lance, babe. Here's the list for the press conference. We're having it in the bar. Petra knows the set-up.'

'Oh, shit, yeah,' you nod. 'The press conference.'

This is Bob's idea. Owing to the general feeling of malaise regarding interviews, and that BFM have firmly gone to sleep on the band despite platinum discs presently winging their way to Mortimer Street, a press conference backstage would kill a few birds with one stone. Plus, it's a firm proprietary gesture at this time of musical guard-changing: in case there's any lingering doubt, *we* are the Thieving fucking Magpies, this is *our* festival, and if you're very lucky we'll answer some of your questions.

'Make sure there's some booze there, yeah?' you tell her. 'Petra's got some bubbly shit.'

'No problem,' replies Heidi. Heidi from the press agency. Or is she Heidi from BFM? She used to work for one, now she's with the other. You can't remember which way round it is. Not that it matters.

You continue walking. Every so often Siobhan from the festival whirls around, flashes a smile and says, 'Almost there.' Black hair, decent figure, nice tattoo. But no. Gradually the flocks of people are thinning. Some bloke you vaguely recognise with a mod haircut and red tracksuit top is chatting to a security guard next to one of the portable huts. He spies you approaching, then flounces over towards you, proffering a cold can of beer.

'Lance! Good to see ya, man. Have a drink on me. Coming to see us later?'

'Coming to see you? Oh – yeah, of course! Which stage?'

'Main,' he smiles. 'Six o'clock.'

'Got it.'

Then as he turns to go, he says something else you don't quite catch.

'Sorry, what was that?'

'Nothing,' the guy says, as he winks and ambles off.

You walk past the security guard ('Good afternoon, Mr Webster,' he says, in what seems an overly formal manner) and realise you're finally in a zone only you can get to.

Oh, and the rest of the band.

And now you're inside the customary portable hut, which is hotter than Hades. 'HEADLINER' written on the door.

'Headliner,' you comment, in the general direction of Siobhan. 'Couldn't they remember our name?'

'Um . . . well,' she beams, 'we use the same room for all three headliners!'

'Yes, I imagine you do.'

She laughs nervously. 'Oh, well! Here's the dressing room. Let's open one of these windows, shall we? You've got all your refreshments here, shower in there, loo . . .'

Craig and Dan have caught up now. Craig ties his hair into a knot and unpacks his bag, making his usual little shrine of deodorant, spare sweatbands, cigarettes, a book (currently something by Terry Pratchett) and drumsticks. He takes an apple from the fruit bowl and chomps into it. Dan immediately begins to undress for a shower, another routine action from when he had usually filthy long hair which needed constant freshening up; he now seems to be experiencing a case of amputee's hairdo. Martin is chatting to someone outside; Petra is bustling around, drawing Siobhan's attention to some items missing from the rider; and you . . . well, you sit down and crack open the beer you've just been given.

Martin appears and sighs.

'Malcolm wants *us* to go check the rigs.'

You look up, perplexed.

'He wants us to check the rigs? Isn't that what we've got Stan and Doug for?'

'He says something odd's going on. They don't want to change anything unless we see it first. Remember what happened in Madrid.'

'Now?'

'Good a time as any,' Martin shrugs.

So you leave to accompany your outgoing right-hand man on this most menial of tasks. Malcolm, your reliable but over-cautious crew manager, leads the way: back past the security guard (who mutters something inaudible as you pass), then a crazy short-cut under guy-ropes, behind catering vans, through a car park where the sun beats down mercilessly on the multicoloured metal rooftops. You can hear the muffled roar of some band hammering out a song you recognise (*'I guess I'm doing fine, guess I'm doing fine . . . Do y' think I miss you? Do y' think I care?'*) as you finally loop round to the massive grey globule that is the main stage, halting by a sealed-off area where all the Magpies' equipment is held. A pale, spotty security chap of about fourteen with heavily gelled hair guards the entrance. Malcolm disappears inside, you try to follow.

'Uh . . . can I see a pass, please?' the guard mutters.

'A pass?' you repeat, incredulous. 'It's my fucking equipment in here. *That's* my pass, pal.'

'I still need to see a pass.'

Martin whips his own from his pocket and holds it out for inspection.

'Sorry, these aren't authorised for this area,' responds the guard.

'Bullshit,' you state flatly, and push past. Martin stays to argue.

Inside the tent a few roadies are standing around, smoking, looking worried.

'Hi Doug, what's all this shit?'

Doug is a dreadlocked, tattooed six-foot-sixer of the sort they don't make any more; been with you since *Shoot the Fish*.

'Something fuckin' odd's happening, L. I changed all Mart's valves before the show yesterday, every single one. Now they're all broken.'

'Weird,' you agree. 'And mine?'

'All the speakers have been unscrewed and ripped on the Twin and the Marshall.'

'Ripped?'

'Yup. In the last two hours.'

'In the last *two hours*?'

'Yeah. I tested it all when we got here, and now they're all fucked.'

You wander up and down, inspecting a few of the guitars, swigging from your beer can occasionally.

'Is Jerry about?'

'Nah, he's having lunch. But don't worry, the drums are all fine.'

You lower your voice.

'What's the security bloke like?'

'Just a kid. Seems okay, though.'

Martin comes storming in.

'We've been given the wrong passes. This guy's never *seen* one of these before.'

The rat you've been smelling starts to turn putrid.

'Fuck it,' you decide. 'Have any of you guys got a mobile phone?

'Malcolm has,' Doug replies.

'Malc!' you shout. He emerges from behind the keyboard rack, sipping a Coke. 'Call Petra. Call Bob. I want a meeting in the dressing room in five minutes with that cock from the festival and someone in charge of security. From now on' – you point at the gear, then at the assembled crew – 'I want one of you guys in here at *all times*. Got that?'

They nod, and you depart. As you pass the security guard you're sure you hear him say something – sounds like 'saul oh' – but as you've no idea what that means, you park it to one side and rush back to the dressing room.

Bob Grant wipes the sweat off his bald head with a hankie, straightens his frankly appalling Hawaiian shirt and knocks on the hut's doorframe as if planning some impromptu DIY. The rest of the band are stretched out in a little patch of sun on the grass, but you're standing, shifting your weight from one leg to the other, limbering up for the fight to come. In your hand is the offending laminate, which you've bent out of all proportion like an expired credit card. Shortly, Petra appears with Rod Blunt (green polo shirt, empirebuilder shorts, looks more like a scoutmaster than a festival organiser) and a thickset thirty-something who introduces himself as Steve, head of security. Bob begins to diplomatically explain the problems you've so far encountered, but after a minute or two you get bored, knock back the rest of your lager and leap in.

'Nah, Bob, sorry to interrupt, but this is far more fucking straight-forward. We are the headline fucking band, the reason this fucking festival *exists*, and someone, I don't know who, I don't really *care* who, is fucking with us. I want it nipped in the fucking bud right now, or you get no show from us. You guys – you talk amongst your-fucking-selves and work out what's going on, whether it's your security guys having a laugh, or someone slipping them a tenner to fuck with our gear, or someone slipping them a line of fucking charlie to turn a blind eye. Whatever it is, it stops *now* or we don't fucking play. I want that kid on our equipment tent moved right to the other side of the site. I want *him*' – you point at the chap guarding your dressing room – 'moved as well. And I want a laminate that's so fucking triple, quadruple A that it gives me the right to walk in on Louise Wener while she's having a shit. You got that?'

It seems they have. They apologise nervously and depart.

'So, what exactly did you need me for?' grumbles Bob, hurrying off.

The backstage bar – a tent normally crawling with industry knobs and liggers in various states of inebriation – is stuffed to the gills with music journalists, such that you can smell them from twenty yards away. They loll on the white plastic garden furniture and nag at their bottled beer while *The Social Trap* cannons out of the speakers, doing battle with what sounds like Judas Priest on the main stage (but you're sure that can't be right). Petra skips over as you approach, finally bearing your new laminates. Someone, either by mistake or for a crack, has obeyed your command precisely and printed four As on it, which unexpectedly makes you chuckle.

'As long as it works, eh, Spalding?' you smile at your drummer, who for some mysterious reason has brought along his Pratchett novel. 'Worried you'll get bored?'

'Yeah, or in case I need the loo halfway through,' he replies. Good old Craig. The only band member who never pisses you off.

There's a muted round of applause as you enter and take your seat: in the middle, as usual, flanked by Craig and Martin to your left, Dan and Heidi to your right. So she *is* with the press agency. Glad you've cleared that one up.

'Okay, one at a time. Let's have it.'

It's pretty much autopilot from hereon in. You like press conferences. There's not the inconvenience and pressure of having to talk to just one person, and you can play off all the daft stuff hacks say in public. It's like playing a gig with none of the music and just the between-song banter, which has always been your favourite part. Petra passes by occasionally, refilling your champagne glass; none of the other guys say an awful lot, but then they never do. Overall, you prefer it that way. Stops them from saying anything stupid, like that time in Zurich when Dan described Switzerland as 'basically part of Germany'.

In the main, the session is a public hearing of the battle currently raging between the older writers (Kenny Mann, Vincent Bates) and the newer ones (Blair Cooper, Toby Johnson, plus that knob from *Craze*) over who can out-hip and out-reference the other. You're a little disturbed to find you usually agree with the older ones, even Mann, whom you and Gloria always detested. You've never laughed so hard as when she socked him in the face that time. 'Hell hath no fury . . .', etc.

But you can't help feeling irritated when some little shit from *Select* smugly notes 'the unexpected success of *The Social Trap*'. Time for a spot of your sleeping-alligator routine.

'I'm sorry . . . "unexpected"?'

'Yeah.'

'I don't understand. Why was it unexpected?'

'Well . . .'

'Did you read that somewhere? Was it in *Music Week*?'

'Well, you've been away for a while, and—'

'A year.'

'But, I mean, since your last studio release—'

'Which sold four million copies, yes.'

'And the musical map has—'

'Ooh, here we go, it's a geography lesson! The musical map. Is that a map that whistles a Black Sabbath song when you stick a pin in Birmingham?'

'No, but—'

'It's never as cut and dried as that, my friend.'

'Sure, but what's your view on the whole Britpop movement?'

'Britpop?'

'Yes.'

'What the fuck is Britpop?'

'Um . . .'

'Brit. Pop. Brit . . . *ish*. Ah! And Pop . . . *ular music*. I get it! Well, *we're* Britpop! The Beatles were Britpop. Manfred Mann were Britpop. The Real Thing, Hot Chocolate, Thompson Twins, The Lotus Eaters, The Associates, The Goombay fucking Dance Band.'

'Actually, they were German,' puts in Martin, above the rising murmurs.

'Well done,' you smile, clinking Martin's champagne glass with yours and knocking it back. 'Spotted the odd one out. Martin Fox, ladies and gents! Petra, can I have a refill?'

Amazingly, the journo is persisting.

'Okay, call it the current explosion of new music. What do you think of it?'

There's a bit of unease in the air and you realise a serious answer might be required.

'Oh, it's all *right*. I mean, I can sort of see why you lot are getting your knickers in a twist over it, that's pretty predictable. But in reality, it's just a decent crop of new bands, and they're all doing fairly decently. It happens. I'm not convinced it's earth-shattering. I haven't heard anything that, like, radically influences me or sends me scratching my head back to the drawing board. But it's pretty healthy, I s'pose. A fuck sight better than the crap around when we first came out. I quite like Sleeper, she writes good lyrics. Supergrass are cool. Will that do? Can I start talking about The Goombay Dance Band again now?'

Heidi picks a serious-looking chap at the back.

'Kai Johansson, *Svenska Dagbladet*, Stockholm. I'd like to ask who you would like to be number one from Blur and Oasis.'

Feeling the need for some variety, you look at your band.

'Guys?'

'Uh . . . dunno,' mutters Martin.

'Blur,' answers Craig, firmly.

'Anyone but Oasis,' offers Dan.

'And you, Lance?' asks the writer.

'Neither. I think both songs are shit.'

'But which band do you prefer?'

'Slade.'

Then you notice that tool from *Craze* has his hand in the air. You're bored. Time for one more scrap, after which it really would be nice to see some music.

'Heidi, pick him,' you instruct.

'Who?'

'The guy over there from *Craze*,' you say over the microphone in a stupidly loud voice, pointing at him, 'who's had his hand up for about forty minutes.'

'Okay, you,' she squeaks. *Craze* bloke smiles cordially, so you smile back even wider.

'Tony Gloster, *Craze*.'

'Tony! Welcome! How *nice* that you made it along. How . . . *difficult* it must have been to drag yourself away from Noel Gallagher's arsehole.'

You're rewarded with a gratifyingly loud blend of laughter and outrage.

'There's no need for that,' frowns Gloster.

'Oh, yes? Just like there's no need for some of those intelligent, thought-provoking things you wrote in your album review. What was it . . . "like a bitter, alcoholic old uncle arriving for Christmas – they're back"?'

'Er . . . it's called a bad review. Live with it.'

'Well, you're right, it most certainly *was* a bad review. And there was another thing that tickled me: "Quite why Webster and others believe they are required in 1995 is baffling." You want me to explain it to you?'

'If you want.'

'Was that what you put your hand up to ask?'

'Well, as you haven't given me a chance to even speak yet—'

'Aw . . . Tony. Poor Tony! Sorry, please . . . ask me what you wanted to ask me.'

'It'll be a let-down now.'

'Just ask, and ye shall be answered.'

'I was just wondering whether you saw yourself as part of, or an alternative to, the current explosion?'

'Oh, booooring,' you moan, having expected something far more fruity. 'Why would anyone want to know *that*?'

'I think it's important. For you, and for your fans.'

'Well, I must tell *you* that I really don't understand why we have to be either, but I would also imagine that none of our fans give the slightest shit as long as we keep making good records. I mean, who cares? Really?'

'Were you ever concerned that the Magpies would be superfluous to the whole thing?'

'Sorry, Tony, I didn't go to university. I don't understand words with more than two syllables.'

'Did you worry that you'd be rendered unnecessary?'

'Hmmm . . .' you think, glancing over at Heidi, 'that one's got *five* syllables. Oh, I dunno. You tell me. Why would we be?'

'Well, you're part of the old guard.'

'The *old* guard. The dear old guard.'

'Pretty much everyone else has been swept away.'

'Swept away! Yes, sweep us away, under the carpet, before Alan McGee spots us!' you cry, swigging a bit more champers. 'Whoever said press conferences weren't fun? Sorry, Tony, I haven't got the foggiest idea what you're talking about.'

'Yes, you have. All your ilk have been eclipsed. The Cure. The Wonder Stuff. The Mission. James. Pop Will Eat Itself. Carter. Jesus Jones.'

'Ha! And you've forgotten Ned's Atomic Dustbin, Eat and Kingmaker, and why don't you throw in Gaye Bikers on Acid and Dumpy's Rusty Nuts while you're at it? Are you getting all this off the back of an old Camden Palace flyer, or what? You see . . . you're looking for answers that don't exist, Mr Gloster. You're reading me names of bands who burned out long before this Britpop thing reared its trendy little head. But we, the Thieving fucking Magpies – head-liners of *this festival*, in case anyone's forgotten – we have *always* been capable of moving on, and we're not stopping now just 'cos there's suddenly a cool new scene for all you cool new people to shake your record bags to. I mean, why the fuck shouldn't people continue listening to us? Why is it such a fucking surprise? It's not as if we're doing something completely contrary to what's happening now. We use guitars. We're British. We write real pop songs about real life. And we still rock harder than fucking anyone. A lot of the new bands rock about as hard as Simply Red.'

You grin at your own gag and glance at the rest of the band. They look as if they're waiting to be called at the dentist's. For God's sake, why don't they ever help out in these situations? You'll have a right go at them afterwards.

But Gloster, unbelievably, still wants to talk.

'But you represent a bygone era.'

'No, we don't, my little friend. That's just what *you*'ve decided, because the goths and grebos used to dig us, and 'cos we're from Reading as opposed to Stockport or wherever. It's total and utter bullshit. I bet you don't ask Shaun Ryder the same question. If you do, he'll probably sit on you, and *then* you'll be sorry.'

'Does a backlash scare you?'

'Hey-hey, it's the backlash!' you whoop, getting up and doing a little jig. 'Welcome back to the backlash, ladies and germs. No, I don't fucking think so. We've already had four of the fuckers. One after each album. We'd survived our first one probably before you finished your GCSEs.'

You turn and nudge Martin in the ribs, which prompts a ferocious glare.

'Wha'sa matter with you?' you hiss at him. 'Why don't you cunts fucking cheer up?'

'What about from the public?' persists Gloster.

'Oh, Tony . . . Tony, Tony, Tony, stop being so bloody tiresome. I want to go and watch dEUS. Please can I go and watch dEUS? Mum?' you shout over to Heidi. 'Can we stop now?'

She cocks her head to suggest you should answer the last question.

'Oh, all right. No, we won't be having a backlash from the public, Mr Gloster, thank you very much. We've got a platinum record, and you can all just fuck off.'

You stand up, and walk straight back to the dressing room without a word. Well, it's an appropriate end to an appropriately dull conference, isn't it? These things are never any fun any more.

Oh, and the band come storming in a few minutes later to have a go at you. Well, that was inevitable. But you give as good as you get, telling them they're all zombies, and that it's by behaving precisely as *you* just did that the Magpies retain their edge, their abrasive style, their reputation for biting intelligence and lyrical wit. Surprisingly, the most sensible comeback to this comes from Craig.

'But you didn't sound intelligent just then, L. You sounded *disturbed*.'

You open another beer and consider this charge. How you'd love to tell him that, in fact, you *are* a bit disturbed. Actually, that you're completely lost; that you feel you've lost a limb since Gloria vanished, and that of *course* you blame yourself for everything that happened, for taking such colossal offence all those years ago when she decided, purely on the strength of one of her cosmic experiences, that she wasn't destined to be with a rock star after all, and that you then turned into such a promiscuous fool, making sure every girl you fucked was as drop-dead gorgeous as possible just to punish her, gradually grinding her down to the point where she started to destroy herself, and then . . . well. You'd prefer not to think about that. But you can't tell the band any of this. Any kink in your armour and you'll be ripped apart. You'd also love to inform Dan and Craig that your day didn't have exactly the most wonderful start with Martin's little announcement; but you gave him your word, and Lance's word is Lance's word. That's one part of your reputation that you *never* want sullied.

The argument winds down and you suggest to Craig that, at last, some music might be a good idea, so – taking a couple of cans for the journey – you stride back out into the sunshine.

At this point, your day considerably improves. You're heading in the vague direction of the second stage (the *Loaded* stage, as Craig corrects you) to catch a bit of dEUS, but, as usual with festivals, there are all sorts of diversions on the way. You're wearing your shades and (a nice effect, you thought) a pith helmet, but the number of fans who still recognise you is astonishing. Or maybe they recognise Craig, then put two and two together. You're not prone to self-doubt, or even band-doubt, especially with the album flying out the shops as it has been, but today's press conference succeeded in making you a little nervy, so the colourful collection of long-haired boys and girls who approach as you traipse along is hugely gratifying.

'Hi Lance, wicked to have you back, geezer.'

'Lance, fucking can't *wait* for later, man.'

'Oh my God, it's you! Can you sign this?'

'Theeeeeevers! Spirit of '89, mate.'

'Or '88?' You laugh.

'Craig!' says another. 'Fuck, you're my fave drummer of all time! Well, after Dave Grohl.'

'It's always after Dave Grohl, innit,' Craig laments.

'That's okay,' you counter, cracking open another beer. 'With me it's usually after Mike Patton, and how do you think *that* feels.'

Some dudes are kicking a football about.

'Lance! On the 'ead, mate!'

You join in for a few minutes, delighted to be in the real world. An insane-looking collection of misfits are knocking out something familiar on the main stage ('*baby we don't love ya, baby we don't love ya, baby, yeah!*'), perfect for a sunny day in the country. Then it's all high-fives and 'see you tonight's and you're off again, towards the red big-top on the far side of the arena.

'Gonna be good tonight, then,' volunteers Craig.

'Of course it is, Mr Spalding,' you smile. 'Course it is.'

The fun continues as you arrive at the *Loaded* stage, where dEUS are midway through administering a shambolically energetic set to the couple of thousand punters who pack the tent. An ecstatic bloke in a Weezer T-shirt gives you and Craig a hug, then runs off to buy you a couple of pints. Some very young girls demand you sign their brand-new Aylesbury '95 long-sleeved tops ('It'll ruin a nice top, though,' you merrily protest). You push on forwards, shaking hands with various people every few minutes, enjoying the band, gleefully allowing yourself to be pushed and pulled as everyone bounces up and down to the chorus ('*she knows where she rolls when she goes for the doorknob*') and supping your pint of snakebite. Funny he got you snakebite. It must be years since you had it. He probably thinks that's all you drink. It's strong stuff.

'Better take it easy, I s'pose,' Craig comments. 'Long time 'til we play.'

'Shit,' you grin. 'Forgot we had to actually play later. Maybe you could get Stan to do it for me.'

'Okay,' he agrees. 'I'm sure Jerry'll do a fine job on the drums too.'

You watch a few more songs then wander out again. Funny old thing, the grand old British music festival: what a bizarre rock on which your career has been built. But it's been good to you. Your career, from such strange beginnings: when an odd but pretty girl called Rosamund gave you that first compilation tape in 1983: Bauhaus, Gene Loves Jezebel, The Cure and The Sisters of Mercy on the first side; The Smiths, Orange Juice, The Pastels and The Lotus Eaters on side two – and you realised, with her help, that you could do it too. You dreamed together; you got drunk together; you even changed your names together. How you loved her. Gloria, that crazy, wonderful, messed-up girl, who remained so bizarrely adamant that she wasn't destined to be yours, but who guided you every step of the way. And how the indie world welcomed you with open arms back then, and how (you believe) you've done your bit in return.

And you realise what a prick Martin is for suddenly rejecting it all. Who knows what will happen now. You've still got tonight, of course. But as you wander across the dusty field – past the stalls, the coloured hats, the endless piles of army-surplus stuff, the burger vans, the herbal pills that never work, the beer tents, the merch stands (the latest Magpies top looks particularly good, you notice, stretched out at the top of the display board), the noodle-eating, pint-supping, sunbathing masses and the ever-changing sonic palette of jagged chords and thumping beats – you realise that in some strange way it feels like you're saying goodbye. You pause, undisturbed for a second, blinking at the gradually setting sun, trying to take it all in, just in case you never see it again. If this really was it – tonight – you figure it'd be okay. No one could say you hadn't had a good run.

You've plenty of fine memories, and enough pounds left in the bank. Some mistakes too, many regrets and a lot of pain, which you know you'll have to deal with over time. But on balance, this is a world which has made you happy.

'You all right, L?' asks Craig.

'Yeah, man,' you smile, watching some fool doing a bungee jump in the distance. 'Nice festival. Glad we picked it, really.'

Slowly the sound from the looming main stage overtakes every-thing else as you make your way back, and you catch a glimpse of the band. You're not sure who they are – neither is Craig – but they seem to be a graduate of the more recent, retro school of thought, competent but not madly impressive, a load of old Rolling Stone chords in search of a decent song. Could it be Shed Seven? No, they're better than this. As are The Bluetones. But it's along those lines. With your slightly superior headliner's cap on, you muse aloud to Craig that it'll 'all be over in six months' – then quietly take it back. Gloria used to gravely warn you about the karmic consequences of slagging bands while watching them. The woman usually had a point, as the next few minutes prove.

Firstly you notice that everyone in this particular corner of the festival has short hair. Then you realise all the clothes are different – tighter-fitting, smarter than usually seen at festivals; velvet suits, shirts, ties. Either that, or more on the sporty side, Adidas T-shirts, vintage trainers. It might be your imagination, but people also seem to be drinking more. Which isn't a completely bad thing; after all, you've been at it all day. That reminds you, there's another can of beer in Craig's bag, so you steady yourself by cracking it open. Another change is that no one's recognised you for a while. Again, not a disaster in itself, but substantially different to elsewhere.

'This is called "Haley's Blues",' announces the vocalist. 'This is for all you lot to shake about to. It's our last song. Have a blindin' evening, enjoy Gene and The Boos, and remember to go somewhere else for the headliner, eh?'

A whoop of laughter slaps you in the face and you feel like you're watching your own funeral.

'What a cunt,' observes Craig, but you're too shocked to reply. 'Come on, let's get outta here. I'm gonna smack him if I see him backstage.'

Backstage. You look at your watch, and then it hits you.

'Shit, hang on! It's six-thirty.'

'Yeah?'

'This is that band! That guy . . . the guy who was talking to the security bloke on our dressing room when we arrived!'

'Which means?'

You squint at the stage. There he is, in his red tracksuit, laying into his Hammond organ.

'It's him. These are the people who are trying to fuck us, Craig. I bet that . . .'

You look around the audience, trying to spot someone you recognise. You're standing handily near the entrance to the VIP enclosure, so you bet there's . . . yes, there he is: Tony Gloster, wigging away in his corduroys and his bloody Graham Coxon spectacles . . . and there's that idiot Blair Cooper, a little further forward, unmistakable with shades on his head and a Creation record bag.

'Fucking *arseholes*,' you pronounce, grabbing Craig's arm and hurrying towards the backstage entrance.

'Lance, I really don't think you should have anything more to drink for a while.'

'Whatever.'

A group of chaps are just leaving the enclosure as you approach. One of them sniggers as he sees you.

'What's so fucking funny, dickhead,' you snarl as you pass him.

'It's all over,' the guy replies, clearly.

Followed by more laughter.

You remain still and think for half a second; then you're off again, storming past the guard by the VIP entrance, holding your pass right in his face.

'Don't even *think* about saying I've got the wrong one.'

He doesn't. What he does say, almost out of earshot as you flounce off, is the same phrase again: 'It's all over.'

'What did you fucking say?' you scream, turning on him.

'Nothing,' he shrugs, innocently.

'Wanker!'

You dash away again. Once inside the enclosure, Craig catches up with you.

'Lance, for the second time today, you are behaving like an utter cock.'

'No, Craig! *Listen!* Call me hysterical, man, but it's a fucking conspiracy.'

'Erm . . . hysterical,' he obliges.

'No, no, *think* about it! Haven't you heard what they've been saying to me?'

'No, all I've been hearing is you mouthing off to people.'

'They're saying "it's all over", didn't you hear them? The prick in the red tracksuit said it, then the security guy by our hut said it, and that little cock guarding our gear before, *he* said it. Hasn't anyone said it to you?'

'Sorry, no.'

'Oh, fuck it . . .'

You glare around at the assembled drinkers and the little queue of girls by the toilet, most of whom are gaping in your direction. It's not something they're used to, the lead singer of the headline band arguing with his drummer in the middle of the backstage area. 'Listen, Craig, whatever you think, do me a favour, will you? Please go over to the equipment tent and check everything's okay. One of our guys should be in there with the gear. If he's not, come straight back to the dressing room and tell me. Will you please just fucking do that for us?'

'Okay! Okay,' Craig says, holding his hands up in surrender and backing off.

You're getting all hot and hassled now, so you whip off your pith helmet. Aware that appearances need to be kept up, you tidy your hair, take a deep breath and walk at a more casual pace back towards the dressing room. Unfortunately, this is the wrong thing to do. Your reduced speed means you can clearly hear, at least five times as you cross the makeshift beer garden, different people saying the words 'it's all over'. Not wanting to look like a total, frantic fool, you ignore every single one of them. Then, just as you've reached the other side, a small female insect pounces.

'Lance, hi! Mari Wechter, MTV Europe.' Here she is, with her beach-ball-sized microphone and her cameraman lurking behind. 'Would now be a good time to have a few words? I'm sure viewers all over the continent would love to hear—'

'Er . . . not such a good time right now, no.'

'Oh, just for a minute. We're very excited to see you and your band back on the festival circuit. Couldn't you just—'

'Sorry, Mari, can we make it slightly later, I need to—'

'It'll only take thirty seconds of your time. We can't wait to see the—'

'Not! *Now!*'

It takes every molecule of willpower you possess to not grab her by the shoulders and shake all the slick, televisual enthusiasm out of her. She gets the message, coughs with surprise and turns back to the cameraman.

'Maybe it *is* all over,' she mutters.

Your patience exhausted, you sprint the rest of the way back to the dressing room where thankfully a different security guard awaits. This is a big guy, reassuringly older, perhaps in his mid-forties, with short blond hair and a slight beer belly.

'Hello, Lance,' he says, warmly holding out his hand. 'It's nice to meet you. I'm going to be doing your dressing room security for the rest of the day.'

'Ah. And your name is . . . ?'

'John,' he replies. 'Great to be working here. I've been a big fan of yours since *Lovely Youth*.'

'Oh . . . right! Well, nice one, John.' West Berkshire accent, you note, just like your mum and dad. You gesture towards the hut. 'Anyone home?'

'Yes, I think your young lady is, as a matter of fact.'

You find yourself a little caught out by his friendliness. However, your initial character appraisal says there's something sincere about him; perhaps not the most interesting man in the world, maybe a slight jobsworth, but he seems trustworthy, which must go a long way in the security business.

'Listen . . . John,' you confide, leaning in slightly, 'do me a favour, will you? If . . . if anyone tries to *give* you anything, like a bribe or anything like that . . . will you let me know?'

'A bribe?' he frowns.

'It's just that . . . there's been some weird stuff happening today. I don't know if you've seen anything . . . have you?'

'Not that I know of.'

'Well, anyway . . . be sure to tell me if anything untoward occurs.'

'I'll do that, Lance.'

'Thanks,' you smile, patting him on the shoulder. 'Oh, and whatever they offer you, I'll double it,' you chuckle.

He looks confused for a second, then laughs awkwardly as you hop up the steps of the hut.

Katie is inside, managing to smoke, nurse a glass of wine, talk on her phone and apply some after-sun lotion to her sunburnt shoulders all at the same time.

'Hang on, he's here,' she mutters. 'I'll call you back . . . Baby! Where've you been?'

'Oh, about,' you sigh, flopping down on the sofa next to her.

'I heard,' she begins, kissing you on the forehead, 'that *someone* lost their rag at the press conference.'

'Oh, yeah? You heard wrong.'

'Well, that's what Dan told me,' Katie adds. 'He said you told all the journos to fuck off and then stormed out.'

'Oh, Christ!' you exclaim, standing up again and opening the fridge. 'Where the fuck is everyone's sense of *humour*? I was *joking* the whole way through that conference, just like I've *always* done, but everyone's so stuffed up their own tight arses at the moment. I don't understand it!'

'God, just take it easy, babe, will you?'

'I've been *trying* to take it easy all fucking day,' you reply, banging your fist on the toilet door, 'but there's some sort of fucking vendetta going on!'

'Right, I'm off,' Katie announces, gathering up her things. 'You're stressing me out.'

'That's the fucking thing about dressing rooms,' you declare, glugging your drink. 'People love to come back and hang out, be in with the fucking so-called in-crowd, admitted to the inner sanctum or whatever . . . but then, they don't like it as soon as there's a little bit of tension. Don't they ever remember it's actually a *workspace*? This is where we bloody *prepare* for a performance! Why doesn't anyone ever fucking remember that?'

'All right, that's enough,' she instructs. 'I'm not just "people", if you don't mind – I'm your girlfriend. Tell me what's wrong. There *is* something, isn't there?'

'Yes,' you nod.

So you tell her. You tell her everything: how someone appears to be *laughing* at you and the band, vandalising the gear, giving out fake passes, slagging you off onstage, telling everyone to mutter 'it's all over' as you walk by. Katie listens sympathetically, but it's this last bit she can't believe.

'How *would* I be imagining that?' you scream at her.

'Will you stop fucking shouting at me!'

You stop.

'And give that a rest for a while,' she instructs, grabbing your beer away.

'Okay,' you begin, more quietly. 'Do me a favour. Come with me. Let's go and have a little walk around. Listen out, and I *guarantee* someone will say it.'

Realising you're in no mood to back down, Katie agrees.

You leave the dressing room, wink at John the guard, and wander off arm in arm into the main enclosure, past the bar, across the sea of white plastic garden chairs, where the drinkers catch the last of the evening sun, over to the side of the main stage (you spend a couple of minutes watching Gene, who you must admit are pretty good) then back to the enclosure, through the public arena and back into the VIP bit . . . and of course, no one says a damn thing. Quite the contrary. People are nice to you. They smile. The guards are all polite. The journos nod. Even fucking Tony Gloster has the gall to come up and say, 'All's fair in love and indie pop, eh?' – at which you grudgingly shake his hand. And with every new person you pass, you feel Katie's mood plummeting further down. When she's finally had enough of walking, just as you're passing the ladies loos for the third time, she turns to you and gives you one of her serious looks.

'Lance, honey, I hate to say it, but you've got some sort of problem.'

'No . . .'

'Baby, listen to me, you have—'

'No! Katie, I *swear*.'

'Sweetness, all you need to do is go and have a lie down, chill out. I'll find you a private space. I think all this is getting too much for you . . .'

'Lance!' squeaks a female voice.

You both whirl around. It's Petra.

'Lance,' she chirps, 'Craig says to tell you all the gear's okay, and Stan's in there guarding it.'

'Ah! Thank *God*,' you gasp, at this most rare piece of good news. You're so relieved, in fact, you can't help giving Petra a little hug.

'Oh, you *arsehole*!' screams Katie, driving her fists between the two of you. 'You complete *shit*! I was going out of my way to be nice to you, and you can't even respect me enough to keep your fucking hands off her in front of me!'

'But, Katie . . .'

'No, you just fuck off,' she cries, holding up an angry warning finger. 'You can *drown* in your little fucking paranoid and miserable world, and take her with you. I damn well hope you're happy.'

And with that, she is off.

Petra's bottom lip trembles.

'Sorry, Lance,' she blurts, and dashes off.

Exhausted, you turn around to the beer garden, where once again an amused audience watches. Setting your controls for the heart of the dressing room, and specifically the alcohol rider, you decide the only possible solution to your woes is to immediately get as drunk as possible.

You've been drunk for gigs before. Actually, you've been *paralytic* before; you've passed out, people have had to slap you and splash cold water over your face in order to bring a shred of consciousness back to your sozzled body. And you've always managed to perform, and perform well: singing almost note perfect, your guitar-playing rhythmic and strong. Only experts would notice the difference. Strange, really, but everyone has their good points. You're sure that if John McEnroe downed five pints of lager and a bottle of wine, he'd still be *fairly* good at tennis.

The ingredient that dramatically alters, however, is how you treat the audience. Stone-cold sober, which only happens very occasionally: you're a bit moody and monosyllabic, only really warming up by the end. A little tipsy: you start getting cheeky and the banter flows. But moderately drunk, you believe, is when you're at your best. Nicely antagonistic, a couple of insults fly, sometimes something controversial like throwing out a lairy audience member, arguing with a bouncer, maybe shouting at a roadie. Keeps everyone on their toes. When you smile at the end of the show and advise everyone to get home safely, that's the pay-off; it's *so* much more effective than if you'd been pleasant all evening. Drunker than that: you start quarrelling with the band and ignoring the crowd, although you still hurl abuse at the little fuckers when they shout out song requests. Again, it keeps people in a nice state of alertness, but perhaps it shouldn't happen more than once per tour. Recently, you have to admit, it's been happening a lot. Thirty-two shows since *The Social Trap* was wheeled out in May: for perhaps half of those you've been smashed. It's been a tough year.

The upshot of this drinking record is that no one is particularly concerned at the state you're getting yourself into tonight at Aylesbury. Craig makes a few comments, mostly because he saw the frenzy you were in earlier, but Martin's been totally ignoring you since the press conference and Dan, judging by the near-empty bottle of rum next to him, isn't an awful long way behind you. Bob comes in to do his usual schoolteacherly routine at around eight-thirty ('Now, gents, remember what we're all here for – keep a little bit back for the celebration afterwards') and Petra looks perpetually worried, but that's probably because she's expecting an ice pick in her back from Katie at any moment.

Nine o'clock approaches, and Heidi cheerfully arrives to escort you to the backstage bar for the Radio One interview. It's at this point that your powers of speech vanish, and all you can do is shake your head.

'Come on, Lance. Perhaps a little of that old sparkle, to make up for earlier?'

'Sparkle,' laughs Martin. 'You'll get more sparkle out of a dead badger right now.'

'Well, *someone*'s got to do it,' Heidi insists. 'Dan? Martin?'

'I ain't going anywhere,' growls Dan.

Martin sighs and goes into his standard martyr routine.

'Oh, all right, I guess I'll have to do it.'

'Hero,' comments Heidi, giving him a peck on the cheek.

'As long as Craig comes.'

'Whassat?' mumbles Craig, who's been deeply occupied with his Pratchett novel.

'Come on, Spalding,' says Heidi, cheekily kicking at one of his trainers. 'Remember, you're in a rock band? Yeah? About to play to, ooh . . . fifty thousand people?'

'It's a bloody good book,' he sighs, sticking his bookmark in and mooching off with Martin.

'Uh, I'll go too,' adds Petra, following Heidi out, understandably not wishing to breathe in the poisonous atmosphere remaining between the two drunk boys.

For a good while neither you nor Dan say a thing; you're too busy nursing your glass of Jack, and Dan his rum, while absent-mindedly plucking at his acoustic bass. But suddenly Dan looks up, frowns, and speaks with a comically slow slur.

'Oh . . . shit. I forgot . . . to tell you. Per . . . seph . . . on . . . ee . . . she called. Earlier. On the phone.'

'Uh?'

'You know. Per . . . seph-on-ee. Gloria's . . . sister.'

'Who . . . whose ph-phone?'

'Yours.'

You actually do own a mobile phone, a lumbering, brick-like device which doesn't fit into any of your pockets, so you tend not to carry it around. You haven't even looked at it since yesterday evening. You drag yourself up off the sofa and stagger to where you dumped your bag. The conversation proceeds with all the energy of two dying criminals at the end of a Tarantino film.

'D-did she . . . s-say . . . anyth-thing?'

'Yeah . . . to call . . . back.'

'Nothing . . . else?'

'Er . . . no.'

The sheer incongruity of the phone call is what shakes you from your stupor. The last time Persephone Amhurst communicated with you was through a solicitor, when you were curtly instructed not to even attempt making contact with Gloria again, or legal proceedings, restraining orders and all manner of other seriousness would ensue. To now be called directly, on your mobile phone, on the day of your biggest British gig in years, seems alarmingly peculiar to say the very least. You open your bag and extract the stout black gadget. You're sure there's a function somewhere for seeing who called last, but it's hard to locate even at the soberest of times.

'Thanks . . . Dan . . .' you splutter, heading out the door.

'Yeah,' he murmurs.

John the security chap still patiently waits where he's been all evening, now puffing on a cigarette in the rapidly fading light.

'Off out, Lance?'

'Yeah . . . need to m-make a . . . phone call.'

'Oooh, dear, you'd better take it easy on the old booze, hadn't you? Big show coming up and all . . .'

'Don't w-worry about m-me,' you drawl. 'I was probably more p-pissed than this the last t-time you saw us.'

'Hmm,' John thinks, as you begin to dial Persephone's number. 'That would've been Langley Park, '93. I was working on the sound desk, as I recall—'

'Sorry, s'cuse me.'

You duck behind one of the tents while the phone rings. That's the trouble with being friendly to the staff: then they think they're your mate, and . . .

'Hello?'

'Persephone.'

'Ah. It's you.'

She's always referred to you as 'you', even for the brief five minutes back in 1985 when you were both making a strained effort to like each other.

'Yes. How . . . are you?'

'Look,' she snaps. 'I'm not going to pretend this is anything other than a message service . . . Frankly, I've no interest in how *you* are, so I can't believe you've any concern for my well-being. Had a telegram from Rosamund. She's had a car accident in Russia. She's recovering but she's lost the baby. She requested that the family tell you, so that's what I'm doing.'

She hangs up without waiting for a response.

Which is just as well, really, for it's another ten minutes before you regain the ability to form a sentence, and this time it has nothing to do with the alcohol.

In the weeks and months that follow, you'll come to realise that all is not quite as it seems. With her usual blend of stupidity and arrogance, Persephone has managed to both under- and overestimate your relationship with Gloria, and the true details of her crash will eventually emerge. But for now, the multilayered news hits you so hard, it's like you've been kicked. Four times. In the balls, the stomach, the heart and the head. By someone with very strong legs. Just, presumably, as the Amhurst family intended. They could equally have sent someone round to beat you up; but then, they'd hardly consider that a *respectable* form of terror. You cling onto a guy-rope in the darkness and reacquaint the contents of your stomach with the outside world: a deliberately violent action with all the follow-through you can muster. You feel such utter, desperate, rock-bottom loathing for yourself and your stupid, worthless little life that you strongly consider lying down and rolling around in the vomit, soaking your hair, soiling your pants and then impaling yourself with an industrial tent pole. There are only two factors which stop you from doing this. One is that there's now comparatively less alcohol inside you and, ironically, you've started to sober up a bit. The other thing is more complicated, but goes something like this: you created another human life, which brings with it certain responsibilities, none of which you've been able to fulfil. Now you believe that life is over, and you suppose the spirit of that life can probably witness your every action, so – put simply – what would it think if it could see you rolling around in your own vomit? Would it be proud of its father? Then you'd have failed it in death as well as life. Years later, you'll come to recognise this moment as the genesis of the paternal instinct that grew so profoundly over the next decade, but right now all it means is you keep your hair and clothes clean. You've also got a show to perform. Although absurd and perverse at this juncture, you suddenly feel a rush of enthusiasm. Yes. This is what I can do. I've fucked up everything else, but I can at least play guitar and sing rather well. Remember that?

You'll also look back in days to come and speculate that everything would've been okay from then on – had Dan not decided to lock the dressing room door.

'Dan, are you in there?'

More knocking.

'Dan! Have you locked this?'

'He closed it five minutes ago,' John the guard tells you. 'Didn't hear him lock it, but there you go, he must have.'

'Have you got another key?'

'No, I'm afraid they don't give us the keys. The organisers will have a spare, but I'm not sure where you'll find them right now.'

'Can't you radio them?' you shout, whacking the door with your fist.

'No, we're on different circuits. You see—'

'Oh, for fuck's sake. Dan! Dan, can you hear me?'

You hear a faint groaning.

'Aw, fuck it, he's bloody passed out.'

You stomp along the length of the hut, seeing if you can climb through the window, but the gap is too small. You shout through it instead.

'Dan, open the fucking door, you dick! We're bloody playing in twenty minutes!'

Silence.

'Well, this is a right old mess, eh?' chuckles John, lighting a fag.

'We could barge the door down,' you think aloud.

'As I've got you here for a moment, Lance, I thought you might be interested to know . . . I *was* offered some cash a little while back.'

'You were?'

'Yeah. Fella came up about two hours ago, bloke in one of them striped shirts, offered me twenty quid to let him into your room.'

'Really?'

'Yeah, but I told him to stick it, y'see.'

'John,' you assert, grasping him by both his shoulders. 'You've got to tell me who this guy is! I need to *know*.'

'I told him to stick it,' John continues, unflinching, 'because I'm an honest man, you see, Lance.'

'Good! Great! But—'

'I'm honest, I work hard, and I don't complain. But what I *do* ask . . .'

'Yes?'

'. . . is that I get treated with a little respect when I'm only doing my job properly.'

You frown at him.

'What are you saying, John?'

'Nice young lady of yours, earlier . . . I bet *she* wouldn't strike a man who was only doing his job properly.'

'What . . . ?'

'I was off work for two weeks after that . . . from stress . . . two weeks, with no pay, and I've got mouths to feed, Lance.'

'John, I have *no* idea what you're fucking talking about,' you shout, turning around and hammering on the door again. 'Dan!'

'Your blonde-haired tart at the Langley Park gig,' John goes on, his voice rising, 'she laid into me when I stopped her entering the sound desk . . . She *insulted* me, called me names I won't even mention, then did *this*.'

He brandishes a Polaroid of himself with a beaten-up face. It looks pretty bad, but . . .

'Fuck off, she could *never* do that to you!'

'Kicked me when I was down, she did.'

'Just shut your mouth, John . . . you're talking shit!'

'It's amazing what someone can do when they're that jealous . . . jealous of the good-looker on the video screen you were diddling. I bet that *really* stung her, knowing she looked like such a freak . . .'

In that one nanosecond, you decide you can either punch him or break down the dressing room door. Wisely, you choose the latter. Dan wakes up from his drunken snooze on the sofa and coughs.

'Whassappenin'?'

'Wake up, you idiot, and don't lock that fucking door again.'

You grab your acoustic guitar and two bottles of red wine, and storm straight out again.

'You've just lost your fucking job, John,' you spit, as you pass. 'Well done. I'm getting out of this fucking place.'

But the only safe place left to go is the side of the main stage, now a hive of activity as The Boo Radleys' gear is wheeled off and your own crew pushes the Magpies' larger stage-set into place. On the road in a strange city, this familiar, almost homely routine conducted by a group of people you trust can usually liven whatever sour spirits you've got yourself into, but not today. Today you're no longer certain what planet you're on. You settle yourself by the monitor desk, open the wine and tune your acoustic: a ritual you perform before every show, normally helping to keep your feet on the ground, but this evening you're suspended a hundred feet in the air with acute vertigo. Bob Grant passes, evidently glad to see that you're at least alive. Stan the roadie passes and tussles your hair. A minute later Doug does the same thing. A nice gesture, but right now you don't understand what nice is.

'All right, L?' asks Pete, the tubby monitor engineer, as he readies his equipment.

'Yep,' you respond, swigging from one of the bottles. But of course, you're not. You're in a galaxy far, far away from all right, sinking back into your previous alcoholic fog.

Gradually the others assemble. You abandoned anything as crap as a group hug weeks ago (in Berlin, actually, when Dan and Craig had a fight before the show), so the inter-band ceremony that precedes this largest of British comeback gigs is practically non-existent. The front-of-house music gets louder (you managed to insist they play the Wilco album), the crowd gets wilder then . . . hey. It's showtime.

'Ready?' grunts Martin.

'Yeah,' you murmur.

And that's just about all you can clearly remember. You know the first song went okay and that you tried to be funny in the next one, but no one seemed to get the joke. You seem to recall singing an Oasis song, for a laugh, then trying to chuck out some of the audience, but the people you wanted to eject outnumbered those you wanted to stay, which was a little surprising. You drank some more, sang some more, then you spotted that idiot in the red tracksuit down the front and did the 'wanker' signal at him. But it all seemed fairly cheerful; a couple of insults, but no more than a Thieving Magpies audience is used to. Then Dan and Martin started to take it all too seriously. What's the matter with these people? Always fucking complaining. In those rare moments you sit down to think about it, it really pisses you off that you spent your whole career dragging them along by their manky ponytails, writing them some of the best songs they'd ever had the pleasure of playing – and, of course, made them a shitload of money – but they've *never* been grateful. And Martin, in the end, didn't even need to admit to the others he wanted to leave the band; he just sat back, happily watching everything collapse as you took the heat. And all you were doing was trying to hold it together. Dan even announced over the microphone (*over the bloody microphone!*) that you were 'being a cock tonight', when all you were doing was defending *them*! Oh yeah, and you saw that knobhead security bloke, what's-his-name ... John ... also down the front, probably not even *working*, folding his arms over his fucking beer belly and pointing at you. So you showed him. If Gloria could punch him, so could you. Fucker, I bet he deserved it that time, too. And then suddenly there were loads of people, all shouting, screaming, arguing, pulling you this way and that ... everyone so *serious*. When all you were really doing was trying to be funny. That was it! But no one was laughing. You looked really hard, all around you, to see who was laughing. But no one was.

And that's when they took you away.

NO ONE LIKES A GROWN-UP POP STAR

I've got to hand it to this Lance Webster bloke. He may be a rubbish drinker, a former womaniser, occasionally arrogant, selfish and frequently nasty to his audiences, but he's really jolly good at making Clive Beresford cry. That's four times in twenty years now, a record unmatched by anyone, even my first girlfriend.

Fortunately, unlike my performance in the toy museum, I do manage to control myself. We are in a major international airport, after all. It's limited to a few tears leaking out and a couple of fulsome blows of my nose, and, to be fair, Webster is doing much the same. Then he scruffs up his hair, lets out a quick laugh and claps his hands.

'Yes, yes,' he sighs. 'All the clichés. [Hollywood hero voice] "*The day my world collapsed . . . I watched in terror, as my whole life caved in before my eyes.*" Fuck, man, I almost feel like a drink . . .'

'Well . . .'

'I said "almost", Clive. The sun is *not* over the yardarm.'

In truth, the thought of a drink doesn't thrill me either, after all that. I study my notes, which are largely unintelligible, but I've a feeling I'm not going to forget much of what he's said.

'You should get a Dictaphone,' he comments.

'I've got one. I just can't find a shop that sells the tapes.'

'Tapes! Come on, Clive. Twenty-first century.'

I stir some sugar into my coffee, starting to feel a bit vague from lack of food.

'It's good calling you Clive,' he notes. 'I never really thought you looked like an Alan. Should have known it was all bullshit.'

I start to apologise, then stop myself. We're silent for a while. After years spent frantically trying to envisage Webster's final few hours as a relevant rock star, hearing their true contents at last seems to have blown a few of my fuses. But either I'm being a bit thick or he's left a lot unexplained, and further questions seem tricky to pose without appearing vulgar.

'So,' I say, gingerly, 'can I—'

'Yep, you got fifteen minutes, journo-boy, might as well use it.'

'How did you discover Persephone was lying?'

He bites his lip and leans back, while I hope to buggery that I've got the right end of the stick. Mercifully, it seems I have.

'It started to make sense over the next few weeks, I s'pose. I suddenly had lots of time to think, as you can imagine . . . No band, no girlfriend . . . no life, basically. I just sat in my flat ruminating, trying not to drink. Failing most of the time. But I kept going back to how Persephone told me the news . . . like I already knew Gloria was pregnant. I didn't, though . . . she never said anything. But I knew Gloria so well . . . better than her own family did, probably . . . and I knew that, despite everything, she'd *never* ask them to tell me she'd lost a baby, not without first telling me there *was* one. So I made up my mind about that bit: Gloria never asked them to tell me a damn thing.'

'Why d'you think she even telegrammed them at all? I thought she wanted to get away from them?'

'Money,' he shrugs. 'Not an awful lot of free healthcare for foreigners in Russia. She had no travel insurance, obviously. Fuck knows what she was thinking, going out there in her condition with no safety net. They wired some cash, sorted her out, then arranged for her to be flown to Tokyo, where a family friend lived. That's where the baby was born. She's bloody lucky her family are so rich. Otherwise she'd have probably died herself, let alone the baby.'

I frown hard, my mind returning to that afternoon in Webster's flat: the framed photo of the little boy, the only flash of colour or emotion in his otherwise blank canvas of an abode. The child would be older than that, surely? But of course, the photo could be from a few years ago.

'So she left Russia for good?'

'Yup.'

'So . . .'

'Yeah,' he nods, following my thoughts. 'Alison whatsit never did spot her in that café. Must've been some other nutter.'

'You read that?'

'Course I did. I read *everything*.'

He pours himself more coffee from the industrial-sized jug we ordered, exhaling heavily. I find it a little implausible, the idea of Lance Webster himself turning to a cheaply made fanzine called *Things That Make Me Go Moo* for information on the whereabouts of his closest friend – but then everything is starting to feel a little back to front today.

'Fucking idiots, her family,' he spits, with vintage bile. 'The irony was, I hadn't even *thought* of trying to find Gloria up 'til that point . . . I hadn't the time, with the tour and everything. But I started looking bloody hard after that, I tell you. Precisely the fucking opposite of what they hoped to achieve.'

'Bastards,' I whisper. 'Why did they hate you so much?'

'Initially, because they're a bunch of upper-class wankers. But as time went by, their feelings became a little more . . . justified, shall we say.'

'But this is what I don't get,' I interrupt. 'It was hardly your fault Gloria was so stubborn about the whole destiny thing. I mean, you guys were in love . . . it must have been bloody difficult for you . . .'

'Not as hard as you'd imagine,' he counters. 'Don't forget, I had my own reasons for not wanting to be tied down to *her*. I was young, stupid and incredibly vain . . . Gloria was attractive, but she wouldn't have exactly been a status symbol. Particularly not during the whole *Bruise Unit* thing, when I had people on my arm like Camilla McBriar and Sally Chester . . . both ended up being models, which unfortunately meant a lot to me at the age of twenty-five. It wasn't until the end, when Gloria really started to get sick, that I remembered I loved her. Sounds fucking crazy, I know, but what can I tell you? I was an idiot.'

'So what did you do?'

He puffs and places his head on the table for a second, each word of his confession clearly a considerable effort. I feel painfully guilty pressing him further, but I guess if he didn't want to continue, he wouldn't.

'Well, I started trying to convince her we should just say fuck it, and be together. This would be . . . autumn of '94, I think. Told her I was prepared to take the risk, and if the whole bloody cosmos came crashing down around us, or whatever she believed, then so be it. And you've got to understand . . . she *really did* believe it. Man, you should have seen what she started to do to herself when we tried to release that stupid song as an A-side . . .'

I brace myself for some graphic description of unprecedented hideousness – which thankfully he doesn't bother with.

'Anyway, I said I'd make huge changes for her . . . give up the other women . . . even the band, if it came to it. Sod it, I'd made enough money, and *The Social Trap*'s recording sessions were . . . well, far from a paradise of creativity. But of course she didn't buy it. So then we had this one stupid night when it finally went too far . . . and that was it. I don't think I saw her again after that. A few months later she was gone.'

My body shudders involuntarily. I remember my video footage of the 1995 Brit Awards, Gloria clearly seen lurking in the background. I glance furtively around the restaurant, not really sure what I'm expecting to see . . . Tony Gloster, perhaps, secreted in a distant booth, taking notes. All I see is a large man in an Arsenal top, irritably trying to persuade staff to give him a steak knife made of something other than plastic. The trials of air travel in the twenty-first century.

I turn back to Webster, who is gazing forlornly at his mobile phone.

'So,' I ask gently, 'did you . . . um . . . did you find her, in the end?'

'*I* didn't. She wrote to me. Sometime around Christmas '95. Didn't mention the baby straight away. She just said . . . she knew her family had been lying to me, but didn't specify what about. I still didn't even know where in the world she was, I had to send my letters via an intermediary for . . . oh, months. Then after about a year she started to mention she'd been "looking after a child".'

He shakes his head and stares into the middle distance, exhausted by the complexity of his own life. After a minute or so he shakes himself out of it, looks back at me and laughs.

'Well, there you are. That's the long answer to the question "why was the Aylesbury gig so shit?". Is that acceptable?'

'Yeah,' I smile, still scribbling on my pad. 'I think so.'

'How close were you, then?'

'I'm sorry?'

'To the stage. At the gig.'

'Oh . . . right down the front, as usual.'

'Did you feel like shooting me?'

'Um . . . no. Alan was the angry one. I think it finally killed his career as an indie kid.'

'Shit, really?'

'Afraid so,' I reply, toying with the idea of showing him the 'black' page from Alan's scrapbook. 'But I think I was a little more philosophical about it. I was completely off my face anyway. Plus . . . well, I was used to you being, um, a bit rude.'

'Thank you!' he cries, jumping up and banging on the table. 'I *said* this at the time to anyone who'd listen, but no one believed me, no one remembered! We used to be *ridiculously* rude to our audiences. Used to tell 'em to fuck off, called them cunts, everything! And they loved it!'

'Totally,' I concur. 'Which is why I was so perplexed by the reaction it got.'

'Well, everything had got so bloody *clean* by '95.'

'That's right. And "moshing" beat "rucking".'

'You what?' he frowns.

'When me and Alan started out, we "rucked" to gigs. Now everyone "moshes", which used to be just a heavy-metal thing. Pisses me off.'

'Ah, well . . . we used to call it "pogoing", so I can't really help you with that one.'

'But . . . the whole business of you being rude . . . I remember my first-ever Magpies gig—'

'Which was?'

'Brixton, spring '89.'

'Ah . . . the "What If Everyone Goes Mad?" tour,' he smiles, looking a bit misty-eyed. 'Not bad, if I remember. Had a row with Martin before the encore. Played the cover of "Bette Davis Eyes" for the first time.'

'That's right. And you screamed at someone for chanting "you fat bastard".'

'Ha! Did I?'

'Yeah,' I laugh. 'Then gobbed at a stage-diver.'

'Ah, the gobbing thing. See? Good clean fun, all that. Never a word of complaint.'

'I suppose we weren't used to you punching security guards, though.'

'No,' he concedes. 'But it's better than hurling bass guitars at them.'

'Nicky Wire,' I respond, catching his reference.

'Right,' he nods – then fixes me with a sudden glare. 'Fucking hell, you're full of shit, telling me you didn't know anything about music.'

'Sorry.'

'Don't fucking apologise.'

'Uh.'

'You're a bloody fool. It made me *so* much more suspicious than I ever would've been. Can't believe you made me go through all those stupid explanations when we were going round the art gallery.'

'Well,' I admit, 'if it's any consolation, it was pretty excruciating for me to listen to.'

'Thanks, arsehole,' he snaps. 'What the hell did you think you were doing?'

'I didn't really know what else to do,' I mutter, pathetically. 'Didn't want you to think I'd heard of you.'

He stands up again, grandly replaces his shades and announces: 'There are some people in the world who've heard of Kurt Cobain, but who haven't heard of me. They exist. But I can take it. I'm a big boy.'

I blink up at him, at a loss for further responses. Then he dashes off – to the loo, presumably.

I exhale and lean back in my chair. I feel pretty drained. His energy has multiplied tenfold compared to the times we sat discussing writing, and it's hard to navigate his ups and downs. It's a skill, I reflect: the feisty rock 'n' roll interview. Every bit as important as singing or playing guitar. A certain amount of his former warmth has gone – the price I've paid, I suppose, for gleaning his darkest, grimmest secrets. There's still heaps I want to ask him, not least about his kid, but I know I'm quite ridiculously privileged to have been told as much as I have. Not just because he's Lance Webster, but simply because he's a human being and I'm just . . . someone he doesn't know terribly well. Which is still the oddest thing. Why the hell has he chosen to tell all this stuff to *me*? I suppose there might be some limited catharsis in getting it all off his chest, but surely he can pay a professional for that sort of thing? Not some weirdo who puts silly notes through his –

Silly notes through his door.

I scrabble around on the table but only find empty sugar packets, Alan's scrapbook, Webster's newspaper and his boarding pass. Then I spot what I'm looking for on the seat, poking out of his jacket pocket. I lean over, snatch up the scruffily folded piece of paper, take a deep breath and open it:

21st APRIL 2007

LANCE,

DEAR LANCE.

I'VE BEEN DREAMING ABOUT
YOU. I FEEL YOU ARE LOOKING FOR
VINDICATION. I CAN HELP YOU, YOU DON'T
KNOW ME, MY NAME IS CLIVE BERESFORD. I WAS
THERE WHEN IT ALL WENT WRONG IN '95, AND I DEFENDED
YOU. I USED TO WRITE FOR A MAGAZINE CALLED "DEFINITELY NOT"
THIEVING MAGPIES RULED MY LIFE AND I HUNG ON YOUR EVERY
NOTE. BUT THEN YOU LEFT. I NEED TO KNOW WHY, THEN I CAN MOVE ON. BUT
I CAN HELP YOU MOVE ON TOO. WITH YOUR HELP I CAN WRITE SOMETHING TO
RESTORE YOUR NAME TO THE ROCK HISTORY BOOKS. I ALSO KNOW OF THE
UNSPOKEN LOVE BETWEEN YOU AND GLORIA, IT'S THERE IN YOUR LYRICS.
PERHAPS ONE DAY YOU WILL RE-FIND EACH OTHER? IF YOU LIKE I CAN
TALK TO YOU ABOUT ALL OF THESE THINGS. I'M NEARBY AS IT HAPPENS—
     NO. 9 OF YOUR STREET
     BASEMENT FLAT.
    WHY HAVE THEY ALL FORGOTTEN YOU?
     —ANSWER ME.
    VORSPRUNG DURCH PEANUT
    Clive Beresford

   P.S. YOU'VE DONE SO MUCH

Webster has returned by the time I finish reading.

'You enjoying that?'

I toss it onto the table with distaste.

'It's . . . amazing.'

'I rather like it.'

'Why on *earth* did I lay it out like that?'

'Probably something primal,' he muses. 'Like, that's the shape your subconscious wants to write in. The Christmas tree of desperation, Freud might call it.'

I pick it up again. I feel like I'm examining my own drunkenness through a microscope. This could turn out to be more educational than expected. I'm astonished that the pissed me thinks this sort of thing is a good idea. Having said that, it's not *quite* as bad as those roadies made out. In fact . . .

'Um . . . funny thing is . . . it's embarrassing, desperate, and really rather sad, but it's not . . . *threatening* at all, is it?'

'Not really,' he replies. 'Just a bit creepy.'

'But, I don't understand. If it's *not* threatening . . . then why did you send your stooges round to see me?'

'Ah. Well . . . I didn't, really. That was Malcolm's idea. He's over-cautious.'

'Oh, my God! They told me what I'd written was *hugely* threatening, and to fuck off, basically, insinuating they'd come back and break my legs if I didn't!'

'Shit,' he chuckles. 'Sorry. I guess they were nipping it in the bud. But I also wanted them to size you up, see what sort of, er . . . *enthusiast* we were dealing with. I've had a bit of trouble with that sort of thing, you know.'

'Um . . . yeah, I know.'

At this point he takes off his sunglasses again, revealing a face with a different tone – far more serious, heavy with intent. His eyes are bloodshot and I realise once again how emotional this must have been for him. But I couldn't be less prepared for the gear change to come. He puts both elbows on the table, leans forwards and narrows his eyes slightly, as if composing himself for some complicated scientific explanation.

'I have to say,' he begins, 'after they visited you, I *was* planning to get in touch.'

'You're joking.'

'No, I really was. But to randomly show up at someone's flat isn't really my style, and as you'd forgotten to give me any other—'

'Fucking hell!' I gasp. 'I never put my bloody email address on it!'

He shakes his head and sips his coffee.

'Then how the fuck did you . . . ?'

From his shoulder bag he fishes out a tatty-looking coloured booklet. A rather familiar booklet, with a poorly printed picture of what looks like Belle and Sebastian on the cover. I reach out to take it. And bugger me with a pitchfork, it's a copy of *Definitely Not*. One of the final few copies of *Definitely Not*, from May 1998 (interview with Cable, review of the second Garbage album). I flick straight to the last page, and there it is: my email address, which I must've had for all of two months.

'Where the fuck did you get this?'

'Gloria gave it to me.'

'*Gloria* gave it to you? How did Gloria get it?'

'Gloria was on the mailing list.'

I gape at him for a few astonished moments, then absent-mindedly flick through the pages. This isn't one of the issues I kept, so it's strange to see the various features again, the editorial, the letters, the appalling photos . . . but to be honest, I'm busier wondering how the hell I could've missed Gloria Feathers among the two-hundred-odd names I sent the rag to every quarter.

'Gloria was a complete fanzine hound,' he continues, 'you surely knew that?'

'Yeah, but . . .'

I notice one of my rambling discourses about Webster himself and snap the booklet shut.

'You used to send it to a Lucille Sanson in Lyon, France.'

'Um . . . perhaps, yes – I do remember sending a couple abroad . . .'

'She's one of Gloria's schoolfriends.'

'No!'

'Yup. She sent stuff on for Gloria . . . to wherever she was.'

I'm flummoxed. I've a feeling I should be realising something important, but my brain's processors are too jammed to function properly. Does this mean Gloria gave it to Webster *recently*, or . . . back then?

'That's who I had to send all my letters to,' he explains, 'until Gloria told me where she really was.'

This is too bizarre. I gulp some coffee, praying it'll have some sort of untangling effect on my brain.

'Which page were you on?' he asks.

'Oh . . . nothing, just some feature about—'

'It's the editorial, isn't it?'

'Uh, yeah.'

'Go on, read it,' he instructs.

I open the fanzine again. Dear oh dear, the thought that he's seen all this nonsense is acutely embarrassing. But he *has* seen my note, so we've kind of hit the bottom of that particular barrel already . . .

I'd like to thank Mary Ryder in Norwich for her letter of last week, in which she put my thoughts into words perfectly regarding Webster's latest incident. He is *indeed* not a man who should be mocked. He's trying, in his own heartbroken way, to say many things to a world which will no longer listen. He's attempting to warn us of the dangers ahead for the alternative music world, when sales figures and chart positions will kill new bands before they've even had a chance to break into their stride. Music will cease to be about passion, intelligence, humour and warmth, but will be governed by the likelihood of a certain song being used in a car advertisement, or by what designer jeans a so-called indie group are sporting on the cover of the *NME*. We'll be surrounded by faceless, charmless dullards with nothing to say and no decent music to say it to. Webster's own wrenching experiences of the last few years should speak volumes to us, but everyone's decided to ignore him or laugh at him instead.

'Fuck me,' I wince. 'What a pile of earnest bollocks!'

'Read the last paragraph,' says Webster. 'Out loud.'

'Oh, God, do I really have to?'

'Read it,' he commands.

I look down, hot and exasperated. Perhaps this is what he means by burying the past: getting Clive Beresford to *read* the past aloud to him in the middle of an airport terminal. Each to their own.

'Uh . . . it just says, "I'm going to close the correspondence regarding Webster for a while now, but I'd like to finish by saying, to him, wherever he is, remember all that you've achieved, and don't ever forget that no matter what the music press or anyone else says, you've composed and played music which has enriched the lives of thousands of confused, frustrated and lonely young people around the world, played gigs that have sent legions of punters home ecstatically happy, and written lyrics that will remain permanently lodged in the head of anyone with an ear for a good line and a spark of wit. You're fragile right now, and you deserve to give yourself a break. Hear it from someone who's been with you since the autumn of 1988: you don't need to fight any more. Take it easy, Zeitgeist man, you'll always be our alternative hero."'

I quickly close the booklet and knock back the last of my coffee. I'm nervous again and I can feel myself blushing. Webster's put his shades back on – his standard interview punctuation mark, I'm now realising – so I'm quite literally in the dark as to his point of view. The sight of those impossibly black lenses on his impassive, feature-less face reminds me of something, but I'm presently too frazzled to place it. By the fact he hasn't said anything, I'd almost guess he's angry. Perhaps because I made him sound like such a casualty. He's not known for being nice to interviewers who point out his weak-nesses, so I grip the edge of my chair and clench my teeth for the ride.

'So, d'you think I liked seeing all this stuff, at the time?' he asks, flatly.

'I, um, dunno . . . I guess I was a little bit passionate about the whole thing.'

'Mmm, it seems so.' He stares back at me, inclining his head slightly. 'And can I ask . . . what exactly were you trying to achieve by writing all that?'

'Well . . . I was trying to . . . y'know. I was angry. At the way you'd been treated. I wanted to, er . . . defend you.'

'You thought I needed defending.'

'Um . . . er . . . well, not exactly *defending* . . . I guess it was more . . . redressing the balance. Trying to blow the lid on some of the . . . um . . . the nonsense that was being written.'

'And you're still trying. Aren't you?'

'Yes,' I nod. 'I suppose I am. That's what I mean when I say I'm after vindication.'

'For me or for you?'

That bloody question again. I shift uneasily in my seat, aware that my sodden shirt is now sticking to my back.

'Well, for you mainly. But it's been difficult . . . not having the full story.'

'And now you've got it,' he states sternly. 'Haven't you?'

'Yes,' I squeak.

He leans back and folds his arms.

'So. What are you going to do with it now, then?'

I've been dreading this. It's going to sound so unfathomably mercenary. How I wish he'd take those fucking sunglasses off.

'Um . . . well, I suppose I'll . . .'

'Huh?'

'Well, I'll start by writing it up, y'know . . . properly . . . so it can be read by people other than just me, and then I'll . . .'

His black lenses are saying nothing. They seem to be getting even darker, but that must be my imagination.

'Then I suppose I'll try to interest some people in it. You know, people who'll appreciate what it all means, and so on . . .'

'Like who?'

'Um . . . y'know . . . the usual . . . I'll start with *Q* perhaps. They might like to do a retrospective feature.'

'Possibly.'

Then it hits me. The video for 'Bad Little Secret'. He wore shades throughout the whole bloody clip, staring straight at the camera, mouthing the words as if in some sort of zombie trance. Their shittest video. Doubtless he decided looking cold, blank and detached would perform wonders with the American market. It worked. And he's using the same tactic to freak me out. It's working now, too. What a fucker.

'Um,' I continue, desperately, 'then there's *Mojo* and *Uncut*, they sometimes—'

'Know any of the editors there?'

'No, but I—'

'Anywhere else?'

'Um . . . ah, yes, a friend told me you're still fairly well-known in the States, so maybe I'll try . . .'

He's shaking his head already. Oh shit.

'. . . *Rolling Stone*,' I conclude pathetically, Alan's words from eighteen years ago leaping into my head: 'You've got to have your strategy worked out, man.'

Webster drums his fingers on the table and looks away, directing his pair of black voids towards the centre of the restaurant.

'And you think these people will be interested in all this bullshit, do you?'

'Well, *I* would be, if I were—'

'And you imagine they'd actually *pay* for it?'

I let out a rather large sigh.

'Look, Lance—'

'Geoff.'

'Sorry: Geoff . . . Look, it sounds bloody awful, I know . . . It's your life. But really, the whole point of me doing it is so you can be vindicated, and . . .'

Here I run out of steam. Arse. He's got me.

Silence.

'I know someone who'd buy it,' he announces.

'Uh?'

He's still looking over at the bar, perhaps eyeing up one of the waitresses.

'Who?'

'Someone who'd make really good use of it, and make it worth your while, too.'

'Who do you *mean*?' I demand, tired of this tortuous exchange. He turns and looks straight back in my direction.

'Me.'

I snigger, disappointedly.

'You what?'

'I'm serious.'

'No, sorry . . . *what* are you saying?'

'I'll buy it from you,' he insists. 'Exclusive rights, of course.'

I've run out of ways to ask what the hell he's talking about, so I stay quiet.

'I've told you what you wanted to hear . . . now here's your side of the bargain. I'll buy it off you for ten grand.'

Oh God. He's gone bonkers again. Next he'll be shaving off his hair and putting on his white suit.

'Um . . .'

'Ten grand. Sterling,' he adds.

'Sorry,' I mutter. 'I'm totally confused.'

Now he's even getting his bloody chequebook out.

'Wait, hang on,' I protest, trying to grab his pen. 'What are you *doing*?'

He drops the pen and again takes off his shades.

'Listen, Clive . . . I don't mean to patronise you, but you're being really naïve. I'll be totally honest: you're not going to get much out of this story. No one will care. Screw any false modesty: who really gives a fuck about me? You might get one of those silly half-page "where are they now" pieces, if you're lucky. As for any money, forget it.'

'But that's not the point, it's . . .'

'And frankly, I don't want everyone knowing all this stuff. I'm not going to be around much any more, but . . . my family's still here, a few friends . . . they'd find it . . . well, difficult.'

'So why the hell have you told *me*?'

'Because you deserved to know.'

I study his face for a moment. I see no humour – and very little of anything else, in fact.

'Is that *it*?'

'Look at it this way, okay? I've been living with this shit for years, and gradually I've managed to patch up a few old wounds. But the one thing I've never done is say sorry, and explain . . . to someone who was there.'

'At Aylesbury?'

'Yeah. And the couple of years after that.'

'But that's just it,' I persist, 'if I write this thing, you'll be able to apologise and explain it to *everyone* . . .'

'No,' he frowns. 'Not in the way you're hoping. Oh, a few people

might say, "All right, well, fair enough then" – and instantly forget
about it. But it'll just mean more embarrassment for me, and the
whole thing'll rise to the surface again.'

'But . . .'

'And there are others involved.'

It's this last bit that shuts me up. Call me slow on the uptake,
but for the first time I have the slightest idea where he's going after
all this.

'But you,' he states, pointing at me, 'are probably one of the only
people left who it genuinely *means* something to.'

He opens his chequebook again, and starts to write.

'Look, Lance—'

'Geoff,' he corrects me again, not looking up.

'Sorry, Geoff . . . I don't think I can—'

'Clive, listen to me. One of the old songs just got licensed for a
big advert in America. Ten grand is roughly what I'll get, and it may
sound insane, but that's ten grand I don't *want*. It'll be a reminder
of a past life, hanging around like a bad smell. And also . . . well,
there are other reasons why I don't want it. It's a single R in
Beresford, isn't it?'

'Um . . . yeah, but . . .'

'Plus, you *have* earned it,' he nods, 'running around like a twat
for the last few months, listening to me prattle on today. Oh, and
the work you did on *Sainsbury Sid*, and who knows what'll happen
with that?'

Bloody hell, Sid the fly. I'd almost completely forgotten.

'So . . . you take this,' he breezes, flinging over the mammoth
cheque, 'and you bloody well *sort yourself out*. You're a fucking good
writer. You should be doing something with it . . . other than
hankering after ex-indie-pop stars.'

I gaze down at the row of zeros in the box, and look back up
at him.

'I still don't understand why you're giving me this.'

'For fuck's sake, Clive, don't make me spell it out to you – I'll miss my bloody plane.'

I can't help but continue to wordlessly gape at him.

'You don't get it, do you? Cast your mind back. I was at my fucking wits' end in '96. My career was fucked, my girl was thousands of miles away with a child I hadn't even met . . . didn't even know what *gender* it was . . . my bloody dad was dying of cancer and I was surrounded by people laughing at me and calling me a cock. It often felt like you were the *only person on my side*.'

I try to respond, but only a feeble croak emerges.

'Gloria started to send me cuttings. Bits and pieces you were doing, a word of encouragement, a letter of support. The way you asked people to write in with their thoughts, gig memories, favourite B sides . . . it all reached me. Yours was the only British review of *Commercial Suicide* that understood what I was trying to do, and appreciated the fucking state I was in . . . I was almost ready to give up songwriting *entirely* before I saw that. Then when things *really* started to deteriorate . . . well, man, you practically pulled me in from the edge of a building. The things you shouted to me at BFM . . . this may sound unbelievable, but . . . fuck it, they actually *calmed* me. No *way* was I going quietly into that police van before you appeared!'

If I wasn't sitting down I probably would've fallen over. I'm waiting for the moment when he says, 'Nah, only winding you up,' and rips the cheque in two.

'But how did you know that was *me*?' is all I manage to ask.

'Well . . . that's the strange thing. I *didn't* actually know it was Clive Beresford for years, until your note came through the door. That line you wrote at the bottom,' he says, opening the scrap of paper again, '"you've done so much".'

'Ugh. Cheesy.'

'Maybe,' he concedes. 'But distinctive.'

I look back at him, a cocktail of nausea and butterflies careering around within my torso. I need an extra hour with him, plus a secretary to transcribe all this hair-raising stuff just in case I convince myself I've dreamed it. And I need a drink. A waitress passes with a couple of beers and I seriously consider lunging for one of them.

'So then this note shows up,' Webster continues, 'at a time like this . . .'

'A time like what?'

'A time when I'm making some major changes to my life,' he responds, in a manner that forbids further prying. 'The note comes through the door, and I realise there's some unfinished business.'

'Are you seriously telling me,' I frown, 'that if I'd simply walked up to you on the high street and said, "Hi, I'm Clive Beresford. Can we talk?" – you would have said yes?'

He sighs.

'Probably.'

I let out a little moan and bury my face in my hands, marvelling at the untold pointlessness of everything that's happened to me since that Saturday in April. The time, the expense, the job, the stress, the lies. Some of which aren't directly connected to Webster, of course, but it certainly feels like it's all part of the same sorry spiral. I look up after a minute, and to my amazement he's actually laughing.

'But hey,' he grins. 'It was so much more *fun* doing it this way . . . wasn't it?'

Once again, words have deserted me.

We sit there for a while longer, batting the various absurdities of the last couple of months to and fro. I'd be quite content to remain here for the rest of the day, but I'm suddenly all too aware that my final seconds with Lance Webster are approaching. That age-old 'if you were stuck in a lift with anyone' rubbish pops into my head, and I wrack my brains for something I might spend the next few years regretting I'd missed my chance to ask. Finally, he stands to go.

'One last question,' I demand.

'You're getting your money's worth, aren't you? Okay, hurry.'

'Why d'you think they all turned on you?'

He looks up at the ceiling, gives a quick hoot of laughter and claps his hands.

'Oh, fuck it, Clive, I dunno. It was our time. We were stubborn, we weren't going away. I think every journo and industry knob expected *The Social Trap* to bomb, and when it didn't . . . they all just thought enough was enough. We simply didn't fit with what was going on. And also . . . oh, I suppose I'd made some enemies over the years. Said the wrong thing, slagged the wrong band, insulted the wrong writer, fucked the wrong girl. So I guess it was a multitude of revenges. But I'm over it.'

'Really?'

'Yeah . . . just. Listen, man, gotta go.'

I wave the cheque at him feebly.

'You know, I'm really not sure I can take this.'

'Don't be a pillock,' he snaps. 'Take it. To be frank, it's either you or the Inland fucking Revenue. But remember – exclusive rights. Not a soul.'

'Okay,' I respond, feeling that only a total moron would argue with a deal like this. 'Thanks,' I add, unsteadily.

'Fine,' he smiles. 'Don't do anything stupid with it. And get your fucking shit together, will you? Quit drinking so much.'

'I'll try.'

'And email me an invoice.'

'Okay.' Ever the businessman.

'Oh, and I guess you can probably tell this crap to your mate Alan.'

'Ha! Well, maybe. Not sure he deserves to know right now.'

'Whatever.'

He slings on his shoulder bag and gathers his paperwork.

'I suppose I'm not permitted to ask where it is you're going now, then.'

'Hey, man . . .' he answers, putting his shades back on. 'I said I'd tell you about *August the twelfth*, *not* the future. You're gonna have to work that one out for yourself. But you guys seem to be fairly good at that,' he sighs, nodding at Alan's scrapbook.

We shake hands. It all seems rather formal – but oddly appropriate.

'Well,' he says. 'It's been . . . different.'

'Alternative?' I suggest.

'Pah,' he responds. 'Always hated that word. Made us sound like poor cousins.'

'Independent.'

'Even worse,' he frowns. 'Right. Better get going. Don't want to get in trouble for holding up the plane, five hours later.'

'Keep away from any cute girls,' I offer, as he departs.

'Ha! Fat chance,' he scoffs. 'You know what they say.'

'What's that?'

'*No one likes a grown-up pop star.*'

He delivers a final trademark Webster grin and bounces off towards his gate.

I remain standing next to the table for a minute, blindly fingering the cheque with something approaching mild dementia. My instinct is to instantly rush out and find a bank, but instead I sit for a while, a strange but not entirely unpleasant daze engulfing me, as I consider what a strange man my benefactor is. But although Webster's certainly got a loose screw or two, the cheque itself is signed, dated and unarguably sane. Of course, in the grand global stadium of rock 'n' roll, people often get bigger cheques for doing far less, while in my tiny little pub venue of an existence the notion that I've truly earned this money seems a little far-fetched. But if Lance Webster wants me to have ten big ones, then bugger it, who am I to protest? My short-term plans remain swathed in their usual fog of uncertainty, however. I have my priceless information – the story it feels like I've spent a lifetime pursuing – but nothing to do with it. It's time to think of something else to write about. A situation I've been in many times before; only this time I've got slightly more money.

'Anything else, sir?' asks the passing waitress, and inevitably the thought of a drink enters my head. But something stops me, and the words 'no, thank you, just the bill' emerge from my mouth almost automatically. Weird.

I pay and amble out among the hurrying passengers and duty-free shoppers, suppressing another instinct when I spy one of the flight-information monitors. I start towards it, hoping to see which badly delayed flight is at last about to depart. But no. That's what I would have done a month ago. Now things are slightly different. *Just let him go*. Wherever it is he's going. Bangkok, Mumbai, Cape Town, Sao Paulo, San Francisco. He had a friend in New Zealand he used to Skype with, didn't he? Perhaps. Or he may just be going on an extended holiday. Or maybe he's going to see Gloria, or Rosamund, as she now might be known again, to finally be the partner and dad he's longed to be. I have a suspicion this might be too straightforward, but then . . . twelve years of long-distance forgiving and forgetting could hardly be described as straightforward. And after all, he's no longer a rock star, so they've actually become *cosmically compatible*. Ha! But who knows? *Let it go, Clive*.

As I get back to the place where the passengers stream into the departure lounge after their long wait, I find myself laughing, as it occurs to me that he never said why he couldn't come to the other side of security. Maybe he couldn't be arsed to move. Or maybe it was another test: to see how much I wanted his story. Who can guess? But on a more practical note, I'm not entirely sure how one gets *out* of here again. Not many people needing to go the other way. A pair of pretty girls stroll by, one of them lamenting to the other that she's 'only got half an hour to shop' before her flight leaves. What's the world coming to? When someone actually seems more excited about their shopping experience than going to a wonderful, far-off place . . .

Like New York.

It's the old cartoon light bulb, the whack of the iron bar on the head, the Zane Lowe interview moment. 'My whole life changed . . . the dry-cleaners . . . just be honest . . . what if I actually did go to New York?'

Well, what if I did?

I look in my jacket pocket. There's my boarding pass, handily tucked into my passport. The flight leaves in forty-five minutes. I look at a departure monitor: it's on time. 'Go to gate', in fact. Not much hard currency, no change of clothes, no laptop, not even a toothbrush. But a cheque for ten thousand pounds. It's a Friday tomorrow. All I need is an envelope and stamp, to send it to my bank manager (who'll probably fall off his chair). Perhaps a quick call to my folks to let them know I'll be away for a bit, and to ask if they can transfer me a hundred quid or so until tomorrow, when my (ahem) ten grand comes in. If I beg them hard enough, they'll agree. Especially if going abroad is involved – always makes my mother nervous. She'll instantly start to worry I've taken up drug trafficking. Maybe a text to Polly, to tell her I'll be paying back the cash for the plane ticket sooner than expected, but that I'll be gone for a few days and she can use the kitchen for whatever foul, depraved activity she likes. I check my phone for Billy Flushing's US number. Could I drop him a line now, to let him know I'm on my way? No, I should surprise him.

I really *could* do this.

New York in the summertime. I walk slowly in the general direction of the flight gate, even spotting an 'I heart NY' mug in a souvenir shop (although who would buy this at a London airport is a mystery). Okay, so I didn't fully 'heart' NY on my first trip, but I've heard it improves with each visit. I could saunter down the avenues and along the streets, snooze in Central Park, perhaps amble over a bridge or two, browse in the bookshops, stop in the cafés, couple of pints of . . . whoah, remember what Webster said. Take it easy. Maybe, just for once, I should be a little careful. If Flushing is to be believed, there could be an army of useful people out there. They'd like to see Clive Beresford the writer, not Clive Beresford the filing-clerk pisshead. Let's set the yardarm for slightly later in the day, shall we? There'll be plenty of time. All the time in the world.

I locate a few cursory items for the flight, post my cheque, call my parents and send my message to Polly, then mount the travolator for the short ride to the gate, a little smile forming at the ends of my lips. I can see the planes taxiing about outside in the sunshine, weaving their way among the baggage buggies and the traffic controllers, everything slightly out of focus through the clouds of exhaust. In the distance, a jumbo rockets into the sky. Perhaps it's Mr Webster, zooming off to whatever awaits at the other end. Lance Webster, the man who crawled through a river of indie filth, to emerge the other side, battered, bruised and a little torn around the edges, but clean, in one piece, and without the bailiffs hammering at his door. And although my mind is still in too much of a muddle to really believe it, it's a tale of survival in which I seem to have played a small supporting role. I give a little nod to the rapidly ascending plane, then turn back towards my own onwards journey.

As I spot my flight gate in the distance, I take my phone from my pocket one last time and, with a final mischievous thought, hammer out the following:

Hello boy. Hope all good. Just to say I'll be away for a bit. But also: I got the whole story from Webster. Every last bit of it. I'll tell you soon. Have a lovely weekend x

I press send, and – picturing Alan's astonished gasp, his abrupt exit from a meeting to immediately phone me back, and his frustration at being greeted only by my voicemail for a good few days to come – turn my phone off.

I reach the end of my ride, step lightly off the belt and stroll towards my waiting plane.

DISCOGRAPHY

THIEVING MAGPIES

MONUMENT / Videopsychomania / The Ballad That Never Ends
February 1987, 7"/12", Abandon

SIAMESE BURN / Inappropriate Girlfriend / I'll Give You Action If You Give Me Peace
September 1987, 7"/12", Abandon (UK chart position: 72)

SOAPBOX / Zeitgeist Man / Marlow Meltdown
May 1988, 7"/12", BFM (UK chart position: 43)

SHOOT THE FISH
September 1988, LP/Cassette/CD, BFM (UK chart position: 18)
Scared of Being Nice
Siamese Burn
If I'm Still Sober, You're Still Ugly
Soapbox
Now That You Are Fashionable
Have You Stopped Talking Yet?

Chopped Heart
I Always Hated Love Songs
Me in a Room
All the Bees Are Dead

SCARED OF BEING NICE / Mad Chicken in a Mud Wrestle /
Celebrity Spares
October 1988, 7"/12", BFM (UK chart position: 41)

WHAT IF EVERYONE GOES MAD? / The Bitch Is Still
Around / Something About Him / Zeitgeist Man (Live)
May 1989, 7"/12"/CD, BFM (UK chart position: 15)

WAR ON THE FLOOR / The Great Kilburn Cop-Out /
Arguably the Last Time
October 1989, 7"/12"/CD, BFM (UK chart position: 12)

LOVELY YOUTH
February 1990, LP/Cassette/CD, BFM (UK chart position: 5
US: 67)
Rancid/Putrid
Tube Screamer
War on the Floor
Look Who's Laughing
When You Were Fun
Lovely Youth
Pit Pony
Little House on the Flight Path
The Hell You Went Through
Camp David
Everyone Behaves Like a Cunt So Why Can't I?

LOOK WHO'S LAUGHING / Jason Got It Wrong / Centrefold
February 1990, 7"/12"/Cassette/CD, BFM (UK chart position: 9)

PIT PONY / With Hilarious Consequences / What If Everyone
Goes Mad? (Live) / Bette Davis Eyes
July 1990, 7"/12"/Cassette/CD, BFM (UK chart position: 27)

ROUNDPEG SQUAREHOLE / King Mother / Roundpeg
Squarehole (Bandwagon Jumping Tie-in Mix) / War on the Floor
(Live).
June 1991, 7"/12"/CD, BFM (UK chart position: 7)

THE COOL AND THE CROOKS / Bleached Whale / When
Girls Fight / Hold Back the Rain
January 1992, 7"/12"/Cassette/CD, BFM (UK chart position: 5
US: 64)

BRUISE UNIT
February 1992, LP/Cassette/CD, BFM (UK chart position: 2
US: 10)
The Cool and the Crooks
Bad Little Secret
Memories of . . .
Walking on the Mines I've Laid
Roundpeg Squarehole
Bad Wiring
Plant Life
This Is What You Wanted
Even If You Were a White Man
Lose It
Maybe You Were Jesus

BAD LITTLE SECRET / The Harridan of Old Brompton Road /
The Cool and the Crooks (Live) / Bad Little Secret (Undressed
Version)
April 1992, 7"/12"/Cassette/CD, BFM (UK chart position: 2
US: 15)

WALKING ON THE MINES I'VE LAID / Mobile Phone /
Lose It (Live) / Maybe You Were Jesus (Live)
July 1992, 7"/12"/Cassette/CD, BFM (UK chart position: 13
US: 46)

MEMORIES OF . . . / Candid Casualty / Leyton Layabout /
Pit Pony (Live)
October 1992, 7"/12"/Cassette/CD, BFM (UK chart position: 17)

MTV UNPLUGGED
April 1993, LP/Cassette/CD, BFM (UK chart position: 5 US: 36)
Roundpeg Squarehole
Have You Stopped Talking Yet?
Bette Davis Eyes
Bad Wiring
Chopped Heart
Hold Back the Rain
This Is What You Wanted
Walking on the Mines I've Laid
Look Who's Laughing
When You Were Fun
Bad Little Secret
Zeitgeist Man

RETRO HETERO / Far from Eleven O'Clock / Back to Blighty
April 1995, 7"/Cassette/CD, BFM (UK chart position: 4)

THE SOCIAL TRAP
May 1995, LP/Cassette/CD, BFM (UK chart position: 1 US: 6)
Contribution
Bells Around the Ankles
Try Blinding
A Good Time Was Had by None
The Happy Sound of Daytime Radio
Scenes from a Nightmare
Retro Hetero
Keep It Out of My Face
Personal Space Invader
No One Likes a Grown-Up Pop Star
Class of 1946

CONTRIBUTION / Dehydrate Now! / Picasso Visita El Planeta
De Los Simios
August 1995, 7" / Cassette /CD, BFM (UK chart position: 7
US: 24)

LANCE WEBSTER

COMMERCIAL SUICIDE
August 1997, LP / Cassette /CD, BFM (UK chart position: 25)
Guardian Or Thief
More Than Ever
Blissful Indignance
Walk-In Disaster
His Fax Beats out the Blues
Laughing on the Other Side of Your Face
Fuck You and Your Opinions
Yes, the Rumours Were True
While You Get Ready for Bed Someone Else Is Just Getting Up
Disposal
The Bad Life

BLISSFUL INDIGNANCE / An Awfully Long Way from
Reading / Chicken Death
October 1997, 7"/CD, BFM (UK chart position: 42)

AUTHOR'S NOTE AND ACKNOWLEDGEMENTS

Although a work of fiction, this novel mentions many non-fictional bands and people. Similarly, it refers to certain events, musical and otherwise, that really did take place. Into some of these I have rudely inserted the appearance of an imaginary pop group called Thieving Magpies. However, a few completely fictional events and undertakings are also mentioned, into which I have even more rudely parked some of the aforementioned *non*-fictional bands or people. In these instances I have attempted to keep to what could have been feasible at the time – for example, The Boo Radleys could certainly have been one of the major supporting attractions at an outdoor music event near Aylesbury in the summer of 1995; Carter USM might have agreed to do a fanzine interview before their Marquee show in the autumn of 1989; Crispin Glover could theoretically have appeared in a 2004 Hollywood comic-book adaptation – and so on. Nonetheless, for me to say they (fictionally) did so remains a liberty, and I'd therefore like to gratefully salute all such bands and individuals appearing throughout the text, expressing my sincere hope that they will view my liberty in the spirit intended.

While we're here, I'd also like to warmly extend my gratitude to a number of people who have given this novel's journey – from one-page Word document to finished book – their assistance, ranging from moral support, via considered advice, right the way through to this-bit's-rubbish-you-should-change-it-style edicts. All of it essential and thoroughly appreciated, thank you: Adrian Weston and all at Raft PR & Representation, Dan Franklin and Alex Bowler and all at Cape, Sonny Mehta and Diana Coglianese and all at Knopf, Sumit "the Great Connector" Bothra, Guy Whittaker, Fin Greenall, Heledd "I was there" Williams, Richard Mays, Jannik Tai Mosholt, Jaime Turner, Iain Baker, Marcus Karenin, Darren Tate, Adrian Boss, Jim Bob, Andrew Mueller, Jonathan "syntax" Goldstein, Colin Midson, Paul Chinnery, Peter Buckman, Michael Ogden & Chris Day, all at MTW, Damian Samuels, Thornton/Lavender and Forcina families, and finally – with lots of love – to Crestina, without whom I'd probably have more in common with Clive than is physically or mentally healthy.